ACTS
OF
GOD

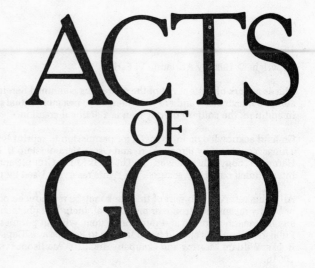

ACTS
OF
GOD

ADRIENNE V.
PARKS

BEECH TREE BOOKS
WILLIAM MORROW
New York

Library of Congress Cataloging-in-Publication Data

Parks, Adrienne V.
    Acts of God.

I. Title.
PS3566.A697.A64   1986   813'.54   85-18588
ISBN 0-688-06052-8

Printed in the United States of America

First Edition

1 2 3 4 5 6 7 8 9 10

BOOK DESIGN BY BERNARD SCHLEIFER

BTB

The word "book" is said to derive from *boka*, or beech.
The beech tree has been the patron tree of writers since ancient times and represents the flowering of literature and knowledge.

TO BILL

Who taught me how to write a love story

THE INDIANS BELIEVE that the world has been created and destroyed four times, the present age being the fifth. The first age was ruled by Tezcatlipoca, the god of the Smoking Mirror, and was destroyed by jaguars. The second age was ruled by Quetzalcoatl, the Plumed Serpent, and was destroyed by a hurricane. The third age was ruled by Chac, the rain god, and was destroyed by volcanic eruptions. The fourth age was ruled by the goddess Ixchel, jade or turquoise skirt, and was destroyed by floods.

The present or fifth age is ruled by the god of sacrifice, Nanahuatl, whose body is covered with sores, and it will end in earthquakes and the stars will fall down from the sky. This will happen "when the earth has become tired, when already it is all, when already it is so, when the seed of the earth has ended."

—*The Anglo-American Cyclopaedia* (1917),
Vol. XXIX, "Mayapán"

PROLOGUE

SHE IS ALWAYS his first wife, the shadowy one, the one people can scarcely remember from the good old days (for she died so young!), the symbol of all their lost hopes, his sainted wife. They remember vaguely that she was small and blond, with blue eyes, although they can't recall her voice; they are reminded of her by cheap postcards, sold by the millions in the souvenir shops. They can look at her on the covers of *Time* and *Newsweek*, beautifully dressed, or deliciously off-guard (it seems to them almost illicit), laughing and playing with the dogs on the palace grounds, in shorts, God help us, in a bathing suit! Making faces and laughing, willfully careless (or recklessly so) of how she would be remembered by the iconographers; elusive, suddenly disappearing from parties, or from the world, always lovely, always young. A myth, or a fairy tale. But they do not remember her clearly.

They remember him more clearly, of course: halted by blood in midsentence, pitching forward, his brains splattered out like black oatmeal on the marble steps of Constitución Hall. There were those who cheered. The obscenity of his death was perfect, for the disturbing beauty of a leader who tried to pull them along too quickly; who didn't care what they thought of him, who sometimes seemed oblivious of the whole world, as long as she was there. El Lorca—who had been handsome even then, slender as a dancer with his jet-black hair, and his lovely hands . . . a little parvenu, perhaps? A little bit of a dago? Although he was then fifty-six. Well, anyway, he was dead. He had tried to substitute

9

his second wife in her place, but he himself had scarcely seemed to believe in it; perhaps it was one of his subtle jokes, the distillate of his bitterness and disillusionment. He had seemed to want his death. She had died too, the woman who had been a pop star; who had seemed like an appropriate replacement, but about whom little was known; had he loved her, had he ever slept with her? Nobody seemed to know, or care; she was a part of his death, like the statues of him they pulled down, the monuments they defaced with spray-painted slogans, the general chaos that followed his assassination. They rampaged through the Presidential Palace, ripping down the flags and tearing down the stiff oil paintings and pulling the sheets off the beds, children gone wild in an orgy of destruction, killing their parents over and over again in an hysteria of relief and guilt. And there had been those who mourned him, although they had been few, and far between: the man who had almost prevented it, and who had hated him as much as anybody; and a priest in the Vatican who had fallen onto his knees and wept.

Father Battiste Tommassi had been self-conscious, even then, of the gesture; but it had welled up within him, and he assumed his ridiculous theatrics were in one way or another the will of God, for publicity for his beloved country. He had mourned *her* more secretly, and remembered her better than most. He had known her longer, longer even than El Lorca, and had loved her more devoutly, and more passionately, although he had never allowed his white fingers to caress her, or his body to know her, his salvation, his sin, his saint. It was he who had started the movement to canonize her—or had it been he? Hadn't it sprung up in a dozen places throughout the country, once El Lorca was dead, the love now simplified because their madonna was again a Virgin, no longer married to a dictator for life, no longer human; a plaster statue, adorned with flowers; and there *were* statues of her, put up around the country; and people claimed to have achieved miraculous cures from them. Touch me, and I will make you whole. I will take away your pain and sin; I will make you devout, beautiful, rich; I will be your film star and your child-madonna; I will be your lover, and I will never grow old—and there were offerings, and sometimes scrawled notes left under the feet of the statues like pen-pal letters; and the plaster became gray with the fingerprints of a million touching hands. She hadn't minded, then; her beautiful face had remained calm and serene despite all of their tears and pleading, remote from either sorrow or ecstacy; and they had preferred her like that, and they had loved her. And so her cult had grown, bigger than the Virgin of Guadalupe; and today she was being beatified, the first step toward canonization.

The rumors were rife. That the President of the United States was going to fly to the Vatican and kneel in front of his Holiness to beg forgiveness (for having caused her death, some said, by denying her last request: that she could come to New York, to Sloan-Kettering, for one last, hopeless operation). That the Lorcanistas were planning a coup, to put that old relic, Quintero de Buiztas, back into power; him who had been ousted by El Lorca himself back in the old days, and who was now nearly eighty, a ghost without even a memory of the past. That the assassins of Ferdinando Lorca were finally going to be brought to justice; or else that they would spontaneously confess their sins, at the moment of the beatification of his wife. And above all, the worst rumor continued to persist: that she was still alive, that her disappearance into the jungle had been merely a temporary retreat, and that she would return to them, their Camila, their *palomita*, their little dove.

Father Battiste Tommassi crumpled the cheap postcard picture of her he had been looking at and threw it into the fireplace. He needed no photograph to remember what she looked like: the color of her hair, unbelievably bright, and the exquisite line of her cheek which had remained with him for twenty years, burning him like a torturer's brand every waking and sleeping hour of his unhappy life. He walked to the window, and stared down with sightless eyes at the crowds jamming Vatican City, as far as the Via della Conciliazione. They were tourists, some; and thrill-seekers and the curious; and hundreds of television cameramen and newspaper reporters, a select few of whom would be allowed into the Basilica to witness the actual ceremony. And there were the thousands of the faithful, for whom merely being here was enough; her lovers too, all of them, he reminded himself with a wry smile. If she could have been there, how she would have laughed. She would have behaved perfectly, of course, convent-

11

bred and always exquisitely polite on the outside; but she would have made some slyly ribald comment behind her hand, and they would have laughed together, waiting backstage, inside this mausoleum: she, and he, and Ferdinando. They had been friends, and how not? Hadn't Battiste Tommassi even officiated at their wedding ceremony, that hurried affair before their flight to the Isla del Viento to escape the police? Whether he liked it or not, he was a part of her myth too, and he put his face into his hands and whispered, "Camila, Camila, I miss you so," just as El Lorca had done in the instant before they blew his brains out.

I.
The Lord of the Smoking Mirror

one

MAYAPÁN—a country of mountains and tropical rain forests, extending from the Isthmus de Tehuantepec to the highlands of the Sierra del Merendón. Discovered by Hernán Cortés in 1517, partially conquered by Montejo the Younger in 1542. Never fully conquered. Principal exports include rubber, oil, and chicle. Principal form of government is nominally democratic. Principal religion is nominally Roman Catholic.

AT FIRST there was only the jungle. Nanacatlan, as the Indians called it, a land of jungle, stretching as far as the eye could see. There were the rich secrets of the oily wells, and the lush wildness of the trees, the thick darkness of the hidden paths, alive with snakes and quetzal birds, and the hot, white, humid sky overhead. That was the land of Hachakyum, Our True Lord, and the people of the Plumed Serpent built their temples and worshiped him, although they called him many names: he was Chac the rain god, who demanded sacrifice; Smoking Mirror, or Kisin, who was death; or the child god, the Niño of the sacred flowers. He was Quetzalcoatl to the ancient Mexicans, and in all of these incarnations he was beautiful. His people were beautiful too, with long black hair hanging down their smooth, supple backs, and a single knotted thong around their waists; men with high cheekbones and a fluid, glottal language that nobody could remember anymore, but which seemed to linger in the impenetrable jungle, along with the whispered laughter and the high, harsh shrieking of the birds. This was Mayapán: which had no boundaries once, except the Isthmus; no cities but the pyramids; no commerce and no king. It lay to the east of Mexico, a secret land, of mountains and steaming rain forests—and farther

15

north, the flat, chalk plains of the Yucatán, jutting out into the clear blue waters of the Caribbean.

In many ways this last terrain was the most representative, although the jungle covered more of the country, mounding up outrageously over the mountains, thick moist valleys, more of it every day, so that the white men would say, My God, what a shitty country, it means to kill us all, it just keeps growing and growing, like the thick green snakes that multiply forever in the rivers. But finally the jungle itself would fade away, and leave only the plains of chalk, the endless flat country covered with small scrub pines, secret wells in the limestone, a desolate country where the crumbling pyramids rose like towers, and could be seen for miles. This was the country as it had always been: mysterious, Indian, and ignored.

When the Spaniards arrived, they sailed farther west, to raze the cities of the Aztecs and found their empire. When Capitano Montejo marched against them, the Maya melted into the trees, and were invincible; one hundred thousand men were lost, before the general conceded, with a curse, and annexed the land for Spain anyway, without having bothered to conquer it. The country was never mapped until the mid-1940's. The priests, those wily Jesuits who had come from Mexico, said, Wait, this is the land that God forgot, if we are patient with the Indians, they will remember us, they will learn to love us. See, first we give them the Madonna and the little baby, just like the Niño, the sacred god of the mushrooms, only soon they will take the piece of dry bread which we offer them, and the wine of blood. Wait, and sooner or later the country will belong to the white men altogether. Truly, General, truly, you will see. The generals didn't believe them, but they didn't care; the land was worthless any-, way, so why bother? Hot, shitty country, what did it hold anyway, but rubber and chicle, chewing gum, for God's sake! And you could lose yourself forever, carving a temporary path with your machete through those juicy forests, losing all memory of reality among those enormous, hanging vines; or wandering in the scrub plains among the chalk and the mosquitoes, hearing the gurgling in the wells where Chac, the rain god, still lived.

The Spaniards made an uneasy truce with the land, compounded of ignorance on both sides. They built their cities, and when these were gradually eaten by the ever-encroaching jungle, they built new ones. They appointed a viceroy, who ruled from Mexico City, and they told the Pope that all the Indians now were good Catholics, but knew better than to believe it. They built a great sprawling port city called Campeche, with high noble houses and warehouses which were never full of anything but rubber and chewing gum, and where the occasional discouraged pirate ship would dock, a city of sad convents and crumbling churches, but what the hell, everybody wanted to get out of it as soon as possible anyway. It was a provincial backwater, where there was always a film of dirty oil washing against the wharf; where exhausted whores dragged their mattresses from street corner to street corner, because it was too hot to go inside; where fine ladies would sit fanning themselves, Oh, this miserable heat, and giving birth inside the closed and secretive houses, crusted with lichens and rusting with the dirty wind off the ocean; and where everybody tried to travel to Europe as soon as they possibly could. In those days, all the Mayapanians looked to Paris, where they could find beautiful clothes and elegant food, not this fish cooked in paper, what peasant could eat this shit, it was only fit for an Indian; and they pined for Europe, and for America—where everybody had a car, think of it, a country as big as the whole world. If they couldn't have that, they would settle for Mexico City; and so they were a nation of emigrés, cut off from the culture they coveted, mired in a culture they despised, and so they lived—and were governed by a series of interchangeable generals; because in that heat, in those storms of mosquitoes and in the absolute lethargy of those endless early years, only the Army could rouse itself to do anything.

The generals left the country alone; they were content in governing the city, in amassing their hoards of stolen gold and jewels, a hundred fortunes made and lost in the unmapped years of their careless despotism, because you could never govern the country anyway; they left the peasants, and the Indians, strictly alone, because what the hell, they were all animals at heart, just like the scrawny horses that pulled the Presidential carriage, because they couldn't afford to honor their President, no, not even by the simple courtesy of buying him an automobile. When each general finally lost his power base, and regretfully left his office, dressed in civilian clothes, sneaking out of the Presidential Palace with a cardboard suitcase, there was always another general ready to take his place; and nobody outside of the city even bothered to learn their names. In the dense jungle, and the flat emptiness of the chalk plains, no word of progress was so much as breathed until 1946, when the neighboring country of Mexico opened a railway line between Campeche and Veracruz, five hundred miles of track, which split the immense desolation and impenetrable isolation of the country like a stroke. President Ramosa, the predecessor of Quintero de Buiztas, who was an educated man, it was said, and who was rumored besides to have married an Indian woman (President Ramosa, whose face would go sad at a Yucatecan song, and who was supposed to have stolen less than all his predecessors put together), expressed grave doubts about this wonderful opening of the country, Just think, now we can be part of the rest of the world, not this shitty little country everybody laughs at. He shook his head, and voluntarily resigned his office, saying, Quintero de Buiztas, my young friend, you are the man in this country with the most demonic sense of humor, and so I leave you my title, God help you, and may you help out our poor ridiculous country while you're at it. Quintero de Buiztas, who was only twenty-three years old at the time, a *mestizo*, and whose famous sense of humor was to see him through the vicissitudes of thirty years in office and an assassination attempt with an Indian's machete, smiled and accepted the job as the perfect outcome of his amazing and always unexpected fate, and by 1967, Mayapán was a part of the modern world.

It was in the fall of that year when the dictator, Quintero de Buiztas, looked down on his city from the balcony of the Presidential Palace and watched the bloodshed in the streets. The rioting had been begun by the students, the striking workers, and extended like a disease to everybody, so that while he stood there on the balcony in his army fatigues and his Castro-style beard, smoking a joint of homegrown marijuana and enjoying the sparkle of the early morning sunlight through narrowed eyes and his steel-rimmed glasses, people were being shot and chopped down by machetes almost directly beneath his feet. He wasn't particularly worried. He had ridden out worse storms than this, revolution in nearby Cuba and the interference of the American Alliance for Progress, and so while he watched the course of the fighting, he was also reading a newspaper. It was only one day old, a rarity in Campeche, and was one of the twenty-five newspapers he read every day from all over the world, with a casual and sightly bemused addiction to knowledge which he'd developed at Yale on a four-year scholarship from United Oil, in the palmy days of his own feigned innocence, and the *gringos'* lack of Americans to educate during the Second World War. This happened to be a copy of the London *Times*, but in addition to the Spanish dailies, he read the newspapers in French and Italian as well, and had the rest translated to him by subalterns, so that he knew the price of *kibbe* in Lebanon, the border disputes in Kenya, the current musical fad in the United States, and the latest fashions on Carnaby Street in London. None of this made the slightest bit of difference to the business of his life in Mayapán, ruled by a dozen or so rich families, the tattered oligarchs who vainly sought, with their few paltry millions, to match the prestige of the coffee plantation owners in El Salvador or the beef exporters in Argentina, but it gave him a cosmopolitan edge over these would-be aristos which he wryly (but keenly) prized. They certainly owned *him*, but in a way he owned them as well: he was their insurance, keeping their investments in rubber and chicle safe, protector of the world's supply of Bazooka and prophylactics, and he knew they couldn't live without him. So they paid to keep him in power, and he pocketed the national treasury and governed with the same instincts of a thoughtful animal which had kept him alive at Yale, and before that for eighteen years on the rough Westside of Campeche, trusting to his fate to keep him alive for the span of his natural life on the balcony of the Presidential Palace. He was forty-four.

He had no fear of his own death, and in fact used to wonder about it. How would it happen? Like so many other events, would he have some premonition about it before it occurred, would one of his aides touch him on the shoulder and tell him, Excuse me, Mr. President, but it's time to die? Or would he be butchered like those poor idiots down there, fighting for a decent wage or a public sewer or perhaps for the sheer love of fighting, who knew? Quintero de Buiztas didn't care. He knew to a fine precision the intoxication of blood, and the intoxication of rhetoric, and he knew as well with an absolute certainty that none of that crap mattered when you had a bullet in your viscera, you only cared about living then, but that was the way the game went. Only the wise played for fun, because it was like dancing, only a fool danced for gain or prestige, the wise man danced because he liked dancing. He turned the page, setting his steel-rimmed glasses more firmly on his nose, and read about how George Romney claimed to have been brainwashed by the diplomatic corps when he visited Vietnam. Well, well, wasn't that interesting. Whenever he read the newspapers there was always something in there to surprise him.

He was interrupted by a knock on the door, and he came away from the window and sat down at his desk, folding the newspaper carefully in front of him, but leaving the window open. Whoever it was already knew about the fighting in the streets, and if he didn't, it wouldn't do any harm to remind him. Dangerous, these Latin American dictatorships. You never knew what was going to happen. You needed a strong man, a *caudillo*, to maintain order, such order as could occasionally be seen. He smiled to himself and said, "Come in."

The man who came in was quite alone, unaccompanied by any of Buiztas' guards, a fact which the dictator noticed but which didn't especially concern him. If this was an assassination attempt, then so be it, but he had to smile if the man who'd been chosen to kill him was this crazy fanatic Juan dos Santos: a brilliant journalist, but well over sixty, with yellowing white hair and a younger, German wife; a young daughter too, Buiztas seemed to remember, so the old goat must still have some juice in him. He was slender and fragile, ascetic and fiery and absolutely consumed by his principles, and Buiztas found him unfailingly funny. He stayed seated behind his desk, but spread his broad peasant's hands expansively, with a big smile.

"My dear friend! I beg you to sit down. Terrible, these disturbances, you've taken your life into your hands just to visit me, and all I can do is sit here and apologize for them. Such violence! Such excess of political feeling! If I were a harsher man, I would chastise them, but what can I do? I'm a liberal at heart myself! What is it that Bolívar said, If it wasn't for his common sense, every man would be a liberal or a democrat? Well, there you are, you see, that's my downfall, I've given the people too much freedom, and just look how they've abused me for it!"

All the while he was saying this he was smiling, and wondering what the hell had brought Dos Santos into his office, a man who hated him as much as anyone else in the country, and more than that, a man who'd made no secret of his enmity, in his newspapers, in editorials, and in free and unsolicited comments to everyone from the Nicaraguan ambassador to the more enlightened representatives sent down from Washington. The old man was looking bad—his thin, pale skin was white and his hands were trembling (very subtly, you had to look hard for it, but Buiztas noticed)—and he wondered, What the hell's going on, smiling to himself while he allowed his features to assume an expression of serious attention. He took note of the dust on the journalist's shoes (which meant he had walked several blocks) and the unaccustomed nick where he'd cut himself shaving. He had large, beautiful blue eyes—even Buiztas, who was certainly no fag, had to admit he must have been some kind of matinee idiol in his youth—and he sat down, which was itself unusual: normally he preferred to stand, the offended populist before the corrupt military dictator. Buiztas was totally incapable of pity; but he was a much better actor than he pretended to be, so he took a flask out of his desk and poured the journalist a stiff shot of French brandy, and pushed it across the top of his desk with a blunt forefinger. "Here, my old friend, you look as if you could use this. Now, take your time. In what way can I be of use to you?" His voice was matter-of-fact, pragmatic yet respectful. He barely repressed a laugh.

Juan dos Santos raised his eyebrows, as he helped himself to the drink. "Cut the crap, Mr. President," he said thinly. "I know all about your meetings with the Cuban ambassador, and the way you're lying to the American government. Now either I can publish what I know in *La Prensa* and blow your deal with El Señor Howard Hughes, or you can help me to get myself and my family out of Mayapán. I'm a dead man if I stay here, and you and I both know that."

Quintero de Buiztas didn't pause for a minute, although his request came as a terrific shock. He had had no idea his meetings with the Cubans were known to anybody, but if they were, well, that was merely another piece of interesting information. He spread his hands again, this time to represent his innocence, and said immediately, "My dear friend, tell me, who can you feel is against you? Has anybody said anything? Who has dared to threaten you?"

Juan dos Santos smiled a little twistedly, as he drained the rest of his brandy. "I can't believe you. *Who* has threatened me? *You* have, Mr. President! My newspapers have been a thorn in your side for twenty years! This is ridiculous! I'm asking for your permission to get out of the country before your people have me assassinated!"

Buiztas was having trouble keeping a straight face, but he managed. "My dear friend! This is terrible—who's been filling your head with such lies! I assure you, from your first word, I've had nothing but respect for your editorials, and for the editorial policy of *La Prensa* as well, which is, as it should be, a free and independent forum for the expression of public opinion. Why—" He had a sudden inspiration. "Would I receive you alone and unguarded, if I thought you were my enemy? I pay you the supreme compliment, of assuming you haven't come here to assassinate *me*!"

Juan dos Santos drew away from him, with the ineffable movement of an aristocrat which Quintero de Buiztas regretted he couldn't imitate, and looked at him contemptuously. "You think we're all animals like you, don't you, Mr. President? Paid murderers, just like you are?"

Of course I think that, Buiztas wanted to laugh, and so do you, that's why you want me to get you safely out of the country, before my men take you out one night and put a bullet in your spine. But we do this little dance. The difference between us is, I love dancing.

"At—at least," Dos Santos continued after a moment, not meeting the dictator's eye, so unused was he to begging. "At least let my wife and daughter be allowed to leave the country. They are wholly innocent of my views, and—my opinions. Mr. President, my little daughter isn't ten years old!"

His momentary cry of an anguished father was neatly diverted by Buiztas, who'd never had any children, and felt vaguely uncomfortable around them. He concentrated instead on Dos Santos' wife.

"Innocent? I wonder. Oh, I know, President Ramosa pardoned her husband, which was easy, as there are very few Jews in Mayapán! But innocent? Whatever happened to Rudolf Heidrich, do you know? Did you ever meet him? Did Lili ever tell you what happened to him?" He chuckled. "All those ovens. Did he take Lili to live with him at Birkenau? I wonder whatever became of him."

For a moment he thought the old man was going to strike him, which was a humorous enough idea but passed like many another amusing suggestion into the hazier realm of what might have been. He studied the old man's pinched nose and stiffened lips and the amazing blaze of those sky-blue eyes, which *could* get angry pretty effectively, it appeared; and he thought that the old *cabrón* must really be scared shitless for his family and suddenly he was bored. He stood up, a big man, strong as an ox, and put his arm around the older man's shoulders to signal the end of the conversation.

"My friend, you have my word, that should you want to leave Mayapán at any time—I can't imagine why you would, but that's your business!—just drive to the airport and go. I'll even call ahead and guarantee you a seat." He patted Dos Santos' arm and felt the old man writhe under his touch; he was going to miss the old *caballejo*, and that was a fact. "Now, I suggest you go home, take a cool shower, have a drink with your wife, and if you want to leave the country tomorrow—just go! We live in a free democracy!" A burst of gunfire from the street below them underscored his words, and Buiztas laughed. "Some people might say too free! But I've always believed that freedom's like a tart—you can never have too much of her! *Adiós, mi amigo*—and speak well of me in Miami, or wherever you happen to end up."

The next day, Juan dos Santos was killed along with his wife when a terrorist's bomb destroyed their car in downtown Campeche. The offices of the radical newspaper *La Prensa* were likewise destroyed by vandals, although neither of these attacks could in any way be traced back to the liberal government of Quintero de Buiztas.

Thus it was, that in that year, when she was ten years old and had yet to see her first vision, when she played with other little girls in the school in Campeche and wore white cotton underwear and little white dresses laundered by her mother, that Camila dos Santos Heirich learned the rules of the dance of politics. It was one of a number of such incidents that year—and was in fact overshadowed by the murder two days later of Tomas Cardinal Fuertes, the Archbishop of Campeche, while he was saying mass. His assistant, a young man of twenty-seven named Battiste Tommassi, became a hunted man, because of the idiotic fact that he could identify the assassins, although at that time he was in no other respect political. So the next day Battiste Tommassi obtained a forged passport, and flew to New York City with the clothes on his back, under the name of Enrique Pratt. All of 1967 was a year of bloodshed in Campeche, and the leader of the People's Rights Coalition, a leftist organization with strong ties to the unions of the rubber and chicle workers, was arrested and held for six months under conditions of the utmost severity, before the young man, Ferdinando Lorca, then only thirty years old, but already marked with the lonely charisma of sorrow, was allowed his freedom upon condition he leave the country forever. The famous poet Porfirio Cheruña wrote a poem condemning "that black year, when all of youth was killed, the best with a sword, the others through despair," and raised his noble voice in protest from the comparatively safe distance of Columbia University, where he was teaching at the graduate school. Camila dos Santos was smuggled out of the country under an assumed name, and brought to live with her aunt and uncle, Ernst and Maria Teppler, who were also living in New York, where she wore silk underwear and went to a private school under the tutelage of elegant nuns, because the Tepplers were rich.

She was a quiet child, with a fleeting, distracted smile as if she were always thinking about something else, and the Tepplers, who were older, found her seemingly happy and spoiled her with their relief. The rest of the world watched in horror as the killings went on in Mayapán, but it was as Quintero de Buiztas rightly surmised, all Latin American countries were presumed unstable, and you had better just leave them alone, as Quintero de Buiztas himself was willing to do, until the violence had burned itself out and those in power could get down to the business of profits again. By the spring there were signs that the worst of the fighting was over.

The oligarchs of the government relaxed. It was the way it had always been: hot sleepy afternoons in the city or driving through the country, past the hanging fronds of the banana trees, the thick green rubber leaves, the rich, moist, sleepy darkness. The country dreamed once again under Quintero de Buiztas, who celebrated his forty-fifth birthday with massive rejoicing, General, it's like we won a world war! And he joked, In a way, we have! Better than a world war! It's a national miracle!

But that night of his birthday, standing on the balcony of the Presidential Palace, he watched the stars, and felt a chill. The ghosts of all his sad victims haunted him, and he sighed, relishing his sorrow with a connoisseur's delight, because he always knew that it was a man's fate to regret, and that a man of true power had more to regret than anybody. He sniffed the nostalgic air of the port, the scent of bougainvillea and petroleum, the heat and blood off the stones (surely, an hallucination?), and let the ineffable sadness of the moonlight spill over him. Almost unthinking, he unbuttoned the twelve buttons of his tunic and the six buttons of his fly and stood naked on the balcony, his matted hairy chest and groin black as a stain against the pure white marble of the building, and smiled at the delicious incongruity that he should be standing there, mother-naked, a peasant's son, for Christ's sake, and who else had more right to be standing there than a man of the people like he was? He stretched out his arms, laughing hugely, and threw his steel-rimmed glasses onto the bloodstained pavement of the square, because what the fuck, a President should be able to be blind, it helped him to govern better, and lay down in his bed inside the mosquito netting of his viceregal bedroom and slept like a stone, The best sleep I've had in years, thank the Lord, he proclaimed. But from that day on, he started to watch for the hand that would depose him, with irony, with sorrow—and with love: because he had learned that all authority yearns to be checked by something, and he knew that the only hand that could check his would be the unequivocal hand of death. He smiled when he thought of it—and smiling, governed as he had done before, because it was too late to change, you could never change Mayapán, a country that was the oldest place on earth, goddamn it, and newly created with each steaming, multihued morning. He smiled, writing hundreds of decrees, because you could always decree that something was something, and he was just marking time in the game.

The hand that he saw hovering over him was slender, long-fingered, and invincible. But in his bed at night, he thought he saw not the remote, merciless conqueror who would kill him, but the loving, forgiving image of a holy child.

two

THE GLEAMING METAL and chrome structures of the city seduced them, initially—those refugees from Mayapán who came up out of the jungle, by plane after the hot sticky train ride from Campeche, exiles in silk dresses or plain brown Indian blankets, their faces scarred by blood and disaster and disillusionment. They initially saw the city, and were lulled by the lights and the sunshine, the clear, dizzying air; they thought, We have come through our crucible, the torture of our lost hopes and fortunes, into the promised land of billboards and American hamburgers and all will be well. It was only gradually, by a cruel process of carelessly dropped hints and pieces of information, that even the wealthiest of them learned that they were unimportant in this new place: faded maiden aunts come into the house of a happily married and successful relative. New York City would shelter, but disdain them. They were *cabecitas negras*, blackheads just out of the jungle. They formed their own community, living on the shreds of hope that fluttered out of Campeche from time to time: the dictator was ill, he was about to issue an official pardon, there was to be a general election, he was going to form a new cabinet, he was going to die. But nothing ever came of it, and after a while the Mayapanian exiles developed their own saying, "That will happen when the serpent flies," meaning, That will happen only when the land itself rises to destroy its defiler, a self-mocking bitterness, because they despised the Indians who still worshiped their old gods.

For those who had relatives in New York, it was easier—or for those who, like Porfirio Cheruña, had created their own lives outside of Campeche: worldly and international, figures bound by no small concerns or parochial identities, but sailing smoothly above them like stately and benevolent swans. The poet and novelist, whose works had won him international acclaim, had shed all trace of Mayapán from his elegant persona and become a citizen of the world: at fifty-eight, with his gleaming white hair and pale, reflective smile, a respected academician—with brisk sales in the United States, where he was a popular guest on the college lecture circuit. Likewise, Ernst and Maria Teppler were able to shelter their niece in comfort, and take her into their international world of banks. Finance and a soft Persian lamb coat wrapped the child of such disturbing tragedy in luxury, and smoothed the consciences in their comfortable, large apartment on East Forty-ninth Street. She seemed to adapt. They summered in Europe (generally Switzerland) and wintered in Nassau or Curaçao, and Camila grew up speaking the multiple languages of a financier's daughter, the convoluted syntax of Wall Street, and the fluent French and Italian and German of her uncle's business partners. She showed no scars, and seemed, in fact, to retain remarkably little memory of her early life and her parents; the psychiatrist to whom her aunt Maria took her pronounced her remarkably well-adjusted, and with a serene maturity unusual in one so young. The Tepplers accepted their good fortune, and left her often thereafter in the care of a succession of housekeepers; she was, like them, above nationalities, and the horrors of the past were best forgotten, whether they had occurred in Campeche, or Dresden, or Berlin.

Camila was sent as a day student to a private Catholic girls' school, and if she was accompanied by bodyguards, that was not so unusual as to provoke comment. Her classmates were the daughters of other rich Catholics, some of them foreigners, whose parents were affiliated with the U.N.: gregarious children as a rule, spoiled with the casual concerns of wealth, a small, nicknamed, and careless society, to whom the affairs of state comprised their gossip about their parents. Camila was immensely popular. She radiated such gaiety, such happiness (the nuns concurred), almost a kind of grace. Camila, giving parties at the Tepplers' apartment, while her aunt and uncle were in Europe (a frequent occurrence): wonderfully naughty, overnight affairs, where the girls smuggled in Harvey's Bristol Cream (and later pot) and listened to "Abbey Road." Camila in the school talent show, the starring role; Camila in the Christmas pageant as the Virgin Mary (making up wonderful ad-lib dialogue, terribly sacrilegious, behind the scenes; convulsing her girl friends). And was it true, was it possible, that she didn't even *believe* everything the nuns taught them, with her wide-eyed, attentive expression, disguising her blasphemy? "How do you *know* the Virgin Birth wasn't a terrific con job?" she would ask. "Can't your parents pull off something twice that good, if they control the newspapers?" But she couldn't mean it, she couldn't really be an unbeliever, could she? her friends reasoned. Why did she go to church that much? And it was true, she was strict and careful with herself, overdoing penances, hundreds of rosaries, so that she spent far more time in the chapel than any of the other girls; then again, maybe she meant it when she said she wrote letters, did the crossword puzzle when the nuns weren't looking. "Yes, Sister Joseph, I'm in a state of grace now, I *think*," with that sidelong, dubious glance that sent the other girls into fits of giggles, because no one was naughtier, no one was *cleverer* than Dos Santos, with her strange voice, comprised of so many different yet oddly harmonious accents. They couldn't figure her out, but they loved her. Then again, she was frequently sick, and this they didn't *think* she faked; and when she came back to school she looked luminous, thin and white, so they wondered if maybe she wouldn't die after all, a virgin like Saint Teresa. She gave her friendship unstintingly, carelessly, so that the ugliest girl at the school could claim her attention as easily as the most beautiful (and she was very beautiful herself)—yet she could be merciless in her derision, bringing her enemies to tears (and she *did* have enemies, not merely from jealousy; she did have people she had slighted, or whom she had unexpectedly *condemned*, for no apparent reason. She did have girls who tried to get back at her).

29

When she was eleven she had spinal meningitis, and was out of school for two months. The little girls visited her: Camila, propped up on pillows in a private room at Cornell Medical, looking *very* small and thin, like a child of five or six, with blue circles around her eyes. They asked her if it hurt. Oh ... she shrugged. Was she going to die? The doctors didn't think so. ... Of course not, her aunt Maria interrupted, she was completely out of danger and would be going home soon, her uncle Ernst had made all the arrangements for a private nurse. The little girls were impressed by the banked flowers (which gave the room a sophisticated, adult look, like the hospital room of a movie star) although they were disappointed that Camila wouldn't have a scar, or a cast they could sign. Well, I could break my arm, Camila suggested, and her aunt got angry and sent the girls out of the room. They didn't know about the agony of spinal taps, then (which were *not* over; there would be two more before Camila was finally released from the hospital), though some of them, much later, would recall with unease the drawn, white, smiling face of their friend—because she *was* smiling, a little wildly, a little out of control, but lit with a secret mirth, a secret knowledge they couldn't penetrate. I've never seen anyone so stoic, the doctors admitted to Ernst Teppler, wondering, slightly uncertain that stoicism was the right word. It's as if she didn't feel it, they confided to their colleagues; she just snapped right out of her body, like those mystics you hear about; I don't know where she went, but she wasn't there, and afterward ... sometimes a great deal afterward ... she came back. Where have you been? the doctors wanted to ask her. What was it like? But she was just a child, and slept like a child, wearied, with a stuffed animal in her arms, a shapeless thing she'd brought with her from Campeche. The doctors left her alone. Certainly, the Tepplers wanted no knowledge of her suffering; they were so busy; and the nurses' solicitude was met with politeness, candor (seemingly), her wide blue stare, her easy smile, I'm *fine*, she laughed, embarrassed ... requests for books, a radio, a television set, she was bored, a deliberate refusal to talk about her symptoms. She seemed so *normal*, the nurses protested helplessly—bright, articulate, interested in boys, horses, her classmates—how could she be the same child with her eyes rolled back in her head, her skin cold, a thready, infrequent pulse, who had so frightened the doctors? Had she done it *deliberately*? Could she control it? Nobody seemed to know.

She lay for long hours looking out of the window, thoughtfully, withdrawn; it was at this time that her dreams began, but she never spoke of them; indeed, how *could* she speak, of something for which there were no words, merely images: wild, chaotic, terrifying . . . yet oddly beautiful. Vivid and frightening, explosions, torrential rain . . . a holocaust for which she was a single, disembodied eye. Their beauty pierced her. Their horrors revolted her. She stared in blank incomprehension when someone, someone she didn't recognize, entered the room, a tall meaningless figure, illusory as a mirage . . . and arranged her mouth into a terrified smile, hoping whoever it was wouldn't guess, wouldn't know that she didn't recognize them. Only gradually would the figure resolve itself into her aunt, her uncle, her doctor, and she would discover herself gibbering inanities, seemingly sane and meaningful to *them*, without having the faintest idea of what she was talking about. Did they know? Apparently not. And *was* it simply a consequence of her illness? Perhaps. She didn't know.

When she returned to school she was frailer, but more popular than ever, more brilliant at lessons, more talented a mimic, a cartoonist, a purveyor of outrageous gossip (which might or might not have taken flight solely within the realm of her own imagination), more the center of her small and intimate circle of friends. Her times alone were taken as the residual precautions of her illness; without ever explaining it, she made her companions believe that the doctors had told her to rest, to take walks alone, stupid but necessary, "recreational" activities which must, perforce, be pursued in solitude. She was then left alone, with her visions (sometimes occurring with horrifying clarity, at midday, at a party, in Central Park, in a class: annihilation, beautiful and overwhelming destruction). Her dreams grew more detailed. She saw huge structures overgrown with vines, a sucking wetness of oily pools, ground so soaked with blood that it welled bleeding around her feet, producing plants of an unimaginable richness: hideous orchids, blood-red gelatinous leaves, throbbing stems—a miasmic wealth and heat, fetid with moisture, dripping with the coiled intestines of the mutilated plants, sharp with the high, metallic smell of death. She would wander through this world, a world so primitive that there was nothing in her but an uncomprehending wonder . . . climbing steps to an enclosed stone chamber of densely painted walls, where she awoke, in the Tepplers' comfortable apartment, in her own sweat-soaked bed, with an immense feeling of desolation. Nightmares.

She grew adept at hiding her terrors and, indeed, all of her thoughts from her companions. Camila dos Santos: who could drink more (beer, wine, or whatever) than her friends (and still not get drunk), who was one of the first to smoke dope (and also to no effect), who was one of the brightest students at the Harley School (indeed, she was something of a prodigy, wasn't she?), who was adored by the nuns, an *angelita*, as the Spanish Sister Juana called her. A gifted child. And so young. So very young.

It was in a break between classes at the Harley School, when she was twelve years old, that Father Battiste Tommassi first saw her, sitting cross-legged on one of the old window seats on the first-floor landing, as he was coming up the stairs. She was totally absorbed in a book, and she didn't see him, so that although he had glanced at her before, in motion, always in motion, the darling of everyone in the school, he stopped now in the bright sunlight at the top of the stairs and caught his breath. He was twenty-nine.

Tall, acne-scarred, big-bodied, without the elegant emaciation which he was to affect later on when he became powerful in the Vatican, he came every day to the school to say mass, and once a week to confess the little girls, giving them penance for their small sins: Father, I stole a pencil from Mary's pencil box, I ate two helpings of French toast for breakfast, I think about boys, I think about girls, I'm unhappy, nobody in the school likes me. He knew all the jokes—lucky you, Father, the little girls, telling you all their secrets in the confessional—but he found them coarse, too fat or too skinny, smelling of their mother's perfume, or sneakers and gym suits, hardly the objects of temptation. When he stopped in his quick stride up the stairs to stare at Camila dos Santos, *la pobrecita huérfana*, the poor orphan, his reaction was purely instinctive. My God, he thought, without a trace of blasphemy, she's the most beautiful child I've ever seen. Who is she? Where did she come from? He approached her, and she glanced up, shyly, and smiled at him, and he took one look at those shining, bright-blue eyes and felt his bones dissolve.

"Hello."

"Hello, Father Tommassi."

He knew she had no need of his company, finding her own sufficient, but he couldn't stop himself from sitting down next to her on the window seat, counting on her innate politeness not to withdraw from him. Nor was he wrong, for she smiled again, that fey, fleeting smile which had nothing of the child in it, yet was honestly friendly, a born politician's smile. He felt a little jolt of surprise. How old was she? Eleven? Twelve? Where had she learned that smile, that bright, flattering attentiveness? She had an exquisite bone structure, with a high forehead and delicate hollows, a face that would be a fashion model's in ten years' time, and her eyes were the clear, light, fearless blue of the sky.

He found himself suddenly at a loss for words. He looked down at his hands and said, "I haven't seen you to talk to, as I've tried to do with all the other little girls. Have you been avoiding me? Don't you—don't you like me?" Stammering. The sunlight very warm, hot, on the back of his neck. The checkered pattern of the mullioned windows on the floor in front of them, red, yellow, his hands colored multihued by that same sunlight (farmer's hands, not a priest's; big, with splayed thumbs, laborer's hands). He was surprised by her laughter, which was high, giggling, a child's laugh, and turned to her with relief, feeling himself less awkward, less embarrassed with her.

"What is it? What's so funny?"

"Oh, I'm not laughing at you, Father—well, I guess maybe, but it's not—I'm not laughing *at* you. You know what I mean. Only—only I like you, and *all* the girls like you, they think you're *very* glamorous, didn't you know that?"

A revelation. *"What?"* And one which was patently ridiculous. "That's impossible! Why should they think that? I'm not— I'm not glamorous. I'm not glamorous at all." A wry smile.

"Oh . . ." She shrugged, glancing at him out of the corner of her eyes, innocently teasing, coquettish. "Because you're a hero, you escaped from a totalitarian regime—oh, you know, all the girls gossip about who's working for the C.I.A., who's undercover for what—I don't know if they think you're in covert operations, but they know you're wanted by the Buiztanistas. Well. . . ." She opened her hands as if the conclusion were obvious, and then burst into peals of laughter. "They say you were shot at! Were you? I know you escaped under an assumed name, because that's what I did too." She dismissed that as boring, unexceptional. "What name did you choose? I called myself Lili Teppler, which was my mother's first name, before she was married, the first time. It's not that common, but it's not so unusual that they thought, Aha, it's an alias! Which would have been fun; but then it would have been a pain in the ass to have been stuck there!"

She smiled, and he remembered her history with a jolt: Juan dos Santos' daughter. And her mother, the former wife of some Nazi, wasn't she? Pardoned by Ramosa ages ago? He shook his head, realizing with a part of his mind that it was *her* history that was glamorous (and did she know that, in some way? Taking it for granted? Her bright funny smile, mocking them both, him *and* her, the gullibility of the credulous?). He had never met anyone so *good* before, so good at being who she was: so unselfconsciously *present*, like a dazzling small flame. (And what had Emily Dickinson said? "The truth must dazzle gradually, lest it blind?") So charming, so happy, so gifted: and it was true that at that time, and for all of his life, Battiste Tommassi was mortifyingly self-conscious, trapped in his own too-large body, vulnerable as an ox. He suddenly felt good, marvelously joyous, sitting there on the window seat talking to this beautiful child: and was it true, that she was precocious? Obviously. And unusually "sensitive"? Perhaps. He wasn't precisely certain he knew what that meant. He felt that he could happily have spent his whole life sitting there beside her on the window seat, and he had a sudden idea.

"I need someone to help me get the chalice and plate ready, when I set up for mass in the mornings. Would you like to help me?"

A great honor, and one whose power he had not misjudged; she stared. "But Father, that's for one of the older girls—"

"Oh—" He shrugged, her own shrug, Mayapanian, and perhaps that was it, a shared kinship between two exiles, which formed the basis for their friendship, or part of it. "I can pick who I like, that's one of the perquisites of the job."

And that was how it began, their unusual partnership; for it *was* a partnership, he was to believe later on, the unexpected complement of two souls (how loving! yet how chaste!). And a necessary source of nourishment to his own famished heart. (A fact which he recognized: "I could have been bitter, before my thirtieth year, but for the influence of her grace; always, in my heart, after that, there was a capacity for grace, for charity"—and with one notable exception, of course, that had been true.) And love. Yes, he thought, why not use that word? Love so piercing that his eyes would secretly well up with tears, watching her reach up to light the candles, standing on tiptoe in the chapel; his secret child—because in the depths of his heart he *did* wish her well, and would abide by her more faithfully than most (save one, her loving husband; but that was in the future). His secret, perfect daughter. He brought her books, and taught her privately, Latin, Greek, the excitement of her mind a foil and challenge for his own, so that he privately credited Camila with his knowledge of several arcane subjects: medieval heresies, a smattering of gnosticism—all very useful to him in the Vatican—God, how trivial! He sometimes missed the sharpness of her mind with a physical pang, up until the last moment of his life. They read everything they could get their hands on, texts from Columbia, where Battiste was a graduate student in the politics department, and the latest news from Campeche: politics, economics, and the philosophies of concrete action—because they were both convinced of the necessity of revolution; they were children of their age. It soon became accepted that Dos Santos was Father Tommassi's pet—with a certain amount of jealousy, cattiness, rudeness—What does he do, does he ask you to hold his thing for him? Does he tell you if priests ever do it? Well, do they? Because of course, the sex lives of priests and nuns was intensely fascinating; and in fact, didn't Dos Santos know some very funny stories, didn't she tell the joke about the nun and the priest getting ready to make it, and . . . ? Although Camila would never say anything bad about Father Tommassi. The nuns found it charming. Surely Camila, of all people, had enough friendship inside her warm heart to go around, and Father Tommassi was so nice, so good with all the little girls. If he had a particular favorite, who could blame him? Didn't they all adore her? Didn't she move inside the charmed circle of their care, their flattery, accepting it as her due, giving her love back, spontaneous, unthinking, generous? Generous to a fault, the bemused generosity of the distanced, the distracted outsider? But that only occurred to them much later, and it never occurred to most of them at all.

It was on Christmas Eve that he gave her a present (although he had given her presents before, holy cards and holy medallions, slipped into the pockets of her coat, on the sly): a beautiful missal, Spanish, covered with white leather, and a mother-of-pearl rosary which she was to keep, and use, throughout her life (even after the silver one she was to receive from the Pope). The headmistress of the school had spoken about it, lightly, to Father Tommassi. Do you think it's wise, Father, to single the child out for such a *particular* gift? Wouldn't it have been better, perhaps, wouldn't it *be* better in the future, to be a little more *discreet*? A little more (with a laugh) circumspect, with the child's reputation? Which had left him with his cheeks burning, a stiff reply, I don't know what you're talking about, a Spanish inflection (two foreigners? Perhaps she had misread the situation?), but what *had* she read into it, what was there for anyone to read? he wondered as he hurried down the hall with his long stride, tall, his pockmarked face stiff with shame, his soutane brushing the floor. He swept into the chapel, knelt, and folded his hands to still his outraged agitation, and felt a warm presence slip into the pew beside him.

"Father?"

"Shh." He finished his devotions, and rubbed the bridge of his nose, glancing at her sideways.

She was smiling; indeed, she seemed to find the whole circumstance very funny, including his discomfort. She shook her head, and even her whisper concealed a giggle. "The sisters are really furious! It's so funny!"

"So I hear."

"I think it's hilarious. Don't you think it's funny? Don't you like shocking people?"

"Not particularly."

A pause, on an intake of amused breath, whispered laughter, during which she hesitated, looking at him. Beautiful girl, rich girl, careless, daring—but she hesitated, looking closely at him.

"People aren't ever going to understand everything, Father," she said softly, whispering. "If you keep expecting them to, you're going to be disappointed."

He raised his eyebrows. "What on earth are you talking about?"

"Oh . . ." Suddenly she burrowed her head against his shoulder, a child's gesture, intimate, trusting. "I really do like my presents, Father Tommassi," she said softly. "I really do." Just as quickly she broke away, brushing his cheek with her lips, innocent, childish. "I've got to go home now. I just wanted to say Merry Christmas." And she was gone, leaving him charmed, embarrassed, desolate, elated. Some of her less charitable girl friends would have wondered whether the effect was deliberate; but somehow, bemused, Battiste knew that it was not. Always, she would provoke and deny love, provoke it and sinuously avoid it. She was deviously innocent. She was infuriatingly guileless. And always, long after the breath had left her body, she would be borne aloft on the waves of unwanted adoration—so he thought, sitting there in the deserted chapel after she had left him. She would be nourished by what charmed her, irritated, baffled her. She would accept it. She would reject it. But she would never understand it. Because the concept of desire was foreign to her: by which he meant, not just sexual desire, but actual *need*. Hunger. Incompletion. Loss.

And sitting there in the chapel, he knew he would feel that incompletion and loss for his private *angelita* for the rest of his solitary life.

three

ON TUESDAY AFTERNOONS, from two to four-thirty, Ferdinando Lorca's graduate students met for a free-for-all seminar in his third-floor office at Columbia University, and there were always a few auditors as well—from the C.I.A., from the State Department, or simply from other departments within the University—since Ferdinando Lorca could always be counted on to intrigue and infuriate his listeners, and walk the thin, fine line between being loved and being thrown out of the country as a political agitator.

He was a tall, slender man with the graceful body of a coordinated athlete, long-fingered hands (which were seldom without a cigarette), a musical, caressing voice, and sapphire-blue eyes, whose expression was at once so far-sighted and so tender that he appeared to be calling each and every one of his students to a beautiful and inspiring destiny. This was true even when he was doing no more than advising them on how to write a thesis, or cut a boring class and attend one of his own. He was thirty-six at the time Battiste first met him, six years exiled from Mayapán and the Buiztanista torturers, a charming, lonely, charismatic man, gaunt and with a slightly forbidding attenuation like an El Greco figure, despite his friendliness and his attempts to be casual:

his bony handsomeness diffused by sweaters, his cuffs rolled up past his slender wrists, yet somehow always impeccable, aloof and remote as an eagle, with his distant sadness, his solitude of a man apart circling his extraordinarily clear blue eyes with sorrow.

It was impossible that he should not have been loved, extravagantly admired by his students; impossible too that he could have lived without it, that adulation which was the unconscious nourishment of his life. Ferdinando Lorca, on a lecture platform, or later standing up in a Jeep, on a troop train, on the balcony of the Presidential Palace: turning to the cheers of his audience and flushing with uncontrollable pleasure, poised as an actor or a dancer. He had the gift of seduction, to make his own needs his strongest, most effective arguments. He ignored university rules by the blithe expedient of behaving like an adult, in an environment designed for children, and smoked dope with his students, slept with them (discreetly), and treated them like fascinated colleagues rather than unruly charges. He was enthralled with knowledge of all sorts (quantum mechanics and psycho-epistemology, as well as his own specialties of economics and political science), but to the life of the mind, he added sexiness and risk: everyone knew that teaching took up only 50 percent of his time, and they were intrigued and enraptured by the hints he dropped of espionage and action concerning the other half. He was in short a perfectly designed machine for the temptation and enchantment of a would-be hero worshiper like Battiste Tommassi, and he did it unconsciously—and Battiste realized that in the first five minutes he spent in his company, minutes that were spent adjusting his chair and laying down his books along with eleven other graduate students around a seminar table while El Lorca extinguished his cigarette and lit another, reached for a paper cup of coffee and took off the lid and took a sip while he was saying hello to three or four regulars and smiling, saying, No, not this week, they still haven't gotten quite bold enough to arrest me, wrist-flipping down pen and pencil and yellow legal pad and glasses on the table, and looking up to look straight into the priest's eyes with a gaze as blue and electric as the spark from an ungrounded wire, while his lean face thinned with surprised recognition and he said, "Why, of course, it's you," and smiled as if they had known one another all their lives.

"So," Ferdinando added, as he sat down and indicated the bloodstained cover of a magazine lying on the table, "who's going to explain to me how the C.I.A. engineered Señor Allende's murder, and how they think the Chileans ought to respond to it?"

The magazine's bloodstains were ink, color-separated over a photograph of the Chilean martyr, and Ferdinando's eyes were bleak despite his flippant manner, tap-tapping with the end of a pencil against the glossy print as he scanned the faces of the twelve students in front of him for their reactions to the week's most lurid headlines. They were a little taken aback by his candor, but only for a moment. One of them, a slight, dark girl of perhaps twenty or twenty-one, with the sharp, violent face of a famished bird, broke out at once, saying, "Look, if we know that the C.I.A. was bribed to rig the elections, if we know that the people from I.T.M. were supplying the military with ammunition and guns—"

"We don't know anything of the sort," a young man drawled, smiling, doodling on a pad in front of him with quick, cartoonlike sketches, and grinning at the young woman as if deliberately to provoke her fury. "All we know for a fact is that I.T.M. made the offer. The reason for plausible deniability is for our friends in Washington to be able to say they rejected the whole idea!"

"Oh, bullshit!"

"*Querida . . . !*"

"Come on, everyone knows they took that money and if you don't think they gave anything back, you probably believe in Tio Sam and every establishment myth since Santa Claus!"

This drew appreciative laughs from the other students, most of whom were Americans, but whose long hair and self-consciously decrepit clothes proclaimed them liberals at least, if not avowed Marxists. Battiste marveled at their innocence, even in their ragged jeans and headbands. They looked like children, and black or white, their skins had the soft bloom of warm shelter and good food: he found it slightly offensive, their dabbling thus academically in horror. He liked the young cartoonist better: his voice was light and pleasant, Caribbean to Battiste's Mayapanian ear, and he had a wide, cynical smile and sharp black eyes, the copper cheeks and straggly black beard of a young *campesino*.

The girl who argued with him was Hispanic as well, although her features showed the strains of Andalusia more than the Amazon: she might have been the daughter of a rich Chilean herself, save that she spoke with abstract anger about the take-over. For his part, he sat incognito, as either a Mayapanian or a priest, in black pants and a white shirt, and because he kept his lips tightly shut (wary refugee) and didn't volunteer an opinion (he'd learned his lesson in Campeche, or so he told himself), he sat locked in his eternal isolation as aloof and shy as if he'd worn a soutane—but without their reticence in front of him, save for his forbidding thoughtfulness. Without his knowing it, his silence made him seem older than the others, more severe and with a firsthand knowledge of bloodshed the others lacked—all save Ferdinando Lorca himself.

"Everyone in the world knows all sorts of things," the young man was saying in a mock-instructive voice, "including the fact that El Presidente Kennedy was not killed by an isolated fanatic, but if you're going to look for proof, it's not going to be so easy. It's like Ferdinando's been telling us—" He reached behind him to tuck strands of his long dark hair back into a rubber band, and Battiste took note of his informality, not merely of clothing but of address. This was neither the typical student's toadying, nor deliberate rudeness, but the easy familiarity of a collaborator, and one who was motivated by a good deal of intelligence and respect.

"—If you're a *gringo*, you have all the dialogue by heart—and if you're a Latin or God knows what, a Martian, I suppose you've got all of *that* dialogue by heart, but it's a different set of words, a different language. Pisita, look: if you were told that the military of a certain country had achieved a coalition of all the political parties, and elected a president by overwhelming popular consent, you'd begin to look for who had counted the votes, and who had received a cabinet post and whose brother had received this or that attractive embassy. That's business as usual in our part of the world. Well, that's exactly the attitude of I.T.M.—for them, this is business as usual! They've got their asses covered, and there's nothing you or I or those poor dead guys down in Chile can do about it! Screwing people is what these guys do for a living!"

This last made even Battiste smile, but the girl was simply

furious. "All right then, that's it, business as usual, and just fuck all the people who get killed or trampled down in the process—is that what you want?"

"Not necessarily!" The young man was laughing so much it occurred to Battiste he might be in love with her.

She threw down her pen and confronted the rest of the group. "Look—this is the same technique that's used by the vested interests all over the place—'It's a different story in that part of the world so don't question things you don't understand.' Well, in Latin America, that's just an excuse for sticking it to the same people you've already been sticking it to for the last one hundred years!"

"Bravo, Pisote!" Ferdinando said, laughing, and stood up to become the peacemaker between them. Battiste noticed that he was very slim: not frail at all, but whip-hard with exercise and an impatient energy. "So. You can't work within a corrupt system, and according to Carlitos, you can't change that system because it's been designed by the other side, so what do you do? Become an anarchist, like your friends in the Weathermen?" There was some indulgent and half-respectful laughter toward the young girl; he must mean it, Battiste thought with surprise. "Allow yourself to be bought off? That's always an option, by the way, you *could* just give up and work for the prevailing rapists, but we'll assume that idea's been tried and found wanting, after the delights of inventing your own recipe for dynamite." He smiled at her, not taunting her at all, and Balliste was struck by the warmth and intimacy in his eyes: for a moment, a privileged instant, he'd made her feel she was his most brilliant student, perhaps the one whose impatience was most like his own. "Come on, give me the party line. 'No isolated urban insurrection can succeed in a primarily colonial environment,' right? All right, Allende tried to extend his revolution into the country, and was brought out of the Moneda Palace in a bag. Tell me. In what way did he go wrong?"

There were little lines of pain or thought around his eyes which had nothing to do with his smile; his slender fingers leaned against the table and lay for a moment against the photographs in the magazine, as if he were pointing to them, bullet-pocked walls and spray-painted slogans, and Battiste felt an answering lurch in his own stomach as he looked at them, because such sights were too recently engraved with shame and terror in his own mind for the geographical difference to matter. He looked at Ferdinando more closely, and tried to guess what had led this artistocratic and intelligent man to risk his life in the hopeless fight for the chicle workers that had led to his eventual arrest. They said they had tortured him. Battiste's eyes instinctively went to the ribs and genitals, both of which were favored Buiztanistas' targets, but he moved like a man who was free from pain: he either had great discipline or a body which forgot the fear of injuries, or both. He was smiling at the girl and coaxing her to answer, perhaps to answer correctly or perhaps incorrectly so he could make a point, and she was looking at him intently, frowning, as if to read her answer from his smooth olive forehead or the tender gaiety in his eyes.

"Action. He should have known the American companies were bound to fight nationalization, and moved to neutralize their ability to attack him."

"Fine." Ferdinando wrote her answer on the blackboard behind him, and turned to face her. "How?"

"How?"

"Yes, how should he have neutralized them? Do you mean kill them? Assassinate all the stockholders in I.T.M.?"

"No." Her lips twitched—apparently dogmatic marxism had not entirely deprived her of a sense of humor. "He could very well have paid them off—that would have been the easiest thing. Or he could have brought some kind of pressure to bear against the American government—I'm not sure what, exactly, but there must have been something—to split the interests of I.T.M. and the United States and make them mutually exclusive." She stopped and shut her lips with a little smile; almost, but not quite, asking him if she'd got it right.

"Very good." He smiled, and wrote her answers on the board as well. "And when the American companies became unhappy with a one-time payoff, when they were used to receiving regular dividends, and the American government realized it couldn't very well have an ongoing fight with the same people who make its business machines and manage its phone lines, he could at least have had the delicacy to pack his bags and retreat in

43

good order like any other banana-republic loser, instead of waiting for Pinochet and his friends to come inside and turn him into a martyr—is that it?"

His smile held the bitter rue of his reluctance to criticize the Chilean president, and encouraged the storm of voices which leapt to Allende's defense. One incipient economist said, "No—he should never have nationalized the copper industry—the other ones don't count, but copper involves too many different businesses—" And someone else was mentioning Cuba and saying they'd certainly nationalized everything *there*, even the rum and the casinos, and Ferdinando lit another cigarette and leaned on the edge of the table, appealing to Carlos and saying, "All right, what do you think about Cuba as a model?"

"Now?" The young man's eyes were merry, and he sat back, crossing his legs. "I think they lost one of the world's great artists and drunks when my parents dragged me out of Havana at the age of ten years old, but I guess they'll get over that! They've got enough drunks there as it is, and they pay their artists less than the capitalists, for all their talk about freedom and economic equality."

The resulting laughter loosened things up, and Ferdinando said, "Well, all right, their cultural shortsightedness, I'll grant you that . . ." and waited until things had quieted down to add, "but what about their economic policies? Does anybody think they're working? Not working? Come on, now, how does their revolution stand up, after twenty years to create a paradise on earth?"

Opinion was split on this point, but vocal, and Ferdinando orchestrated the two arguments without taking sides until the girl with the sharp-boned, famished face lit another cigarette and threw the match into her coffee cup with an impatient gesture, saying, "All right, we know perfectly well what you're leading up to, that marxism doesn't work, that it just means colonialism from Moscow instead of Wall Street! Well, I say give me colonialism by the workers rather than the capitalists, and I'll be better off being exploited by people who are at least nominally on my side!"

Ferdinando collapsed into his chair at the applause which greeted her accusation, and said, laughing, "My God, Pisote! I

never said that! You've got a better grasp of the principles of rhetoric than I do!"

"Well, I just get mad," she said, smiling a little and tossing
her cigarette into her coffee cup after her match.

"I can see *that*! Well, now that I've been accused, I can see
I'd better come up with some answers." He smiled and thought a
moment further before he spoke. "Of course socialism's the obvious answer—the only way to stop being a colony is to own your
own land, and the quickest way to throw out the big corporations
is to incorporate yourself. Fine, but where do we go from there?"
His bright blue gaze searched them each curiously, as if both
challenging and expecting them to answer. "Does the next step
have to be marxism? Apparently. There's no other ready-made
path, although I for one would like to see one. There *has* to be
some alternative besides jumping straight into Moscow's lap, the
minute you've wrestled yourself out of the avuncular embraces of
Uncle Sam, but I'm damned if I can see it! Can you?" His fine
eyes were honestly baffled, asking them for answers as much for
his own sake as for the minimally important rationales of tests
and grades, and he scanned their faces, young, trusting, and came
to rest for a thoughtful moment on Battiste's attentive, acne-
scarred face before moving on. He looked down at his hands and
shrugged.

"Well, there you are, there's your omniscient teacher for
you. Of course I have opinions—what thinking man wouldn't?—
but even if I were to possess a whole glittering theory of anticapi-
talist action—how should I express it? Here?" He nodded to
include the cluttered office, the starkly modern walls lit by fluorescent lights (because though it was scarcely four o'clock in the
afternoon and late September, the sky had grown cloudy and
dark, presaging rain), the incongruously small, leaded gothic
windows, and his lips twisted. "As a matter of fact, I have no such
theory. I think Allende was a martyr, but not to the socialist's
ideal. He was a martyr to unreality, to the hallucination that the
United States doesn't exist, that it isn't a capitalist system. And
that it would simply *tolerate* a socialist democracy in this hemisphere—it won't. Chile was too much of a figurative bogey, but it
was also too much of a literal one: it offered the one real threat

you can make against an exploitative system, the visible existence of a choice." He shook his head, and through his bafflement there could be glimpsed a trace of wry humor. "He certainly made them call in the Marines down there! God, strafing the palace with aircraft and machine guns—that's one way to get yourself into the history books, make them destroy the entire country as a way of tearing down one single man. Perhaps that was Allende's point. You can kill me, but you'll have to admit I touched a nerve—the diseased tooth between what this country *says* it believes in, and what it actually supports. That's something to be said. I wonder if he realized that. I could see him, in that case, opting for a deliberate suicide, rather than letting himself be butchered pointlessly in some Sala de Interrogaciones."

His face darkened as if he'd come upon a memory he'd rather have sidestepped, but his hesitation was lost within the new storm of discussion occasioned by the question of whether Allende had been murdered (as the left contended) or had committed suicide. El Lorca made a casual comment about the Americans' love of a conspiracy—ever since the Kennedy assassination, they refused to believe that anyone was buried in the graves assigned to them—but for the most part he was silent, tapping with his pencil on the yellow legal pad in front of him, and Battiste was silent too, watching the thin lines of tension which bracketed his mouth, his white knuckles as he played with the pencil, tap, tap, tap, his eyes contemplating the bloodstained poster on the cover of the magazine. When the bell rang for the end of class, he was distracted for a moment, and then looked up.

"Well, let's call it a day, shall we? I'm sure we can solve the world's problems next Tuesday, when I also promise to teach you something, and earn my salary and your degrees, not necessarily in that order. All right? Oh—" He turned gracefully from tossing away his empty pack of cigarettes, and made an apologetic face. "I'm afraid I won't be in town for the latter part of this week, so the meetings I've had scheduled with individuals will have to be put off till next Monday and Wednesday, I'm afraid something unexpected has come up. You can call the department office and set up a time, and if your advisers balk at your slothfulness you can tell them it's all my fault, and you're thinking of getting the University to revoke my green card." He smiled and turned away from their laughter with the perfect timing of an actor who knows better than to overstuff his audience with infatuation, and modestly started putting away books, that was it, the performance was over for the day, and Battiste stood up reluctantly to leave with the others when Ferdinando turned to him and said casually, as if it were the most habitual thing in the world, "Why don't you join me for a cup of Mayapanian coffee, after penitentially drinking this stuff all afternoon? I know a place over on Columbus Avenue that sells the real thing, it's like fragrant ambrosia after this horse piss from Chock Full O' Nuts, and besides I'd enjoy the company."

"I—I'm afraid I—"

"You've got to be going?" Those startling blue eyes looked at him with teasing directness, and he said after a moment, "No you don't. You haven't got a single thing better to do than come and have coffee with me, so why don't you do it?"

Battiste swallowed to hide his confusion, and only succeeded in becoming more confused. "But I—I don't know what we'd have to talk about—"

"So? Don't talk about anything, if you don't want to. God knows *I* talk enough to put ten people to sleep, *and* prevent them from getting a word in edgewise, so you'd better come with me and have ten cups of coffee and not utter a sound, and by rights I should find you the perfect companion."

While he was talking, he finished straightening his office and put the lights out, and turning to the priest as if he were introducing himself, he held out his hand. "Come on. I promise not to rape, seduce, or molest you in any way—nor to involve you to international espionage—that is, at least not unless you want to. I've got two hours until my plane leaves for Santiago, and I'd like to spend them in the company of someone who comes from the same flyspeck on the map as I do, it'll put into perspective what is a probably useless and possibly foolhardy gesture." He turned behind them to lock the door of his office, saying, "You can't be too careful, they might have to seal this with tape and only open it after they've recovered my body—"

And only then did Battiste realize what he was talking about and stammered, "You mean you're flying to Chile—tonight? In the middle of everything that's going on down there?"

"Well, it's rather *because* of everything that's going on down there that I'm flying down tonight," Ferdinando said, pausing on the steps outside his office to open his umbrella against the drizzle and offering to share it with Battiste.

"You see," he added, as they crossed the campus like any two academics, chatting on the way to a faculty dinner or class, "I got caught in the middle of some rather delicate negotiations with Allende myself, and there are some papers of mine that I'd just as soon General Pinochet didn't have, if it's all the same with his secret service. Not that they'll ever amount to anything now, but for old times' sake, I'd prefer the Americans—and also the new Chilean government, as far as *that* goes—not to know exactly what I've been up to."

He smiled at Battiste—who was staring at him with the openmouthed amazement of someone who'd give up any pretense of not being surprised—and unbent enough to add, in a private whisper, "Don't be too taken in by the James Bond trappings. Most negotiations between heads of state and out-of-work radicals are pretty boring, the only interesting aspect in this instance was getting to see firsthand the mess Allende made of his labor relations. I could have done much better than him, but unfortunately—or fortunately, as it turned out—I wasn't in a position to put in a bid for his job."

Battiste felt himself swimming in a sea of unfamiliar possibilities not all of which could be true—he felt as if he couldn't be sure of anything with this vital, demanding, challenging man who walked beside him with the quick step of a man in a hurry and, at the same time, the easy grace of long friendship, a man who spoke to him as if he didn't have a secret to hide in the world, but who spoke of secrets that could have affected the destinies of nations—a man whose lean, handsome face had the sharp, hard attractiveness of a bird of prey, yet whose eyes were the color of drenched violets, and whose long-fingered, graceful hands were the hands of a musician or an artist. Battiste felt lumpy and awkward by comparison, stolid and slow-witted and unintelligent beyond belief—my God, couldn't he think of a single thing to say that would recommend him as having a brain in his head!—and he mumbled, as they entered the coffee shop and moved from the cold dampness outside of autumn rain, to the warm, fragrant

48

dampness of wet wool and fresh pastry and cappuccino steam, "Don't you—I mean, didn't you say you didn't approve of marxism as a system, I mean socialism—I mean, didn't you say it wouldn't work?"

"What I say in class and what I do in the so-called real world are two very different things—unfortunately," Ferdinando said, putting up his hand to indicate a moment's silence while he ordered two coffees from the waitress. "The Russians like to flatter themselves that they're doing more than the Americans to subvert Third World countries, while the Americans like to flatter themselves that they're doing less. I let myself be courted by both sides, and I flutter my eyes and tell them how *macho* they are and all that stuff, but I very rarely have to 'put out' anything and I find out a lot of useful information in the process. Also—thank you—" for the coffee, and he put a teaspoonful of sugar into his cup and stirred thoughtfully. "The game of political analysis is all very well, and you can sit on the sidelines and talk about who's doing what to whom and get all worked up, but it's really just playing with yourself under the sheets, and rather distasteful to a man who has any real balls and would like to be out taking part in the action—" He drank a sip of coffee and added, looking up with a smile, "I hope I don't offend you with my metaphors, I'm somewhat out of practice tailoring my language for a priest, you'll have to forgive me. Or do all priests use bad language now? What's the prevailing opinion since Vatican Two?"

Battiste felt the back of his neck getting hot, as if he'd been found out in the shameful secret of his priesthood, and he looked down at his cup while those intent eyes probed his feelings like a scalpel and then he heard that mellifluous, carrying voice say, "I thought Cardinal Fuertes was a good man, but he could have done more good for Mayapán if he'd had the common sense to remain alive. You've got nothing to be ashamed about."

By which alchemy more pain than Ferdinando could possibly have known about was erased, wiped out, because Battiste had never even admitted to himself his irrational guilt that it had been his superior, rather than he, who had been assassinated. He felt his heart swell gratefully in his chest, and he savored the sensation as he did any kindness directed toward him, sipping his coffee and trying at the same time to pass the matter off as a small thing. "It's nice of you to say so, considering the suffering you went through for *your* beliefs! I know it's inexact, but I'll always feel as if I got off more or less scot-free!"

The minute he said it he sensed the tension in the other man, as nothing visible, but merely the sudden stillness of a turning inward against memory, the momentary tightening of his lips which gave his face a stonier appearance, and the complete absence of expression which made his light, vivid eyes grow suddenly dark blue and opaque. He didn't say anything, but stirred and then sipped his coffee, and after a moment he said, "Well, it's not a course of study that I'd recommend to the average student, it can let loose more possibilities for recanting than it hardens into idealistic resolve, and even when it doesn't . . . well, let's just say it teaches you some things about yourself that you might have preferred not to know."

Battiste wavered, tact warring with kindness and curiosity in equal parts, and when the silence continued unbroken between them he finally gave in and said hesitantly, "What do you—what do you mean?"

Ferdinando drank the rest of his coffee and reached into his pocket for a fresh pack of cigarettes before he answered, and when he did his lips curved again into his familiar ironic smile, a little bitter perhaps, but also ruefully gentle. "Thus does the inveterate *poseur* pretend to a dignity of conscience he does not, in fact, possess. . . . I just meant that it might be better for all concerned if I did *not* reach the position of the late Señor Allende— or the unfortunately still-living Señor de Buiztas, take your choice. However. That's *probably* less likely than the eventuality that I'll *get* there, so one way or another the world will simply have to put up with me and live with that." He smiled at Battiste and lit his cigarette, looking for a moment at his watch. "So, tell me a little bit about yourself. Where are you from in Mayapán? What's your background? I have twenty minutes before I have to leave for the airport and I hate silence. So talk to me, tell me something to distract me from my own yapping."

Battiste stammered his way through a few banal facts, and such was Ferdinando's interest, his flattering, natural, unforced way of drawing him out, that he forgot for a little while his innate, crippling shyness and talked freely, indeed volubly, about himself. It turned out that Ferdinando was not such an aristocrat as he imagined him to be: they came from the same rough Westside of Campeche that had also spawned the dictator Quintero de Buiztas, the area of slums and small, two-story houses where dogs fought and ran wild in the vacant lots, and men fought and ran wild too, the true desperadoes, because they had given up hope. They discovered they'd taken similar routes out of the dead end of Campeche: Battiste into the Church and Ferdinando with a scholarship from the military. They discovered their mothers had had the same first name: Leonor, or in Battiste's case Leonora, and even El Lorca's background was not unmixed Spanish, for like all the *porteños* he was a mixture of French and Italian and Spanish like Battiste. In Ferdinando's case he even had some Indian ancestry, which accounted for his dark, high-cheekboned face and jet-black hair, along with the incongruous lightness of his eyes.

"It's true, I'm a mongrel." Ferdinando laughed. "God knows I'll never win any prizes for my pedigree."

Their parents were dead, in Ferdinando's case dying young, and he glanced down at his long fingers, hesitating, when Battiste asked him how it had happened. "A tram accident," he said slowly. "My mother fell, and was pinned between two cars. My father tried to rescue her, and one of the wheels crushed his spine. It took him six hours to die in the hospital, while I was with him." He looked off into the middle distance thoughtfully. "The only thing he couldn't believe, up until his death, was that my mother was no longer alive. He simply ruled that out. That was a fact that didn't exist in his universe—his death, all of that he could handle. He simply refused to believe that my mother had not survived the crash."

Battiste looked down at his own, big-boned hands, and said with some embarrassment, "I'm afraid my father left us when I was fifteen. I don't know what ever became of the old bastard." He laughed suddenly. "Do you know, I've never called him that before, but of course he was. I was always too afraid to hurt my mother—but she's dead now too."

They were silent, together, for a moment, remembering their histories, as the rain fell with greater intensity outside the window of the café and the place began to fill up with people. There were students from the University, but Ferdinando remained unnoticed, deliberately so, leaning slightly farther over the table and shielding his cheek with his long hand. A student knocked against their table in passing, dropping a book and not realizing it, going on with his companions out the door, gesturing with a bottle of Budweiser. Ferdinando bent next to the table and retrieved the book. It was a copy of *The Shadow Jaguar*, the first book by the poet Porfirio Cheruña to gain international fame and acceptance, and was by now a classic text in Spanish-American literature. Ferdinando Lorca smiled as he riffled through the paperback's dog-eared pages.

"Look, this is what really endures in our culture, the tricks and illusions of this old fox. Have you read him?"

"Not his latest," Battiste said, a shade too dismissively, for he admired Porfirio Cheruña's writing. "He teaches here at the University. Do you know him?"

"I've met him a couple of times," Ferdinando said lightly. "He's a pretentious old relic, and cruel. He's vicious with his students. Yet I can't get over his once being able to write this—"

He quoted from the book, in his beautiful voice. " 'I can stand on the pier at twilight and feel nothing, not the slightest stir of remembrance; no, nor when I stand in the shadow of those ancient walls, am I troubled by your love. I am unmoved, nor is it the sudden scent of bougainvillea that undoes me, jungle country, yet I am ravished by your beauty, old and new, without a clue to your mystery, I lie down once again, helpless, in the land from which I was born.' " He paused and then said as he put the book down, "That's what endures, rhetoric and sentiment—and love, or whatever phrase you want to use for it—love of one's country, of one's past, for God knows what—love of the future, of the possibility that you could do something better than anyone else, do something nobler, make something make sense, perhaps just make something look different than it ever has before!" He stood up and laughed. "All from the pen of a third-rate scribbler who never put together six decent lines in his life! There's our ridiculous country for you! No wonder the *gringos* think we're fools—I think we're pretty foolish myself most of the time. What else can you do with a silly country like ours but laugh?"

He did laugh, but without any animosity or rancor. There was a wealth of tenderness in his laugh which embraced their country and their past in equal part, but remained specific enough to implant the incipient love in Battiste's breast as though it were set in cement. He put his hand on Ferdinando's arm and said rapidly without pausing to consider what he was saying, "Look, why go to Santiago, you said yourself it was a useless gesture and you'll run too much of a risk. Let somebody else go, *I'll* go if I have to, they'll never kill a priest and if they do so what, what's the loss, but it's ridiculous for you to go down there and get shot for no good reason whatsoever! It's too much! You can see a way out of this mess for our country, and that's too rare a gift for you to waste it getting yourself killed for some fool who couldn't even manage his labor relations!"

Ferdinando looked at him as if he'd suddenly lost his mind, with touched delight but also with considerable surprise, and when he'd finished he gently prized the priest's fingers from his arm and shook his head as if saying no to a child, murmuring, "My God, you're as bad as Pisote, all you people have nothing better to do than to kill yourselves. Shall I tell you how Pisote got her nickname? It's the name of a clever little animal that lives out in the jungle among the ruins—but it's an animal that's very hard to *catch*, and if Pisote didn't share its attributes, she'd be dead by now, with all her idealistic bomb-throwing. I assure you I'm not going to get myself shot for anyone—least of all Salvador Allende, who's dead anyway, so what would be the point? I'll be back in town in three days, and I'll give you a call when I land. Perhaps—" He hesitated, and added, "Perhaps there are some things that you might like to do to help in our fight to oust the dictator Buiztas? Would you like that? Would that satisfy your appetite for sacrifice and bloodshed?" And he smiled at him.

There were many reasons why Battiste should have said no. Perhaps Ferdinando was even making fun of him, but the sparkling gaiety in his eyes convinced Battiste that his heart had already signed up for the duration with this spellbinding, lonely, charismatic man, and it would be ridiculous for the rest of his awkward body and his possibly useful mind not to follow suit. He gave Ferdinando his phone number, and watched him write it down on a matchbook, saying to himself, "My God, now I've seduced a priest," without it occurring to Battiste that there was anything more in his comment than self-mockery. It didn't seem possible that he might have been watching a perfectly crafted performance, tailored to an audience of one, by an actor so in love with applause that each performance attained a kind of truth. He was too infatuated at the moment to think clearly, to imagine any duplicity in his hero, or to care. Only later did he begin to think in those terms—to think that Ferdinando might have been wooing him, might have said and done all the perfect things to convince him of his integrity, his sincerity, his brilliance—but even then he had to admit that that was only half the truth. Because Ferdinando was so in love with love that he actually went out and *did* the things that procured it: taught students or championed the chicle workers, or, in this case, went to Santiago on a fool's errand simply to protect a dead fool's reputation—and his own. When Battiste thought about their first meeting later, that was a factor that he always had trouble adding in.

But at the time it seemed the most natural thing in the world. He shook Ferdinando's hand and wished him well with the Chilean fascists, and when he came back alive and telephoned him that same night, Battiste found himself enlisted in the Movimiento Revolucionario de Mayapán and plotting the overthrow of the dictator Quintero de Buiztas, and having the time of his life.

four

WHEN SHE WAS SIXTEEN, Battiste helped Camila enroll in Columbia University.

It was the obvious solution, and high time too, because by that point the nuns had despaired of teaching her anything more. She was polite, she was always exquisitely well-behaved, but she was bored to the point of distraction and consequently a bad influence on her schoolmates. And for her part, Camila was excited at the prospect of attending a university, without bodyguards, as she herself demanded: "I refuse to be a freak. If they want to kill me, let them kill me." Battiste was ecstatically proud of her. She was his pride, his crowning achievement as a teacher, and he wanted to show her off before a larger audience. Besides, as he himself diffidently assured her aunt and uncle, he was also a student, in the politics department, and could look after and advise her; her aunt and uncle were casually pleased. They were off on an extended visit to Europe, on business that would keep them in Germany for the better part of the next few years, and more schooling seemed the perfect solution to their solitary niece's disposition. They wished her well. She would have the run of the Turtle Bay apartment, she would have a housekeeper and a maid, and Battiste, and she was certainly mature for her years. They flew off to Bonn and forgot about her.

And yet she was uncertain, for a moment deathly afraid, when the day came for her first day of classes. Her dauntless courage, which had seen her through the deaths of her parents without a whimper; which had seen her through the long journey from Campeche and the sea to the vertiginous mountains of Manhattan skyscrapers, and which had enabled her to withstand the awkward love of Father Battiste with a steadfast belief in its innocence, momentarily deserted her when she stood on the busy campus in front of the ivy-and-chrome buildings for the first time. She felt the press of people, the curious stares of strangers, and her small hands trembled as she pressed her books against her child's white cotton blouse and wished she hadn't come. She wanted to run away—but she was the daughter of warriors, and she refused to give in to her fear for a minute. Straightening her shoulders, she smiled her dazzling white smile and sailed into the room designated for her first class, because there was nothing in the world but yourself that could kill you, so what the hell.

Her first class was with the poet and preeminent literary celebrity of the University, Porfirio Cheruño—because Battiste admired his work in spite of all El Lorca's reservations, and because he was Mayapanian himself, a walking vindication of their native culture, even if he *had* spent the last twenty years of his life in New York, and was proud of his Spanish and English blood. He was a popular teacher (the spiteful said because he was easy), and the large airy classroom was crowded when Camila dos Santos walked down the central aisle like a beautiful statue, with her heart in her mouth, and found a seat down in front, where for some reason there were a number of empty chairs. She sat down and crossed her legs. She was prepared henceforward to learn everything she could.

Porfirio Cheruña was suffering from indigestion that morning. He had dined unintentionally the night before on a bouillabaisse containing shrimp, and the iodine flavor of the fish had left a metallic taste on his palate which still lingered. He was also acutely annoyed by his schedule, which necessitated his arrival at the University an hour earlier than usual, scarcely correct for a man of his advanced age. He was sixty-three. He smoothed down his vest over his still flat stomach, checked the crease of his trousers, and set his steel-rimmed spectacles carefully on his nose—spectacles which were exactly the same make and style as those worn by Quintero de Buiztas, although as between the elegant, epicene college professor and the swarthy dictator there could not have been a more disparate comparison. Then he took a deep breath and was ready to face all of those awful, eager students. He hoped that he would have a few mildly interesting ones this semester.

He knew that he did, from the moment he saw Camila. He directed his remarks to her, the way he always did to students in the first row, and as the class went on Camila began to feel vaguely uncomfortable. She put it down to her shyness, but the avidity with which the old man looked at her, the subtle blandishments of his voice, and the thin, rather pitiless line of his lips disturbed her. She found it difficult to concentrate. After the class was over, she stood up, and as she was about to leave Professor Cheruña called to her. She went up to the elegant and frigid and disquieting old man, whose clothing had the faint scent of cologne and whose skin had the dry, preserved texture of rice paper, stretched taut over his beautiful bones, and allowed him to take her cold hand and murmur, "Ah, Señorita, I had no idea I would be so fortunate, to teach someone of such beauty!" and allowed him to invite her to lunch.

She was afraid of him. She was afraid of his international fame and his blue-veined hands, his cosmopolitan assurance in the restaurant he took her to just off Fifth Avenue, where all the waiters recognized him, and most of the patrons; he shed his identity of a college professor as easily as a dowdy skin, and became a celebrity. She allowed him to order for her, feeling young and underdressed in her simple white blouse and skirt; she ate her soup, her filet of sole and cheese and fresh fruit cup as if she had been eating sand, but she caught a glimpse of herself in one of the gilt-edged mirrors of the restaurant and was surprised: she looked older, with a long slender neck and thoughtful blue eyes, a mature woman, making her schoolgirl's outfit perversely sexy and fashionable. Her companion dominated the conversation. Speaking about literature or wines or himself, he had an exquisitely trained voice (he had studied extensively with actors, preparatory to his many appearances on television), and his bony, prehensile fingers slid under her skirt behind the cover of the tablecloth, quite plainly mocking her to scream within the confines of a crowded restaurant.

She pressed her legs together against that intimate assault, widening her eyes without uttering a sound, but he merely slid his hand a little higher, leaning toward her across the table as if he wished to make a particular point, while his fingers probed and caressed between the warm skin of her inner thighs. She was too frightened to protest, as his hand took greater and greater liberties with her, holding her eyes with his own behind his ice-cold, steel-rimmed spectacles, so that he knew as much by her expression as by the ease with which he suddenly reached her underpants that she had decided to let him do what he wanted to her.

He amused himself a moment longer, then withdrew his hand and looked at his watch. "I'm afraid I must run, I have an appointment, but allow me to get you a taxi to see you home." He stood up. Somehow, she stumbled to her feet, and followed him out of the elegant restaurant into the bright glare of the street, which hurt her eyes, while he spoke all the while of inconsequential things, and put her into a cab on Fifth Avenue and paid the fare without touching her again. As she rode home inside the enormous interior of the taxi she examined her feelings. She was embarrassed, and shocked at him, yet unavoidably flattered, and frightened, as if he had threatened to hurt her. She considered telling someone—certainly, Battiste—but in the end her embarrassment won out and she decided not to tell anyone. Her next class with Porfirio Cheruña was three days later, and she trembled as she sat in the front row, wearing a light print dress that showed the beautiful line of her throat, but he ignored her. Two days later, she received a note at her desk: "Please give me the great pleasure of having dinner with me tonight at La Côte Basque. Your admirer, Porfirio Cheruña"—to which he had added a postscript: "Please break my heart, and wear the print dress." She accepted.

And to her surprise, their dinner that night was thoroughly enjoyable, with Porfirio telling her funny stories and coaxing her into a general recapitulation of her family's history (which she easily managed to keep light, smiling her beautiful smile), while they ate snails and steak tartare, sipping wine and deciding against dessert, that they would just have coffee. As the waiter set the cups down Porfirio reached across the table and gently took her hand. She stiffened but refrained from drawing away.

"Don't be afraid, *pobrecita*, I'm not going to hurt you. I just want to thank you for giving me a most enjoyable evening, of the kind an old monument like myself can rarely enjoy anymore. You can understand that, that I would enjoy being seen with a beautiful young woman—still with the ability to appreciate your fresh loveliness, my sweet, despite the difference in our ages and situations at the University—does that shock you? You must become more sophisticated, *querida*, and learn to accept a man's admiration as a compliment, his visible applause, so to speak—importunate, perhaps, in a man of my age, but not lightly occasioned—I assure you, I am not usually so moved, so extremely moved, as I am by your extraordinary beauty tonight. . . ."

And all the while he was speaking, his fingers were lightly, slowly caressing her palm, and his eyes held her hypnotized, paralyzed with embarrassment, unable to look at his fingers which had moved in that same, exploratory way between her thighs.

He didn't let go of her hand, or cease his lightly tormenting caresses, as he gave the waiter a hundred-dollar bill, left the change, and drew her to her feet, nor did he let her go after he had placed her coat lightly over her shoulders, gently massaging her shoulder blades as he got in beside her in the cab. She heard his address on Sutton Place through a haze, but she wasn't truly afraid; but rather curious with a suffocating anxiety and a light-headed feeling of inevitability as she felt his fingers sliding up her skirt again, inside the public darkness of the cab, caressing the inside of her legs, her belly, her thin cotton panties and then she heard the first changed sound from him, a soft moan, which seemed to escape his lips against his will.

He told the taxi driver to go around the block, while he slipped down her panties, drawing her slightly closer to him on the vinyl seat, still not touching her in any other respect but slowly insinuating his fingers into her body, stroking her in an unbelievably private way which left nothing in the universe but the gradual amazement of her feelings of drowning and being violated at the same time, ashamed of his intimate knowledge of her and gasping at the unexpected pain and pleasure. She closed her eyes, letting his fingers increase the swampy reverberations which were keeping her there, pinned to the seat of the taxi—when suddenly he withdrew his hand and got out his wallet to pay the cabdriver, quite as if nothing had happened, as they pulled up to the curb in front of his address. He helped her out of the taxi, and they rode the elevator in silence to his penthouse apartment, where he helped her undress, and when her slender, childlike body was shivering naked in front of him he held her on his lap and manipulated her more thoroughly with a rubber phallus until she was awash in a sea of pleasure and the crotch of his trousers was soaked with semen. She became his mistress for four years.

Even for a man of his wordly stature and his immense contributions to literature, his white hair and his benevolent identity as a popular sage, the sudden acquisition of a sixteen-year-old mistress would have been cause for some comment, but Porfirio Cheruña was a skillful actor, and moreover he had the entire weight of his spotless reputation on his side. She was not the first little girl he had seduced, and his publishers and his readers had never been offended by the breath of scandal, or the suggestion that their beloved storyteller was anything less than what he seemed, although they wondered why he had never married. It took Camila some time to realize the true nature of his desires. Initially, she found herself ashamed and secretive, embarrassed by her pleasure, upset by the meticulous calculation with which he caressed her and called her his little whore, and confused by his refusal to behave toward her in the normal manner of a lover, until she realized he was more moved by her excitement—while he remained detached, watching her, relieving her frenzy or cruelly prolonging it—than he could ever be by any satisfaction of his own. Their secret united them in a silence consecrated by the shameful nights when he would force her to her knees while he fumblingly opened his trousers, sitting at the big desk in his study where he wrote his books, stroking her hair and calling her his *querida*, his little sweetheart, while he searched for the cleanliness of a relief that always eluded him. At the University, he was immaculate as always, and she used to wonder that this composed and somewhat severe old man could be her lover who had driven her wild with his caresses the night before, dying of his love for her, making her stand on a low table in his living room like a pale living statue, while he gently touched her, oh my God, yes, yes, parting her sex with the very tips of his fingers so that he could see the exact moment of her involuntary contractions, ah, *querida*....

She also wondered at the sharpness of his cruelty toward her in class, the stinging humiliation of his criticisms, until she realized that this was neither shame nor excessive fair play on his part, but the desire to find her more tractable when she was alone with him. That was when she determined to outwit him with the full power of her mind, and achieved such spectacular successes at the University in such a short time that there was no way he could criticize her without revealing a suspicious partiality on his part. But she did not succeed in extricating herself from his malign influence, and indeed, as time went on, felt herself falling more than ever under his spell, breathing the steamy air of his old man's love like the miasmic effusion of a pestilence, and drowning in the secret flattery of his perversity.

Her relationship with Battiste fell to pieces. He couldn't understand her blushes, her evasiveness and the dark circles which began to hollow her eyes with a wistful sadness, and because he was incapable of imagining her in any circumstance of less than immaculate innocence, he effectively forced her to lie to him. He forced her to lie when they had lunch together at the University and he refused to listen to her conversational gambits of, What do you think, Father, is it wrong to force yourself on another person? He refused to understand what she meant, she told him she had to go to the doctor and he evaded the cause of her illness literally putting his hands over his ears, saying, I don't want to hear anything about this, while he smiled and his eyes winced and he looked at her with his mute adoration of an adoring father and begged her with bantering laughter not to hurt him. She gave up. They still saw each other almost every day, on the way to a class or sharing a sandwich on the steps of Low Library, and he probed with discreet inquiries the distance that he instinctively felt opening up between them—and she dug deep into her inner resources and managed to simulate an innocence that she no longer felt, and was able to convince him of her continued happiness, a small price to pay, so she felt (in any event she had no means in her heart to refuse him), for the peace and serenity she gave him, and more and more often she felt herself to be nothing but an ambidextrous whore. Sometimes the unreality of her two so-different lovers made her head spin, and as time went on, the attenuation of being his *angelita* for Battiste and his secret harlot for Porfirio Cheruña made her own self become very thin and frail, and her blue eyes became large and clairvoyant like the eyes of a plaster saint in a church, and she started at any sound. Her friends and teachers attributed her distracted uncertainty to the natural anxieties of youth, and were encouraged in this by Camila's own stubborn secrecy; she couldn't explain her situation as anything other than an entrapment, but it was an entrapment of her own devising, because she was bound by the shameful necessities of love. It was around that time that a visit from her aunt and uncle informed her of their decision to remain in Europe indefinitely, and it was then that Porfirio Cheruña suggested that she move in with him.

He was, as always, exquisitely careful of his reputation. White-haired, and favoring a cane in public, he presented himself at the Tepplers' apartment and outlined, in his beautiful voice, his reasonable proposition: that their niece's brilliant progress at the University should not be impeded by a sudden change in residence, and that his own enormous apartment on Sutton Place was far too big for him to live in as a feeble old bachelor. He proposed to act as her unofficial guardian, along with a fictitious sister and an equally fictitious housekeeper, and so convincing was his enactment of the extreme fragility and decrepitude of old age that no one more grandfatherly and gentle could have been imagined. Camila watched the performance with a grudging admiration from the next room; she particularly admired the slight tremor of senility which he managed to suggest with his beautiful, torturer's fingers, and the smile of his implacable lips. She was terrified at the prospect of living with him, and unable to wrench herself away from a perverse attraction to his unbelievable suggestion. Ernst and Maria Teppler asked for her opinion, and she was able to say calmly that Señor Cheruña was extremely kind and generous, and that he was very famous and she supposed no more impeccable companion could be found for her in her dear aunt and uncle's absence. So it was decided. On her first night's residence in the apartment she became unexpectedly hysterical, and Porfirio Cheruña was forced to swab her forehead with alcohol and rock her like a child in his arms in order to keep her screams from being audible through the walls—and only much later, after they had both fallen asleep on the sofa, was he able to awaken her and obtain the sweet passion from her which he desired, and which was becoming more and more necessary for him in order to stay alive. He was very careful with her that first week, loving her gently without hurting her and solicitous of her desires as a suitor, and gradually she relaxed and became less afraid of him. Her eyes were still sad, and her slenderness made her cheekbones stick out with a painful, fragile beauty, but she was able to smile with the incredible serenity which enchanted everyone who looked at her—although her smile was no longer radiant as the sun, but had the paler, more numinous quality of the moon at the wane.

Battiste suffered. By an almost supernatural act of faith he managed to convince himself that her presence in Porfirio Cheruña's apartment was innocent; but he knew her too well to believe that she was happy. The gap between them which he himself had forced left him too embarrassed to question her directly, and her own pride erected a brittle facade of lies, which enabled them to speak to one another but only on the most trivial of subjects. She hid the pain of her occasional wounds from him, straps on her wrists, shameful, internal pains from his endless probing of her sex, and occasional wilder blows from his cane, his hands, which he soothed later with remorse, a washcloth soaked in warm water, and the secret cruelty of his love. She had become Porfirio Cheruña's acquisition, like his collection of Mayan antiquities, as she realized fully the first time he had a party in his apartment and she was displayed for his friends, cold-bloodedly, the flattering light of the fire warming the soft curve of her hips and the nipples of her breasts which she attempted to cover with her hands. No word from Porfirio, but rather a strange intuition on her part made her gradually lower her arms, aware of the rapturous vulnerability of her audience. For the first time she experienced the heady thrill of being absolutely powerful, in that context, over men who ruled the world: highly placed men of business, and politics; the Mexican ambassador, and the president-elect of El Salvador; the American Secretary of Defense—slowly turning to allow them to be imprinted with the distracting memory of her satiny thighs, their devastation before the naked body of a young girl. She was never to forget that introduction into the teasing game of power, or the secret pleasure she derived from it—pleasure which was cold and slightly forbidding, because it left only a sterile emptiness inside of her, and a little silt of mud. Many years later, she was to feel that same pleasure on the balcony of the Presidential Palace, and to flee from it in horror.

But in those remote years when she was seventeen, when she had yet to realize her incredible destiny and was still tasting with small bites the bittersweet fruits of depravity, she was also leading a false life of normality outside the hot, moist prison of Porfirio Cheruña's apartment. Since the tensile strength of her will was so strong, then, that it could sustain her through anything, not having been worn away yet by the sands of pity, and the terrible years of love and struggle when she was fighting for power in Mayapán, she bore up under her humiliation with a sense of humor, and even managed to keep her balance, not knowing how she accomplished that feat of acrobatics from one moment to the next. It was around that time when she was walking across the commons in front of Low Library, with Battiste, that they saw from a distance a tall man in his shirt sleeves stop Porfirio Cheruña and speak with him, and even from a distance the quiet authority of the younger man could be seen to give the older man pause for a moment, as he held up his hand, shaking his head, smiling his thin false smile, and hurried away from him—while the tall man in his shirt sleeves followed him with his eyes with a look of piercing intensity, his light eyes sparkling in his dark, thin, incisively handsome face. So affecting was that clairvoyant look that Camila didn't know what to do, she felt a painful blush staining her cheeks, and she asked Battiste almost at random who he was.

"Who? Where, *querida*?"

"There, that man." She pointed, not wishing to be seen pointing, and added, "The tall man, with the blue eyes," although from that distance she could not possibly have seen what color his eyes were.

Battiste looked where she pointed and felt a momentary twist of not unpleasant jealousy—his own love both yearned for and hated the idea of sharing Ferdinando with anybody—and he said thickly, "That's Ferdinando Lorca, the man I was telling you about. Come on, you ought to meet him, you'll love him, everybody loves him and he'll love you, you were made for each other."

"No, I don't think so," she said, hesitating and drawing away, the frightened blush ebbing from her cheeks and leaving them very pale. "I don't think he'd like me at all—"

"Nonsense, you're the most beautiful creature in the world, he'll go crazy for you—"

"No—" She pulled away from him and stood biting her lip, not torn by any indecision but a wild yearning, for what she didn't know, and finally she said, "No, he sees through Porfirio, he'll see through me and he won't like me—I'll disappoint him too much—" And then she ran away from Battiste into the anonymous sanctuary of the library, with its labyrinths and its books in a thousand languages from cultures all over the world, written by the crabbed hands of panting old men in the desperate insomnia of their desires, in the hot air of midnight, in the steaming senility of their studies with their pants pulled down around their knees, because goddamn it it was too much, and there were some pains that were just too terrible to be borne.

five

T HE BRACKISH POOLS, and lush black decay of the jungle, the mysterious wells in the vast northern chalk wastes of the Yucatán finally woke up the dictator Quintero de Buiztas after twenty-nine years of his improvisatory stewardship and he authorized the *gringos* to make a test, just a little test, of the country's resources and untapped reserves just to please an old man, because of course there was nothing there—with the surprising results, which surprised everyone but Buiztas, that the entire country of Mayapán, border to border, was swimming on one of the world's largest reserves of oil.

It was an upsetting discovery. The unenthusiastic scientists, whose job it was to look for riches in the most godforsaken countries in the world, checked and rechecked their findings and finally revealed that what had seemed a political fact was in essence a mirage, an illusion of time and luck: no monopoly existed for the Middle East and small-fry Mexico, and here was a whole new player in the games of energy and extortion—in effect, a whole new ball game. This was made more complicated by the fact that Mayapán had no industry: barely the wherewithal to get the electric lights going in the Presidential Palace after a flash flood knocked out the generator, and for three days the entire government read by candlelight and drank warm beer. Ninety percent of the population still did their business in public latrines and washed their clothes in public sewers because the Army was always talking about putting in nationwide plumbing and never got around to it; and 95 percent of the kids in the poor quarters had worms and parasites, and green skins like pallid fish and great big soccer-ball bellies from eating dirt and garbage and all kinds of shit; and 98 percent of the country was calmed in terror or lethargy or the combined exhaustion of the two and that was a conservative estimate, Mr. President, the only Mayapanians with any hope at all were the foreigners who had any money, and the expatriates plotting revolution outside the boundaries of the country. And suddenly here there was, this enormous lake of riches, just when the world and especially the *gringos* needed it! and no way in hell of getting it out of the ground.

The dictator moved to solve this problem as best he could, but either his greed, or his personal distaste for pale, sweating northerners in Harvard ties who spoke better Spanish than he did, made him make a mistake—a crucial mistake, as it turned out—and attempt to fund the whole operation himself. Of course he couldn't do it, but he was ruthless in his acquisition of enemies' lands, farms and coffee plantations which had slept uneasily in their owners' hands after they had insulted him, Mr. President, is it true you smoke horse dung? Is it true you murder your friends because you aren't intelligent enough to argue with them? He took any excuse to foreclose on old debts and he made himself remember others that he'd barely paid attention to at the time because everybody criticizes their President, what matters are deeds not words, but now he made himself remember, he made himself imagine slights when he couldn't think of one, he used any pretext he could think of to bloat himself with wealth and amass a huge fortune, not for his backers, but in his own name— Buiztas Enterprises—because he was going into business producing gasoline for the Yanquis.

It never got very far. The supplies took months to arrive, and there were untold difficulties trying to transport and reassemble the rudimentary machinery in the slippery jungles where the Spaniards had gotten lost in that green madness, dying of fever and disgust in their heavy armor—which was lighter than the pumps and steel girders that fell into the river, slipped off the trucks, and became the property of the thick vines and the sucking water holes, the macaws and the monkeys, and showed up at their destination six weeks late and covered with a tenacious coating of mud. He was still involved in the hopeless enterprise of building his private industry when he felt the walls of his office shake and the ground move under his feet, and for a moment he thought it was cannon fire, that this was the biggest insurrection in the world, at last, the one that would really topple him, and he relaxed for an instant and shut his eyes, happy that they had finally dropped the other fucking shoe, when his inkstand fell off his desk with a crash and his orderlies rushed in with the terrified news, It's an earthquake, Mr. President, my God, the whole Westside is on fire.

It was one of the worst in a decade, and it wouldn't have been so bad if the country hadn't been pushed to industrialize, so the silent Indians had been moved out of their jungle villages and brought into the towns, the shanty Westside of Campeche had grown in the last few years into a vast encampment of corrugated metal shacks, and nothing had been done to keep pace with even the most minimal needs of sanitation so that when the earthquake hit and there were two hundred dead, no, two thousand, my God what a disaster, it was more than that, a lot more, as the Red Cross doctor said grimly, fearlessly confronting him, because your city is a pesthole, Mr. President, it's an open sewer, and if you lose half your population to cholera you'll get off easily, I'll be surprised if you don't all drop dead. Relief medicines were sent in, planes of supplies from the United Nations and Catholic Charities, but somehow they didn't seem to get to their destinations, there were bureaucratic mix-ups and most of the medicines ended up on the black market; there were problems in rebuilding because it seemed all the heavy machinery was being used somewhere off in the jungle; there were uneasy denials from the government until someone had the temerity to say it out loud, He's selling it himself! the President of the country is selling us medicine at 200 percent inflation to finance the same construction company that's rebuilding our houses, it's his own company, Buiztas Enterprises! He's getting rich because of us! But there was nothing to be done—and even his greed may not have been truly greed, but rather the terrible lure of the oil that was seeping up through the ground, just think of it, more riches than you could really imagine—enough money to fix everything and really put us on the map! When every day the death toll mounted, and Mayapán became more of a plague spot, and a joke, in the eyes of the civilized world: ripe for insurrection, as Ferdinando said to Battiste while the two of them were working in New York.

Battiste had joined the revolutionary movement, and worked Xeroxing leaflets, recruiting volunteers, and raising money among his wealthy Catholic communicants. He was deliriously happy. Ferdinando was the sun around which their entire solar system revolved: even when he was covered with ink, while repairing a printing press (he had a deft, innate ability with complicated machinery), or showing them how to dismantle a Soviet-made carbine, he could convulse them with laughter and inspire them at the same time. And he drew talented planets into his orbit—the girl Pisote (whose real name was Francesca Estaban, a wealthy Argentine who'd decamped from Buenos Aires in emulation of the mythical Che), the cartoonist Carlos Molina, and increasingly, Battiste himself. All worked in close contact with the man they loved, and not merely helped but contributed the fertile inspiration of their own minds to the revolution they were trying, step by step and concept by agonizing concept, to think up.

They kept close watch on their quarry, the dictator Quintero de Buiztas: noting his most trivial movements. He was aging, afflicted with a swelling of the prostate which made urination a painful and frequent necessity: that year his most visible public act was the construction of numerous portable latrines all over Campeche, for the purpose of allowing him to relieve himself when he went on his daily tours from the military barracks to the customshouse. Almost immediately, these public *pissoirs* became known as "Buiztanistas," and the rebels made good use of them, in cartoons, in leaflets, and in doggerel distributed in the capital and abroad. The kidnapping of twelve Nicaraguan diplomats, and the resulting payment of one million dollars ransom by the Somoza regime, was covered extensively in the revolutionaries' newspaper: allowing, as Ferdinando admitted, "the carrot of greed to be held in front of the mule of our countrymen's anarchistic tendencies," and resulting in at least three other kidnapping attempts. Ferdinando was everywhere, organizing their shaky alliance with the rebels in El Salvador, their necessary rapprochement with the repressive government in Guatemala, their friendly relations with Papa Doc, and their cordial, though noncommittal, flirtation with Fidel Castro: promising little, but hinting much to each regime in turn, and avowing simply his intention to do one thing—restore democracy with free elections and land reform for his country—at which point he would step down, retire to private life . . . or sometimes, when he was feeling more candid, admit that he would allow himself to be elected to some office, perhaps a seat in the Chamber of Deputies, where he could have some impact and perhaps do some good for his fellowmen.

He had never been more dynamic, or more beautiful, than at that time. Throwing his arms around the startled Battiste to embrace him . . . or thoughtful, almost withdrawn, leaning his cheek on his hand and smoking a joint while they stayed up late at night, sorting leaflets.

"Did you ever think how long he's lasted?" he asked, smiling, perhaps teasing Battiste. The priest raised his eyebrows.

"How long who's lasted?"

"Buiztas. Thirty years, more or less. God, it's a lifetime—half the people we're hoping to liberate have never known any other authority. It's unbelievable!" He drew the sweet smoke down into his lungs, held his breath, and released it, passing the joint to Battiste. "Do you think I should emulate him? Grow a beard and pretend to pick lice out of my hair just like he does?"

Battiste smiled. "I wouldn't believe it for a minute. You wouldn't be convincing as a pig, it's not your style."

"Oh, no? You didn't see me crawling out of the harbor in 'sixty-seven, you might have changed your opinion." Ferdinando laughed, packing the smeary black leaflets into boxes with his long, deft hands. "I can match even our beloved leader for smelly characteristics—try spending some time in La Miramar Prison, it's a great equalizer."

He had grown more easy, talking about his imprisonment—at least with Battiste; the priest didn't know whether this ease was one he attained with everyone, as a way of making them feel flattered, or whether his was a special case. Still, the image of his beautiful friend, with his clear blue eyes and his slender, visionary's face, in the hands of the Buiztas thugs was painful to Battiste, and he looked away without answering.

"It's a good question," Ferdinando pursued, taking the joint back from Battiste but not smoking it, his eyes focused on the middle distance. "The man is a *caudillo*, successful, a bandit like all his kind. You don't argue with success, you study it, and see what makes it tick. No, I'm serious. I'm thinking about Mexico. The people were offered an illusion of democracy, and when the time came, what happened? The riots of 'sixty-eight. Bloodshed. Three hundred dead. The invisible committees who run things can't afford to have the people truly participate—they might lose their jobs!—but one man, one man alone ... I don't know. One man alone might risk the impossible originality of mob rule ... with the knowledge that the mob *might* tear him to pieces. That's where Buiztas is shortsighted too." Ferdinando paused, the smoke barely moving between his lips. "You have to be willing to take that chance, and know that, eventually, you'll lose. They'll kill you. That's what makes it fair for all concerned. That's what makes it fun."

Battiste laughed a little nervously. "You're crazy. Who do you want to be right now, Buiztas or Robespierre? I'm not sure."

"Oh, I don't know—" Ferdinando said with sudden whimsy. "You're forgetting our addictive capacity for violence. Mayapán is an Indian country, we don't need Robespierres, we can kill our kings and priests and everyone else quite well enough by ourselves! And if we need any help, we can always call in the Marines and the United Fruit Company! Shit, I don't know!"

And then he laughed, hugging Battiste, admitting for once to human weakness. "God, I'm stoned. I'm full of shit. Nobody's going to kill anyone. You take me too seriously, you know that?" Suddenly, intimately, pressing his forehead against Battiste's. "Idolater. You'll get in trouble for that. I'm not Jesus Christ. I'm not even one of your fucking revolutionary clergy. I'm just another son of a bitch. You're going to have to remember that, because from time to time I find myself in danger of forgetting it."

Around that time Ferdinando introduced Battiste to their arms broker, an unexpectedly wistful man named Jorge-Julio de

Rodríguez, who despite his Spanish name was half Maya Indian, and who had known Ferdinando since their childhood. Jorge-Julio had stayed in the Army, as a captain, and eventually a major, but was so devoted to Ferdinando that when the latter had said, Come on, my friend, let's castrate that old devil in the Presidential Palace, he had not hesitated for an instant: throwing away his career, his rank, and very nearly his life amid the sweaty plotting in basements before the 1967 riots, and after Ferdinando's release, finding some way to get to New York, working as a parking lot attendant now for the self-effacing motive of staying near him. He was a gentle man, tall and thin with sad eyes and a long black moustache, and nobody knew very much about him except that he could speak the old Indian language, knew about guns, and, surprisingly, could bend a spoon into a circle with one hand. Tonto, some people called him, but for the most part he was respected. He was working with the girl Pisote on the acquisition of small arms, and revealed to Battiste that their main purchases of guns were organized by the Vatican.

"What!" Battiste exclaimed when he told him.

"Oh, it's true all right. The Vatican oversees a lot of operations in which they don't have direct control. They pass information along, and if they want to they profit, but it's mostly the information itself they want." Jorge-Julio shrugged, smiling his sad smile at the priest, and wiping his forehead with dirty fingers. His hands and face were always soiled with machine oil. "I don't know whether it's for their investments, or for simple curiosity. Come along sometime if you want."

Battiste went, to one of their rendezvous in a Cuban restaurant over on Eighth Avenue, which served Chinese and Mexican food. There, eating black beans in Szechuan sauce, he watched as the tall arms dealer talked to a girl behind the counter, a matter-of-fact transaction, and when he sat down again at the table he asked him with a pained smile, "Is that it? I would have thought the selling out of St. Peter's would have required a little more haggling."

Jorge-Julio smiled. "They're not selling out St. Peter's, they're just grown-ups." He spoke softly, and drank deeply from his bottle of Dos Equis, wiping his moustache. "It's like anything, the first time is scary, like buying dope or shooting a man, but it gets easier. It gets too easy. You have amateurs risking their lives, doing all kinds of stuff. It's a funny world." He shook his head, looking down at his blackened fingernails, his hands holding his knife and fork, and his mouth twisted crookedly. "I have to smile sometimes. I spent all my life in the Army, now I'm buying surplus matériel from the North Vietnamese—captured supplies they took out of Saigon in seventy-two, probably manufactured by the same *gringo* firm that's supplying Buiztas right now. If people knew what went on in the world they'd have a fit." He took a bite of black beans and said, chewing, looking up, "Well, here he comes, right on schedule. Let me talk to this guy, would you? He takes a little getting used to."

Battiste looked around behind him, too obviously to be casual, to see a well-dressed man with kinky brown hair coming toward their table, holding up his hand and smiling a wide smile.

"Hi," he said, taking out a cigarette and pulling up a chair with one hand. "All right if I join you for a moment?"

"Sure," Jorge-Julio murmured into his plate of black beans without looking up. "Who's going to stop you?"

Battiste found himself looking at the man curiously, which in itself was unusual, since he looked perfectly nondescript, in a nice suit, an ordinary, snub-nosed face, and a friendly smile; a salesman, perhaps; just a regular businessman on his lunch hour and in that case, what was he doing in a dive like this?

"So," he said, reaching between them to tap his cigarette out in the ashtray. "What have you two guys been up to?"

"Oh, you know, same old shit," Jorge-Julio said indistinctly, shoveling black beans into his mouth. Battiste was amused by his suddenly exaggerated Hispanic inflection: he might actually have been the greaser parking lot attendant he pretended to be during the day. "You still making your mother sit on a sharp stick?"

"Oh, come on, Julio, you know my mother died years ago," the man said without missing a beat. "I thought maybe we could be friends. Your boyfriend Lorca sucks up to me enough, so why can't you guys do it?"

"Señor Lorca is a very polite man," Battiste said mildly, getting up to get them another beer. "Maybe he doesn't want to hurt your feelings." He brought back a third beer for the nondescript businessman, who took it with a smile.

"Thanks, pal, you read my mind. I don't believe we've met. Hi, I'm Bill Mynott, I'm with the C.I.A."

Battiste's handshake was firm, although his gaze shifted for an instant to Jorge-Julio. The latter raised his eyes to the ceiling and made a face as though he had tasted medicine. Battiste let go of his hand.

William Mynott, C.I.A., took a long drink of his beer and said, "No point in playing games. Julio here knows me, and he'll tell you the minute I go out the door, so what's the point? How many guns you buying this week, Julio? Or do you really think I can't find out on my own?"

Jorge-Julio methodically finished every last black bean on his plate, and crossed his knife and fork in the middle of this plate before answering. "What Señor Mynott doesn't tell you is that he was thrown out of the C.I.A. six years ago, and has no more reason to be around here than some cockroach—less reason, since a cockroach lives by what it dirties. That's what Señor Mynott doesn't seem to be able to remember without my help."

"Ha ha ha, the kid's got a great sense of humor." He laughed complacently, sipping his beer without seeming at all put out. "Fuck it, you know. If Julio wants to be an asshole then I say let him, no skin off my nose, you know what I mean?" He turned to Battiste with an open, friendly expression, and the priest was struck by how shiny his eyes were, silvery, with pinprick pupils, like ball bearings. "He knows we do these little covert things from time to time, and it might be a good idea for me to disavow all knowledge of operations right now, so he plays this little game. Now me, I like to break a few rules. Tell people the truth. Some people may not like to hear it . . . like Julio here, he likes to believe he's going to be the next Augusto Sandino, don't you, Julio? But fuck it. So, are you a member of this bunch of crackpots, or are you just along for the ride? I mean Jesus, I recruited guys in the Hmong in Laos, and picked up stray rebels with Zavimbe, but a lost cause is a lost cause whether you're black, white, or purple, you know what I mean? So, like, what's your angle in this? You look like a smart guy. You going to make money off these bozos or what?"

Battiste raised his eyebrows and said levelly, "I'm a priest. I'm familiar with lost causes. Any other questions?"

"No shit? Well, fuck me," Mynott said, not at all abashed. "Jorge-Julio's getting religion, I say great, convert the mother-fucker!"

He shook his head and stood up. "This has been great, gents, I'm really sorry I can't stay." He finished his beer and set the bottle very carefully on the table, as if afraid it might spill. "You guys should do this on television, you're better at blocking than the Dallas Cowboys. Have a nice day."

After he'd left, Battiste raised his eyebrows pointedly at Jorge-Julio, who wiped his mouth with his napkin, and could be seen to be laughing.

"Well? Are you going to tell me what that was all about or should I guess?"

"Oh, shit, he's just a fucked-up *gringo*. Listen to me, I sound like him. You want to get us a couple more beers and I'll tell you? All right," he said as Battiste came back with the two beers, and suddenly his face looked older, worn, the face of a laborer or a veteran of combat, although he was still faintly smiling.

"Bill Mynott was fired from the C.I.A., like I said, and he's crazy. I mean, he did a lot of work for them, helped them train the men in SAVAK, and he was a junior G-man on the Bay of Pigs, but he went nuts and he's out. Although no one's ever out, they probably still use him. He was castrated by the Khmer Rouge, and I guess they feel obliged . . . I don't know. He got very into drugs."

Battiste remembered. "His pupils were very small. What does that? Heroin?"

"I don't know. I don't even know what it all means, or what's on his mind. He's always jumping around like a *cucaracha*, that's why I called him that." He shook his head like a man puzzled by a riddle, and his dark sad face, with its long black moustache and its carved mahogany cheeks of a man who had spent all his life facing danger, assumed a perplexed, almost gentle expression. "I'd kill him if I had to. There's not a lot of men I'd say that about anymore. I've killed enough men to say that. But him I would kill, to protect Ferdinando. I don't want Ferdinando to have to put up with a *cucaracha* like that."

That might have been their credo—although no more self-reliant leader could have been imagined, and he didn't want their protection but their love to inspire him. So caught up was Battiste in his dreams of a pure-hearted revolution in those days that he saw no dilemma in confessing the little girls at the Harley School with oil from sixty Russian-made machine guns under his finger-nails, drinking the heady moonshine of illegality as they drove over to Queens late one night to take delivery of two hundred grams of cocaine to be converted into money for the revolution; he did it, led by the sinewy strength of his beloved friend El Lorca and the occasional glimpses of his adored child, Camila . . . I wish you could meet him, you'd love him as much as I do, but she prevaricated, No, Father, not just yet . . . touching his hand in the corridor outside a class, or kissing him lightly on both cheeks—those cheeks which were growing lean and losing their fat because he kept forgetting to eat, it was true, his body felt strong and muscular for the first time, and he was accosted by six gay men on the subway, much to his secretly delighted surprise.

He was able to help with the practical plans of revolutionary leadership, Which delegates to the U.N. should we contact? he asked questions, and pretty soon it became apparent that of course Father Battiste's ideas were correct, because the tautologi-cal training of the Jesuits gave him an edge sometimes equal to El Lorca's own, and he had always carried within himself the seeds of a self-mocking Richelieu. My Eminence, Ferdinando called him, delighted, you'll make cardinal before you're fifty . . . and Pisote and Carlos and Jorge-Julio applauded him: them, the two of them, Battiste and Ferdinando—bowing in the cellar of a house on 135th Street where they were all drunk and stoned, smoking Thai sticks, Christ how he loved them. For the first time in his life he used all his mind to manipulate events, rather than exam-ine his own sins, and when events moved to his will he was dou-bly freed, from hesitation and doubt, the hesitancy of an untried skill and the doubt of an untried heart. He felt ardent and free . . . and that lasted a matter of months. Gradually, his doubts came back, his sense of sin and his private sense of worthlessness, and as much as he tried to trace his sorrow through the labyrinth of memory he couldn't truly explain it. All he knew was that it began again around the time he introduced Ferdinando to Camila.

six

IT HAPPENED BY ACCIDENT, because Battiste had not been expecting to see her. He'd been talking intently to Ferdinando, in the same coffee shop where they'd first conversed, and he'd been facing away from the door so that when Ferdinando put down his coffee cup and said suddenly, "My God, who's that beautiful girl over there?" he turned around for a moment uncertain who it was himself—although he knew before he actually saw her. He knew with an instantaneous lurch in his stomach that the meeting he'd been trying to set up and dreading was going to take place, and he motioned to her with his hand to come over and join them.

She was wet, from the November rain outside, and had come into the atmosphere of freshly brewed coffee and lights almost as if she would go out again, until Battiste waved to her again and said, "What are you doing there? Come here and have a drink, you're wet to the skin."

Shyly, she approached the table. Since moving in with Porfirio Cheruña, she had attained a measure of serenity, but her exhaustion was wearing her thin, and her unearthly beauty was taking on the painful transparency of a shadow. She was starting to become more often light-headed: she dreamed occasionally of killing Porfirio, and more frequently of killing herself. When she came over to the table with her breathless smile, taking a scarf from her head, with her pained sharp cheekbones and her gasps sticking her skin to her ribs, she saw El Lorca, who stood up, and whose eyes met hers with a look of such startled recognition that she didn't know what to do, Excuse me, but you must be the daughter of Juan dos Santos, my God, you resemble him so, it's uncanny, and at the same time his smile was so amazed at her presence, his piercing eyes so blue, that she lost the thread of inconsequential chatter which she was stringing together and felt as if her bones were beginning to melt. For his part, Ferdinando was simply amazed. Here was Juan dos Santos come to life, in a girl whose translucent loveliness combined such vulnerability and light and pain that she seemed the physical embodiment of their raped and beautiful country—and even if she had the mind of a moron, he was determined in the first instant he set eyes on her to get her to join their movement. As he spoke to her, as she sat down, as he warmed her with the charm which was as instinctive a part of his being as his breath, he felt himself a prey to conflicting emotions: sheer exhilaration that she was intelligent! My God, they could use her! curiosity about her unhappiness, liking, combined with the recoil of an instinctual isolate, and a frank appreciation of her as a beautiful and sexually poignant young girl. Battiste, watching them both, felt the twist of jealousy tearing him apart from both sides, and at the same time he thought, Well, of course, how could they help not to like one another? Camila ordered a coffee and combined looking down at her cup with shy glances at Ferdinando, who took her wet coat from around her shoulders and asked her with serious attention if she was warm enough, would she like something to eat, would she like a cigarette, he asked, proffering his own pack, and to Battiste's surprise she said yes—it was the first time in his memory that he'd seen her smoke.

"Did you know my father, Señor Lorca?" she asked, lighting her cigarette.

"I knew *of* him more than knowing him," Ferdinando said, taking the matches away from her and lighting her cigarette for her. "Forgive me, I like these little *macho* gestures. We met one another several times of course—I believe I also once met your

mother. I wrote some articles for him after I got back from Nicaragua, and he was kind enough to lend me some money when I
couldn't get hired by any reputable firm."

"Yes, he was pretty disreputable," she said, smiling.

"You know perfectly well I didn't mean that."

"Yes, I know, but he was. He could never trim his sails,
that's why they finally killed him. I gather you're not very good
at trimming your sails either, are you, Señor Lorca?"

"Well, I'm still alive."

"Just barely. Oh, I didn't mean that as a threat," she said,
smiling her light, pale smile and taking a sip of her coffee to cover
her lovely embarrassment. "I just meant that you had risked
death too. Forgive me, I don't seem to be expressing myself very
well."

"I think you're doing just fine."

Watching them, Battiste sensed the flirtation without quite
grasping its motives, although he knew he was watching a seduction—akin to his own?—and the emergence of a hitherto unknown Camila, neither child nor victim, but a smiling and
tentative young woman: although her blue eyes, which were
lighter than Ferdinando's, kept looking at him with shy pain and
sadness as though she was afraid that he was going to disappear.
They spoke about the earthquake and the weather, classes at Columbia and the Mayapanian revolutionary movement: idle chat
that became less idle as serious ideas were exchanged, and Battiste
sat at the table and put in a word now and then and felt himself to
be suffering a private calvary, which was made up of exquisite
embarrassment and which in any case was being effectively ignored by both his companions. Camila and Ferdinando talked for
perhaps twenty minutes, while the coffee shop filled up with
people and the twilight fell imperceptibly outside . . . and then
she broke off, starting because of the time, remembering who she
was and where she had to go that night with the force of such intense pain that it took all of her strength of will to keep from crying out, to keep the memory of a smile on her pale face as she
shook her head saying, No, she must go, that was all right, please
don't accompany me. She stood up, and her pallor was so complete that Battiste was really frightened for her, although she had
the illusion of hallucinatory gaiety which her girl friends might

79

have remembered from the months she spent in the hospital. She put her scarf over her head like a banner, and her eyes as she said Good-bye, Señor Lorca, were the eyes of a drowning woman, and then she was gone. A beautiful girl . . . who was Porfirio Cheruña's mistress, his little whore, and whose insides were permanently scarred by the insidious probing of his fingers (which all the warm water in the world wouldn't cure), who was the addiction he worshiped and the instrument on which he performed with his detachment, his artistry—his torture, which had left her unfit for normal human contact, and which had incidentally left her barren by the age of seventeen. (A supposition. For that, or perhaps for no reason, an autopsy was never performed on her body; but the fact was that she never conceived a child.)

She rode back to the apartment on Sutton Place in a taxi, with the heaviness of unshed tears making her tired. Once there, she composed a letter to her aunt and uncle, whom she had not seen for over a year: the egregious lies in it nauseated her, but she persevered with it until she heard the key in the lock, the quick light steps of the old man in the hallway, calling, "*Querida*, come here!" and she stood up, leaving her letter in plain sight (for it soothed his occasional fears to see what she wrote to them), going to relieve him of the many packages he was carrying.

"My God, what did you buy for me," she murmured. "It looks like you purchased the entire store."

He delighted in buying her presents, but only if she would delight in receiving them, like a small child, his daughter (he would run his bony fingers through her soft hair), *Querida*, you'll bankrupt me, he would complain, while she tried on fur jackets, gold necklaces, tore tissue paper to reveal feather-light silk scarves, shoes for her small feet (he would put them on for her), occasionally books, and once a full-length, fox fur coat. He also bought delicacies for them to have for dinner, preferring to dine with her alone, in the big penthouse apartment, on oysters and stuffed squab (prepared by a caterer—he never cooked), champagne and truffles, the rarefied fruits of the land and the sea which they ate by candlelight, just like a wealthy father and his beautiful daughter, until the time when he could no longer resist the swampy pull of his testicles, the heady fragrance of her body with its scent of flowers and he made her leave her place, please, with your fingers, just there, yes, stroke me, death tearing at him with its claws and he bit his lips against the pain of angina, expiring in the labyrinth of the wonderful toy that he possessed, that he could play with and enjoy as no man had ever enjoyed anything since the world began.

Tonight as always she took the packages, jars of brandied peaches and crystallized violets, fish poached in wine all ready to be put in the oven and tasting like the fare at the best French restaurants, she put them in the kitchen, his coat which she hung up for him like a dutiful daughter, packages from Saks and Harry Winston, which she put down on the sofa in the living room without opening them and sitting, asked him casually, "Tell me, Porfirio, Ferdinando Lorca, what do you know about him? Who is he? Do you know who he is?"

The old man turned peevishly from pouring himself a cognac. "Why do you want to know about that lunatic? He's a radical, one of those people who always wants to blow up everything!"

"Surely not everything."

"Yes, I tell you! He's got a fringe coterie of would-be revolutionaries behind him—the discontented who are easily stirred by any demagogue's rhetoric: Buiztanistas, Lorcanistas, Sandinistas, it's all the same. You know—" He paused, and his eyes behind his steel-rimmed spectacles regarded her thoughtfully. "You look very pretty tonight, my dear. All of a glow. I don't know that I shall be able to resist you."

She raised her eyebrows, quelling the knot of fear in her stomach with difficulty. "Really? I thought we had gotten beyond the point of casual compliments."

"Oh, certainly not." He brought her a cognac, over ice, and her hand shook as she took it from him, but she came from a race of subtle fighters and had learned how to negotiate for small victories, an accomplished little *putatita*, little whore. "Tell me, Porfirio, this man, this revolutionary—he's Mayapanian, isn't he? Like you and me? Well, what do you have against him—surely he's harmless? Mayapán's a joke for its injustice. Now in the aftermath of the earthquake—"

"Ha! You've been reading the leftist newspapers, have you? *Querida*, there is no such thing as a righteous government, don't you know that—communist or right-wing, C.I.A.-supported or backed by the Kremlin, *querida*, it's cut from the same cloth! Don't you believe my heart bleeds as much as the next man's for the dying in Campeche?—but you don't see me rushing to support this or that governmental coup, and why not? Because I know that whoever comes to power after Buiztas will be just as corrupt and venal as he is. It's in the blood of politicians—and all revolutionaries are politicians, regardless of their slogans. I had no idea you were susceptible to the blandishments of the *descamisados*, or whatever it is they call themselves now—all those liberators of the people, with rolled shirt sleeves and satin underwear! You're a charmingly naïve little girl, my dear, but I thought you were a bit more *au courant!*"

Camila smiled. "I don't think Ferdinando Lorca wears satin underwear, Porfirio. Somehow I just can't picture it."

"Ah? Then he's a communist, my dear." The old man laughed. "Did you know that when I was a young man, I joined the Communist Party in Paris? It's the party of *les très grands naïfs;* perhaps you should join it, my dear, but it is not the answer to Mayapán's problems—nor is Ferdinando Lorca, for all his solicitation of my services, which I naturally refused. Ah, dear, dear, come here and sit on my lap. The world is full of leaders and fools, and you are my one refuge of sanity, please don't acquire a political conscience, I beg of you!"

She prevaricated. "*Is* he a communist, Porfirio? I, that is— people say, he doesn't seem to give that impression."

"My dear, how should I know? I make it a practice never to read political literature, the ink comes off on one's hands and the syntax is generally abysmal. Let me get you another drink. What on earth brought on this spate of curiosity in you, I'm quite breathless trying to keep up with you. Did you meet Lorca by any chance? They say he's quite handsome, in a patent-leather kind of way. I'd be interested to hear what you thought of him."

Camila's eyes regarded him with limpid honesty in the soft light. "I never met him. Is he handsome? Perhaps I'll look him up."

A shadow like the suggestion of unhappiness crossed the elegant face of Porfirio Cheruña, and was gone in his smile of an enigmatic pharaoh. "You know I'd never let you, *querida*. I'd flay the skin off your little bird's back before I would run such a risk of losing you, my incredible little darling."

"I'm touched." She absently tore the brown paper on one of his packages, revealing a white silk blouse. "How pretty. You really must stop giving me all these presents, Porfirio, you'll spoil me. Is he wanted by Buiztas? Is that why he isn't working in Mayapán?"

"Who? Lorca? Ha, now there's a thought! They'd shoot him on the spot. I suppose Buiztas doesn't want to risk an international incident, extradition making him a *cause célèbre*. It's an interesting paradox: the more effective he becomes as an agitator here, the more he risks being repatriated as a political prisoner! I must say it all sounds terribly complicated."

"Yes." She gave up picking at the wrapping of the second package with her fingernail; there was no point in opening presents which you couldn't have, and she felt tired, achingly tired, of the whole game, the whole bloody business. "Get me another drink, Porfirio, would you?" She smiled at him thinly. "You're a good guardian. See how carefully you take care of me? I don't know what I would do with myself without you."

The spread of disease in Mayapán was escalated by the rain, which turned the roads into paste in the little villages of corrugated shacks, green children brought into the local *farmacias* covered with the sores of age-old diseases without a name, It's a disgrace, the little children are *dying*, Mr. President, but Shh, the President is reading the newspaper, he can't be bothered, his prostate is driving him crazy—and so little by little even the Indians in the interior, who had never cared to know who the President was, or who the cabinet ministers were, began to say, This Buiztas is a bad man, a crazy man; and Quintero de Buiztas, who certainly wasn't crazy, scented the metallic smell of danger and began to take harsh measures with the writers of slogans on walls, the people who happened to have the wrong color paint under their fingernails, because it didn't matter who they caught, as long as someone was found face down in a pile of his guts on Sunday morning to ensure the good behavior of everyone else. His secret assassins toured the countryside in beat-up Land Rovers equipped with army-issue machine guns, and the people in the villages called them "Buiztas' hunting dogs," with a certain amount of awe, because there was something to be said for a man who could maintain order when God Himself had attacked His capital city and sent plagues to all His people, God forgive them, for the sin of not shitting in an indoor toilet, for not washing their clothes in disinfectant because there was none to be had for under twenty dollars a bottle, for the terrible sin of being angry, fed up with all this crap of a paternal government that never did a thing for them, not a thing, except for finishing them off fast, when they might have died slowly of old age or starvation or malaria. They begged to tell the President that they had had enough, if he didn't mind—interrupt him from his perusal of *Le Monde* to tell him We're angry, but of course he knew that. He had lost the easy carelessness of former days, although he still had his demonic sense of humor, and so he killed with greater fury than before, irritably, like a man who know's he's running out of time—and still the stink in his country grew, the stink of anger, which had yet to find an outlet beyond the suicide, helped by the machine guns, of an occasional fed-up man.

Camila knew of these things, and didn't know. She rarely read the newspapers anymore, or anything else; there were too many words in the world, too much illusion of words that told you nothing, but imprisoned you; beautifully phrased words in the elegant voice of a wicked old man who more than ever, now, was going a little crazy. She wondered if he had ever had free rein with all of his compulsions before; she doubted it. I'm the embodiment of his fantasies come to life, she thought bitterly, but she was fading away, her body more than ever a child's body of tiny breasts and hipbones pointed beside her hollow belly, she laughed, I look like one of the children of the provinces, look at my skin, it's the color of green leaves, I'm turning into a plant. Locked up in the plush apartment, from which he would rarely let her leave; turn over, I want to . . . ah, yes, again . . . his artist's touch . . . while her hand held his flaccid penis, old man's skin, please, please stop . . . but he knew the exact moment when her body would betray her, Now, *querida*, perhaps you'd like me to stop, oh no?, oh no? She would lie in bed with him at three o'clock in the afternoon, on the sheets that smelled of patchouli cologne, and listen to the scratching sound of "La Vie en Rose" playing on the record player, love songs from his decrepit youth in France as a member of the Communist Party, Edith Piaf, La Môme Piaf. He would turn her body into a single nerve, and then he would sit back and look at her, saying, What would the nuns say if they saw you, *querida*, they'd think you were a whore out of the jungle, one of those crazy women who want it anywhere, in the mouth, in the behind, you name it. I'm leaving, put your panties on, here, you make me sick . . . until she would stammer, No, please don't go, you can, I'll let you . . . I *am* going crazy . . . I love you, Porfirio . . . please don't leave me. She would accept his humiliating diagnosis, that she was unnatural, that most women didn't have these feelings . . . and so it went. She would go for days when even water would revolt her stomach, and after a while she gave up wanting to go outside, she was afraid, she gave in, and she began to be convinced that the only way she would ever leave the apartment was through the escape of death. She grew so pale and still that finally her lover and jailer grew afraid, but still he didn't take her to a doctor—because he was afraid by then that a doctor would take her away from him.

He sat on the edge of the bed and talked to her. "You are not feeling well? What is it, *querida*?"

She shrugged, turning her head away from him on the pillow. It was exhausting, too exhausting to talk about anything. She felt as if she didn't care anymore.

"But you *are* well?" Porfirio persisted, plainly demanding it. "Tell me. You know I'd do anything in the world for you."

She turned her huge blue eyes to look at him, dully. "Let me go," she whispered. But of course, that was the one present he would never give her, and she closed her eyes before she should see his pain, his prevarication, Don't you love me, don't you want to stay with me? because when all else failed he was adept at playing the wounded child himself.

She began to have a fantasy that she was existing, snail-like, curled up inside the shell of her body, where nothing could touch her, incognito, Anne Frank inside the attic of her smooth white forehead. It helped to see Porfirio and herself from a distance, when she could even pity him, unable to keep his hands off her; how much it must bother him, she thought in a rare moment of lucidity, not to be able to control himself, not to be cool and detached but trapped in the sick sweet mania which seemed to have no end, but would suck him down like the irresistible pull of quicksand, urgent, desperate. This doll he held in his arms, she was so pretty ... and he didn't mean to hurt her ... but Camila was far away, even when he forced tears from her eyes; it wasn't really her ... and soon she had trouble getting out of bed, her knees buckled and she had trouble walking, she was so weak ... but it wasn't really her, she was asleep inside her shell, curled up inside herself like a fetus, dreaming on a salt sea of oblivion. He *did* get a doctor for her, then: but it was one of his friends (he had so many friends!), and he thought she might be slightly anemic; he gave her a tonic; she heard them talking, through the buzz in her head like cicadas, Be careful, Porfirio, you know I don't approve ... but it didn't matter, this weakness spared her, she didn't have to pose for anyone, she didn't have to help him entertain his guests ("She's enchanting, Porfirio, your *ward*, do you say?"), she lay in her bed and heard them talking, all his powerful acquaintances, chatting, having drinks ... and there was no one there who could help her, no one who would have risked his wasp's anger, his reputation as a benevolent man. He was one of the powerful men himself—certainly more powerful than the Mayapanian ambassador—and she knew that he would never have spared a colleague, had someone tried to intervene on her behalf.

Finally one night he came into the bedroom in his long silk robe, switching on a bright fluorescent light with a narrow shade which he brought next to the bed, breathing lightly with a faint, shallow sound, an old man's breath, as he stared down at her hollowed face, her eyes shut, like the face of a woman anesthetized in a hospital. She was aware, but she couldn't move; it was very strange; but she knew somehow that this strange immobility of hers was a novel excitement for him, as he carefully drew back the sheet and removed the light *camisa* she was wearing, letting his fingers travel exquisitely over the pale, cold skin of her belly, murmuring gently, beautiful, yes, beautiful ... she wanted to move, but she was also afraid, fearful that she would reveal the secret hiding place of her mind to him ... and then she felt him rubbing himself furtively over her body, like a man masturbating, while he whispered please, oh please, oh please ...

She couldn't move, and she felt his desperation, perhaps his misery, as he tried to insinuate himself still soft, between her legs, please, but it wouldn't work; she felt his hands fumbling, trying, only now, please, once, like a normal man; his hand moving rhythmically, yes, in time to the frantic beating of his heart, oh yes, until a thin trickle sour as urine yes splashed across her belly, and she heard him crying, swallowing tears of relief and self-pity, because he had never obtained such satisfaction as he had from a paralyzed girl, white, under the fluorescent light, as if she were already dead. She heard him gasping for breath as he switched the light out, leaving her uncovered, like a statue, as he staggered from the room and her mind reeled and saw the vileness of the shock, and retreated from it, and only then could she open her eyes with the absolute conviction that she had to get out of there.

She dressed in the first clothes she came to in the dark, a thin dress and shoes and a raincoat, no hat, no stockings, putting them on in silence with shaking fingers terrified that he would come in and find her, but everything was silent; she let herself out of the apartment without being discovered, took the elevator to the lobby and walked out into the street in a daze. A thin rain was falling, scarcely more than a mist, and the cold air hurt her lungs and made her shiver; her coat was too thin; there were people all around her, richly dressed citizens who looked at her curiously with her uncombed hair and her pale, unpainted face. She looked, then, not like the star of the posters she would soon be, with her face on the cover of *Time* magazine and on the billboards, but like a patient released from a mental hospital. She walked without thinking, gradually faster and faster, hearing her steps on the pavement and feeling the delayed fear, walking from Sutton Place into the neighborhood of the big office buildings, deserted now, tall skyscrapers and shining, empty streets; and farther, to an area of cheap nightclubs and strip joints, neon signs which oddly enough warmed her, where her sleepwalker's demeanor was accepted as natural, What's with that one, oh she's just stoned. She felt her heart beating so fast, as she looked at the cheap posters, for kung fu movies and sex shows, thinking, Where will I go? For as her mind cleared, she realized she had no place in the world to run to, no money but a few dollars change in her pocket. She went into an all-night restaurant, amazed by the stink of grease and ammonia, and ordered a cup of coffee, going into the ladies' room to smooth her hands over her hair, looking at her shocked face in the mirror, thinking, Where will I go, where will I go? The police? But who were they, but the ones who put bombs in automobiles when they had to, everyone is in the pay of the powerful, there's always someone, it made sense to go to the police but it didn't make sense in this downtown sewer with a sticker on the mirror, JESUS SAVES, and she thought about Battiste and wished she knew his home address but he wouldn't understand, he would make her go back, hadn't she herself said, He's a nice old uncle, we have a good time? The white-robed nuns wouldn't understand, nor would anyone at the University; she felt the hopeless nostalgia for the first time of just how helpless she was, and the horror of his old man's sighs drove her trembling out of the bathroom, leaving her coffee on the table, out into the street, stumbling against drunks and *machos*, Heh, chiquita, you look *muy seductiva*, Where can I go? where can I go? she whispered, until she stopped and a flush crossed her pale face, because she remembered a conversation with Battiste, guiltily revealing his revolutionary activities, We meet in the apartment of my friend Ferdinando, 309 West Fifty-sixth Street, you must come sometime, of course we don't keep any of the guns there. . . .

Camila smiled for a moment, thinking that that was a pity. She counted the change in her pocket, and hailed a cab, not giving herself time to think, time to wonder what he would say, it must be three o'clock in the morning, but he would know what to do, he was a fugitive, in his own way, he knew about the way of the world. . . . And when she was standing opposite his building in the rain, she could see there was still a light on in a top-floor apartment, and she knew instinctively that that was his, he would seek the top story like an eagle, always. She paused for a moment to look at the light, and then she went inside and found the apartment number on his box, F. Lorca, and she took the elevator with her heart beating because she had only met him once and perhaps he wouldn't remember her, but she had nowhere else to run to, and so she knocked on the door, and he opened it after a moment in a bathrobe and said "Yes?" and then, "My God, what is it, what's happened to you?" and put his arms around her without an instant's hesitation—and she felt his heart racing, his strong arms and his hard chest, that pillowed her head like a lover's, and the sudden intake of his breath, as he tightened his arms around her, and then his firm lips as she raised her head because she suddenly knew why she was there, why she had had to come to him, her only home, her only lover and she felt his lips, his gentle hands, Shh, don't cry, it's all right—and a madness which was perfect sanity, because in that disordered apartment she had finally found the other half of her life, her only husband, and the man she would love with perfect faithfulness until the hour of her death.

seven

Explanations came later: as he held her in his arms, muffling her hysterical sobs against his chest, and listening to the whole sordid story.

He got it in bits and pieces, augmented by delicate questioning: and as the general outlines of her horror began to become apparent (murmured by her, so that some things were barely audible) he swallowed a blinding rage which surprised him by its intensity, and began at the same time to savor this brand new world, where she should be here in his arms, at three o'clock in the morning, a beautiful, shivering bird whom after all he barely knew. He got her to sit down, trying to take her coat, which she refused to give up but hugged wet around her body, so he sat down beside her, and held her close to his body to warm her, feeling an unexpected surge of sexual tenderness as they sat together on the couch in his disordered apartment, it occurred to him he really should have cleaned up, but then who expected visitors at three o'clock in the morning, he murmured to her, You've caught me when I wasn't expecting company, and all the while she was shaking uncontrollably and he held her feeling a diffused but delicious intimacy that he realized was entirely on his part. She was too shaken to be aware that she was sitting with a strange man, in his messy apartment, with no more clothes on than were required by the rules of minimal decency, and he looked down at her bright hair as she pressed her face to his chest with a quizzical smile pulling up the corners of his lips. Come on, you really are going to catch cold, he said, shrugging his robe down on the sofa beside her, and he went into the bathroom and dressed again, trousers and shirt from the hamper, whatever he could find, and when he came out of the bathroom she was curled up on the sofa like a child and he put a blanket over her and sat down beside her, occasionally running his fingers over her hair, suffused with a light, warm happiness and a perilous desire to laugh, thinking, Now that I've got you here, what in the world am I going to do with you?

She stayed with him for two weeks. She awoke, and he carefully fed her milk, grilled cheese sandwiches, valencia oranges section by section, listening as she spoke sometimes with exhaustion, sometimes with hysterical violence, letting out the black vomit inside of her that was consuming her because goddamn it that *bastard*, he tried to *kill* me! ... And such was his patience of an expert lover (or it may have been his instincts of an expert hunter) that he didn't interrupt her, even when she lay exhausted against his shoulder, murmuring some inconsequential detail over and over with the tired persistence of amazement, because it helped her to remember and name what had been done to her— just as it helped to cement the bond between them, that she should tell all these intimacies to *him*. He never made her feel uneasy or embarrassed with him, sensing that her pride would run from any recoil on his part, even in her desperate state. He was gently matter-of-fact with her, teasing her to eat something or drink a small glass of tequila, Come on, you can't be Mayapanian and not drink this stuff, we all drink like fishes ... making her listen to music, and pulling her up to dance with him. ... Come on, of course you can dance, here, I'll show you ... making light of their enforced isolation like two fugitives, and always watching with the thin, veiled care of a doctor in case she took a turn for the worse, and he would have to let her go and put her into a hospital. He encouraged her to read the many newspapers he brought home, and the political journals ... watching the news on television, he gave her back her world very deliberately refashioned according to his own perceptions, but he sensed an answering chord in her as well: in many ways they were very much alike. When she made a comment about the fifty-year amnesia which had made Augusto Sandino once again attractive to the Salvadorans, he caught his breath and had the uneasy sensation that she had uttered his thought a scant second before he'd thought of it himself. In all ways he improvised a treatment for her, made up of his own self-interest, and enlightened, without his even being aware of it, by the delight he took in this slim, pale, lovely girl who inhabited his life and his apartment as though she'd always been there: and so without meaning to, he made her whole, and looked into her eyes with an unexpected resonance in his own heart, my God he'd found a friend, among all these disciples, somebody that he could really talk to! And smiled at all her new-made loveliness, which he held trembling between his hands.

Only then did he allow himself to kiss her, sliding his hands to caress the softness of her breasts, the unimaginably narrow hollow of her waist, aware even as he did it that he might be destroying all his handiwork because she might have been too hurt, too scarred by what had passed to withstand him, but he couldn't resist, he had to taste the sweet fruits of the scenario he'd spent two weeks of passionate effort trying to construct, and although he wanted her as his political ally, he also wanted her quite definitely in his bed. She started, but didn't draw away from him; and when he hesitated, willing to stop, she drew his hands again to her, unbuttoning her thin dress with a sudden boldness so that he could see, not only how fragile and thin she was, but the proud symmetry of her body, straight-backed, the slender body of a warrior. He marveled, running his hand down the curve of her belly, drawing her to him on the same old sofa where he had held her shattered fragments two weeks before; he felt her own hands sliding beneath the robe he wore to explore tentatively the boniness of his rib cage, the strong muscles around his spine; he undid the sash of his robe to help her, and slipped it off; and then for a long moment they simply looked at one another: naked, fingers outstretched, barely touching breasts and shoulders, faces, smiling mouths. The lean incisiveness of his cheek, and her eyelids, lightly veined, like the roseate nipples of her breasts. The stern beauty of his face, softened by tiny lines of humor around his eyes, and her face, upturned to him like a flower: a smiling flower, which wore the traces of pain and weariness as lightly as cosmetics. Her light-veined eyelids fell over her eyes as he pulled her to him roughly, and covered her mouth with his: and she gave an involuntary moan when he entered her, and pressed her hands against his back as though never to let him go from her, and bore the weight of his ardor with an uncompromising courage which transformed itself into the first act of pleasure she'd ever freely given and received, and when he gripped his hands in her hair and cried out she felt herself to be filled with a clean, light air, and a thin haze of sweat sprang out on her skin and covered her body with moisture.

Afterward, they talked. Ferdinando got up and found his cigarettes and lay down on the sofa again beside her, catching his breath: and she discovered he was a discursive, gentle, playful conversationalist after sex, the kind of man who would use words to bridge the gradual relaxation of his body, the way another man might take a nap, or bathe with his companion. She lay still and savored the aftershocks of pleasure; trying not to think that this beautiful man who lay stretched beside her, and whose heart she could still feel racing along with the intimate, playful tenderness in his voice, would soon be up and giving himself freely to a million different ideas, and a million different people. She kissed the damp hair on his chest and thought, This has to be enough, because she already knew with the wisdom of absolute clarity that she loved him more deeply and completely than he loved her. She couldn't feel any regret about this: she couldn't feel anything but happiness in his presence, and her main fear, the simple fear of a child, was that she should be forced to leave him, no matter how many other people she had to share him with. It was that which made her say, when he asked her if she could make sense of a life that brought him a slum apartment and obscurity, but the leisure to make love at four-thirty in the afternoon, that it seemed to her to be the most sensible life in the world: and when he smiled at her and said she was prejudiced, and besides students had an easier schedule than their professors, just look at her, she shook her head slowly, and looked at him for a long time with her clairvoyant, light-blue eyes. "You're talking nonsense, you know. You were born to lead a country, you weren't born for obscurity. These last few years have been special. And in any event, I think you hid out for these last couple of weeks deliberately, so you could be with me."

He was a little shaken as always by her intuition, as well as delighted by her prophecy. He laughed, leaning back against the arm of the sofa. "You're getting very cocky, for a little girl who's just been properly made love to for the first time."

"Oh, is that what it was?"

"Yes, I thought you might have been aware of it."

"Sorry, I've got no grounds for comparison. You'll have to give me a few more examples, and then I'll be better able to judge."

He turned his face against her shoulder and laughed with the most magnificent sincerity he'd felt in years. "My God, I love you, *querida*!"

She felt as if a slimy, cold presence had insinuated itself between them, and she shut her eyes. "I love you too, but please don't call me that again."

"Why not?" He looked at her, his alertness coming back at her pallor, and then after a moment took his finger and traced it down the contour of her cheek. "Is it as bad as that?"

She shook her head, smiling, shaking it off like a nightmare or something that would kill her if she let it. "It's nothing. I'm fine. Forgive me? You can call me anything you want."

"How about *mi angelita*? You look like an angel, with all that blond hair." He smoothed his fingers over the soft hair at her temple, and kissed her there. "You make me feel like Rumpelstiltskin. How'd you like to join our movement, and have Angelita be your revolutionary name?"

As simple as that. And for a moment, she looked at him, divining that his motives might not have been unmixed: and he held her eyes with a smile that said, What if they were, we've both been made extremely happy by the eventuality, and you know you want to join us anyway, you're a radical's daughter, it's in your blood. And in a way that was true, although not as simply as he suggested it: it was there in her smile, a recklessness which exceeded Ferdinando's own, although he was the first person with the wit or the luck to notice it. She smiled, in slow recognition of it herself. "Blowing things up?"

"Don't tell me it's never occurred to you?"

"Never consciously."

"Well, think about it consciously. But only with me. I don't want you blowing things up indiscriminately. You're far too effective a weapon for me to give you away. I think I'm going to keep you exclusively to myself."

And because he was basically telling her the truth, she felt no disappointment in learning what she truly meant to him. She was filled with a clear radiance as she sat with him later on at his kitchen table, drinking a cup of coffee, and she put her elbows on the table and smiled at him saying, "Well, *mi general,* what do you want me to do?"

"Well, let's see. . . ." He cast his eyes in mock consideration at the ceiling. "You could help us get guns—no, Pisote's already doing that. You've got to meet Pisote, by the way, you'll love her. More to the point, she'll love you, perhaps you'd better not. Well, what else? You could help your friend Battiste get money from conservative Catholics . . . he's remarkably good at that, by the way, you'd be amazed at his talents. Why, what are you laughing at?"

She bent her head over her cup to hide her nearly helpless laughter, which had come upon her suddenly, with all the sweet sharpness of hysterical relief. "You, making fun of Battiste! Christ, between him and Porfirio, I haven't known whether to turn myself in to the police, or apply for a job taking away the sins of the world. Perhaps both!"

She looked up with sparkling eyes, to meet his, grown slightly darker, and he looked down at his hands as she said, still laughing, "What? What is it? Have *you* thought of a job for me?" And when he didn't answer, she took his hand and said very quietly, "What is it?"

He looked at her, slowly shaking his head. "You know, you're quite extraordinary. I really don't want to take advantage of you."

"You can't take advantage of me."

"You want to bet?"

"Yes," she said smiling, and leaned her cheek on his hand.

"Because I love you. You may not want to hear that, but you've got to have been aware that something like that was going on all this time."

She didn't see his slight smile, although she felt his lips gently brushing her hair. And so, when he told her his idea, she conquered her terror with the same quick certainty with which she'd stared down so many unpleasant realities, because after all there was really nothing so bad but it could be seen in its context as a matter of degree. It made sense; and the happiness she felt was such a strong, palpable presence that any amount of pain seemed tolerable, even if that pain seemed tolerable only with the strongest exercise of her will. She had gotten control enough of her voice by the time she looked up to say, "You're right, of course I'll go back to him. He knows everyone in the U.N., everyone in Campeche, he'll be a gold mine of information—" and there was no way she could be talked out of it. Deceiving Porfirio, who could send Ferdinando back to prison in Mayapán, and certain death; who could be coaxed into revealing the secrets of his own business dealings with the Buiztanistas (despite his much-touted liberalism); who deserved her lies (and perhaps that was a secret motive unadmitted even to herself). Ferdinando took her back to the apartment on Sutton Place that afternoon in a taxi, and kissed her good-bye, whispering, "I'll have Battiste get in touch with you soon. He'll tell you where we can meet." There was a tender gaiety in his eyes as he held her face in his hands and asked her, "Are you sure you'll be all right?" and it made her heart stop. And so she smiled at him, and stepped back, waving from the doorway: a slender, fragile girl in a light dress and a raincoat, with translucently pale skin and soft blond hair whipped by the November wind around her face, and then she was gone—and Ferdinando Lorca pressed his fingertips to his eyes and told the taxi to take him uptown to Columbia, because he had a class, because life had to go on, although her leaving had touched him more than six months spent with the Buiztanista torturers, and he felt appalled at what he was forcing her to do, even while he was forcing her to do it.

Camila rode the elevator up to the penthouse with a numbing calm. Perhaps he wouldn't even be there? Perhaps he would have guests? She laughed, soundlessly in the elevator, a cruel, rather breathless laugh as the door opened. That would serve him right, if he had guests. Perhaps there was nothing more to it than that—the knowledge of what a monster he was. There was nothing more he could do to her. She was no longer a child. What the hell could he force her into if she wouldn't let him?

At least that's what she thought, until she opened the door. The apartment looked immaculate as always, and there was the sound of a kettle whistling, which told her he must be in his study with the door closed. She felt a shiver of horror as she realized how much of her was tied to him, how much they knew about each other: but there was no point in dwelling on that, she told herself firmly as she shut the thought out of her mind.

She opened the door to his study without knocking, so that the sound of the whistling kettle, at first, made him look up—and then he froze, gazing at her without any expression at all. She didn't know in that instant what she had expected: perhaps his fury, perhaps tears, doglike whining, but not that blank cold stare of his ice-gray eyes that flayed her to the bone. He was the same as always, thin, immaculate, with his steel-rimmed spectacles on his nose and he remained immobile for a very long time save for one bone-thin hand which shook with a very faint tremor . . . he put the pen he was holding down on his desk . . . he continued to look at her, with that same imperious blankness which hid whatever rage or relief or guilt he might have been feeling, and his hand trembled as he said, "Well, *querida*, imagine seeing you here."

She took a deep breath, against a viscous substance that had lodged in her throat like tar. "Hello," she murmured, and then taking another deep breath she said, "Yes, I've come home for a rest. I've been away seeing friends. I hope you don't mind?"

"Not at all. It's—nice to have you back." He continued to stare at her as if she had arisen from the dead, and he said, perhaps unwisely, "I alerted the police about your departure."

"You did?"

"Yes, I—"

"Somehow I just can't picture that," she said softly. "I just can't picture you going to the police because I'd left. Well, you'll just have to tell them I'm back, I guess." She sailed into the room,

97

pouring herself a brandy from the decanter and gulping it down. She was making up her dialogue as she went along, and the sensation was delirious, like playing Russian roulette. "Shall I take that kettle off the stove, and make you your tea?" Her heart was pounding in her chest like a sledgehammer, but she went on. "I could use a cup myself, you can't imagine how cold it is outside. I'll leave your tea by the door for you when it's steeped, I don't want to disturb you. I shan't be in for dinner tonight, but I just thought you might like to know I was back."

Which *was* how Camila came back into Porfirio's life, but with a difference. It was a difference which at first he found difficult to credit. She was still scrupulously polite with him; and he knew she was still afraid of him, but somehow that fear had ceased to matter. She was able to retreat behind her mask of a charming stranger whenever she wished: she was inventing her role of an impervious diplomat without knowing the circumstances in which she would play it, and at times he had the uneasy sensation that she was playing with *him*, as when he asked her in exasperation, "What the hell happened to you?" and she stared at him with her limpid blue eyes, clearly uncomprehending, saying, "I don't know what you mean. I'm the same person that I always was. I'm me. Isn't that what you want?"

And of course that was what he wanted—which was both his torture and his strength. At first he simply assaulted her with the insidious compliments and intractable rigidity which had previously been enough to subdue her; then, when she revealed a new skittishness and lack of understanding of his desires, he took sterner measures. He lay in wait for her with his harsh sarcasm and his imperious orders, his imaginative invention and the hundred cruelties with which he tormented her from the first moment he saw her in the morning to the time when she locked her bedroom door to him every night. In his mercilessness there was an element of masochism, since this was the only way he could show her how much she'd hurt him. He wore her down with trivial meannesses and unimportant details, while his cold eyes continued to regard her with his implacable intention in a million different circumstances of their daily life, and his thin lips were pressed down on the secret they both knew: that he would stop afflicting her and would give her the momentary betrayal of her body which he could deliver with his most contemptuous touch, if she would allow him the intoxicating pleasure of doing whatever he wished with her. Finally, about ten days after her return, she was so exhausted by her anxiety that she felt it was better to face her fear than to continue to die in that impossible uncertainty. She came out of the shower to find him waiting for her in the hallway and instead of turning away from him she bore the intensity of his eyes with a scornful expression. Sensing his desires, she let her robe fall from her shoulders and endured his scrutiny with a scornful smile. She followed him into his room and when he made a slight gesture with his eyes more than his hands that she should stretch out on the bed she did so, wounding him with the ineffable sensuality of her movements, and the scornful way in which she put one hand behind her head. She opened her body to him as if mocking him, while she was dying of shame, and the same expression of anguish gave his face a spiritual quality as he sat down gently beside her on the bed, running his hands over her, murmuring, You really haven't got any morality at all, have you, *querida*, you can't stop yourself from behaving like a little slut, can you, and she told herself that wasn't true but she couldn't believe it. You can't stop yourself from enjoying this no matter how much you'd like to, and she shook her head fighting tears of shame which he took to be tears of pain as his fingernails probed and pinched at the most intimate secrets of her body, you can't, oh God, you can't tell me to stop any more than I can tell myself to stop, oh Christ, *querida*, and she found a new level of detachment as a practical maneuver while her insides were torn to pieces, and a sad and rueful wonder while her mind lost its moorings and wandered in a realm of shadows, and the flinty strength of absolute self-disgust, while her body sank aching into a swamp of sensation, and her spirit fluttered like a caged bird around a prison of love and necessity, and helpless ambiguity, and sweetest shame.

But in the mornings he avoided her: he slept late, or left early, leaving her a note, The milk is in the refrigerator if you want a bowl of cereal, she saw him at the University and he barely glanced at her, he was dying by inches in the labyrinth of his mortification at possessing yet not possessing her, but all she could think of was, I'm free of you, I'm getting free of you; which in a way was true. In their unreal estrangement of being virtual strangers in that big apartment except for certain designated times, she managed to keep up her charade with him, and also her spirits, which were in danger of foundering in the winds of so many different realities. She saw Battiste on campus, and he took her to meetings where she met Pisote and Carlos Molina, Jorge-Julio de Rodríguez; and she and Ferdinando pretended to know each other slightly, but she was aware that everyone there was in love with him: so she didn't feel jealous of the others, but vertiginously free to be whoever she wanted to be as when Carlos first met her and whistled, "Dos Santos, huh? Can you put out a newspaper like your old man?"

"Better." She laughed. "Just get your ass in gear and get me some cartoons, and you'll see what I can do!"

It was a time for being in love, for all of them. Camila turned nineteen, and they gave her a party; cheap wine and cake at Pisote's apartment, throbbing with loud music, and there were radical-lesbians kissing in the corners when Pisote said, "Shit, we can't talk in here, come out and sit on the fire escape."

Where there were some boards laid down, and faded cushions and even a stained *futon*, on which they sat, New York twelve stories down, in the courtyard behind Pisote's building. "God, how I hate this place," Pisote said, lighting a cigarette. "Do you like it?"

"New York?" Camila asked. "America, or your apartment?"

"Shit, I don't know." Pisote laughed. "Why are you making life so difficult, I'm just trying to put the moves on you, half the fatal femmes inside are dying in there with their tongues hanging out, thinking, Who's this bitch Pisote think she is, getting her all to herself out there on the fucking fire escape, just because it's her fucking apartment?" Pisote grinned her hungry urchin's grin, fine-boned olive-skinned face, bringing her lips close to Camila's ear, and whispered, "How come you're not drunk? You must've had six glasses of wine, a pile of reds and two joints, and you're not even drunk. How do you do it? If I had a head like yours I wouldn't be into half the shit I'm in most of the time."

She laughed, stretching her arms over her head, the tip of her cigarette and her eyes glowing in the deceiving light from the street, city light, reflective in the courtyard. "You may not believe

it, but I could have any of the women in there, *and* most of the
dudes, yeah, skinny little no-tits me, but you are one fuck of a
beauty, you know that, and I look at you and I feel like I never
saw anyone like you before. You know that?" She drew on her
cigarette, red red lips because she was into what she called her
"spic look," red plastic miniskirt and lots of mascara, black stockings and stiletto heels, and expelling the smoke she said, "Who
the hell are you anyway? Are you gay? Are you straight? That
fairy Jesuit father thinks you're some fucking Saint Teresa,
doesn't he?"

"Yeah, I guess so," Camila said, leaning her cheek against her
knees. "Who are you? Can you answer that question any easier?
Because I'm not Saint Teresa, I can tell you that."

"No, somehow I didn't think so." Pisote's eyes sparkled,
perhaps with angry tears, and she threw her cigarette into the
courtyard—"Bombs away, let's set fire to a wino"—and shut her
eyes. "I mean it, I hate this fucking city. I hate not being able to
speak Spanish without cops thinking I'm a prostitute or a rene-
gade chicano fruit-picker. I miss the sun. I miss being able to
wear bright colors and dance barefoot and fuck around, and people who think America is something more than just the United
States. Do you think we'll ever get to Campeche? Do you think
I'm full of shit? Do you think I'm pretty?"

Camila moved very quickly, to take Pisote's face between her
hands and press her lips against her forehead, a strangely ritual
gesture, and suddenly Pisote was crying, stupid fucking tears that
she couldn't control any more than a baby's as she snapped, Goddamn it, why are you so beautiful, you make me feel like a little
kid, a *puta*—but Camila wasn't listening. Her eyes staring beyond Pisote's head were rapt in the suddenness of a vision, terrible and as abrupt and unexpected as death: fire, falling from the
sky, a great red fireball rising over the city in a sky burned black
with ashes, silence, the limitless ache of the end of the world in
those vivid colors of purple and rose, yellow like the staining of a
bruise across the battered sky with the great red eye of the sun
grown ten times too big, as it sank over the charred debris of the
world. She heard the whistling of the wind of ashes sweeping
over the desolate silence, an hallucination so clear that there were
no words, nothing on earth had any meaning, the sorrows or the

joys, revolution, love, the hectic concerns of idiots, and looking down at Pisote's bowed head she heard words that were hers but had nothing to do with her mouth saying, "It's all right, it's all right to love whoever you want, for that short time between the first breath and the next, between the first stroke and the last, it's nearly midnight or close to that for all of us. . . ."

She didn't know what she was saying, as Pisote looked up, touching her face, her eyes black-circled like a raccoon's with smeared makeup as she whispered, "Do you mean it? You understand—you make me feel like I can't behave myself, like I'm going to make a fool of myself in front of you. It's not, it's not like I want to sleep with you, I mean I wouldn't *mind*, but I know better than to make an asshole of myself. It's just that, to want to be near you. . . ." Suddenly giggling with self-deprecatory relief, wiping her fingers across her eyes so that all the makeup came off, she looked younger, really she was very young, perhaps twenty-three or twenty-four, a girl, like Camila, no street-wise bitch but Francesca Estaban, whose parents owned half of downtown Buenos Aires and whom she hadn't seen for six years. "Fuck, I don't know why I get like this . . . I must be more ripped than I thought—" And then, because Camila was still staring with a bemused, blank expression into the courtyard, "Hey, thanks for letting me make an ass out of myself. You're all right, you know that? I don't know exactly what planet you're coming from, but you're all right. Listen, can I get you a drink? You want a cigarette or a joint? Happy birthday, hell, I'm great, I'm giving you one hell of a birthday party. Come on inside and let me blow my nose, shit, they're going to think we've been snorting up an ounce of coke out here the way I'm sniffling."

Camila floated in a haze of distraction through the rest of the party, and for several days thereafter. She asked Porfirio one day, while he was sitting at his desk, "Excuse me, but do you mind if I ask you a question?"

"Yes? What is it?" With a fairly normal tone of irritation; she'd interrupted him while he was working.

"General Fuertes, he's the brother of the murdered cardinal, isn't he?"

"Yes, what difference does that make? You know perfectly well he didn't share his brother's politics, he probably arranged

102

for his assassination by Buiztas' guards, if he had any concern at all for him! You've met him here. Why on earth do you bring him up now?"

She set his cup of tea down on his desk; she still did little acts of kindness for him, dutiful Camila, with the fine hint of contempt in them, to make him uncomfortable. "He called, that's all. Nothing special, but he wanted to come over. I thought we could have a party."

Porfirio stared at her as if the touch of her hand, her presence, were infectious. "You whore. Why are you tormenting me? Are you trying to kill me, is that what you want?"

She shook her head, her eyes innocent, baffled. "What on earth do you mean? I thought you might like to know what's been going on in Campeche, that's all. All those rumors, men being armed in the jungles. Buiztas is going to make a deal with the Sun Oil people." Which was pure fabrication, but which made him stand up, playing with his glasses. So he *does* have some stake in Buiztas Enterprises, she thought with satisfaction. That explains a lot.

"Who told you this? Fuertes? Never mind. No, you're right, my dear, I'll call him, have a few people in. Maybe tomorrow night. You wouldn't—you wouldn't like to assist me, would you?" Almost humbly, which she didn't trust for a minute; his little boy's act was his most duplicitous. "You're my greatest asset, you know that, you don't realize your incredible charm, you're so . . ." His eyes raking her from top to bottom with a feverish nostalgia, so that even poised and fully dressed, she stiffened. "You're so pernicious," he whispered, making it sound like a compliment. "If I didn't have you there, they would notice your absence—as if I had neglected to provide the appropriate wine, or a particularly delightful morsel to eat."

Which of course had been what she wanted: although she managed to make her acceptance sound conditional, she might or might not be there, a casual young girl. Porfirio, how delightful! Miss dos Santos, how we have missed you! I heard you were unwell? All right? You look radiant, so lovely in that dress . . . a clinging pale silk through which her body could occasionally be glimpsed, teasing, her eyes bright and watchful. She reported to the others in the house on 135th Street: "General de Campo and

General Fuertes, and the Argentine ambassador's aide, who is this incredible faggot and proceeded to get drunk and make a pass at General de Campo, and two or three others—nothing, a Cuban poet—and a man named Villada, he's a Nicaraguan: tall, very thin, very well dressed, with his hair combed like that across his forehead."

She showed them with her hands. "He spoke about the rioting in Mérida. They know that the people have guns, but they think it's sporadic; they assume it's Soviet-backed, just causing trouble, drop a few hand grenades into the water every now and then and see if the sharks manage to kill each other. That was Villada's metaphor. Then, he said, the Soviets would come in: but they don't expect a concerted uprising, because they assume the Russians can't be bothered to organize the people. Apparently they've discounted an extensive network outside the country. They seem to think that the Mayapanians *here* have given up—in the words of Señor Villada again, they're cranks."

Her bright smile flashed in the dimly lighted basement, as she took off her expensive fur coat, and pushed her hair out of her eyes to lean over a map. "Look, here—they know about the six men in Tenabo, those guys who went crazy and hit the general post office. They're aware that they were armed by somebody, but they don't connect it with the riots in Mérida, the arms cache the attaché discovered in Progreso—which was put down to drug smugglers, as we expected—and the outbreaks in Lerma and Seybaplaya and Sabancuy. It's miraculous! We could explode a bomb under Quintero de Buiztas' behind and they'd put it down to an isolated incident!"

She laughed, glancing around at all of them, like a child pleased with herself, but her eyes were on Ferdinando, and his eyes on hers; orchestrating one another, giving one another tiny, infinitesimal clues.

"Did you ask them?"

"Of course." She shook her head. "You can ask people anything if you're a woman, the best they'll assume it to be is polite interest."

"And there's no belief in a united rebel army?"

"There's no belief in a united rebellion whatsoever, it's a mess down there, Buiztas' men are shooting at random, they shot three nuns yesterday. Yes, it's true." She turned to Battiste, re-membering to tell him. "There's a growing feeling that they must placate the Church, after that papal warning against outside in-tervention beyond the boundaries of charity—because of course with all the food and supplies being shipped in they have no idea what's coming from where. But there's a feeling that the bishops and the episcopal delegates to that meeting in Port-au-Prince will come out with some statement condemning the Buiztas regime *and* its supporters. I think there's some suggestion that Villada send somebody in there to buy them off."

"What!" Battiste exclaimed in astonishment. "They're going to buy off the congress of *bishops*?"

"Yes, it's interesting, isn't it? I was wondering, do you want to fly down there and keep an eye on things?" She raised her eyebrows, merely suggesting, perhaps deliberately naïve, and they remembered suddenly that she was rich. "I've got my own account that has nothing to do with Porfirio. I could easily buy you a ticket."

Carlos Molina laughed, showing all of his back teeth, like a horse. "How about throwing in a couple of trips to Jamaica while you're at it? We could bring back some great ganja!"

Ferdinando calmed them all down, thinking, grinning to himself. "It's not a bad idea. Can *we* bribe them to get even more upset—Camila, what do you think?"

"It's a piece of cake—"

"Now wait a minute!" Battiste exclaimed. "I don't know if I can go along with bribing my superiors in the Church to protest on a violation of human rights policy!"

"Aren't they going to protest anyway?" Pisote asked blandly. "We'd just be *encouraging* their consciences, not creat-ing them for them!"

"Besides, perhaps I was imprecise," Ferdinando said quickly. "I didn't mean we should offer them a check. Surely there are other ways—*you* must know—ways of convincing them, influencing them, perhaps merely by distributing our evi-dence. God, slaughtered nuns! The deliberate rerouting of drugs, kids dying by the side of the road—"

Battiste looked at Ferdinando sideways, but Camila knew he was just pretending to be dubious. So he *does* want to go there, she thought, but he can't admit it: he's ambitious, she realized with sudden surprise. She'd never known that about Battiste before. She touched his arm, pressing it warmly.

"Come on, you know what to say to them. Appeal to their hearts. All they want is the merest suggestion to cast them into the role of heroes, calling down an interdict on Campeche and excommunicating the Buiztanistas!" Her eyes twinkled. "And you can assist them with their business. At least buy them a nice meal. It's good publicity. I think you might even enjoy it!"

So it was decided to send Battiste to Port-au-Prince, well funded, and supplied with two sets of documents: generalized information on the iniquities of the Buiztas regime, and more detailed plans of action, to circulate among the radical Jesuits. He came back in a week, with eleven avowals of definite support, and the wholehearted condemnation by the Caribbean bishops of the atrocities committed by the government of Quintero de Buiztas, human rights violations and a scandalous disdain for the rudiments of public health and safety, my God, what a sacrilege, which was cited with approval by the United Nations, and which made it to the front page of *The New York Times*, excerpts on page A12—along with a photograph of the bishops in front of the National Assembly which included the first public picture of the tall, severe-looking priest who was identified in the caption as Fr. Batista (sic) Tommassi, S.J. The plans went forward for the anticipated rebellion in Mayapán, although no specific date was mentioned: they were afraid to foresee the culmination of their years of toil, even in the privacy of their own minds, and so continued to talk about it jokingly as something that would be lucky to happen in the next one hundred years.

During that time Camila and Ferdinando were in almost daily contact, but never without the presence of half a dozen supporters; and while he continued to be amazed and delighted by her quick mind and her adept, instinctive talents at deception, he rarely thought about her except as one of his co-conspirators: their fleeting intimacy had been a transitional thing, serving the purpose of converting her to their cause, and there had been the end of it. Yet he continued to think about her. He thought about her in the privacy of his shower and of his bed and in those brief, somnambulant moments when he was walking along the street or riding on a subway; he thought about her in the midst of action and in the midst of discussion and staring at her in some God-awful rathole where they were plotting revolution, he thought that in a life of brief women and essential loneliness he had never felt so disturbed and elated as he felt with this slender girl who was young enough to be his daughter. He wondered if he was turning into another Porfirio, another child molester, and he tried to shake his growing warmth toward her in loves with other women who were older, or younger, whose minds made him wince or whose intuitive sympathies approached the clairvoyance of angels, but they all turned into Camila; and he found himself lost in the exasperating delight of knowing he could ask her to do anything, without in the least diminishing her essential love for him, which was of the quality of pure joy and which contrasted so strongly with all his contradictory emotions: darkness and hunger, impatience, rage, sharp pride and leaping ambition. He thought it might be possible to lose some of that darkness with her, without knowing for certain that he wanted to lose it. Battiste for his part could not have helped but know what was going on, but he tried not to see it: for fear of taking sides, but also for a more confused feeling of anguish, which he refused to acknowledge even to himself.

But they were all too busy for contemplation, and Ferdinando and Camila were among the busiest: rolling up their sleeves and writing, telephoning, coordinating, planning the intricate details of a revolution two thousand miles distant, made up not of numbers but of desperate, poorly educated men and women, who went crazy, attacking government outposts and jeopardizing their comrades by mistake, or indolence, or the crafty placement of government spies. They learned to work together so well that they came to anticipate one another's actions, and they learned the fun of friendship without even thinking about it, and finally they learned how to laugh in the face of all convention, as when Porfirio came upon them talking outside of Low Library.

"So," he sneered, "Ferdinando Lorca. I see you have met my ward, Camila dos Santos?"

Ferdinando inclined his head, speaking quite formally despite his little smile. "I have only just had the pleasure. Where in the world have you been keeping her, Porfirio?"

His voice was so light, there could not have been an insult, but Porfirio stiffened, replying with a short laugh, "I can no longer keep her anywhere! I'm afraid she has unsavory friends. But perhaps you wouldn't consider them unsavory, Señor Lorca. Perhaps you would like them very much!"

"Is that true, Miss dos Santos?" Ferdinando asked her mildly. "Do you have many unsavory friends?"

It was his eyes that saved her, just in time, smiling at her so that she replied, swallowing, "I don't know what my guardian is talking about." She regained her breath and added, "Señor Lorca, Battiste said you might be joining us for dinner tonight? I should very much like to continue our discussion about the political situation in Guatemala, if you have any time for it."

"I should be delighted." Ferdinando smiled. "It isn't often I get a chance to dine with one of the luminaries of our culture, as well as a close friend and a very beautiful young woman."

Which was how Ferdinando happened to join them for dinner that night at the Four Seasons, much to Porfirio's scarcely concealed irritation: and afterward for drinks, an oddly assorted party, with the old man, the stiff, uncomfortable, miserably unhappy priest, and the beautiful girl and the darkly handsome man. "Miss dos Santos," Ferdinando asked her gravely, "would you like to dance?" And so she felt Ferdinando's warm fingertips take her hand, and there was a limit to discretion because oh yes, she would like very much to dance—and then she was in his arms, moving step for step and gracefully, gracefully as trained ballroom dancers, as if they'd been doing this all their lives, smiling, laughing, to hell with the whole world, Ferdinando drew her close, his eyes and his lips smiling down at her, and looking up at him her face was very pale, very bright, with her magnificent blue eyes fixed on his as if they were the only two people in the room. My love.

Over at their table, Battiste was talking quickly, frantically, but not so persuasively that he was able to distract the sick, rapt stare of the mesmerized old man as he watched because he knew, of course he knew, there was no way he could not have known, the piercing sweet expression he had longed for and never seen, for himself, on Camila dos Santos' face.

eight

IT WAS ON THE EIGHTH DAY of December in the thirty-first year of the tyranny of the dictator Quintero de Buiztas in Mayapán that the revolutionaries moved, in a single concerted hour of incendiary bombs, dynamite, and bullets to knock out the central power plant, the main offices of the telephone company, and the oil refineries along the wharves on the south side of Campeche. They stormed the main offices of *Los Tiempos*, the government-controlled newspaper, and smashed the presses, putting sixteen writers and secretaries to summary execution against a wall with machine gun fire; hacked their way into the military barracks and fell to hand-to-hand combat with the soldiers; but it wasn't the surprise attack they had anticipated because they were beaten back from the barracks by mortar fire; the offices of *Los Tiempos* were strafed by aircraft from the La Jola Air Force Base and three hundred insurrectionists were crushed beneath the collapsing walls, burned alive in the fires of napalm and gasoline which poured into the gutted building; and intense fighting continued for six hours at the central power plant so that the only unalloyed victories of the revolutionary strike force were the telephone company and the oil storage tanks, a raging fire covering the Southside wharves but what the hell, we can always get more oil and who needs the telephones anyway, we've won, we've beaten them back, those lousy bastards, Quintero de Buiztas exulted. Then the second wave hit, twelve hours later: outside the city, at the air force base, which was sparsely guarded, a few lazy soldiers and technicians who surrendered at the first shot; they put the base to the torch, millions of gallons of aircraft fuel, rising up in a holocaust like the end of the world Just look at that, my God, and some of them said, We should do that with all of it, burn up their oil and boil the oligarchs in the broth of their own gasoline. They hit the military bases at San Pedro, the army training camp on the Isla del Carmen, and faded back into the jungle, A few hundred of them, certainly no more, Mr. President, and he shook his head, No, there's a lot more; and over the next three days there were sporadic raids on Paraiso, Comalcalco, and then a devastating strike against the city of Cunduacán far to the south, seizing the oil rigs, barricading themselves into the fortresslike Santa Rosa refinery and setting up their own citadel with cassavas and fruit and enough rum to drown a regiment of radicals, Goddamn it, that's enough, Quintero de Buiztas shouted, This time they've gone far enough, as he ordered his troops to retake the Santa Rosa refinery without concern for casualties, I don't want to see a single man alive on either side after the last shot is fired. He chewed his fingers and paced his office in his military fatigues and his steel-rimmed spectacles, issuing orders with the quick incisiveness of a man who's backed against the wall, because when a man's got a knife in your balls you don't mince words, and acting on the impulse of his fateful intuition he knew it was not his time to die yet, he snapped, Get me the *americano* army base in Guantánamo, and navigating the treacherous waters of United States diplomacy he made a deal, Ten million dollars in aid, gentlemen, within twenty-four hours or I call in the assistance of the Cubans. He fought them back—but they welled up between his fingers like the blood from a bad wound, more and more of them, because this time the contagion of rebellion was strong enough within the country and infected enough from the outside that you couldn't heal it with the old bromide of Kill the dog and you get rid of the rabies, because there were too many dogs and when even one of them got away with it, even with the death of a single Buiztanista, they all thought, That's me—and so they no longer believed in their own deaths, up until the moment of their annihilation they saw themselves as necessary casualties toward an ultimate victory and Buiztas thought, Goddamn it, there's somebody else's mind at work here, these sons of bitches couldn't have thought of such a thing on their own. He pondered long hours at night, trying to think who that other person might be—because he honestly had no idea, there were hundreds of candidates among the political thinkers he had exiled, tortured, had killed; any one of them or their followers might have spawned the antagonist he sensed now, smelling of blood and the animal stink of a slaughterhouse, smelling of bullets and the clean, harsh smell of the disinfectant they used in the public hospitals against the threat of infection, and now the doctors poured it onto the wounds of the soldiers because they didn't have any other medicine, and poured it down their own throats because they didn't want to live anymore, what the hell, it was as easy a way to go as stand out in the street and wait for a stray bullet to blow your brains out, long live the revolution. And Buiztas stood alone in his offices inside the Presidential Palace fingering the twelve buttons of his military uniform while he tried to place that disinfectant smell—like the smell of blood, mixed with the French perfume smell of the fishmonger tarts down by the waterfront, but it wasn't quite like that; he followed his dog's keen sense, through the labyrinth of his Presidential Palace; he searched through the giddy night of the moon's darkness and the scent of the bougainvillea until he found what he was looking for in his own bedroom, it was his Presidential aide, doused in perfume and lopped like a dead steer on the welter of the Presidential sheets, and despite the best efforts of the disinfecting cleaning girls he was already beginning to rot.

The revolutionaries in the Santa Rosa refinery held out for six days, until a seismic charge shook the ground from the Isthmus de Tehuantepec as far as the Presidential Palace in Campeche, rattling the windows and breaking china, and people ran out into the streets thinking it was another earthquake, my God, but it was worse than that, because the governmental forces had made a final attempt to oust the insurgents and rather than be taken alive, the revolutionaries had preferred to level the entire refinery with dynamite. Goddamn it, Quintero de Buiztas said when he heard of it, that's the way to do it, gentlemen! My heart-felt congratulations on being men with something more than talk between your legs, but that didn't stop him from moving against the rebel forces with far greater ferocity than before, to prevent their being taken for martyrs; he contacted the United States Secretary of State, and in secret conference revealed to him the presence of communist instigators in his country, he made it up, his invention took flight and he described agents captured in last week's fighting, a high-ranking Cuban official, a light-skinned man who was obviously a Russian and spoke Spanish out of a guidebook, he had no idea if any of this stuff was being believed, but he got what he wanted: an announcement to the world, at the next press conference, The United States doesn't rule out military intervention in the crisis in Mayapán. He sat and soaked in a hot tub of eucalyptus leaves, fighting the pain of his enlarged prostate, Let's see them fight that, those sons of bitches, but sighing with the wistful certainty of shit I'm getting old, because he had never before needed the help of the *gringos*, he had fought his own battles and now they were going to fuck up everything, just watch them, with their superior weapons and tactics they were just going to get involved in his country and make a mess of everything. He half liked the revolutionaries—his own people, smelling of the same stale sweat that caked his own armpits, not the Old Spice and deodorant smell of the Yanquis. His men moved with the superior Yanqui weapons to crush the rebellion in the jungle: the desperate commandos in their wicker masks, who struck at bridges, twenty yards of the Pan American Highway just south of Cuauhtémoc, they were ill-equipped, they were sometimes no more than children, but there was a tenacious thread of suicidal madness in them that made Buiztas feel he was hacking his way through a swamp of blood, bone-crushing exhaustion with a machete in his hand, as he killed them one by one, yet he liked them, they were crazy sons of bitches, he thought they were full of shit but he admired them. His men moved gradually into the villages, turning the tide of the war; arresting the brave young men in their wrinkled green uniforms, faces caked with dirt and the sweat and stink of lying hidden in mud hollows and latrines to escape the government patrols; they dragged them out; they shot them at point-blank range with exploding bullets that shattered the skull, leaving them in the middle of the road, there, you see what happens to those who oppose the system; they jumped into their battered Jeeps and took the more important prisoners into the cities, where with electric cattle prods they searched for the illusive disinfectant smell of his first dangerous enemy, until they could report to Buiztas, He has a name, Mr. President, and his name is Ferdinando Lorca, and he has the languid bony implacability of a whore with a gun in his hand, he has the gentle fragrance of the bougainvillea and sea breeze mixed with the acrid smell of gunpowder just as you imagined it, and Buiztas laughed, of course, that fairy—because he had honestly forgotten all about him, until that fateful instant, but the name made perfect sense. It fit perfectly into his half-mad sense of his own ironic destiny, so that he said, Get me that man from New York, I want to carve his corpse up with my own hands, get him here within twenty-four hours. But, General, they said, that's impossible; the Americans won't let you have him; and he shook his head, looking out the window—yes they will, the Americans will let me have anything I want, they've invested too much in me to stop now and he might have been right but he hesitated, growing tired of his own interminable orders; get out of my sight he told them, and they hurried out the door. He sat alone, in the darkening shadows of his own Presidential office with the banners of the nation by his desk and his spectacles all alone on the green felt blotter, he stared out of the window, watching the sunset over the ocean of his pockmarked realm of bullet-scarred walls, the great square maintained free of crowds because no one was permitted to stare at the President; he rubbed his nose, drinking in the show of the great painted sunset dripping into the water like the gradual bleeding of a wound in the sky; he sighed, feeling the weight of his years and the ache in his balls and the terrible hollow feeling of why should I give a shit anymore—all he felt was a faint curiosity about this man, this beautiful El Lorca, so that if he could have had him there at the moment he would have said Good for you, take the nation with my blessing, because he finally understood what his predecessor Ramosa had meant: that it wasn't disillusionment that made you quit, it wasn't rage or fear, but the sheer deadweight of boredom, the endless round of diplomatic cock-sucking to keep your ass on the throne of power. He knew that tomorrow he would demand this El Lorca's extradition—and he would get it; the Yanquis couldn't afford to turn him down—but now in the elegiac languor of his vast cynicism he imagined inviting him in. Let him come. Let him take the country, if he could—he would drown in the deceptive jungles of his own glory, and if he didn't? Then he would blaze like Jesus Christ in his innocence: and Buiztas had to admit to a faint curiosity that he should blaze like that. What would it be like? A living contradiction to all his street-fighter's instincts, and the bitter weight of his accumulated wisdom.

He heaved himself up from his chair, and pouring himself a glass of rum from his private store, aged pirate's rum, he toasted with his glass to the invisible enemy outside his walls, through the open window where the salt breeze was blowing in from the sea. Let him come, with bullets and a wave of sanctity, like the feeble peasants believed in their kerosene light reading smeary literature that had been printed by the *norteamericanos:* let him come with healing blood and incarnadined love, and Buiztas would fight him with his thirty-year wiles of a dog in the manger, and let the best man win. Here's to you, you son of a bitch, he said, laughing, I hope the country sinks its teeth into your ass the way it has into mine, and drank, and spun around on his heel throwing his glass away as his aides marched into the room, laughing, Get me the American ambassador, gentlemen, I want them to send me the head of El Lorca on the next banana boat.

nine

So that actually, when it happened, it happened quickly. The event which was to change so many lives, defining them: giving them purpose, and more than that, "style," the peculiar glamour which was to invest them all the rest of their lives: their hurried, "secret" marriage. Like something out of a fairy tale. The lovers who would be loved by so many thousands: like film stars, like mother and father, the President and the First Lady of Mayapán. Ferdinando Lorca and Camila dos Santos were married in a quick ceremony at five o'clock on the afternoon of Thursday, the twenty-second of December, with Carlos Molina and Francesca Estaban standing by as delighted witnesses, and Father Battiste Tommassi performing the ceremony in the deserted chapel of the Harley School, which was closed for the Christmas vacation. And by that time Ferdinando was a wanted man.

It became a part of their legend, embroidered upon but never bettered: the hurried phone call from Battiste ("He's all right, no, the Department of Immigration's trying to stall it, they'd prefer not to let Buiztas extradite him no matter *how* many charges he's trumped up") and his painful, twisting attempt to soften the stark reality of Ferdinando's suggestion: "I need an alibi so I thought how about asking Camila to marry me? I'd do better with a wife, they'd never expect me to leave town on a honeymoon, and I can use her wherever I end up." He tried to stammer and hedge, making it sound emotionally precipitous ("He needs you beside him, he says if you were willing to take this chance for him . . .") but he hadn't counted on her joyously pragmatic heart, which went to the core of the matter without a moment's hesitation: "Yes, of course, it makes sense, it's the only way to keep him out of the hands of Buiztas, tell Ferdinando of course I'll marry him!" She then made a second phone call, either from the study phone in Porfirio's apartment (while she rifled his desk for ready cash; the police found the broken lock), or more probably from her aunt and uncle's apartment: shrouded with dustcloths and wall-to-wall silence, sitting at her uncle Ernst's gunmetal desk while she searched for the number—overseas? Or would she have been able to reach him in the United States? That shadowy figure, who was to enter their lives for the first time: and whose name had come to her immediately, simply, from some far-buried memory of the past. (Her mother, in a long black dress, strapless, evening gown? In the long living room in Campeche, filled with the water-patterned light off the sea, dancing with an old man to Duke Ellington's "Creole Love Call." Had that been he?) The shadowy man whom no one ever knew very much about, save that he was rich—one of the richest men in the world, they said—and immensely old, German. An industrialist? An automobile manufacturer? Or had his plants made other things, outbidding Farben for the semi-survivors of Auschwitz? No one knew. No one even knew where he lived, or how he lived: in style, or in seclusion, or in the villa on Isla del Viento, perched like a fortress of pink stone by the sea, a beautiful place, accessible only by helicopter, ten miles off the coast of Mayapán. Their benefactor, their Mephistopheles (and he was certainly called both), the man whom she telephoned and who agreed to help her (but why? But she never would explain). Alfred Linz. Who made a fortune off his connection with the Lorcas. And who might have been—? But no one knew exactly who he might have been. A friend, or a relative. Perhaps.

Battiste brought Ferdinando to the Harley School, letting him in with his own key (for setting up for early mass; for working late; he had keys to most of the rooms in the school, the nuns didn't know of his connection with a "famous" Mayapanian revolutionary). He felt an indefinable emotion as he and Ferdinando crossed the hall, below the big main staircase, with the mullioned window and the faded window seat halfway up; light streaming through the window to illuminate Ferdinando's lean, handsome face; and the peculiar mystical silence of the empty school, smelling of chalk and incense, the quiet of the usually noisy halls. This is where we first met, he wanted to say to Ferdinando, but he couldn't say anything. He felt embarrassed by his own emotion, so he was relieved when Ferdinando looked around him with a chuckle and said, "It's beautiful! Is this really where they educate Catholic women, or have you started sneaking catechism lessons to a bunch of Protestant boys?"

Battiste shook his head. "No, it's true. They're mostly diplomats' kids, they expect a level of gothic stuffiness."

"Well, I should say so! This place looks like the annex of the Harvard Club! Did you really pursue your priestly vocation here?"

"I still do," Battiste said, blushing, and added, "it's a good cover, they all think I'm the soul of nonviolence!"

Ferdinando smiled at him, in the half-light of the hallway, which threw his face into shadow and left only his eyes sparkling with light. "You still are," he said, without explaining his pronouncement. They went into the headmistress's study, where there was an electric coffee maker, and Ferdinando volunteered to make them some coffee. He hesitated, holding a scoop of Maxwell House in his hand, as his eyes suddenly focused on the middle distance. "I just realized, I'm actually going to get married in . . . what is it? Three quarters of an hour? My God, what a picture! I ought to be scared to death."

"Well, are you?" Battiste asked through a tightness in his throat, sitting on the corner of the headmistress's desk and trying with all his strength to keep his voice light.

"Of course not. I adore Camila. Marriage sounds like a wonderful thing to try. God knows I've tried practically everything else."

He finished starting the coffee machine and turned to look at Battiste with his amused, gentle, wonderfully intelligent eyes. He said softly after a moment, "Well, how does it feel to be my best man?"

Battiste had trouble answering, though he tried not to avoid his eyes. "I'm not your best man, Ferdinando, I'm your priest."

Ferdinando continued to look at him for a moment longer with the same light, thoughtful gaze, and then he smiled. "So you are. And you don't approve of this."

"It's not my place to approve or disapprove."

"You think she could do better. Well, perhaps she could. But let me assure you I *do* love her, and I was under the impression that you didn't think too badly of *me*."

"I—I think you're great," Battiste said, wincing at the banality, and went on, with ghastly jocularity, "I think you're both great! You're two of the best things that ever happened to me, I just don't want . . . I don't want either of you to make a mistake," he finished lamely, which wasn't the truth at all, but he found himself unable to tell him the truth while he was standing there next to the coffee machine.

Ferdinando looked down with a little smile. He said, seemingly for no reason, "You know, the first time I slept with a woman was when I was nineteen. You'll think that very old, but I was a romantic, and she was no Westside tramp, but a girl of good family . . . a rebel . . . my God, how I loved her! I was scarcely her first man, but I thought, You know all the things, well, perhaps you don't . . ." He shook his head, as if looking back through the glass of twenty-one years, very deliberately not looking at Battiste. "Anyway . . . we drifted apart, and I made up for lost time, but I'll tell you, I still can remember that woman, and all the women I've loved since then, and none of them can hold a candle to Camila. That's a boring expression, isn't it? But it's true, she *is* like a candle, isn't she?" He looked at the priest with tender compassion and said, "You know, I'm capable of a lot of things, but lying down with tragedy has never been one of them. I won't make her unhappy."

Battiste felt as if he would make a mistake if he said anything, did anything beyond looking at Ferdinando with a painful, terrible intensity and then he felt as if that was stupid, and he forced his mouth into a sick smile which by the time he stood up from the desk was real.

"Well, I can't give you more of a homily than that. I'm not going to advise you against birth control, or counsel you on bringing up your kids in the Church. How's that coffee coming? I feel as if I could use a cup, and Camila will be here before long."

Which was true, at that moment she was on her way across town in a cab to join them, although Porfirio didn't learn of her disappearance till that night, and didn't report her missing to the police until the next day. He waited until his anxiety of the next morning convinced him she wasn't fooling—and by that time he knew, of course he knew, that she was gone, obviously gone to join El Lorca, whose beauty burned the old man, twisting in him like a knife, deeper than bone. *Christ*, where had he taken her? His beloved, his—addiction. He couldn't grasp the fact of her disappearance, his monstrous loneliness—his pain! He couldn't—*couldn't* be experiencing a blank like this, a void which was unpremeditated, not of his control! He couldn't imagine it!

That night, trembling, after he knew for certain she had gone (and he had been in elegant, serene control all day; immaculate; in a charcoal-gray, pinstripe, three-piece suit, impeccably tailored; because his tall, thin figure was still graceful—and he was always aware of how he looked. He had been careful to behave "reasonably," with the police, with everyone, that day), he shut his eyes, and shuddering, slammed his fist against the glass of the dining room table, cracking it, burst knuckles, the sobbing self-pity of his own tears and blood. He went coldly crazy, a bizarrely calculated rage, tearing at the books in his study, fragile figurines, terrified by a shaking senility which haunted him with the specter of irrationality, making him break things as a way of proving he was still *in* control, still—alive. He systematically drank brandy, Courvoisier in a medicine glass from the bathroom, and broke the lock of her closet door, tearing down her clothes (because she had taken nothing; all the presents he'd given her), throwing them on the bed—fur jackets, dresses, blouses—and pulling open her drawers to tear at the piles of her underclothes, brassieres and panties and slips, raw silk that hurt his fingers, throwing them all on the bed—he shuddered, and feverishly unbuttoning his fly, unbuckling his belt, he held the cool, soft material against his flesh, trying, for the first time in his life, to soothe the pain of his loneliness and loss. He sank to his knees next to the

119

bed, pressing the sheets against his face, hunting for her smell; wadding them against his groin while he stroked her pillow with his bloody fingers, murmuring, *Querida, querida*—and his brain seemed to clench like a fist, exploding through his head; he pressed his face with his palms, pleading, Oh God, please don't let me die; and the morning found him, trembling and sick but himself again, oh God, yes, he was himself, cold sober and icily rational—staring at his flaccid, naked body in her full-length mirror, while his eyes took in the evidence of a minor stroke: one eyelid drooping, half his mouth stiff, there, when he moved, a slight limp. Himself. Naked. His bitter smile. Ah, *querida*, how unfortunate for you I'm not dead. He looked at his naked body in the mirror, a tangle of gray hair on his chest, his belly—he ran his blue-veined hands experimentally over his stomach, down his thighs—gagging with revulsion, he shut his eyes when his fingers encountered his penis, his testicles—his shame, oh Jesus, when would it ever end? And swallowing, a lump like blood in his throat. Yes, *querida*, how very unfortunate for you that I'm not dead. How very very very inconvenient for you. . . . He shut his eyes.

But by that time she had gone—taking a taxi to the Harley School at four-thirty the previous afternoon, slender and young and radiantly beautiful, her long blond hair pulled back from her face, in a dark-blue, "Russian"-style coat and boots. She stepped into the shadowed halls of the school, where Battiste took her hands and allowed himself to touch her cheek for a moment with his lips. Embracing her . . . Pisote is here, and Carlos . . . their embraces too . . . and the quiet of the chapel, with two candles lighted, darkness outside . . . and Ferdinando standing next to the altar, very still, with the candle flames lighting his eagle's beauty, proud, and a slight, secret smile just touching his lips, as she approached . . . willow-thin, so small . . . scarcely more than a child, but with an incandescent loveliness that made him stretch out one long-fingered hand . . . his prize . . . his fingers laced with hers, and he drew her to him with a sudden swift movement of a predator, covering her mouth with his, his long hands holding her fragile beautiful skull between his palms, his wife . . . and she turned in his arms, seeking his mouth, like a flower seeking the sun.

II.
The Plumed
Serpent

one

ALFRED LINZ JOINED THEM for dinner every night, but other than that, they had the days to themselves—swimming, or lying in the sun, on the quiet beach on the Isla del Viento, stretched out naked in the dazzling sun of noon. Ferdinando, with his eyes shut, the taut, lean incisiveness of his face relaxed for once, his hair disordered across his forehead, lightened a little by the sun to brown, drying in the breeze. He had one arm thrown behind his head, and a blithe narcissism (she'd had no idea how much he loved to go naked) because he knew very well she was looking at him (and he had a lovely body, there was no point in denying it—long and slender, brown, sensual, a lovely line, even in repose). Camila moistened one finger, and drew it down his chest, and across his belly, and he said without opening his eyes, "If you tickle me, you will live for approximately thirty seconds." So she brought her body to hover over his, lightly kissing him, so that he opened his eyes and pulled her down on top of him, feeling the astonishment of her fragile shoulder blades beneath his hands; the incredible lightness of her body on top of his, like a child, turning in his heart like a small secret wound with the unexpected delight and sweetness he felt in being with her—warmed by the sun which possessed his flesh,

123

with an astonishment that sometimes shaded over into awe, because there really could not *be* such a person, there, so featherlight, so young, in his arms—holding him so tightly (it seemed as if her bones would crack), taking him into her, so freely, so recklessly—holding his soul so delightfully inside her body, until it pleased her, finally, to let it fly back into his own breast again.

They went swimming in the crystal water, clear blue, indigo; swimming far out, over the reefs, sometimes snorkling, for you could see shoals of fish—fire red, blue, green—El Lorca was an excellent swimmer, and he taught Camila how to swim for hours without tiring. They were left alone, in the sprawling pink villa set among palm trees and gardens by the sea; rising at any hour, there was always fruit and cheese, wine, bread, tequila, left by the invisible army of servants on the table outside their room; there were always fresh towels, newspapers, magazines—but they never saw anyone, until the evening. They joked about how they must do it, spying on them: "We must give them plenty to spy on." Ferdinando smiled, and he might have meant it both as a comment and a suggestion. Long, dizzying days. Camila, naked, swimming off a reef; Camila, wrapping herself in a towel to stand on their balcony to look at the sea; Camila, scented with Arpège, in a long, filmy white caftan, the wind blowing her hair: she was like a darting, sometimes slippery fish herself, or like a bird, one of the shy quetzals that Linz kept in his garden, hidden among the leaves save for an occasional flash of green. She was unselfconscious, putting suntan lotion on her nipples, to keep them from getting burned by the sun; she was suddenly hieratic, bronzed, turning to face the sunset on the terrace like a Mayan goddess; she was occasionally serious, her blue eyes looking very light in her suntanned face, leaning her cheek on one hand, staring at him as if she were trying to memorize him. She was all women and every woman he had ever desired—and if there was a part of her that he couldn't know, it was very slight; he certainly knew her better than anyone else. He caressed her beautiful face and held it between his hands, stroking with his long fingers the delicate temples, the soft downiness of her hair; and he wondered at the serenity he felt with her, whom he had married so lightly, and so flippantly. She soothed the ache of inaction and laid the balm of patience on his heart, so he was able to enjoy the magic of the island like a child, and wait for the future to reveal itself.

They had dinner with Linz, in the high-ceilinged dining room or, more frequently, out on the terrace, dizzily high over the ocean, a wide, whitewashed eyrie of stone to which they would make their way, casually, sipping drinks, at six-thirty in the evening; and he would arrive punctually fifteen minutes later—a little wizened, desiccated old man, plainly dressed in an old black suit and a white shirt stiff with starch, tiny, scarcely over five feet tall, with long, yellowed teeth, and half his body maintained (apparently) by machinery.

His hands had been operated on, plastic joints replacing the bone destroyed by arthritis—still, he showed them, flexing his fingers, it wasn't the same; he had been a gifted pianist once, but you couldn't replicate that skill. He had had several organs replaced, and was the first (and only) surviving recipient of an artificial kidney (not yet generally available, because of the extraordinary expense). His eyes, clear, watery blue, were also the result of surgery: an unbelievably delicate operation, whereby the optic disc was replaced (from a donor) and a new lens inserted (plastic) along with a new iris—his eyes had originally been brown. His voice was high but clear, really quite beautiful, and he had an encyclopedic knowledge of world history; spoke English and Spanish fluently; and had a doctorate in philosophy from the University of Halle-Wittenberg (he declined to give the date of his enrollment).

He was a thoughtful host, and a charming dinner companion. Well read, well informed. They followed the course of events in Mayapán by radio, by satellite TV and shortwave transmissions, Telexes from his many offices. There, off the coast of Mayapán in the warm shimmering sunset of a cloudless day, shading to opal, almost (one could have imagined) within sight of the troubled shore of their troubled country, he sipped martinis as he sat with them, nibbling caviar and sweet butter (Camila joked with Ferdinando that he must also have acquired a much younger man's stomach, in one of his many operations); and he saw through their charm, and the obvious delight they took in one another, to the pain in Ferdinando's eyes as he looked out to sea; the hunger of his longing for his country; his power, and his country's freedom. Alfred Linz said nothing. He had a wonderful chef. They dined on native dishes, venison and *cazon* and moro crab, flavored with sour oranges and *achiote;* they presumed he was merely humoring their Mayapanian tastes, but he seemed to enjoy these Yucatecan foods himself, dousing them liberally with *chile habañero* sauce, which made his Mayapanian guests blanch. They drank French wines, or Mayapanian beer, Alfred Linz laughing and saying it was better than anything you could get nowadays in Germany.

There were many things about him which were unknown, but little about which he was secretive; he seemed open-minded and reasonable about all things, willing to discuss (in general terms) the effects on his businesses of the price hikes of the Middle East nations, the valid claims for autonomy of the state of Israel and the P.L.O.; the rebuilding of German industry following the war (his voice casual, dispassionate; it was *a* war; there had been many wars); and the corresponding problems in American industry—"Forgive me, *United States* industry," he would say, smiling. "Which is really a contradiction in terms. The United States still sees itself as a nation state, the bastion of democracy *et al.* It's really very naïve. Today, Germany, Japan—especially Japan, that country which was forced to learn the face of the twenty-first century at Hiroshima, a useful lesson—see themselves as corporations, a worldwide nexus of corporations, dispassionate, self-interested . . . it's really a very clean world, very sensible. Misaki, Loder, Phipps International . . . I.T.M. . . . ?"

"And Linz?" Camila murmured, leaning her cheek on her hand. She was very beautiful, in the early evening light. The blue hour . . . and she was wearing a long navy-blue dress, like gauze, that floated around her body; two pearl earrings, and her long blond hair loose down her back. She was teasing him . . . perhaps. Because she was so young, a girl, a family friend, she could tease him, question him more lightly than Ferdinando could. She drifted to the edge of the terrace, looking out over the darkening sea far below them, the waves' phosphorescent colors breaking on the beach, pearly white and silver and pink. She looked like a lovely, fragile toy, a lovely frivolous ornament in this setting (and Linz admired her skill, at pretending to be just that), sipping her drink, the ice cubes tinkling in her glass. Her smooth forehead was pleated with a little frown, as she gazed down at the sea.

"You know, they still need dreams, they still need leaders," she said, seemingly casually, taking up the thread of their previous conversation. She leaned her hands on the low white balustrade, staring out toward the sea and speaking very slowly. "They still need nations to believe in, and national—what? Identities? The people in their tar-paper shacks and their roadside stands, the coffee farmers out there, the rubber growers. They still need the illusions of 'us' and 'them.' "

"They still need what governments have always given them, which is security," Ferdinando said mildly, coming to her side and taking her hand. His light, musical voice was playfully rueful, deliberately casual; he was wearing a white guayabera shirt, the sleeves rolled up over his slender, muscular arms, and only Camila could hear the underpinning of pain, the breath of defeat in his poised, extraordinary voice. Or perhaps Linz heard it too? "I tried to give them security, and instead have brought them, not peace, but a sword. It's an unfortunate irony. I offered them freedom, but that freedom must be enjoyed within the confines of the Miramar Prison."

"Not necessarily," Alfred Linz murmured. "You're assuming you know how things are going to work out. You can't. All revolutions occur like acts of god, which is to say, by lunatic actions that no human being could possibly understand or predict. All any man of rationality can do is attempt to stack the deck." He smiled, sipping his drink. His expression might have been merely politely interested, or benign. "Let's be theoretical for a moment. How much would it take, to launch a decent assault against the major government strongholds in Mayapán? Sixty million? Eighty? Give me a figure. How much would it take, to give these people in their tar-paper shacks and their picturesque coffee plantations the illusion of a *bona fide* revolution? A national identity?"

For a moment, Camila and Ferdinando couldn't answer— smiling stiffly, in sheer amazement. "What, to give them a national identity?" Camila laughed, turning to lean against the stone balustrade. "Why, you could do that for nothing! They have it already, it's in their blood, in their faces. All they need is someone to pat them on the back—" she hesitated, her face going thoughtful and blank. "To pat them on the back, and tell them it's all right, to *be* who they are, *cabecitas negras.* Shift the world south and make them the center of the universe. No more *norteamericanos.* They'd love you for that, and they'd make you a god." She smiled, and shrugged, sipping her martini. "*That* could be done for nothing. What costs money is ammunition and guns, buying off the army and the Americans."

Linz shook his head, smiling at her, chiding. "No, you two children still don't understand. There are twenty men who hold the real power in the United States, and only sixteen of them are Americans. Charlie Cox is also on the board of Deutsch-Telegraphieren and Linz Industries, despite the fact that he flew a bomber against the Axis and leveled Dresden. These things are easily forgotten, when you're the senior vice-president of United Oil—he's also good friends with the Libyans, although he'd die rather than let them hear of it in Washington. The Americans who count could easily be convinced that it is in their best interests to see a change of administration in the Mayapanian government."

Ferdinando lifted his glass to his lips, and sipped, without a tremor, perfectly relaxed. It was not a completely unexpected proposition, as he had to admit to himself, although it had come more suddenly and straightforwardly than he had imagined it would.

"Why?"

"*Why?*" Alfred Linz looked honestly surprised. "You're talking about a country that harbors the potential for the richest oil reserves in history—as well as rubber, coffee, bananas, tourism—and you ask me *why?*"

"Why me? Why not Buiztas?"

"Well—" Linz touched a napkin to his lips; he had a slight tremor in his mouth, which caused an occasional trace of saliva to wet his chin; and he was self-conscious about it. "Let's simply say that I don't know Buiztas. He doesn't know me. He knows some people, mostly within his own country, and he's an old-fashioned man. He still believes in nation-states, the U.S.A. and the Russian Bear. And Mayapán a colony in the middle. He's botched one of the biggest oil strikes in recent memory, so that instead of swimming in riches and underbidding OPEC, his country's involved in a wasteful interior struggle with its own people, and his economy still compares unfavorably to Panama's. And more than that?" He smiled gently. "Let's just say that Buiztas isn't married to the daughter of two dear friends of mine. And he's a fool. He would not be able to guarantee me a favorable return on my investment."

"And you believe I could?" Ferdinando murmured, sipping his drink. He was elated, almost drunk and calmly, coolly excited; his fingers felt cold around his glass, as he held it steady, although the wind blowing lightly over the terrace was pleasantly warm.

Alfred Linz smiled at him. "I'm not going to flatter you, Señor Lorca," he said mildly. "You are an extremely gifted man, a gifted public and private speaker. You have a power over your listeners, which I have not seen since the early days of Fidel. To be fair to you, I was once held in the grip of another such charismatic speaker—in Germany, but that is neither here nor there. You may even believe in what you are saying, the freedom which you offer, which is certainly a help in giving a convincing performance. But you will never achieve your goal by counting solely on the will of the people, and if you try, you will only succeed in leading your followers to the slaughter. *I* have the power—and my colleagues. And, still, governments have the power, but their power is waning, and it has—how shall I put this delicately—too many strings? Whereas my help has practically no strings. Just guarantee your cooperation in Mayapanian investment, industrialization—which is certainly what you want— and your country is yours."

"As simple as that," Ferdinando said lightly, smiling. "You make it sound like a business transaction."

"It *is* a business transaction. Even the noblest experiments must be financed."

"And financiers need guarantees, a guaranteed interest, in case of default?"

"Up to a point. They also *need* investments, if they are to maintain a competitive edge. Yes, I think you have a grasp of economics which has eluded many of our elder statesmen, but as I say, they have a tendency to live in the past. I, on the other hand, live in the future—even though that future contains my own death."

He spoke of it conversationally, as one might refer to any trivial, imminent occurrence, casually, no problem of his. It occurred to Camila that their whole conversation was unreal—poised so high, above the darkening Caribbean, with the sound of the waves a soft pulse in the distance. Tiny moths fluttered around them, but kept their distance; there was a barely noticeable, kerosenelike odor from the torches burning around the terrace, starkly modern, to keep the insects at bay. It had gotten very dark, and there were even a few stars out in the sky. She leaned on the balustrade, abandoning her attention to the conversation, because it was so obviously going to happen; a part of her must have known, on the level of blood knowledge, that Linz would finance their operation, make this offer. From high on this Mount Olympus . . . he was so old, so frail, that he himself could never go anywhere . . . but he could send *them* down, into the hot steamy jungles with their ancient wells. And he was *so* rich, so *unimaginably* rich . . . was it an illusion, she wondered idly, *did* one make a mistake, when one imagined one could do anything with money? One could certainly remake a country. One could certainly remake it, in one's own image . . . until? Until what? Until one could remake it truly free? But what was true? Standing there, so high up, she could spread her arms in her light silk dress and feel the winds which had blown from Managua, San Salvador. Was that it? Betrayal of her own people was idiotic gibberish, and besides she wasn't betraying them . . . even if they were her own people. But she felt guiltily like a child being given a present she might not honestly deserve . . . it was fun, intoxicating . . . appalling . . . just to think of all that money. Enough money to buy the whole world.

"What you are offering me," Ferdinando was saying slowly, still smiling coolly, "is collaboration with an industrial entity, a source of capital, from the very inception of a government. Without the accompanying alliance *with* a foreign government. The truth behind all treaties—"

"Exactly." Linz nodded. "The truth behind all alliances is

money. Why not ally yourself with a group of private investors to begin with, and preserve Mayapán's autonomy?"

"In name," Ferdinando said drily. "We're none of us an island, with the possible exception of Isla del Viento."

So it was decided—but had it ever been in question? Dining, that night, on *paella* and chilled white wine ("Field Marshal Rommel always enjoyed this wine," Linz told them with a straight face, "but Reichsmarschall Goering preferred a sweeter wine, and actually used to flavor it with a teaspoon of sugar."), Ferdinando was in excellent spirits. "I'd like to propose a toast, to our delightful backer, the 'angel' of our benighted enterprise!" And later still, laughing, with Camila, deciding to go for a midnight swim . . . the ocean warm and buoyant . . . his arms circling her, he whispered, "Well, what do you think, shall we accept his offer?" Standing in water up to their shoulders, under the imminent, Mayan stars, with his strong arms around her and his vivid smile and his heartbreakingly blue eyes fixed so delightedly on hers, she pushed aside her momentary disquiet as excitement and put it out of her mind, as she felt the current of his ambition, vibrating in his body like a pulse.

"Of course." She laughed. "Why do you think I brought you here?" And she laced her slender arms around his neck, and brought her lovely, salt-wet face up to his face for a kiss.

two

So IT WAS seemingly inevitable that they should come to power, seemingly inevitable that their destinies should shape and inspire a country, with the ease which can only be bought with cash: endless supplies of cash. In gold, in silver ingots and blue-chip stocks—and in diamonds, Linz's favorite currency, instantly negotiable, tax-free, and private. It was seemingly impossible that the Movimiento Revolucionario de Mayapán could be revitalized from the ashes of the abortive December uprising, but it happened: paid for by a grant from Linz Industries, interest-free, and with a seemingly open-ended period for the repayment of the loan. Within two weeks of their flight from New York, Camila and Ferdinando were planting the seeds that would later flower into their triumph in Campeche—and one of their first actions was to send word to Battiste to join them on Linz's private island.

He came, arriving by helicopter, looking incongruous in a bright Hawaiian shirt (he had been forced to pose as a tourist coming through Dallas), bringing with him the extensive files of the Mayapanian Revolutionary Movement enough documentation to give "60 Minutes" a record sweep in the ratings, as he wryly admitted, describing the desperate wooing of CBS, following the Lorcas' precipitous escape.

He looked changed, paler and more tired in the two weeks since they had seen him: or it might have been the change in *them*, which took his breath away, as he ducked under the helicopter's slowing blades and into their impatient arms. Tanned and vibrant and almost obscenely happy, they moved with the greater assurance of knowing each other's movements, and spoke as if reading each other's thoughts: and Battiste, who had never been that close to anyone, felt the difference in them as a bittersweet pain in his chest. The strain in his pockmarked face, and surely, could it be, the one or two strands of gray in his thick dark hair, might have been no more than the visible face of the city they had left behind: New York, where they had all been refugees. He smiled shyly, and there might have been tears in his eyes? (but surely it was the wind from the helicopter; he wiped them quickly away) and accepted their kisses (Ferdinando's as well as Camila's), smiling and biting his lips.

And he *did* love them, even if they hurt him more than they could imagine. He changed, and went for a swim with them, and floating out beyond the reef, with their hands lightly resting on his shoulders, he felt a salt-lightness in his own body, buoyancy, that was totally unexpected. Warm and free from guilt, indistinctly sexual: for a moment he wasn't a priest, wasn't bound by vows of celibacy or any other vows; he was a thirty-eight-year-old man, with normal strength, normal desires, and he held hands with them and felt happy. Breathtakingly brief, the innocence of Eden. He knew it couldn't last; and since he was barred by everything he loved from loving them, he saw their happiness as through a window, and pressed his fingers close against the glass, with the wistful pressure of a prisoner touching the window of his cell.

Afterward, they lay stretched out on the sand, eating mangoes, while they talked about their plans.

"You've got to take over the New York operation—keep up our contacts at the U.N., and keep the people there together, until we can get you some money," Ferdinando said, licking his fingers. "We'll be able to deposit checks at Morgan Guaranty, which is partially owned by Linz International, and you can draw them in your own name. I want you to get in touch with the Israelis— our contact is a man named Lewis Roth—and arrange with him for arms shipments; we'll be buying them from the Russians, but naturally, we can't go direct; remind me to give you his phone number. Now, as soon as you can, I want you to move a number of our people down to Washington—rent a house in the suburbs, Bethesda, Chevy Chase—we'll get a list of influential lobbyists whom we can use to build up support, so, when the time *does* come, everyone will see that it's in their best interests—"

"Wait a minute," Battiste interrupted. "You want me to horse-trade with the Senators—in Washington—"

"More or less." Ferdinando smiled. "You won't find it so hard, half of them are in Linz Industries' pockets to begin with, and the rest of them are friends of mine. We're not asking them for aid—which should delight and amaze them all no end. I think you should have a cover. What if I arrange it with the reverend fathers to get you a lectureship at Georgetown?"

"Wonderful," Battiste murmured. "I'm to become Teilhard de Chardin by way of John Ehrlichman and Jimmy Hoffa, before you're through with me."

"Oh, not so much." Ferdinando laughed. "I also want you to meet with the major columnists: we'll promise them exclusives, and take them into the jungle with us: they'll love it. I'm arranging for publicity inside of Mayapán myself—twenty thousand short wave radios, to be distributed free throughout the countryside, isn't that nice? All tuned exclusively to our programming. We can broadcast from here, on the island."

Battiste looked around him, at the smooth white sand and the dazzling sun, the palm trees, soft blue sea—the lovely pink house almost obscured through the trees—and felt an irresistible desire to laugh. It was all too extraordinary! They had worked with nothing, and nearly brought about a revolution! Giving the people a few guns, a few scraps of hope: and now El Lorca was going to give them short wave radios, and the U.S. Congress—it was like Christmas, it was insanity!

"Now"—Ferdinando smiled—"within a month this will be academic, because we'll have our own people establish in Campeche, but initially we're going to need to make contact again with the unions, set up a safe base of operations through them? Can you arrange it?"

Battiste nodded. "It's the same network we used for smuggling in our supplies, most of the key people have escaped detection—but are you sure it's wise, putting your own people in the country? I mean our visible leaders—would—would—surely you're not thinking of going there yourself?"

"That *is* the eventual point, isn't it?" Ferdinando said, laughing. "Of course right now, it would be suicide—but the people must have their leaders with them. If I cannot send myself, then—my beloved surrogate?"

Camila smiled.

Battiste stared at them both in horror. "No," he blurted out before he could think better of it. "No, absolutely not, I won't permit it!"

"Won't permit it—?" Ferdinando murmured. "What on earth—" He smiled at him, his extraordinary eyes quizzical and just slightly irritated. "What on earth do you mean, you won't permit it?"

'I mean I—I won't permit either of you to risk yourselves, like that, I—I'll go." Battiste discovered that his fingers were sticky with mango juice, little grits of sand sticking to them; he laughed, trying to make a joke of it. "I'm a mess, I'd better go wash my hands." He got up and walked into the water, up to his knees, rinsing his hands and discovering to his mortification that he was trembling. He turned around to discover El Lorca standing quite close beside him, holding out a white linen napkin— "Would you like to have this to blot yourself?"—and he stared at his friend, shaking, for once utterly unable to hide his feelings.

"You wouldn't make her go—would you?" he whispered. His fingers touched the napkin, groping, like the fingers of a blind man. "You wouldn't—let her risk that—" He stopped, swallowing, and felt a blush staining his cheeks, even his chest (big white body, hateful, compared to Ferdinando's thin, tanned frame), as he let go of the napkin in embarrassment.

For a moment, the water lapped around the knees of the two men, and Ferdinando's eyes remained level, a clear, slightly colder blue. "I think that's a matter between Camila and me. I don't see how your opinions enter into it."

Battiste narrowed his eyes, as if in pain. "I can't have any opinions at all, can I? It's all between you and her."

Ferdinando sighed, and turned to look back at the beach, where Camila was sitting. She waved to them, and gestured to her watch, the sun (which *was* burning Battiste's skin, he could feel it), and smiled at them, shaking her head.

"Look," Ferdinando said, "I know how you feel, but we're never going to get anywhere if we continue to fight over Camila like two dogs fighting over a bone in an alley."

He held up his hands to forestall Battiste's immediate denial, and his eyes were amused again, although they were still a little ruefully angry. "You don't have to protest anything, I'm not accusing you of anything, but it just gets ridiculous having to defend my actions every step of the way! Give Camila a little credit—this was her idea! She stands the best chance of being safe, she was a child when she left the country! Besides, Buiztas is too blind to be afraid of a woman, he's too much of a *macho*. I need to have you in the United States, and I need to be free to organize the army myself—in Honduras, or Mexico, or wherever. So what other options does that leave me?" He smiled and squeezed Battiste's shoulder. "Besides, who do I have that I can trust, besides the two of you?"

Battiste swallowed, shifting his shoulder beneath Ferdinando's strong fingers. "I know," he whispered, "I mean we'd all be willing to risk our lives—so what's the problem, Camila's the most courageous person I've ever met—" And he looked away from him, unable to meet his eye, toward the knife line of the horizon.

"Come on," Ferdinando said, "let me tell you my plan for a possible scenario."

And so Battiste was drawn, against his will, into the complicated schemes to force a devaluation of the Mayapanian peso (arranged through Linz's agents in Germany) and Ferdinando's arrangement with a man named Ottavio Moroque, a Cuban refugee, to train a mercenary army in Honduras.

"You don't approve, Eminence?" Ferdinando asked him, challengingly—almost with exhaustion—for they had by then been talking for hours. Camila had gone back up to the house to change, and they were sitting under a canvas awning, in two canvas chairs, drinking rum. "You believe our revolutionaries should be exclusively homegrown?" He sighed. "No outsiders? No Cubans?"

"No," Battiste said, sipping his drink and considering. "I think it's a good idea. The Cubans are good fighters. Everybody else uses them. But I'd better arrange a deal with an American arms manufacturer. Even if we don't need him, it'll look good, in order to keep everybody guessing."

It was decided that Jorge-Julio de Rodríguez would accompany Camila to Campeche, and from there on, into the jungle, the little villages. "There's a convent in Campeche, affiliated with the Maryknoll people," Battiste suggested. "They could go as a priest and a lay sister—after all," he added, abashed, "you know all priests and nuns look alike!"

"That's wonderful!" Camila said, laughing, drawing her black fringed shawl around her shoulders—a lovely airy lace, threaded with gold, through which her bare shoulders gleamed—as they climbed the white stone steps to Linz's high terrace, overlooking the sea. "I've always wanted to put those years of training to some sort of use—eight million paternosters, dear God! All those hours wasted otherwise!" She walked to the balcony, looking down at the ocean, which was a soft, wind-whipped gray tonight; a mist coming in, over the terrace; a mysteriously cooler night, as she leaned her bare arms on the white stone balustrade, beautiful, pensive. A calm descended on the three of them, which was so illusory as to be almost cruel.

Battiste was remarking on the dizzying height of the terrace; quite at the top of the house; which was itself quite high up, built on this rocky cliff, like a fortress. It was windy and *almost* vertiginous—impressive but *almost* frightening; although the view was splendid; as he came and joined Camila and El Lorca, leaning on the balustrade. "Look how far away the sea is—"

"How far below us."

"Yes."

"Do you really *know* who Alfred Linz is?" Battiste asked, and instantly regretted it, because *he* didn't know; he was a child in the world of international finance, multinationals, his information gleaned from the leftist press, naïve, and probably baseless. "I mean—I mean they say—he's been involved in—are you sure

137

you want to become involved with a man who's so—notorious? In a secretive kind of way—I mean a reclusive kind of way, you know, living here, this—this *castle*—fortress—" He spread his hands, speaking softly. (Because of course the man himself could appear at any moment, couldn't he? And he could imagine his own embarrassment!) "He's almost deliberately shy—of course I imagine he's very old—but he's one of the best-known shy people in the world, and there are lots of stories about, well—shady deals—the business with United Oil, of course during the Second World War they couldn't *afford* to be involved with him, could they? And afterward it was only natural that they should look *somewhere* for investment capital—in the Middle East—a friendly government in Iran—but still—"

He stopped, blushing painfully, knotting his big hands together as if he were praying; he realized what he was doing, and stopped, putting his hands in his pockets; he was wearing his clerical black, dog collar and all, and it occurred to Camila how much he resembled a pained Reformation priest: Martin Luther, upbraiding the sins of the worldly Catholics. She touched his arm.

"Alfred Linz was a friend of my family's. I really don't know the whole connection—my mother's family was widespread, all over, in Hamburg, before the war—he may very well be a relative of mine, although I can't imagine it! But he's just a man, you know—he's not a monster, Eichmann in his glass booth—I wonder if anyone's really the monster we'd like them to be. He's just a very smart businessman, who's managed to keep going for a long time—by a combination of luck and investment capital and drugs! I don't mean he sells them," she added, bursting into laughter at his shocked face. "I mean he's a walking supporter of the chemical industry! He must be ninety years old!"

"And still in control of the corporate direction of Linz Industries *and* Linz International," Battiste said, wincing, as he looked down into her smiling, laughing face. "There was a major crisis a year ago, when Venezuela nationalized its oil fields, when forty-six workers were shot. Thirty-two corporate executives lost their jobs, but Linz remained untouched."

"Well, he couldn't very well have fired *himself*, could he?" Ferdinando laughed. "I think you're looking for difficulties, because the idea of such a windfall is so unexpected. But necessary, and welcome. Do you honestly think we could have gone on fighting indefinitely, without allying ourselves with anyone?"

"You certainly don't have to worry about that now," Battiste found himself saying sarcastically. "Linz has enough money to break Morgan Guaranty Trust—he certainly can afford to break a small government like Buiztas', and install his favorite pup—candidate in his place!"

Ferdinando's smile was still warm, only slightly frozen, as he asked him, "So, you believe I should decline his offer. Is that it?"

"No—" Battiste stopped, catching his breath on his automatic prevarication, because of course, what *was* he suggesting but that they should refuse his help—this mysterious, enigmatic old man who (it was reported) had been a Nazi; made obscene profits from the war; was worth more than General Motors and I.T.M. combined; and had toppled governments before (so they said)—Iran in the 1950's, Argentina under Isabel Perón, Chile under Allende—could it be? Was it possible that he was standing, in this soft night breeze which nonetheless chilled him to the bone, on this high stone terrace with his friend and hero Ferdinando Lorca—the man who had mourned the death of the marxists, and gone to Santiago, when it was patent madness to have done so— lean and tanned, poised, relaxed, in the pay of Linz Industries and United Oil, and plainly delighted with his good fortune? He hesitated and was about to speak, when they heard the punctilious step and careful, old man's breath of their host on the terrace behind them, and they turned around as he said, "Ah, Father Tommassi, I'm glad you got here. Are you all primed to join us in our second brainwashing of the Mayapanian people? The first was, as you know, accomplished by the Catholic Church."

Battiste flew off to Washington three days later, sunburned, with a dozen forged passports, roughly $500,000 in a bag in unmarked currency, and messages for the ambassadors of Panama, Mexico, Venezuela, and West Germany. Ferdinando arranged to fly to Havana and Tegucigalpa the following week, and from there to a private airstrip near the Mayapán–Honduras border, to oversee operational setups with Ottavio Moroque. That Friday evening, he said good-bye to Camila.

"Book a room for me in Campeche, will you?" he asked her,

joking, as they waited for Linz's helicopter to refuel—Camila looking very young in a blue cotton skirt and blouse, low-heeled shoes, and a scarf tied around her hair, which was dyed brown for the occasion.

She had gazed at herself in the mirror that morning, emerging chrysalislike from a towel, and burst out laughing. "Oh, I can't! I look like a Campeche whore! It looks ridiculous—I can't do it!"

"Yes, you can," he told her solemnly from the bed, and he reached up and caught her hand and pulled her down beside him. "Don't you know that assuming a vocation means a mortification of the flesh?"

"Oh, shut up—"

"Denial of vanity—you're really far too suntanned, you know, to be a nun—you'd better not let anyone else but me see you naked. . . ."

Now they stood in the breeze from the ocean and waited for the breeze from the helicopter, and the sunset was bleeding magnificently into the sea and they realized that their honeymoon was over. Ferdinando looked at Camila. She was gazing off over the terrace with an absolutely clear profile—no terror, or what was there so well-schooled as to be absent; none of the piercing pain he suddenly felt at having to say good-bye to her, this quickly and perhaps this irrevocably. He turned her in his arms, and she looked up at him with such absolute joy that it took his breath away. He recognized that he could ask her to walk through fire for him, and she would do it: and somehow that fact brought him both pleasure and sadness. He kissed her on the tip of her nose, and sought for a light tone.

"Well, are you all set to become Our Man in Campeche?"

"I suppose so. Although I don't know how well I'll do in the masculine gender, I haven't had a lot of practice at that."

He smiled down at her. "Are you frightened?"

She shook her head. "I don't know why not. I suppose it's just lack of imagination. I can't picture them doing any harm to me. Oh, I know, intellectually I can quote the statisics that I'll be shot on a dirt road, by people who don't even know what I'm doing there, but it seems ridiculous to be afraid of *that*! And so long as you're looking out for me by long distance, what harm can come to me from the Buiztanistas? Besides—" She laughed. "I'd have to survive just to see you again! You've given me a wonderful excuse for living, and I'm not about to shortchange myself for a minute!"

"My pleasure," he said, with a faint thrill of guilty amazement as he gazed down at her softly lit face in the deepening twilight, and he kissed her as the rotor blades started and blew a stronger wind across them and he let her go and handed her up to the pilot.

He stood and watched until the helicopter was far away in the sky, and when he turned away he felt cold in his light shirt and rubbed his hands up and down his bare arms, and he went back inside and poured himself a stiff drink.

three

CAMPECHE WAS BROILING under a sun as hot as June when Camila dos Santos Lorca arrived (under an assumed name) from the Aeropuerto Quintero de Buiztas. She came in a taxi, one of the old ten-peso cabs which she remembered from her childhood, and which resembled nothing so much as a getaway car from a movie from the 1930's; assaulted by the smells of fried bananas and cheap empanadas, which you could buy even in the airport; fresh fruit and salt air and hot tar from the pavements, the chalk smell in her nostrils on the drive into the city; and remembered it all: the palm trees blowing on the sea wall, the vivid green of the watered lawn in front of the old Palace of the Viceroys (now a national museum); pelicans and longtails flying for scraps in the harbor; the old stone houses, and the new office buildings (taller than she remembered), the statue of Christopher Columbus in the middle of Campeche's most notorious traffic circle (around which they circled for several minutes, while her driver cursed in a patois of Mayan and Spanish) and the white-painted iron gates and bricked square of the Presidential Palace, its white-painted walls still chipped by the recent addition of bullet holes.

Since her passport proclaimed her an American (Sister Mary Francis Morton, from Garden City, Long Island), she was able to ask the cabbie (in good but not excellent Spanish) to drive her around a little, she wanted to see the city. So she saw the sights: the old Grand Hotel, looking seedy, tiles fallen from its Mayan frieze facade (for there were few tourists in Mayapán now, and businessmen stayed out at the Holiday Inn). She could remember having ices in its dim interior, bought by her father on the days when he could take an hour or two off from the newspaper. The beautiful Madre de Dios cathedral, gleaming white stone and Spanish-style fretwork: that still looked good, and no wonder; it was on all the halfhearted travel posters that peeled from out-of-date agency walls in the States: Visit Mayapán, the country where history comes alive! Yes, indeed, Camila thought: where they shoot you in the street, that should be enough history for you. She could remember the embassies, shaded by cypress and pine trees, palms, philodendrons, out along the Avenida Montejo; where it was always cool (the combined effluvia of a million *gringo* air-conditioners); and as they drove along she shaded her eyes with her hand, as she turned and looked out the window of the taxi. The Saudi Arabian embassy was closed, as was the Iranian; the American embassy was still open, but there were no cars in the driveway; they were hedging their bets, and besides, they couldn't risk any more kidnapping attempts: they had become too common in Latin America of late.

As they turned down the Avenida Cortés, she leaned forward a little . . . that had been the *La Prensa* building a little farther down the street, hadn't it? A converted mansion covered with bougainvillea, where in the summer they had left the windows open, birdsong and the fragrance of flowers mixing with the smell of machine oil from the presses and the printer's ink; but there was no sign now, and anyway, she wasn't sure of the address. There were billboards all along the Avenida now, Pima soft drinks, Emmo gasoline, and it didn't look the same; it was getting built up with residential houses, where once there had been long stretches of palm trees and open sky. She leaned back against the sticky seat of the taxicab and closed her eyes. She was home. And it was all right, she hadn't fallen to pieces or been shot, or been translated back to herself at ten years old, skinny frightened kid in a borrowed overcoat hustled onto an airplane; she was a married woman; and the Buiztanistas would never expect the daughter of Juan dos Santos to come back to the country at all. She was in the States, wasn't she, or in Europe? Probably sailing off Skorpiós with a rich Arab or some Kennedy kids—other casualties of too *macho* fathers, gunned down in the line of duty. She smiled. The tragedy of the Buiztanistas was a chronic lack of imagination.

She had the cabdriver drop her off at the Catholic hostel on the Calle Fuertes, hefting her suitcase onto the sidewalk (packed with three changes of underwear and stacks of five- and ten-peso notes, bound with different-colored rubber bands: pink for Campeche Province, yellow for Quintana Roo, blue for Yucatán, white for Los Cuchumatanes). She paid the driver and as he drove away, she looked out across the roofs of the downtown shacks, small one- and two-story houses, corrugated roofs and pastel-painted walls, the three blocks to the sea—where the sun was sinking in a vivid splash of gray-blue, soft pinks, vivid red—and smelled the evening smell of fish breeze and cooking beans, cat urine and garbage, which was the aroma of the poorer quarters of the city. She narrowed her eyes, trying to make out something: some kind of a bird, flying around and around the roof of the Presidential Palace (which was some distance away): long lazy wing-flaps, up and then gliding down; in no kind of a hurry, a clumsy flight which had nonetheless the power of its immense size. She thought it was a condor, it was so big, until she realized it was a vulture.

That afternoon, although she didn't know it, Quintero de Buiztas had executed seven political prisoners, firing the pistol himself through their left temples and leaving them tied to their rudimentary posts on top of the Presidential Annex. By nightfall there were a dozen vultures, and by the next morning they took what was left of them down and buried them, but news traveled fast and by the next morning everyone knew what Buiztas had done. What a monster, no better than a Mafia murderer, some kind of a President for this shitty country to have. Jorge-Julio de Rodríquez told her about it over their evening meal, sipping a

Dos Equis, which the generous nuns had thoughtfully provided, and wiping his long moustache with a napkin.

"I think he's going a little crazy, because there's no reason to do things that visibly. Apparently two of them were foreign journalists, and a third was the assistant to the Minister of Finance—they say he was robbing Buiztas blind, and the journalists were in on it—but it's still a stupid move. How did you get here, did you have any trouble coming through customs?"

"No, it was fine," she said, sipping water and leaning her chin on her hand. "I see you got here without any trouble."

"Oh—" He shrugged, eating his dinner, and thereby discounting his own dangers in leaving the United States. He had a self-deprecating shyness in front of her that made her smile, and he hid his hands from her, despite their scrubbed cleanliness, curling his fingers around the utensils as he ate.

"He got it hushed up with the foreign press, so it shouldn't be too hard to break the story whenever we want to. Tell Ferdinando I'll get him a statement from the commander of the guard if he thinks he can use one."

"Oh, sure, we're going to tell the world a lot of things about Señor Buiztas." Camila smiled and took a bite, adding, "How did you happen to find out any of this?"

"Oh—" He shrugged again, smiling his sad smile at her. "You know I'm half Indian. We're good at finding out things we're not supposed to."

He had a red, ridged scar running along his neck, which looked new, and which seemed to embarrass or irritate him, since he kept touching it and hiding it with his fingers. She raised her eyebrows in slight concern, and he hung his head.

"I got it fighting in a little town called Los Palmes, it's way up in the highlands, there was this crazy Buiztanista there who was banging the hell out of all the local girls. He got an idea I wasn't on his side, and pulled a switchblade on me when I tried to stop his fun with a twelve-year-old *virgen.*"

Camila put her head on one side, and said in her soft, poised voice, "Did you save her?"

"Oh—" He shrugged, taking another sip of beer. "She'll probably get married, have sixteen babies in fourteen years." He suddenly broke into a grin. "Of course I saved her. So—now I'm the one who sheds a little blood, eh? A *virgenita*—it's the insects right now that are driving me crazy. I should get some calamine lotion."

Camila laughed. "I think it makes you look fierce, like a bandit."

"Bandit my ass—fighting with a strung-out Buiztanista, who gets in under my guard with a little *pachuco* knife!" He went on to explain that all the Indians in the interior were taking drugs, smoking native-grown ganja and selling it to the *gringos*, hashish and pills and booze smuggled in by the traders. "*Claro*, it's no worse than New York, but it's no better—and they're bloating on Faygo red-pop and thinking they're modern, with no hospital facilities within two hundred miles, and the kids so full of parasites their bellies look like cannonballs."

"Can't anything be done? The Peace Corps or the Red Cross?"

"It's too expensive. No, really, I guess the main thing is they're selective—they'll take the *gringo* diseases, and the *gringo* junk food, but not the *gringo* medicines ... it's really a mess. Don't get me started on the Indians, we've got enough crap to deal with out in the cane fields and the coffee *fincas*, where we may be able to get the people into the commercial centers to demonstrate or to vote. Out in the jungle it's nobody's game—not Buiztas', or Ferdinando's, or anybody's—not even mine, and I was born out there."

He took her after dinner to a cantina, a little tin-roofed shack at the end of a dirt road under some dusty palm trees, where the music was loud and funky. He wasn't sure if she'd like it, but she insisted, and sat drinking shots of Flor de Cana rum until he was amazed at her head. She confessed to him that it was almost impossible for her to get drunk.

"Pills, dope, you name it, I'm immune—but it's handy, when you want to be sociable and still not make an ass out of yourself. If I ever have to have a bullet out of me, like a soldier with a shot of bourbon, I'll be out of luck!"

She watched the dancers out on the floor in the middle of the shack, tapping her foot in her low canvas shoe, discreetly watching faces, and Jorge-Julio watched her. Classic bones, and even without makeup she had the kind of face that would be remembered, in cantinas, from the back of a train, anywhere. Those clear blue eyes. Firm lips, and a trickle of sweat into the hollow of her throat, a face so strong it was not afraid of being vulnerable. Wow. They would have to keep her out of the sun, or else take hair dye with them to touch her up on the road, in the strong Mayapanian sunlight the brown was already beginning to fade and the gold to show through. They'd be lucky to keep her alive for a month, and it was that night, in the quiet of his undemonstrative soul, that the sad-eyed, thoughtful Indian resolved to guard her if necessary with his life.

They met the next day with Luis García Mores, who owned and ran the only television station in Campeche. Luis García was the descendant of one of Montejo's bloodiest captains, a thin-faced Castilian who had bequeathed his neurasthenic handsomeness and cold, aristocratic hauteur to all of his olive-skinned descendants: but it was a useless nobility, because MAYA-TV and MAYA-AM, and -FM, were going nowhere with reruns of *The Name of the Game* and garbled and inaccurate traffic reports. They met García in his villa out in the Maldonado district, walking across manicured lawns that were watered by an interior sprinkler system, into the cool dim patio with its hushed whisper of the sea, an immaculate white stucco and red-tiled oasis overlooking the ocean: where in the shade of flowering shrubs and resinous eucalyptus trees they sat with Don Luis and drank lemonade and nibbled French pastry brought by his barefoot Indian servant, Jesús.

Camila began by complimenting MAYA-TV's coverage of the recent political "disturbances." She said that given the difficulties of taking crews into the interior, with outdated video cameras and clumsy, nonportable tape machines, it was really extraordinary, the shots they had gotten. She sighed that it was unfortunate that they could not afford the new portable Ikegamis, Betacams, or a one-inch editing facility; she said that it was too bad, their having to take a network feed out of Florida, the reception was so bad, now if they had a satellite down-link just think what they could get, soccer from Buenos Aires and tennis from Wimbledon; and why stop at that, why not an up-link as well, so they could produce their own programming for worldwide syndication, and what would it take to build a really state-of-the-art facility in Mayapán, eight, ten million dollars, what did he think?

Don Luis García Mores tried not to choke on his almond croissant, as he heard himself being bribed with more money than he could possibly imagine, to betray a crass dictator whom he hated anyway, simply by denying him access to his airwaves. He dabbed at his forehead with his Givenchy handkerchief, and tried to calculate the amount of money he owed everybody already, and what life would be like with not only that debt erased, but wonderful new equipment and kickback deals from the record companies, easy listening on MAYA-FM, and a marvelous new production house, under the protection of a sympathetic government that appreciated the power of the media. He stammered, and couldn't believe it, and Camila continued to spin her sweet-sugar fantasies like an enormous, imaginative pastry around the amazed and impoverished executive—and inside of an hour he was tasting broadcasting immortality, nibbled out of the palm of her hand, and had agreed to twenty-four-hour programming of Lorcanista propaganda, the moment she said the word.

While they were walking down the white-graveled driveway toward their battered, rented Fiat, Camila asked Jorge-Julio if he'd had any idea what she was talking about.

"Frankly, no, little *mamá*."

She smiled at him. "Neither did I. Isn't it amazing how you can lie, when you put your mind to it?"

They had a different opportunity to lie the next day, when they met with Lejo Costamendez, the big burly giant who was the head of the Truckers Union. They'd arranged to meet Costamendez in his warehouse out by the Furillo Estuary, an oil-slimed backwater next to a parking lot paved with blacktop, where the big rigs of Costa vans fueled up before the long jolting trips to Mérida and Managua. They'd arranged to offer Costamendez a deal: bigger kickbacks than he was getting from Buiztas Enterprises, in return for a general strike, to coincide with student demonstrations in all the major cities in the country. The problem was that Costamendez was friends with the dictator; more than that, they were business partners: Buiztas Enterprises acted as a cover for a thriving business in cocaine distribution, oganized through the offices of Costa Trucking, and Buiztas and Alejandro Costamendez split the profits. There was no way they could call a halt to Costamendez's millionaire moonlighting without calling down the wrath of the heirs of Meyer Lansky, so Camila and Jorge-Julio had decided their best offer would be a combination of threat and greed: bigger profits in the long run for Lejo if he kicked out Buiztas and ran the operation solo; and an absolute guarantee that the Miami books of the business would be turned over to the F.B.I., if Costamendez and his truckers didn't play ball.

It was a good plan, but it almost didn't work because Costamendez was seducing his secretary when they first arrived, and being possessed of the conviction that women didn't really exist above their waists or below their knees, he was amazed and scornful and excited when he first saw Camila. Jorge-Julio and she were standing in the open doorway of the warehouse, a big steel slab raised horizontally on well-oiled wheels, and when they first arrived, Camila, as she glanced up, had to resist a strong image of the door as the blade of a metal punch or guillotine. She stood a little back from Jorge-Julio, willing to let him engage in formalities with the sweat-stained thug who was emerging from his office, zipping up his trousers, while a little girl with the café-crème skin of a *mestiza* buttoned her blouse and retreated behind the door. Costamendez plainly didn't think much of Indians, except as siesta playmates, and he sneered at Jorge-Julio, who was holding his panama hat deferentially in his hand, his dark patient face revealing his willingness to be treated like shit if he could get what Ferdinando wanted.

"So, d' you decide you want a job, after all these years?" Because Costamendez knew Jorge-Julio slightly, and thought all Maya Indians looked most appropriate behind the wheel of a truck.

Jorge-Julio shook his head, smiling sadly. "You know I hate driving," he said. "I wouldn't be any good for you."

"Huh, that's for sure. I see which one would be good for me." He smiled, leering at Camila, who stood her ground, staring up at him with the full electricity of her intense blue eyes, so that when he was no more than a step away from her, he stopped, as if momentarily uncertain whether to assault her or be afraid of her.

"Señor Costamendez," she said formally, "you don't know me, but I know you, and you know my husband, Ferdinando Lorca."

That stopped him in his tracks.

"Señor Rodríguez is his associate. We've got some private business I think you might be interested to discuss." With a little smile. She was so thoroughly without fear that she unnerved him; smiling quite pleasantly, so he laughed, showing his brown teeth: "*You're* married to Ferdinando Lorca!" And put his arm around her shoulders: "I know your husband well, he's a brave man!" Translation, Camila thought: He's an idiot, and by rights he ought to be dead. So? Quintero must be slipping. Well, that was all right, if he thought that, he would be more receptive to the idea of changing horses.

"Shall we talk?" He indicated his office, but Camila didn't favor the companionship of his preteen whore, and so turned in his grasp, saying, "Sure, why not, but how about out here, since it's cooler?"—a few degrees' difference, in the aroma of gasoline and hot tar, but he agreed; slipped back to his office for a moment, presumably to dismiss the girl; and came back out beaming, his strong bull's face laved with sweat, to take her arm again. They threaded their way among the rows of parked trucks while she and Jorge-Julio deftly outlined their plan, Jorge-Julio talking, while the trucker refused to let go of Camila's arm, and squeezed her breasts, insinuating his arm around her waist.

To his credit and/or his cupidity, Lejo Costamendez heard them through, encouraging them with bursts of laughter and grumbled agreement, slipping his hands where he shouldn't, but Camila had survived Porfirio Cheruña and wasn't unduly worried. She could tell Jorge-Julio was getting nervous, two steps in the rear and continuing to outline the Lorcanista position while Costamendez leaned her up against the door of a Costa van and tried to establish his *own* position vis-à-vis her slender thighs, but she continued talking to him calmly, gently, pleasantly, telling him in rounded figures that the *minimum* increase in his profits would be 200 percent; that there was no point in going to a *gringo* jail, when he could become a self-made multimillionaire; that Quintero de Buiztas would be nothing without *his*, Alejandro Costamendez's, financial and moral support—and finally assuring him (quite fictitiously) that Jorge-Julio had a twelve-inch knife and would willingly castrate him if he didn't pull himself together and behave himself. At which point Costamendez laughed hugely, gave her breasts a parting squeeze, just to show he wasn't intimidated by some lousy Indian, raised his hands to the unarmed Rodríguez to show him he truly meant no harm, and wrapping another paternal bear hug around Camila's shoulders, walked her and Jorge-Julio out from behind the cab of a Mack truck straight into the barrels of six Guardía Buiztanista rifles.

They all froze. Camila threw a quick, noncommittal glance in Lejo Costamendez's direction (because if he had already told the Guardía who they were, they might as well make a run for it; if, on the other hand, he'd merely summoned them for a "disturbance," it was well worth the gamble to see what he would do). Costamendez was looking surprised, smiling uneasily, and sweating like a pig, so she guessed that he hadn't identified them to the Guardía, and was of two minds now as to where his bread might be most thickly buttered. The young lieutenant of the Guardía dropped his pistol a fraction of an inch and saluted, and she watched greed and prudence chase each other across the beefy face of the trucking magnate while the lieutenant snapped, "You reported an intruder, Señor Costamendez. Capitano Furo's apologies for the delay, we came as soon as we could, the President has made it clear we are to be at your particular disposal, but there is a bridge out on the Coba road . . . and . . ." The young lieutenant spared a moment's military precision to moisten his lips, and decided against elaboration. "We came as soon as we could, sir."

Camila raised her eyes to Lejo Costamendez's, who would, undoubtedly, rather have looked away. He bore her gaze uneasily, wincing, but unavoidably smiling; embarrassment pulling his mouth into an idiot's grin because her eyes were still completely unafraid (only she knew the fiction behind *that*), calling his bluff with a sort of polite intellectual interest, as if wondering, Well, Lejo, you've been a crook all your life and I'm not asking you to stop, but are you going to let this fragile, beautiful *señora* who's offered you a fortune be turned over to the men's-urinal hospitality of the Guardía, or are you going to stand by her and have a little guts for a change? He spread his hands again, pink moist palms, as he had to Jorge-Julio showing he meant no harm, and smiled so hard that his back teeth glistened.

"Boys, boys, you took me too seriously. A little trouble. . . .

Señorita Merlano, the little *puta*—you know the little bitch?—she's been stealing me blind, so I called up the Guardía as a joke! Capitano Furo's a new man—he doesn't know enough to recognize my little jokes—but if you check with Colonel Horales, he'll tell you it's the easiest way to get rid of a troublesome whore! Call out the Guardía for her! But in this instance, not even that was necessary—she ran out ten seconds after I'd made the phone call—so you see it's quite all right, everything's fine, it was a false alarm, nothing serious, I was only joking!"

It was doubtful whether the Guardía believed any of this; doubtful too that it made that much difference: *they* didn't care if Señor Costamendez wanted to play stupid jokes on their superiors, Furo and Horales. It was doubtful that Costamendez himself knew for certain what he was going to say, until the hearty reassurances oozed stickily from his lips; and then, of course, he knew that he *was* going to betray his former partner, and stick by the dauntless (and intimidating) Señora Lorca. Jorge-Julio held his breath and his tongue in mute admiration while she called his bluff, actually smiling and taking his arm, laughing, "Ah, Señor Costamendez, you will break all our hearts!" causing the guard to falter to parade rest, salute, and huff back to their Jeep; and then releasing his arm and coolly saying, "Thank you," and that was all. A moment later she and Jorge-Julio were opening the doors of the Fiat and driving away at a leisurely twenty-five miles per hour over the rutted gravel road that led to the highway: and having turned onto its heat-slick surface, streaked back toward Campeche at race-car speed while they dissolved in laughter, and felt that they had cheated Death not once but twice, because they had made Death treat his own plans for killing them as a joke.

Their third interview in Campeche was with Nucho Ortega, who was the head of the Federal Workers Union in Mayapán: a bureaucratic job that had leeched so much color from his face he resembled a pale, punctilious ghost; and implanted in him such a hatred of the Buiztanistas that he practically talked *them* into dynamiting the Presidential Palace. He was a young man, with willowy good looks and a prodigious memory for figures, and Camila filed his name away for future use by Ferdinando once it came time to put the government back in order. Then she and

Jorge-Julio de Rodríguez packed their clothes and their campaign handouts and headed for the interior.

Where they began quietly, speaking to small groups in mission huts, in the social halls of flat, parched towns and in remote, rain-soaked villages up in the hills, on the slopes of the verdant coffee plantations and under the corrugated tin-roofed lean-tos put up by the banana companies, listening in silence to the complaints of the workers, the small landholders, speaking very little, then, while they let the people grope for words, shape the accumulated bitterness and despair of thirty years into hesitant speech, and find the unaccustomed, exotic satisfaction of complaining about something without getting shot. Camila and Jorge-Julio listened ... although sometimes he found himself watching her face instead; knowing in advance the tales of want and cruelty, hopeless ignorance which he had witnessed firsthand and so needed no reminder, as she did—listening intently, seriously, rarely interrupting. Instead he watched her face, observing her wince, recoiling inside from some particular horror; watching her restrain her tears, for fear of wounding the pride of some—or allowing her tears to flow, tender reassurance for some others, timed with the nicety of an actress, never too much. He watched the occasional film of exhaustion cloud her eyes, still listening, nodding soberly, when she had had her fill of misery and could absorb no more; and he watched the mysterious alchemy by which she could transform their misery to laughter—traveling with them, through their pain, and out the other side. Taking them with her, with her smile, into a world where pain was triumph—making them laugh with her, their lives redefined and meaningful, simply by the experience of having met her. She did this largely unconsciously. She had no idea of her power; jolting along over the rutted back roads in their mission Land Rover, she watched for birds, peeled and ate bananas, and had no idea what she was going to say to people until the moment when she said it. She still treated their work largely as an adventure; she still washed with Madame Rochas soap wherever they stopped at night, rinsing out silk underwear in the mildewed basins of Catholic hospices in the middle of the jungle, eating thick tortillas filled with bean paste, with the knowledge that she could fly back to Isla del Viento at any time, and drink champagne. But it may have been that freedom in her—so Jorge-Julio thought, anyway—which made her such a magical figure to the poor farmers and workers whom they met; even without benefit of the Lorca name (which at first they concealed) she became a subject of comment in the little towns through which they passed: the pretty madonna who listened to their troubles, with the golden hair. For as Jorge-Julio had anticipated, the sun bleached her hair inside of a week back to its shimmering blond; so quickly, in fact, that a less ingenuous man would have wondered if Camila, bored with anonymity, had abetted nature and deliberately washed away the dye.

four

THREE DAYS AFTER Camila's arrival in Campeche, Ferdinando caught a commercial flight from Miami to Tegucigalpa, where he was met by Capitano Enrique Zacapa of the Honduran National Guard, and Ottavio Moroque, late of Havana, Cuba.

They met him as he was coming out of the airport, flight-bagged and inconspicuous, which was more than could be said for Capitano Zacapa, who was dressed in a glaring white uniform and all his medals; and Señor Moroque, who was dressed in combat fatigues and an Australian bush hat, and smoking a Havana panatela in an ivory holder. Ferdinando took one look at these two and his heart sank, while his sense of the ridiculous rose: if these were the men who proposed to launch a "secret" invasion from the mountains of the Sierra del Merendón, they might as well take out an ad in *The New York Times* while they were at it. He acknowledged their waves and cries of welcome with a polite smile, and let them take his bag (two changes of linen and a toothbrush, which Capitano Zacapa carried as if it contained the national treasury), and let Ottavio Moroque take his arm (which he held uncomfortably tightly, fawning on him and calling him El Jefe), while they escorted him to a waiting Hertz. It was only

later that night, when they took him out to celebrate at the Trop-
icana Disco, that he confirmed his suspicion that he was being
entertained by the two most flaming poofs in Latin America:
when Capitano Zacapa emerged in full Dolores Del Rio drag, and
danced the flamenco (quite well, as a matter of fact) in front of
two dozen clone-look *gringos;* and Ottavio Moroque introduced
him to his "ward," a cream-skinned Mexican boy whom he volunteered to lend him for the night. He was neither surprised nor
offended when Ferdinando declined his offer, and between them
the two lovers showed such good judgment on military matters,
and such good humor between their mincing, and their waving,
and their whispered, bitchy asides, that Ferdinando revised his
initially unfavorable impression of them. They finished out the
evening with high-sounding expressions of Castilian rhetoric and
bravery, and wished him good night by planting twin chaste
kisses on his cheeks; after which they twined their arms around
each other's shoulders, and drifted off into the jasmine-scented
darkness behind the parking lot of the Tegucigalpa Hilton.

The next day they flew out to a training camp in the Sierra
de Opalaca, near a small town aptly named La Esperanza. There,
over the course of the next two weeks, light-plane loads of young,
poorly educated, strung-out professional suicides arrived to join
the glorious army being put together by Señores Moroque and
Zacapa. They ate, drank, screwed the passive Indian women, and
learned the many ways of inflicting death by bullet, bayonet,
hand grenade, and plastic explosive; and (since Zacapa and
Moroque were pragmatists at heart) learned how to avoid being
shot, stabbed, eviscerated, or blown to pieces by the myriad
deaths they handled and learned to wield, eventually with considerable skill. Because their commanders offered them no motives
aside from greed, they thrived; they grew hard and well-trained
and no more lax in discipline than any other army in the field, far
from barbers and civilization and in close proximity to twelve-
year-old whores and fields of *sinsemilla.* Ranks of pup tents
strewed the plains, while Generalissimo Ottavio Moroque
tramped the bush in Castro-esque field garb and shouted fond
obscenities, and Colonel Enrique Zacapa sat in his field tent and
filled out duty rosters and applied lipstick. They had a combined
force of four thousand men by the end of the month, ranging

from sixty-two ex-Green Berets (all in their thirties, tough as nails, and blandly prepared to slaughter gooks in this or any other hemisphere) to Mayapanian exiles, intellectuals, and Indians from the remote interiors all up and down the Central American isthmus: Cuna from Panama, Miskito from the coast of Nicaragua, and Mayapanian Lacandon, whose high-cheekboned beauty and wide eyes recalled El Lorca's own striking features. They came, some of their own volition, some prepaid, some for idealism or bloodthirstiness or boredom or just for the hell of it: and trained on the best supplies and the best equipment Linz Industries could provide, until they were bonded into a single, brutal, ruthless entity, loyal unto death to Ferdinando Lorca, and with no other morals whatsoever.

Ferdinando watched, but didn't actively participate in the elevation of his persona into an excuse for barbarism. He was a skilled soldier: and, as became apparent during the march on Campeche, a brilliant military technician. But his experience was theoretical, and he allowed Zacapa and Moroque pride of place in the practical exhortation of thugs. He made infrequent visits to the troops, but when he did was courteous, self-effacing, and invariably created a near riot of partially manufactured but largely heartfelt enthusiasm: he was a regular Joe, eating the same food as they did, a glamorous father-figure still young enough to be an older brother to some of the older men. He was good-humored and quick to praise, knew everybody's first name, and swore like a Campeche stevedore—in short, he was as faultlessly seductive in a rain forest in Honduras as he had been in a classroom at Columbia University. Then too he was still nominally a virgin to fame: they caught him when he could still be surprised by spontaneous cheering, and it could make him burst out laughing. It was a time that could not come again for any of them, but it was a time to inspire them all to feats of unexpected effort: a time of valor and high hopes, which seemed (sometimes to them; eventually, certainly, to Ferdinando) superhuman and extraordinary, theatrical, and more than a little unreal.

He spent many days up in a light plane, surveying the terrain; the mountainous country which formed the southern border of Mayapán was an area he had never seen, and his scouting expeditions were more to satisfy his own curiosity than to establish routes of transport: most of his army would be parachuted up closer to Campeche in any case. For these expeditions, he was usually accompanied solely by a pilot: a flat-faced Maya half-caste named José Luaro, who spoke little, but was obviously well-educated. Ferdinando tried to draw him out. He offered him a cigarette, and a shot of brandy; he offered him the stray leavings of his mind, impromptu between the puffs of a Camel, at seven thousand feet, random jottings not just about their projected war, but about their country as well: the people, his hopes to form them into a harmonious and patriotic whole, not split between class and class. (José Luaro briefly smiled at that, banking on a high turn with the sun shining in his face, white teeth bared in a grin of almost lupine sarcasm; although he was always respectful, quiet-voiced, whispering his spare questions: Do you want to go on to Quezaltepeque, Señor Lorca? Do you want to refuel there, or shall we go on to Jilotepeque?)

He revealed to El Lorca, almost as an afterthought, that he was a priest: raised by the Franciscans, educated by the Dominicans, poverty and brilliance mixing with his mud-slimed heritage as a *campesino* to make him a fighter, ignoring the dictum "Thou shalt not kill." He revealed little else; El Lorca, for all his charm and his offhand curiosity (after all, they *were* trapped together in a creaking Cessna for six hours out of every day; there had to be *some* distractions besides the scenery), couldn't win his confidences, and gradually assumed that he was merely dull-witted, one of the army of people who say nothing because they have nothing to say. He still gave him cigarettes, and the Maya brought him once a bottle of *aguardiente*, the fierce, cheap Indian cane liquor that tasted like distilled liniment, which they drank gravely, shot for shot, and got roaring drunk, buzzing the jungle on either side of the Chamelecón River. This was unusual; for the most part, José Luaro was scrupulously correct, and so it was with some embarrassment that Ferdinando Lorca asked him to take him to the ruined Mayan city of Copán, buried in the Honduran highlands somewhat off the beaten track of tourists, and just then being excavated by a team from the Peabody Museum of Harvard. This had nothing whatsoever to do with the war in Mayapán, and everything to do with his personal interest in the site: he had never seen the ruined city, he had heard that it was very beautiful, it amused him to visit it in the company of the reserved, Catholic José Luaro, whose forebears had built it, and he happened to be in the neighborhood. Luaro smiled his momentary, wolfish smile, revved the plane, and took off over the mountainous jungle. Ferdinando watched the dense trees pass underneath the window, split by rivers, valleys, a lush and virgin and wonderfully hostile land. How appropriate, he thought, that our country should be so unyielding, so stubbornly mysterious; it would never be known, mapped, explored fully, because it was always changing. A little after noon, with the heat of the sun steamed by 100 percent humidity and the sweat pouring down his back and sticking his white shirt to his body, they cleared a hill and saw the valley of Copán below them, snaked by the Copán river, shaved by the diligent pruning of government workers so that the vivid green jungle was somewhat kept at bay—and visible through the encroaching vines, and the wilderness of wild orchids, the crumbling city of Copán, pyramids and ball court, mantled with a fine green mist of vegetation.

There was a slight breeze when they landed, bumping onto the improvised airstrip and being met by a tall, sunburned Englishman who introduced himself simply as Lloyd, and who volunteered to show them around the place.

"We don't get too many visitors this time of year, the universities bring some groups in, but mostly in the summertime. This area here is the ceremonial ball court, where they played a game rather like a cross between soccer and basketball. There's a remarkable wealth of detail work here, it's much better than anything you get down in the rain forests, well, of course, that's simply the climate, we don't have the same organic deterioration as you get down at sea level. Directly to your left, that great step pyramid is the Staircase of the Inscriptions—hieroglyphs telling the Maya obsession with time—some plumed serpents—they're fairly unusual in this latitude, it's a more common motif as you work your way up north. It's an extraordinary piece of work—absolutely unique in Mayan archaeology. It's eighty-six feet high, sixty-three steps in all. . . . There's a marvelous view from the top, would you like to see it?"

Ferdinando smiled. He turned his head to survey the peaceful scene, trees massed in green seclusion all around them. He was attentive, almost respectful in the uncanny silence which pervaded the ancient ball court, despite the clamor of parrots and monkeys from the nearby jungle. There was a feeling of great peace to this forgotten city of lime-green stone, cool, aesthetic, very soothing. He smiled again to the friendly Englishman, turned, and walked slowly between the banked walls which had once formed the sides of the playing field; trying to imagine two teams of lithe, brown-skinned athletes fighting for control of a ball of hardened rubber: the single-minded beauty and exact discipline of their play so symmetrical beside the unplanned chaos of war. He stepped up onto the banked wall, feeling the good leverage it would give to a man, running, trying to pass a ball to his teammates. It must have been a sharp, fast-paced game. The trees whispered in the light wind in the distance. José Luaro had stayed back by the plane. There was no one there who knew who he was, no one to pin him down to an identity as El Jefe. He ran along the side of the banked court and jumped down onto the flat stone floor below, breathing lightly.

"Yes, I would like to see the view from the pyramid, if you don't mind."

The sunburned Englishman smiled and held out his hand. "Certainly. It's a bit of a breathless climb, but the results are certainly worth it."

Step by step, Ferdinando followed the archaeologist as they scrambled up the carved facade. It was badly eroded, and they skirted the inscribed treads and worked their way up the sides, reaching for a handhold on the worn figure of a god or priest. Finally, scraped, streaked with sweat, they emerged onto the top of the pyramid, and turned to look out over the jungle spread around them, the quiet of the Great Plaza and the eastern court of the Acropolis, the whole softened, ruined, smoothed from the shapes of man-made structures into the softer shapes of the jungle, infinitely poignant and lost and wild.

El Lorca bent, and cried out as something flashed by his ankle, stabbing pain. He crouched down and felt his bare ankle, which was swollen, but not so badly as by a scorpion bite. He winced, and managed to smile at his guide.

"I think I've been bitten by a snake. Do you have any antivenin?"

The Englishman squatted and examined his ankle. "I'd better make a cut, just to be on the safe side. We've got some serum in the first-aid kit—half a sec, let me just get my knife out—" He made a quick crosscut on the site of the wound, sucked, and spat. "I'm afraid you'll have a bit of a climb down, do you think you can make it?"

"Of course," Ferdinando snapped. "I feel ridiculous, getting bitten by a snake. Even a *gringo* would have worn boots for tramping in the jungle!"

The Englishman, whose own feet were Orvised to the mid-calf, was nonetheless compassionate. They made a quicker journey down than up, but Ferdinando was still bone-white by the time they reached the ground, and there was a film of sweat smearing his bony temples. He waxed eloquently furious while the Englishman and an assistant daubed him with alcohol and shot him full of antitoxin, and then José Luaro appeared, smiling slightly, to ask, "Well, did you enjoy your walk?" and El Lorca glared at him with scarcely disguised antipathy.

"Just get me out of here. This was a ridiculous self-indulgence to begin with, and I've managed to pay for it in a suitably ridiculous fashion. Just get me back to La Esperanza."

José Luaro ferried him back to camp. He was laid up for three days with a high fever and a higher degree of impatience, swearing, hallucinating, unable to read or write, and so bored, as well as immobile, that his associates began to fear for their own self-esteem as well as for his health. Ottavio Moroque and Enrique Zacapa were beside themselves with worry, and he insulted and ridiculed them. José Luaro disappeared for three days, and Ferdinando forgot himself enough to refer to him as "that Mayan idiot," an insult for which he apologized obliquely, once he was back on his feet. He was carried far out over the jungle, and up into the sky, in crevices of his mind and back into the basement of the Miramar Prison by the action of the poison in his system, and when after three days he began to recover, it was only slowly, almost tentatively, that he could bring himself back to the real world. He looked out at his army from a great distance. He couldn't remember what they were for. But gradually it came back, it all came back, and he took up the reins of his reason, and smiled at them again. He was El Lorca, and these were the people who were working for him, and would put him into power.

But he retained a certain antipathy for the jungle ruins after that, which stayed with him for the rest of his life. It was scarcely conscious, but he was heard to remark on more than one occasion about his countrymen's obsession with their past, and their willingness to turn it into an industry, when they were unwilling to accept any other kind of industry and indeed set up innumerable delays and obstacles to anyone who was interested in bringing them forward into the twentieth century.

five

I N THE FIRST WEEK in May, Camila Lorca
and Jorge-Julio de Rodríguez caught the daily train up into the
highlands of Los Cuchumatanes Province and started to organize
the coffee workers.

It was a seemingly impossible task, because the coffee workers had been bred from infancy to the docility of cattle and the
hopeless apathy of clinical depressives, by *finca* owners who had
held their fathers and grandfathers in the bonds of virtual slav-
ery. The laws of Mayapán and the unwritten laws of the region
made all attempts at unionization more punishable than treason,
and in any event most of the *campesinos* were literally starving to
death, and as Brazil's "Red Bishop" Camara had recently put it,
"People with no reasons for living will not find causes to die for."
Nevertheless, there had been some success of late on the part of
the Catholic lay workers, and in response to their charity, these
missionaries were starting to disappear: singly or in pairs, occasionally in groups, most often called out of their houses for a police inquiry and never seen again. Their superiors protested, and
their governments, when they were foreigners, but the government of Quintero de Buiztas was so shaky at this point that he
had stopped responding to official communications. Privately, he

joked that they were asking for it. He simply obliged these religious masochists, by letting them share the fate of their beloved lord and savior. They ought to thank him. How many other countries had a President so tolerant of religious differences that he allowed zealots to be crucified, with or without their consent?

This was the climate in the primordial beauty of the coffee *fincas*, lush green forests on the highland slopes of volcanoes, bright blue skies above, blood-smeared earth beneath the trees. Camila and Jorge-Julio de Rodríguez got off the train at Solala and everywhere around them there were the signs of plenty alchemized into hardship, natural riches hoarded by a terrified few and prefab poverty silted up for the terrorized many. They were welcomed at the Capuchin mission, which was run by two priests from Baltimore; given a tour of the nearby shantytown and mission hospital; given a cup of precious bottled water and a quinine pill apiece, and left to their own devices to hammock in fitful slumber for the afternoon, the shrill calls of children and the clucking of chickens audible through the windows along with a breeze from the beautiful dark-green hills. In the early evening, they rose and shared a frugal meal of beans and tortillas with the two American priests, and then joined them for their climb up the slope of the mountain in the gathering twilight, the trees rustling with nesting birds, past narrow plots of corn and bean rows, shacks filled with naked children and strident, combative dogs—climbing on an overgrown dirt track now flat as a road, now steep and strewn with rocks, to a flat clearing hacked by bulldozers from the side of the mountain and then abandoned, where the priests set up an altar on a cardboard table and said mass. There were perhaps three dozen worshipers there, primarily men. The women could come down to the church, but the men were afraid of being seen by the authorities, their actual or supposed radicalization would be guessed by their attendance at the Capuchin mission, and the priests themselves were reluctant to be seen too obviously fraternizing with the male *indios*. So they materialized out of the gathering darkness, flat-cheekboned, strong-nosed Maya faces, and gulped the host, praying for rain and safety for their wives and children, as they might have prayed four hundred years ago to the *chacs*, the rain gods—but perhaps they were still praying to the *chacs*, knowing in their hearts which gods had any interest in looking out for them. Jorge-Julio watched them impassively, and Camila stood with him. Neither the priests nor anyone else in the region had any idea of their identity, and they were now far away from the sea, far away from even the illusory borders of safety: high on the arched spine of a country whose blood was still volcanic, the terraced plots of scavenged land and the rich coffee soil alike volcano-born, and violent. They knew they could easily die here. And if they succeeded in their work, they would incite these people to run forward out of the darkness toward the probability of their own deaths.

The priests had accomplished an impressive task in educating the *campesinos* in a short time to a rudimentary knowledge of written Spanish and modern agronomy; where they had not done so well was in instilling hope, because the liberation they promised was a slow process, and dependent on an eventual ally in the government, to combat the power of the oligarchs. That was where Ferdinando would excel over Jesus, Jorge-Julio said in a rare moment of lighthearted blasphemy: he would give them results in a hurry. But the organizational setup of the Capuchins was sound, and Camila decided to adopt it intact: training of seminar leaders at the mission schools, and dissemination of the information in small *comunidades de base*. There was no system or premeditation to her observations: one of the striking characteristics of the Lorcanista revolution, in its early stages, was its receptivity to the inspirations of chance. Camila and Jorge-Julio merely used what they discovered intuitively: Jorge-Julio, holding the head of a chloroformed Indian while a priest seared, with a hot machete, the stump of his amputed arm; Camila, helping a terrified Indian woman bury the aborted fetus of her child in the scruffy ground behind the ramshackle church; Camila and Jorge-Julio, teaching their brightest students to parrot back the rights guaranteed to them by the constitution of Mayapán, and never put in force since the declaration of independence. These might have been incidents in their education as any two bleeding hearts—save that they already knew the prescription for the health of their country, and were in no wise reluctant to tell even the most anguished victim that he or she was being helped by the Lorcanista party: that Ferdinando Lorca was the answer to all their problems, and that no amount of violence, guile, or covert

165

damages to the oligarchs' landholdings was inappropriate in a noble cause. They recruited in droves. They had trouble finding enough material to make quadricolored armbands (in red, black, white, and yellow, the Mayapanian national colors), which their converts kept hidden out of sight, along with their weapons and their newly forged identity as patriots, until the signal came to move. Inside of a month, they knew that when the time came, given twenty-four hours' notice, solely by word-of-mouth runners, boys and girls, spreading out from village to village, the entire Cuchumatanes region would rise *en masse* to support Los Lorcanistas. They knew that the priests would be on their side. And they knew that the hacienda owners were aware of their peril, and were desperate enough to fight it with all the means at their disposal.

An indication of their desperation came on the hot May night when Camila and Jorge-Julio, returning in twilight to the comparative luxury of the Baltimores' mission, from two days spent traveling among the dirt villages, were met at some distance from the house by a Maya woman who whispered something inaudible to Jorge-Julio and faded back into the forest. Jorge-Julio stopped Camila with his hand on her arm, and they squatted down in the dirt by the side of the road while a government Jeep beamed the trees with its headlights, and a covey of men hustled the two priests naked out of the house and dumped them into the waiting cab. Wheels ground dust from the road, and the apparition faded into the night—as did the priests, who for all Jorge-Julio's dogged inquiries and Camila's probing (via Battiste's contacts in Washington) had apparently become an illusion: an unfortunate hallucination on their parishioners' parts, because it was conclusively proven by the government, with citations available upon request, that two priests from Baltimore in the Cuchumatanes region had never existed in the first place. Quintero de Buiztas' government was very sorry about the misunderstanding, and even offered to send some priests, of his own choosing, whenever he got around to it. Camila and Jorge-Julio, in their spurious identity as lay workers of the Chuch, found themselves called upon to offer spiritual comfort, and an outlet for the feelings of rage and grief which seethed among the people who had loved the Capuchins. There was an impromptu work stoppage called among the coffee workers, men slipping into the forests and sometimes burning their fields before them, and harsh measures of revenge taken by the landowners, which threatened to escalate into the kind of pointless civil war that would have weakened the Lorcanistas' chances, by making them seem to be merely an accident in a time of political disturbance. Camila and Jorge-Julio discussed the situation, while they were sitting drinking the last of the priests' medicinal rum in the shambles of the dismantled dispensary, and it was then that they hit upon the bold, rash, inevitable idea of starting the revolution there, because there was no way they could keep their identities a secret that much longer, and the people's rage in that district seemed too perfect as raw material for them to miss such a golden opportunity for amateur theatricals.

Which was how she and Jorge-Julio determined to organize a massive rally in Solala, which Topsy-like just grew, from a few dissident leaders until it included every dissatisfied worker in the region; and which attracted Guardía platoons like flies, so that by 2 P.M. on the twenty-fifth of May the main square at Solala was jammed with people, and ringed with soldiers six men deep, with their carbines at the ready and their safety catches off. The crowd shimmered in the heat, and Camila had no idea what she was going to say to them, but she began by speaking very calmly, telling them she understood that they had all been having a hard time, that it was nobody's fault, certainly not the fault of their poor neighbors who had sold their sons into the Guardía, and it had undoubtedly been the best decision, in order to feed their poor families a few more grains of rice or kernels of corn to keep them on this side of starvation. She told them that she understood their problems—and the undoubted insult of being talked to like this by a woman (who was only suited for cooking and keeping a good house running, as she herself fervently believed), but that the bad men who inhabited the capital, and who had no more care for the people of Solala than a fat Wall Street broker, had made her frightened for the people of her country, frightened that they would be hypnotized by the evil energies beamed to them by the wicked people in Campeche, and that they would be turned against themselves in an evil sickness like that of a mad dog that goes around biting itself, its owners, and everything else in its path.

"It's true," she said, "I don't come from the highlands, and so I may have misunderstood. But isn't it true that many of you have been incited brother against brother, to kill one another? Isn't it true that you see no way out, that your manhood demands some action, for your wives, your little children, and the oligarchs have left you no alternative but to fight, if you are a worker, and to kill the workers if you are a *guardianista?* Isn't it true that you want some other way, some way of regaining your dignity as men, and saving the lives of the brothers who may have taken a different path from you—only to survive, only to put some food on their tables and some hope into their children's lives? Oh, my dear brothers and sisters—" And here she spread her hands quite reasonably, without the least show of theatricality, so that the people were impressed by her sincerity. "Isn't it true that you want peace for your country, peace and freedom where all men can have enough to eat and a little clothing of human dignity, without being exploited by people who care nothing for you, who care nothing for your children, or your country, and who only care to manipulate you like toys for their own wicked ends?"

She then went on to explain—still quite reasonably and diffidently, because she was aware of the vast prejudice in the square against a slip of a girl, in her linen skirt and jacket, talking to men who could have been her brothers, her fathers, her grandfathers—she went on to explain that the reason she had come to Solala was to tell them about a man, a wonderful man, a man who was willing to help them. This man knew about their suffering, and grieved for them. He had sent her as a messenger, because he could not come to them personally—but he would come, never fear! Now she would like to tell them about this man. He was a man of peace, and he knew about their suffering; he had been imprisoned by the Buiztanistas, and he had been exiled from his beloved country. Yet he had not been hardened! He had not turned into a monster, like the dictator Quintero de Buiztas—yes, she had the courage to name his name!—because he was a man of peace, of love and compassion for his people. He knew what to do to help them. He had spent all his life studying to help them, and now he was organizing an army, which would come, soon, to pull their wicked leaders down from their thrones and cast them into the ocean! Wouldn't they join him? And she spread out her hands again, hungry, slender arms, like a joyous starving child who says there is food here enough for everybody. Jorge-Julio stood below the rickety wooden platform in the center of the square, with his hand on his revolver just in case anyone tried to hurt Señora Lorca, but he was staring at her openmouthed, as fascinated as any of the *solaleños*. She explained that she was not the light of this man, but she was here to bear witness to that light—and a muscle pulled at the corner of her mouth as she kicked into overdrive, speaking more quickly, smiling her bright winner's smile as she told them that was why she was here, yes, even a little girl like her, whom they had no reason to listen to! She knew she was insulting them by even thinking she could share in their pain, but she couldn't help coming to tell them the good news—that there was a man who was going to help them, and he was coming to help them soon. Would they like her to tell them his name? Would they like to know the name of the man who was going to liberate them? Reverently she lowered her voice. His name was Ferdinando Lorca, and he was a man of the country like them (a lie), a man of the poor, who knew the sufferings of the poor because he had been poor himself! He was a man of gentleness, a scholar, yet a soldier, a man who wasn't afraid to spill blood but who preferred to sweep them all to glory, to a life where their birthright would be peace and respect and the joy of living in harmony and righteousness with their fellowmen!

And he was something else. She spoke more softly still. He was a man who understood that all men are brothers. Now this might be difficult for them to believe. Not just the poor people of the highlands, but *all* the people of Mayapán were brothers! And more than that! All the people of the world, regardless of their countries, regardless of their beliefs, were united in a common bond of strength and needed no outside help to reach out and grab their own destiny! She unbuttoned her jacket and spoke in a rising crescendo. They were the freest people in the world, if only they realized it! They could compete with anyone, trade, buy, and sell—and yes, form alliances, for mutual assurance of gain—with anyone, another country or a private corporation, without the middlemen who had for centuries kept them low. *This* was what El Lorca gave them! They were *all porteños*! And all *campesinos*! And all *solaleños*! Yes, even she! And Jorge-Julio, watching her, realized that she had become carried away by her own rhetoric—or by something else, a distant look in her eyes as if she were speaking lines being dictated to her by another power, or perfectly, vividly, impossibly scripted in advance. She stripped her jacket off and threw it in the dust, and her two-hundred-dollar white silk shirt was grimed and stuck to her back and under her breasts with sweat. They saw the sweat running down her face and she shook her long blond hair loose from its comb, and reached into the crowd, saying, "Somebody give me a scissors, you can't pick coffee with hair like this!" And when somebody handed her a scissors she shook her hair to one side and hacked it off in great ragged clumps, until her hair was as short as the hair of a *campesina*.

Then she stood up straight, with her chest heaving and her hair straggling around her face, and a great roaring cheer went up from the crowd below her, and those nearest her reached up in a blind, avid struggle to touch her, to touch her hands, and the coat which she had thrown down was seized by the crowd and torn to pieces as souvenirs. Guardías dropped their guns and embraced the peasants, who dropped their machetes, and men who had been lifelong enemies embraced one another with tears of unashamed emotion running down their faces, and Jorge-Julio was jostled to one side and experienced a moment of blind panic, as he lost sight of her, swallowed up by the crowd. He fought his way through to her, elbowing people aside and very nearly shouting for them to leave her alone: when she reached out her slender arm to him, and her bright smile beamed to him, and she whispered, "Get me out of here before I faint, would you?" But she didn't look as if she were going to faint. She looked wonderful. She looked radiant and highly amused, tickled to death and perfectly delighted by the results. In village after village, all up and down the crown of that desolate country, the experience was repeated, and the crowds cheered for her, and she grew more and more confident in inciting and accepting their love. She woke up the souls of people who had been asleep for three hundred years, and she bloomed as a consequence. Jorge-Julio saw her drinking water from a canteen a few days later, the sun warming the golden hairs on her strong, tanned wrists as she held up the rusted canteen to drink, and had his own vision of her as his ideal woman: a beautiful fighter, someone who wouldn't be beaten by any mortal power in the world.

six

FERDINANDO LANDED at Progreso, less than 120 miles from Campeche, with a force of six hundred troops on the morning of July 18—a date which was to become famous years later as a national holiday in Mayapán, after the Lorcanistas came into power. He was forty-one years old. He came without a weapon (although his men were armed to the teeth), with a sweat-stained uniform on his back and a clean one in his baggage, and he came with the absolute conviction that he was going to win: with an assurance which radiated out from him like a warmly attractive glow, so that he appeared to be a man on a holiday, having the time of his life.

As a matter of fact, he was. The inherent dangers of being a marked man and a known dissident gave an added fillip to even the most mundane of rebel activities—like attacking the *cuartel* at Progreso, six men who surrendered without a shot. And the knowledge that he was once again in the same country as Camila gave him an added source of amusement: they were able to communicate now by shortwave radio, crackling broadcasts which could be picked up by the hundreds of new Lorcanista radios in the country, and which quickly became the favorite national soap opera: as they talked back and forth, trading possibly spurious rebel victories to the deliberate provocation of the Buiztanistas, and mutual endearments to the titillation of their civilian audience.

His force was comparatively small, because he wished to maintain the fiction of a totally grass-roots revolution: cadres had landed almost simultaneously at the Maya ruins at Tulum on the coast, at Payo Obispo on the Rio Hondo, and at Dzibalchén and Iturbide in the interior, but in each case, their arms and training were blended with the extant local resistance into a semblance of spontaneity—thus "Mayapán for the Mayapanians!" became a convincingly jingoist slogan, and the extent to which their revolution had been prefabricated, and shipped to Mayapán ready for final assembly, was conveniently ignored.

In truth, the revolution was both more and less certain than it appeared to be. At any moment in the next four months, a sniper's bullet could have bankrupted Alfred Linz's investment and left the whole movement leaderless; at the same time, the women who braved the government patrols to bring supplies and their bodies to the brave *muchachos* who were hiding in the hills, and the men who threw down their trowels and seized their machetes to join the rebels, were in themselves less important than they were led to believe—especially by El Lorca himself, who was everywhere, joking with a wounded man at midnight and up at dawn, to give an individual word of encouragement and praise to each and every member of his unit, so that the joke began going around, Why is it better to have El Lorca on your side than the Pope? Because El Lorca knows more about the shitty life of a fighting man. He threw himself into the creation of this new role with the single-minded concentration of an artist: slogging through mud up to his armpits; grim-faced with his lieutenants Zacapa and Moroque, while they were planning the next day's campaign; jubilant with his men . . . inspired in no small measure by the success of his wife, who was becoming famous ahead of him. In this there was not the slightest suggestion of jealousy (in fact, he listened with delighted amazement to Jorge-Julio's report from Cuchumatanes Province, haltingly decoded by Colonel Zacapa, and then spent half the night putting it back in code to send on to Battiste in Washington) but merely his enthusiasm for one of her many good ideas, which he then put into practice and am-

173

plified. While they were thus individually engaged, the Lorca/ Linz/Tommassi publicity machine was hard at work putting them front and center in the public's consciousness, by means of radio spots, television, poster art, and print, so that the wonder was not that people in Mayapán fell in love with the Lorcas, but that someone (on either side of the political fence) did not remark on the extraordinary degree of premeditation and precision which accompanied Ferdinando and Camila's "precipitous" rise to fame.

Carlos Molina had been smuggled into Campeche shortly after Ferdinando's arrival in Progreso, hustled into Don Luis García Mores' mansion, and given the full facilities of MAYA-TV's art department and the National University Press to turn out radical art by the truckload. Soon every telephone pole and whitewashed wall in Mayapán was blazing with three-color portraits of Camila and Ferdinando, as well as uncomplimentary cartoons of Quintero de Buiztas, and unflattering sketches of the prominent oligarchs sequestered behind his back. They even began reprinting and reissuing books of Porfirio Cheruña's poetry in Spanish, so that the inflammatory and (as Ferdinando knew) insincere verses of the greatest Mayapanian poet could be read again, in cantinas and in chuches and on the sly in the hallways of the Presidential Palace, reawakening dormant patriotism with the ersatz rhetoric of the calculating and cynical old man. Don Luis gave Carlos the keys to his building, his house, and his safety deposit box in the Federal Bank of Mayapán, and then decamped to visit friends in Los Angeles until the danger should be safely past. The rebels contacted a Madison Avenue advertising agency to design them a campaign, a slogan, and a logo (two clasped hands surmounted by a coiling snake, with wings), and when it became too difficult to smuggle their videotaped messages through customs, Pisote showed up and started producing them at the studio herself. She also started putting her sharp-boned face and big, serious eyes on camera, for lack of another spokesperson, and rather enjoyed the experience. She was able to wear all the colors she wanted, get dramatic effects with lighting and makeup—Carlos helped her set the gels—and on video her famished beauty was striking, and her voice low and throaty and seductive; she sang the old Yucatecan songs and accompanied herself on twelve-string guitar, and was able to produce a dozen spots before it became too dangerous and she had to shut down production and go into hiding with the Maryknoll sisters.

Battiste stayed on in Washington, where he had succeeded in interesting network executives and correspondents from *The New York Times* and *The Washington Post* in their story; invested heavily in the reelection campaigns of three important congressmen and two Senators on the Foreign Relations Committee; and paid the fare for two syndicated columnists and a documentary film producer to be sent to Mayapán to record the story of the rebellion. The Buiztas lobby didn't have a chance against the combined incomes of Linz Industries and Linz International, and more money was coming in every day: from United Oil (which was interested in Mayapán because of its subsidiary, Emmo gasoline), Misaki Corporation, I.T.M., and Deutsch-Telegraphieren. He kept in touch with Ferdinando via telephone through Linz's satellite up-link, sending bulkier information through the diplomatic pouch of the Mexican ambassador, whose office was cautiously on their side. Their private conversations were (perhaps fortunately) not available to the shortwave listeners who tuned in daily for the Camila–Ferdinando show—and went on far into the night, while they talked about a variety of things, politics only peripherally. Ferdinando might ask Battiste nostalgically what movies were playing, what bands he'd heard, and what new restaurants he had discovered, trying to remind himself that there was a world beyond the scrub-jungled camps where he and his followers were lodged itching and smelling like God knew what . . . and a side of himself that was interested in other things, besides killing and being President. Battiste, for his part, could beam his mind via satellite into the mosquito-humming darkness, and sit by his friend, listening to the low voices of the *compadres* and consoling himself for his safety and inaction. It was a poignant connection for them both—and occasionally they talked about Camila, what she had said to Ferdinando on the radio that day, how well she had sounded, sweet-voiced and sharp-minded as ever. It was probably just as well that their subsequent mythographers couldn't hear them talking like this, but it helped them to maintain their sense of reality; and in many ways these were their freest and most spontaneous conversations, exempt from the complexities of heartache, and the tensions of their creation of their public selves as heroes.

All this heroic publicity was pouring like a tide of filthy sewer water into the halls and reception rooms of the Presidential Palace, as far as Quintero de Buiztas was concerned: and he watched its gradual rise with a galling twist of amusement, observing how it had risen to the level of his ankles, as he splashed across the Sala de Recepción, where someone had left a Lorcanista newspaper, and into the little office of Capitano Profuma, commander of the Presidential Guard, where the *guardías* quickly took off their headsets and pretended not to have been listening to the Lorcanistas' radio program. He saw how it had stained the walls, leaving a sea-track of slime on the outsides of the palace, where each morning's new white paint imperfectly concealed the night's spray-painted artistry of Viva El Lorca and Muerte a los Buiztanistas. He felt it come mouth-high in a taste of grit and blood, when he learned that the girls whom Capitano Profuma had been corralling for him for the last thirty years— and who had at first come willingly, thrilled by the prospect of sleeping with a President; and who had then come with good-humored resignation, satisfied that it was the simplest way of keeping out of trouble—now had to be coerced at gunpoint, because they were superstitiously afraid of sleeping with a dead man. And he felt it break over him in a wave of pure hilarity, when one of the girls he'd had brought to him, scarcely fourteen years old and skinny as a foal, appeared after he had undressed her piece by piece, trembling and terrified, stark naked and with her arm circled by a Lorcanista armband. He stared at the girl and then burst out laughing—and then he threw her dress at her and ordered her out of the room: Go fuck the rebels if you love them so much, go fuck donkeys or go fuck yourself and he laughed so much that tears ran down his cheeks because shit, if the little *putas* of the country wear El Lorca's colors inside their clothes then I really am done for, the whole country is sick with the disease of Lorcanistitis.

That was when he sat down and started to think seriously that this infection might last longer than he'd originally supposed: and he had certain precautions taken, all with perfect reasonableness and sagacity: the construction of an elevator separating his private quarters from the rest of the palace (he borrowed the idea from Batista), the installation of increased security agents, and the importation of Negro whores from Port-au-Prince who spoke not a word of Spanish. He soothed the terrors of his oligarchal backers while tactfully suggesting they export their valuables to Daytona Beach, and he even went so far as to suggest to certain American companies, in which he himself held stock, that they move their assets into their Panamanian bank accounts, and their dependents to Mexico, where Señor el Presidente could recommend a number of good hotels.

For years he had been putting small sums away in a numbered Swiss bank account (almost without thinking about it) and now he stepped up these contributions to his private old-age fund—but he showed no indication of leaving Campeche himself, and in fact gave concrete evidence of his very real plans to stay. He renewed his subscriptions to his numerous magazines; he redoubled the guard outside his quarters; he kept his private collection of firearms cleaned and loaded ... in short, word began to spread around the palace of El Presidente's intention to withstand a siege. Publicly, his generals were behind him. Privately, they even went so far as to offer him the keys to their apartments in Miami, or the telephone numbers of their friends in San Juan—simply out of nostalgia for the military despot they had served with allegiance for thirty years, and who now seemed patently bent on committing suicide.

Buiztas rebuked them for their lack of faith; they backtracked, and he threw them out of office. In their place he hired a new staff made up of cronies from the seamiest backwaters of his past: old drinking companions from his regular Army days, former pimps, the managers of gambling casinos, and even a half-mad oratorical begger who had been a fixture of the Plaza Columbia for twenty years, whom he appointed as his new Secretary of State. Historians shook their heads, and remarked that Quintero de Buiztas, like Caligula, was finally going mad; sycophants praised him for taking the reins of government thus completely into his own hands; and hopeful idealists saw him (albeit ineptly) trying to turn the federal bureaucracy over to at least a few of the people. What no one realized was his plain in-

177

tention to create such a mess that his successor would spend the next fifteen years simply trying to unravel it; and he almost succeeded—the records of the national treasury ended up in the mulatto housekeeper's room for safekeeping, and his personal physician, Dr. Horacio Lazcal, stole the Presidential Seal from the lunatic Secretary of State and hid it under his bed in his modest house on Calle Soledad, till he could give it to Battiste Tommassi. But his scorched-earth government failed: not for want of incompetent ministers, but because of the sudden and spectacular success of the rebels.

This happened in, and around, and in the environs and finally in the houses of a little town named Tenabo, less than twenty miles from Campeche: where the Buiztanistas had seen fit to lodge their entire reserves of troops in training—sixteen-year-old soldiers for whom this represented their first time away from home, drilling in the arts of bayonet and mortar under the watchful eyes of commanders too green, or too cowardly, or too well-connected to be sent into battle. There were some eight thousand men in Tenabo—the estimates varied, depending on the loyalties of the census takers—and they were taken, dead or alive, in eight hours of intensive fighting by eleven hundred rebels and approximately four hundred guerrillas, under the personal command of Ferdinando Lorca. He accomplished this with the loss of fifty-six men and another eighteen wounded: the divergence in casualties being the result not of any intransigence on his part, but the fanatical loyalty of his followers. He accomplished this with the loss of two tanks, twenty-three rifles, six mortars, and four light bombers, against nearly ten times that amount of ordnance extravagantly mismanaged by the enemy. And he accomplished it by assiduously risking death at every moment, seeing for the first time the interminable hours he'd spent memorizing military strategy in Madrid finally put to their fullest and most serendipitous use; and blithely showing off for his wife and his even more absent friend.

They started on the night of October 2, just after darkness had blanketed the scrub jungle outside the town with thick muddy shadows (the rainy season was just starting to taper off, leaving the sinkholes brimming and the roads rutted and sticky with drying muck). Their first targets were the large army outpost at La Merced, just to the south of town (a regular army installation, where they had tanks which the rebels hoped to commandeer) and two smaller posts at Cristos and Las Villas, both on the northeastern periphery, near the radio tower and the wealthier houses of the city. Ferdinando moved his men up to surround these positions, himself leading his six platoons against La Merced, while Comandantes Moroque and Zacapa took four platoons each against the northern installations. When their troops were in position—mines set in the long road leading up to La Merced, and air and tank support keyed to coordinate with the ground fire there and at Cristos and Las Villas—Ferdinando got on the shortwave radio and called the commandant of the main army training camp at Mont Alegre, in the center of the town.

"Tenabo is surrounded," Ferdinando told him conversationally. "You can lay down your arms, or you can take them up with us, to fight the rapists who are fucking with our beloved country. Of course, you can also use your weapons to fight us, but if you do, I have to warn you that you're going to lose."

The commander of the Mont Alegre training facility was a courageous man, and he demanded to know—also quite conversationally—who the hell Ferdinando was, and what he was going to do after the Buiztanista garrison cut off his balls for him, as well as those of his (euphemistically coprophagous) men.

Ferdinando explained that he was Ferdinando Lorca, commander-in-chief of the rebel forces, and that his men had an extra set of balls apiece. He went on to give some (quite accurate) coordinates regarding his own forces, giving the commandant plenty of time to locate them on a map, and meanwhile glossing on the paternity of the particular commandant in question to such good effect that that officer ended up screaming obscenities at him and hanging up—at which point Ferdinando calmly switched to the rebels' own frequency and signaled his men to begin the attack.

The first platoon moved down, firing from a slight rise before the main gate of La Merced, where they'd been screened by bushes, lobbing hand grenades and pop-popping shots which were immediately answered by blind fire from inside the *cuartel*—which was easily evaded, as the rebels faded back into the underbrush. Meanwhile, a similar opening pavane was performed at Cristos and Las Villas—firing, and retreat; no casualties (as far as they could tell) on either side. The men around La Merced now decided (since it was becoming a fine night, with a glut of stars and a fresh, mild, rain-cleared breeze) that it was time for a little singing; however, the song they chose was calculated to bring little joy to the men inside the *cuartel*: it was a variant on a popular Mayapanian love song, roughly translating, "Soon we will be together, soon all our waiting will be over and you will see me!"—sung badly but with admirable gusto in a taunting, jeering voice until the gates of La Merced swung open, and three Jeeps and a family of T-17 tanks came trundling out to provide a baritone accompaniment to the warbled tenors and sopranos of the rebels. Instead, the first tank hit a land mine and skidded sideways, plowing into the muddy slope of the side of the road and tipping over on its side. Gasoline poured from its ruptured tank, and a well-placed rebel shot ignited a lurid illumination by which the Lorcanistas could see the other tanks milling, Jeeps disgorging men with rifles and machine guns, and a man writhing in the dirt with his body blown away from the waist down. The rebels popped more shots, but held their concealed positions in the jungle undergrowth, hearing the drone of planes and the distant shots from the northeastern sector as a counterpoint to the shouted orders, thin and frantic at that distance, as more men and Jeeps poured out of the gates of La Merced and one of the Jeeps set off another land mine, and then Ferdinando (who had been slightly concerned with their ability to draw the enemy out, and distract them until the planes flew over, but who realized now that he should never have worried because the Buiztanistas could always be counted on to do precisely the wrong thing) felt an intoxicating glow of heroism snap like an electrical current through him, and he breathed through his mouth till he had it under control, and then called to his men and led them out from under cover just as their air support arrived and started bombing the gates of the undefended *cuartel,* and within fifteen minutes the garrison of La Merced surrendered.

The firing continued, distant and sporadic, at Cristos and Las Villas, and the planes turned north to supplement the attack of the rebels there. Ferdinando coordinated his men at La Merced, accepting the loyalty of the dozen or so regular infantrymen who professed a desire to join him, and locking the rest of the enemy forces into the mess hall with plenty of cane liquor, but no clothes or weapons, until such time as they could support the revolution, or be tried as traitors or hailed as heroes (depending upon who won). Then he got on the radio and called the commander of the Mont Alegre garrison again.

"We're at La Merced, and a number of your boys are being slaughtered at Cristos and Las Villas. There's still time for you to change sides and welcome us. I just thought you might be interested."

He sat back and examined his fingernails while the commandant swore at him for five minutes in incoherent fury. Meanwhile, his men were raiding the stores of La Merced for ammunition and supplies, and rolling the tanks out, squat turtles, one by one into the street.

"We've got the ordnance from La Merced, and that, along with our own stores, should enable us to blow the excrement out of you, you must be aware of that. Are you sure you want to break the hearts of all the mothers of your brave boys, simply to prove the point that you're pigheaded enough to die like a dog, in the service of a worthless cause?"

Ferdinando paused in this reasonable argument to glance at a message from Generalísimo Ottavio Moroque, commander of the attack force at Las Villas, to the effect that they now held the radio tower and were transmitting all of this, not merely over shortwave but to every radio listener in the country.

"Señor Whatever-your-name-is, let me make you an offer. You don't agree with our political philosophy, but a democracy is the best of all possible systems and there must be a number of your downy-cheeked trainees who would rather join with us than fight. Why don't you ask them? They're all probably listening to this broadcast. I'll give you a minute to go to your window and listen—there, do you hear it? Democracy in action? You see, every man can make a decision on the matter for himself, and based on the most enlightened of circumstances, a clear and present knowledge of the situation. I'll give you another five minutes before we start. We'll be coming up . . . let's see, coming up Calle

Palmira and then turning onto Avenida Quintero de Buiztas, which will take us to the front gate of Mont Alegre in a little over an hour, I should imagine. Do you think that will give you enough time to prepare a welcome? I should add that it's our desire to kill no one, and that anyone who comes out into the street in the next hour carrying a Mayapanian flag, or wearing a Lorcanista armband, will be treated as a patriot and accorded the highest honor by my men, who will embrace them and call them brothers and sisters. . . ."

Then he signed off, and ran back out to the front gate, where his men were waiting, and jumped into the back of a Jeep and gave them the signal to start. The men who fought their way in from the radio tower had a difficult time of it (since the wealthier citizens of Tenabo felt themselves ideologically constrained to oppose rebels whom they had heard were communists . . . and since they didn't have the publicity advantage of a radio announcement of their route), but the Lorcanistas who rode in the caravan that night with Ferdinando Lorca, down Calle Palmira and along Buiztas, took two hours to reach the Mont Alegre garrison because they were being cheered as heroes. The people of Tenabo (who had heard his voice on the radio) came out of their houses to applaud a popular leader who had done what Quintero de Buiztas hadn't been able to do in thirty years: appeal to their imaginations. They jumped up onto the hood of his Jeep, climbing in beside him to shake his hands and embrace him; and he let two young girls sit in the back of the Jeep while he got down and walked along with the crowd—and those who had them wore Lorcanista armbands, and those who didn't improvised: waving torn strips of red, black, white, and yellow cloth, pieces of paper and the labels off popular brands of soda water, condoms, and fertilizer, all of which happened to be printed in the national colors. It was like a wonderful parade—and when they got to the corner of Avenida Quintero de Buiztas, they were met by the men from the Cristos garrison, who had capitulated and were escorting the men of Colonel Enrique Zacapa's four platoons in triumph through the town; and Ferdinando came forward and solemnly embraced Colonel Enrique Zacapa, whose face was streaming blood into his smile, and pressed his shattered cheekbone against the shoulder of his uniform so that his breast was ensanguined and smeared with the colonel's heroic blood. Then he took Colonel Enrique Zacapa with him (when the latter flatly refused to ride in the Jeep) and put his other arm around the shoulder of Generalísimo Ottavio Moroque, and walked down the Avenida Quintero de Buiztas toward the Mont Alegre training facility, and when they got there they found that the cadets had opened up the gates, and hung an enormous Mayapanian flag from the porch of the commandant's quarters, and the commandant had put a bullet through the roof of his mouth and the town was theirs.

Ferdinando's actions at that time were characteristic: he declared a general pardon for all those who had fought against his men in the evening's conflict, and offered anyone, enlisted or civilian, the opportunity to leave the town and join the Buiztanista forces in Campeche. Since this was scarcely twenty miles away, and offered scant security—and since the more conservative cynics in Tenabo didn't believe him—there was a less-than-general movement to decamp. So Ferdinando went further: he offered anyone who wanted it safe-conduct out of the area entirely, and furthermore, his personal guarantee that those taking advantage of this noncombative opportunity would have it in no way held against them—their Mayapanian passports would remain valid, their visas intact, and they could return to their homes at any time with no stigma of cowardice or unpatriotic hesitation attaching itself to their names. He was having too much fun to risk people's lives who didn't enjoy the excitement; and so contagious was his fun (although it was called by other names: courage, leadership, and so forth) that most of the Tenabians opted to stay behind him and follow him into Campeche. He posted guards and radioed Carlos Molina in the capital—spread the word to Lejo Costamendez and Nucho Ortega, they would need a general strike in twenty-four hours, Costa trucks to snarl up traffic and government workers out *en masse*, full programming on MAYA-TV (satellite porn movies and Lorcanista slogans, keep the people occupied instead of going to work), get Pisote to handle the telephone company, all communications down but ask her to please refrain from blowing them up as we'll only need them after we've taken over the government. He contacted the second-in-command of the Guardía Civil, Nucho Ortega's brother (and a man he claimed could be trusted), and told him (there was little point in secrecy now) the same terms he'd offered the *militares* in Tenabo: Join us or fight us, but if you fight us you'll risk your men needlessly, and if you join us you'll risk a Quintero de Buiztas last-ditch tantrum-style purge, and if he'd take Dr. Lorca's time-honored prescription he'd lock the doors of the Guardía barracks and counsel his men to play dominoes until the whole change of government had been effected. Major Ortega seemed receptive to the logic of this suggestion, and volunteered to see what he could do. Then Ferdinando drank two thirds of a bottle of rum standing up in the guardroom of the Mont Alegre barracks to try to anesthetize his victor's high, and lay down to sleep for three hours until it was time to begin their final, implacable drive toward the capital.

The next morning, the country was frozen in the snow of a gentle and inexplicable paralysis. Trucks didn't run, and government workers stayed away from their jobs because of attacks of green vomit or unavoidable deaths and illnesses in their families. More than that, the trains and buses didn't operate, cars didn't start (Capitano Profuma was distraught to discover himself stranded six miles out of town at his mistress's house, and he had to hike his way, sweating and swearing like a sailor, over the dirt roads back to the Presidential Palace), and even the passive beasts of burden, horses and oxen and soft-moving, sloe-eyed cows, were rooted to the ground and wouldn't budge; bicycle tires went flat moments after they'd been inflated, and men and women of all occupations found themselves afflicted with boils and bunions, corns, pulled tendons, and sciatic agonies which made walking any distance a virtual impossibility, they were fervently sorry, but given the mess things were in it was just more trouble than it was worth to move. Nor was the country merely immobilized: telephone and telegraph lines were silent, and people experienced a ringing in their ears somewhat akin to tinnitus: in fact, the ringing was rather pleasant, like a carillon of small bells, and went away when they turned on their TV sets and watched the Lorcanista advertisements and the marvelous X-rated movies which were being programmed all day long. The people of Campeche took it as an excuse for a holiday—in fact, their spirits were extraordinarily light when they woke up that morning, and men who had been wearied by love felt a youthful stirring for their wives and sweethearts, and women who had felt themselves overwhelmed by the cares of the day found the time to perfume their bodies and perform acrobatics they'd never before imagined, and children ran out into the street and found all sorts of marvelous things: stray puppies and kittens, toys, vendors of ices and fritters who gave their wares away for free, managers of broken-down circuses and trained animal acts who for no good reason had decided to bring their amusements into the city: because life was short, and it was a beautiful day for a festival.

The Lorcanistas benefited from this euphoria, while being themselves affected by it: Pisote found herself singing as she led a group of commandos into the telephone offices, where they were served coffee and cakes by the all-night operators who had themselves shut down the telephone system, all but a line from the Presidential Palace, which they took turns listening to. Carlos Molina left two technicians to get stoned in master control at MAYA-TV, and himself got on the radio on MAYA-AM/FM and broadcast reports of the rebels' progress toward the capital— all secrecy was abandoned, and the cheering crowds, who were out in the streets anyway, welcomed the anticipated army less as the cause of their celebration than as an excuse for it. The rebels' vehicles, tanks and Jeeps, all of course worked to perfection. Colonel Enrique Zacapa dressed in a beautiful wine-colored gown, and a new soft, flattering wig, and looked very striking despite the bandage on his face; Generalísimo Ottavio Moroque favored Colonel Zacapa's uniform, which was bloodier than his own, bandoleroed with ammunition captured at La Merced, which, it now appeared, they would not need to fire. They collected so many supporters on their twenty-mile march to Campeche that by two o'clock in the afternoon their singing could be heard for miles, hoarse choruses punctuated by fireworks and gunshots into the air, shouted slogans and quotes from the poetry of Porfirio Cheruña and the revolutionary rhetoric of El Lorca. They found a priest, a gentle old man who seemed largely terrified by their approach, and put him up front in the first Jeep with Ferdinando, to show their peaceful intentions and their undiminished respect for the Church. Ferdinando did it because he thought it would make Battiste laugh when he told him about it afterward, and because he was afraid the old man would have a heart attack, trying to follow them on foot—naturally, the mission Jeep which had served the priest faithfully for sixteen years this morning wouldn't work. So he put the trembling old man into the seat next to him, because the elation of the people of Campeche was as nothing compared to his own elation, which rum and exhaustion couldn't mitigate for an instant, and he wanted somebody to share it with, some company, as the people shouted his name and wept and called him liberator; even if it was only for a moment, and part of their euphoria; and part of an hallucination that would pass, as all things would pass, when this the sweetest day in his life was through. Shortly before 4 P.M., when they were still four miles from town and moving at a snail's pace because of the crowds, he received word that there was an even larger crowd approaching the city from the south, and that this crowd of Indians and men and women from the interior was being led by a woman, with the short hair and plain print dress of a *campesina*. Then his heart became agitated with his piercing loneliness, and the remoteness of his spirit which had never known another mate besides her; and he had to resist his desire to leave the parade of his followers and hurry ahead (as she was resisting) because that afternoon belonged to the people who clamored to get close to them, who celebrated without even knowing why it was they were celebrating. As the long rays of sunlight lingered through a day of cool, light breezes, and as twilight drew on they brought out torches and flashlights and (through a sudden miracle at the power company) some of the streetlights came on (although they still couldn't get any electricity into the Presidential Palace) and the people who crowded the streets pushed up onto the sidewalks to allow a path for the Jeeps and trucks to pass, and they headed toward Plaza Columbia, where there was a huge bonfire, made up of governmental leaflets and regulations and all the shit that the Buiztas administration had dumped down on the people for thirty years, and through the haze of smoke and sweat and gasoline Ferdinando caught a glimpse of a slight figure standing on a flatbed truck, guarded by a gaunt man with a long moustache and the high, flat cheeks of a Maya Indian who was holding a machete and appearing almost to threaten the people who struggled to get close to her, to tear her apart with their adulation while she reached down to grasp their hands, kissing them telling them yes she loved them yes while her frail body of a twelve-year-old seemed to shimmer in the seething light of the city's unrestraint, she seemed to disappear and Ferdinando put aside the congratulatory hands which were clapping him on the shoulders, which raised him up on a cushion of cheers from the back seat of the Jeep beside the priest and strangled him with the applause of Put me down, you idiots, and they put him down, and he fought his way to her side and up onto the flatbed truck and stopped Jorge-Julio's machete with his sinewy fingers grasping his wrist, laughing, Stop that, you fool, do you want to run this government by yourself or what? and then fell into the well of darkness of the only love he really wanted in the fragile incandescence which he held clasped tight in his arms while he buried his face against her hair, feeling her heartbeat pumping life back into his body, and her incredible vitality warming him in the shadows of his solitude and the lonely unreality of having won Campeche and everything he'd ever dreamed of grabbing in the world.

seven

BATTISTE ARRIVED IN Campeche the following morning, this time wearing a cassock and bringing with him the elegant white robes and gold scapular which he wore that afternoon for celebrating mass on the steps of Madre de Dios Cathedral for five thousand people, more than the Pope drew when he came to Campeche two years later, with the white hot sun burning down on the soldiers and peasants and mercenaries and Indians of the Lorcanista revolution, whose bloodstained and sweat-grimed faces were caught by television and still cameras and wire-serviced around the world: prize-winning journalism recording the strength and dignity of the Mayapanian people, as lit by Carlos Molina with a script provided by Vatican II. The magical immobility of the city still held, now somewhat formalized by the change in government. In fact this change itself was *de facto*, rather than *de jure*, since all night long, while the Lorcanistas celebrated and burned every memento of the Buiztas regime they could get their hands on, while the Guardía Civil stayed closeted in their barracks, and the ministers of state either hailed the revolutionaries or hid beneath their beds, no one entered the Presidential Palace—which remained dark as a tomb (even after electricity had been restored everywhere else);

guarded by taciturn peasants and Cuban mercenaries who would have fired on anything that moved except nothing moved, not so much as a breath of life stirred the brocade curtains behind the windows of the first-floor salons, or showed between the cracks of the second- and third-story windows, which had been barricaded with steel plates against attack. By seven o'clock the next morning, Ferdinando and Jorge-Julio and Generalísimo Ottavio Moroque and Colonel Enrique Zacapa had had time to bathe, shave, and drink a mug of black coffee apiece, and they decided it was time to pay a call on the ex-Presidente.

The *guardías* who were standing or sitting on the main staircase leading up to the first floor, their weapons halfheartedly ready but their courage and conviction leeched from them by the night's sounds of celebrations from outside, blinked at the invading forces when Ferdinando and his men, a dozen or so officers accompanying him and a hundred more waiting outside, pushed open the heavy white doors and demanded that they give themselves up. One, a skinny lieutenant with the fertile acne of an eighteen-year-old, came forward and rather sheepishly saluted, with one hand, still holding onto his rifle with the other.

"General," he explained, unsure of Ferdinando's title, but deciding to err on the side of flattery, "we'd like very much to surrender, but we've taken an oath to defend the President with our lives, and we would be less than men if we didn't take our words seriously. Can you guarantee us that the man we're guarding is no longer the President of Mayapán?"

Ferdinando cleared his throat (it was the first time he'd had to articulate it formally) and smiled at the young lieutenant as he said, "You have my assurance that the military despot Quintero de Buiztas is no longer President of Mayapán. You are free to act as you wish."

The young lieutenant saluted again, his face wreathed with smiles, and handed Ferdinando his rifle. "In that case, I have the honor to surrender."

The formal rooms, which until recently had swum in the brackish waters of Quintero de Buiztas' suspicions; and the beautiful reception halls, which had been stripped by his terror to the iron-plain necessities of an embattled bunker, were thrown open to the light and air; and as the curtains were pulled and the windows opened one by one, there was the sound of cheering from the massed crowds packed outside the white-painted gates along the Avenida San Cristóbal. They found kitchen workers and laundrywomen, maids and gardeners hiding in the back recesses of the building; and they reassured them that a new age *had* in fact come to Mayapán, when all would be free and no one would have to live in fear. They found not a single committed Buiztan-ista in the building; given the circumstances, self-protection had formed a bond with latent idealism: inside the house of the dicta-tor they were hailed as conquerors. But they found no minotaur inside the labyrinth; Buiztas himself seemed to have disappeared. They made their way to the second floor, and there discovered the contraption out of a black Feydeau farce: the wrought-iron, two-man elevator, plated with bulletproof steel, which Buiztas had had installed as the only method of gaining access to his pri-vate apartments. The elevator was immobilized eight feet off the floor, permanently arrested in flight, and the controls were jammed from above.

Ferdinando burst out laughing. "Gentlemen, I think we've found our quarry. Let's see if we can get this damned thing to work!"

They jimmied it, hit it with their rifle butts, and pried open the wrought-iron cage which encased its gleaming steel interior. Generalísimo Ottavio Moroque finally suggested they use plastic explosives, and they were on the point of trying that when Fer-dinando managed to insinuate his long fingers inside the eleva-tor's wiring system and short-circuit the locking mechanism, starting it with a jolt. They laughed and started the ride up to the third floor, two men at a time, Ferdinando and Jorge-Julio first, the tall, lugubrious Indian still carrying his machete. The elevator let them out in a small antechamber wallpapered in red brocade, with leather furniture that resembled the decorations of a bank; Ferdinando pushed open the heavy oak door, which gave easily with barely a click of the latch, and they found themselves in a long white room, sparely and elegantly furnished, with a desk in front of the balcony at one end, and a tall, heavyset, bearded man sitting behind the desk, looking at them through a pair of steel-rimmed spectacles.

Ferdinando stepped forward into the room. Such was his

vanity, or perhaps his sheer enjoyment of the moment, that he came unarmed—although Jorge-Julio was guarding his flank with his blade and pistol, and Generalísimo Ottavio Moroque and Colonel Enrique Zacapa had arrived via the elevator and were standing, armed with rifles, waiting in the doorway.

"Mr. President," Ferdinando murmured, "I have the honor to inform you that you have resigned your office as of this morning. Please be so good as to come with me."

Quintero de Buiztas' face was impassive: the big, strong features, his unruly beard (shot through with gray, as was his hair, Ferdinando noticed with surprise; and he had not expected the glasses, which gave him a bemused, faintly professorial air). A muscle twitched in the side of his mouth, and they heard a creaking, gritty sound—which was the grinding of his teeth, clenching in the back of his mouth.

Finally he spat—not at Ferdinando, more generally, among the papers on his desk—and said, "Who the fuck gives you the right to be so insolent with me?"

Ferdinando came forward another step, his blue eyes shining, twin blue gas flames in his deeply tanned face, and said, still very quietly, "I'm another son of a bitch, just like you, Mr. President. But if you don't come with me now I'll kill you, and the people will celebrate and even Tio Sam and the Russian Bear won't dare to come forward and accuse me of doing anything wrong."

There was silence in the office for the space of half a minute, while the two men regarded each other. Ferdinando, slim and elegant and whip-hard with his glory and his victory, Buiztas slovenly and rumpled, in his khaki uniform that was actually not that different from the uniform of the rebels—feeling how his nose ached with the pressure of his glasses, and how the savor of life had disappeared since the days when he was a young man and had accepted the leadership of the country from President Ramosa, because he had the worst (or best) sense of humor in the nation. His lips twitched again—this time with honest amusement.

"Very well, if you're honestly committed to being this stupid, there's nothing I can do to talk you out of the actions of a madman. I did the best I could, let everyone here witness."

Then he stood up and took off his sash of the Presidency and took his gun out of his pocket and his knife off his belt and handed them all to Ferdinando in a little pile. Then he stretched his hands up over his head and laughed.

"You doing this to give your little *puta* of a wife a present?"

Because of course there had been a photograph in the morning's newspapers (special edition) showing Ferdinando and Camila embracing like lovers on top of the flatbed truck the night before; and perhaps the dictator Quintero de Buiztas had recognized her as the daughter of his old antagonist Juan dos Santos, because she had the same ethereal look of a burning martyr, which was the look of a crazy idealist, which was the look that he had seen in his dreams of the one who would destroy him and which he could see no trace of, in this handsome, olive-skinned man who stood before him now: who was merely a Westside street-fighter, just like him, so he took a chance and insulted him and when Ferdinando moved to strike him, he stepped in close with a concealed knife and cut him deeply in the side.

Ferdinando's fingers stanched the wound while his other arm went up, blindly, to block Jorge-Julio's machete blow which threatened to split Buiztas' skull. His face was white, but he managed to smile because no, it would spoil the victory if they killed Buiztas like this. He was a *macho* himself, and he was scarcely kind, but he knew that the greatest insult they could offer this *macho* dictator would be his ignominious life, spared for him in the perfect contempt of their clemency. He wasn't about to deny himself that pleasure.

"I shouldn't have put on my clean uniform," he managed to joke. "Now I'll just have to put on another one."

He grinned and deliberately refused to allow the occasion to become melodramatic, steadfastly maintaining that he had not been hurt that badly (and in fact the wound proved to be comparatively minor). Perhaps Buiztas has intended it as such: he laughed bitterly as he was being led away, and said something like "You'll need four more, in your hands and feet, but don't worry, the job will give them to you," but they couldn't tell for sure because he was laughing too hard. They brought him downstairs (all three of them, crowding into the tiny elevator) and drove him away in an old Alliance for Progress van, across the stenciled handshake of which had been spray-painted the letters of the Frente Lorcanista de la Liberación de Mayapán, and for the whole drive to the Miramar Prison he was still laughing.

So Ferdinando attained power—and immediately gave it up, to a civilian/military junta, who convened a national convention. They refurbished the dusty phrases of the Mayapanian constitution and called for national elections, which the Lorcanistas were certain of winning, but El Lorca wanted the legitimacy of very visible elections to scotch the rumor that he was communist-backed or United States-backed, or backed by anything beyond the invisible support of Linz Industries, which guaranteed him a landslide victory. There followed a disjointed time, best symbolized by the black-and-white photographs that appeared daily in the world's newspapers, the color photos that appeared in *Time* magazine and *Newsweek*, the televised tableaux which were beamed around the world: El Lorca and his wife, standing on the balcony outside of Buiztas' study, he in his newly bloodied uniform (with his ribs taped) and she in a variant on the Lorcanista khaki, trousers but a white shirt; Ferdinando and Camila (the image was repeated constantly) raising their arms above their heads, hands clasped and smiles flashing. Ferdinando alone, as he drank the cheers of the people that night, shirt-sleeved as a civilian (read: as a political candidate), standing on the steps of Constitución Hall, where the most perceptive observers could notice the phenomenon that became so striking later on, his transformation from a man apart to a man of the people, smiling and affable: light-filled as Lucifer. Camila (observed only by Battiste) slightly removed from the chaos of those next few days—slightly distracted, looking up startled when Ferdinando called to her, and her smile bloomed, slightly bemused (as though she watched a separate reality, beautiful? or frightening?), freezing suddenly when the people's cheers seized her, that night on the balcony of the Presidential Palace—before her terror melted, in compassion, in resignation: tears sparkling in her light-blue eyes while she stretched out her arms to all of them, accomplished, expert at extracting and prolonging their adoration.

Naturally, they won—the Lorcanista delegates sweeping the legislature and Ferdinando Lorca elected by an unprecedented majority (some of the Lorcanista leaders were enjoined to vote for the other candidates, to avoid too suspicious a mandate). Ferdinando took the oath of office, like the American Presidents, out of doors, standing with Camila on the wide marble steps of Constitución Hall while the president of the Chamber of Deputies administered the oath and pinned the quadricolored sash across his breast: a slender, intense, attractive man in a business suit, sweat barely beading his upper lip, while his impacted followers below him streamed perspiration and waved flags and cheered.

Then they held a lavish inaugural ball—which lasted all night, with thousands of guests and two full orchestras providing continuous music; a guest list which included the American Vice President, the Russian Deputy Premier, fourteen film stars, and sixty-eight foreign ambassadors: the entire Presidential Palace thrown open to the balmy air of the night and the steel window-plates discarded, and *guardías* dressed in smart, new white uniforms, armed with ornamental dress swords, and allowed to alternate in two-hour shifts so they could enjoy the party. Generalísimo Ottavio Moroque came in his own new white uniform, his chest covered with medals, and maintained a stern demeanor, even when murmuring obscenities to the young *guardía* who'd been appointed his personal bodyguard. Colonel Enrique Zacapa came ostensibly as his date: the beautiful Doña Rosario Zacapa, and danced a waltz with the Russian Deputy Premier before the latter found out that he'd been whispering Slavic endearments to a transvestite war hero. Carlos Molina showed up in a full-dress tuxedo, with his long hair tied back with a black ribbon, and no shoes and socks on his feet. Pisote wore a long red gown, which left her shoulders bare; a ruby necklace that had been in her family for three generations, and which as a fervent socialist she'd always pretended to scorn; and a tumble of white gardenias (a gift from Ferdinando, his smile piercing her along with his casual joke, that he couldn't give her a medal, not in that dress, as there'd be no place for him to pin it on). Don Luis García Mores was back from Los Angeles with a perforated ulcer, from worrying about his TV station, and spent the evening drinking milk. Nucho Ortega was there with his brother, now commandant of the Guardía Civil, and surprised everyone by outshining Señor Lejo Costamendez in seducing a voluptuous

Italian film star, leaving with her in her Fiat before the second round of toasts had been exchanged.

Ferdinando and Camila and Battiste had a private drink upstairs, in Quintero de Buiztas' study, before going downstairs at the beginning of the evening.

"So, what do we do now?" Battiste joked, sipping sherry, while he sat in one of the big, soft gray chairs that Ferdinando had had installed in the long white room, softening the impression of classical rigidity further with thick white carpeting and pearl-gray curtains, the latter open onto the balcony to let in the warm night breeze and the sounds of music from downstairs, laughter and fireworks and louder music from the streets outside. Ferdinando and Camila sat in the two other chairs, and by inclination was well as policy, they had left the lights out, to avoid drawing a crowd to stand below the window and cheer.

"It feels good to relax and savor the moment of victory, let's not spoil it with *gringo* Puritan ethics." Ferdinando smiled, and reached out to touch his wife's hand. "Tomorrow we'll roll up our sleeves and get to work, I promise you. Camila and I have already thought of more reforms than the legislature can handle."

"I wouldn't be surprised. What are you going to do with Buiztas?"

"I'm not sure. Feed him to the sharks, or keep him imprisoned in La Miramar on public display? I may very well let him go, he's a *corazón* with no teeth anymore, he shouldn't be that big a threat to public safety!"

He sipped his martini, laughing. "Alfred Linz sent us his regrets, and six cases of his Nazi wine! I told him I was going to serve sugar with it!"

He had to stop and explain the joke to Battiste, who was slightly disconcerted by his nonchalance. Warm and gentle, Ferdinando stood up and rather formally bent and kissed his friend on both cheeks, startling him more than he had intended.

"Why did you do that?" he asked him, blushing despite all his strength and his newfound, Washington-bred sophistication, which still couldn't control the heartbeat that leapt like a physical reaction, like a jolt of electricity, through his chest.

"Because I felt like it. Didn't anyone tell you that I'm the President now, and can do what I like—and because this victory belongs to all of us, my friend, all three of us in this room, and *this* is my inauguration—here, with the two of you?"

It was a lovely sentiment—and Camila smiled, wondering to herself if he meant it. Like all good actors, he had the power to be convinced by his own rhetoric. They touched their glasses, tall, awkward Battiste in his black cassock, holding his glass in his big, strong fingers, wishing good luck to his friends with a lump in his throat; and Camila suddenly felt sorry for him and kissed his cheek too, brief, fleeting touch which still reminded him of the kiss of a holy child, even though she wore lipstick and her slender body was radiant in a long white iridescent sheath, with diamonds at her ears and her throat and her fingers. She knew better than to prolong the contact, so she laughed, slipping her arm through the priest's, on the one side, and taking her husband's arm (Ferdinando, her husband; who was the President of Mayapán) on the other, and they went downstairs, and the orchestra played the Mayapanian national anthem, and she and Ferdinando danced, and there were a profusion of well-wishers and popping flashbulbs which left an incandescent glitter in the back of her mind and somewhere in the confusion she touched the icy fingers and loose parchment flesh of a wicked old man, who was there as a national monument, of course he would be there, Porfirio, and she trembled with a terrible pulse-leap like a sledgehammer, betraying her as she turned toward him with her heart in her face her bowels turning to water drowning with love as she always had . . . but it wasn't him, it was another man, who kissed her hand and murmured, "Señora Lorca, allow me to present the felicitations of my government."

And so she fled from him, down the corridors of smiling diplomats and through the shoals of flattering attachés to the strains of the music to Ferdinando, who turned to her and realized with immediate concern that something was wrong, What is it, can't you tell me? And who then smiled at her with his shining blue eyes and took her outside, to the long columned porch of the Presidential Palace, where the cheers of the people met them like a blow with the concentrated love of a million souls for the beautiful couple whom they would love forever and ever, and she gave herself up to the delirium of love, and the commencement of a shimmering, hallucinatory dream.

III.
The Chac Mool

one

THE NEXT MORNING, it began—the years of working, of carving a brilliant, modern state out of the miasma of the primeval jungle, and the eventual decline: from their bright dreams to the lesser but still extraordinary reality: Mayapán, with a strong (albeit mortgaged) economy, and a secure and (apparently) democratic government. Ferdinando Lorca called a meeting of his closest advisers and key Mayapanian citizens for nine o'clock on the morning after his inaugural ball—when everyone was hung over, and many arrived still wearing the rumpled party clothes that they'd napped in for an hour or two at most: but everyone showed up, by eight-thirty, assembling in the long public reception room on the first floor of the Presidential Palace, which had been turned into a conference room, with a long table and plenty of chairs—and they found food and drink thoughtfully provided, hair-of-the-dog tequila and coffee and scrambled eggs, and Campeche sweet pastries, piping hot—and precisely at nine o'clock Ferdinando came in without any fanfare, dressed in a plain dark suit and carrying a briefcase and a cup of black coffee, and sat down at the head of the table, saying in his quiet, carrying voice, "Gentlemen, let's get to work."

For the next three hours, they unraveled the tangled mass of duplicity and sloth in which the Buiztas tyranny had enmeshed the government, working so well that by the noon hour the outlines of a competent and practical regime began to be visible through the surrounding silt of bureaucratic debris. Ferdinando led the discussion as he had conducted his seminars at Columbia, thoughtfully smoking a cigarette, writing an occasional note down on a yellow pad: saying little, but guiding the conversation so that each one of his informants was given an opportunity to shine—and incidentally to tell the thoughtful, attentive President all he knew about his particular area of expertise. Nucho Ortega described the low-level bureaucratic organization of the government; Dr. Imeldo de Rogua, the gray-haired, wealthy patriarch of the Mayapanian cabinet, where he had held the post of Minister of Finance for twenty-eight years as a personal fiefdom inherited from his father, outlined the upper-level pecking order which had been allowed to develop, more or less at random, during thirty years of neglect at the public trough. It was a pecking order Ferdinando intended to abolish, but he heard the old man through in respectful silence, as he heard Admiral Ramirez on the state of the Mayapanian Navy (Admiral Ramirez who, like the Ruler of the Queen's Navee, had never been to sea, and who owed his nautical appointment, so wags said, to his having successfuly navigated the oceans of his own alcoholism for the better part of six decades). Felix Innocencio Agudo spoke, briefly and precisely, about the state of the nation's economy; as president of Mayapán's largest bank, the well-dressed, superficially casual Agudo had a power only slightly less than Ferdinando's own, and during the course of his succinct remarks the two men took the measure of each other's character, and decided they could do business. Agudo smelled the Linz money on Ferdinando, and Ferdinando was amused and respectful of Agudo's predator's instinct. When the banker had finished his report, he stood up and bowed politely to the new chief executive; Ferdinando thought there was a twinkle in his eye.

"Excuse me, Señor Presidente, but if the other gentlemen will pardon me, I have urgent business to attend to back at my bank."

Ferdinando inclined his head. "Certainly, Señor Agudo, we

can understand your hurry. Please feel free to drop in anytime. This office is always open to you."

Agudo smiled and, picking up his briefcase and notes, quietly left the conference room. There was a slight ripple of conversation following him; it had been a small show of favoritism, requested and indulged, in allowing the bank president to leave early. More to the point, the conferees had the distinct impression that El Presidente's office was *not* going to be open to everyone, and that he was deliberately informing them of the intention of his government to favor private investment, the exploitation of the oil resources in particular, over other concerns in the first months of his administration.

Ferdinando allowed them a moment, nicely timed, to receive that impression—and then spoke again, mildly, as he turned over the next sheaf of papers in front of him. "Señor Agudo is a man in a hurry." He smiled. "Perhaps it's his new wife—*la estrella* Juanita Marquez is, I am told, a very beautiful woman, and quite demanding of a man's most assiduous attentions. We must make allowances for these little things."

Since everyone there knew that El Presidente's own wife was beautiful and young, his joke was doubly barbed, as he had intended it to be, catching his own vanity with Felix Agudo's, and putting everyone at his ease. His next words shattered them.

"Gentlemen, apropos our finances, I've decided I can no longer afford all of you. Oh, don't be concerned—everyone dismissed will be found jobs in the private sector, but our little country has always taken the easy way out in terms of padding the payroll, and now we're going to have to learn to do it less obviously, like civilized countries. Since I'm not in a position yet to judge your relative merits—being, as it were, a newcomer to your estimable society—I'm going to give each of you a chance to shit or get off the pot: either you'll have your staffs cut by one third, by this time Monday morning, or I'll be forced to cut them for you—which I'll do, I might add, working from the top down. Now—" He paused, and lit another cigarette, smiling at them all gently, his vivid blue eyes nailing them to their seats around the table. "With all these newly unemployed relatives and girl friends, I propose to organize a department of land redistribution, to begin at once, breaking up the big *estancias* and giving small tracts of land back to the *campesinos*. This is going to provoke an outcry, comparable to five hundred oligarchs being gang-raped in a men's privy, so our next order of business is to find a way to grease our prong so it slides in easily and doesn't provoke any traumas. Any suggestions?"

There was dead silence around the table—since most of the cabinet members were themselvess *hacendados*, pinned to embarrassed silence by his deft use of a metaphor, unable to protest. Finally Nucho Ortega cleared his throat, smoothing his little blond beard nervously with his fingertips.

"We—we could pay them," he suggested, wincing as he said it, as if he expected to be struck for offering such an outlandish proposition. But Ferdinando merely nodded thoughtfully.

"I was considering that, but I don't know that even *my* investors have quite enough capital for *that* on hand." He spoke the words easily, "my investors," and placidly didn't elaborate. "The landowners are in a position to name any price they choose, and if we don't meet it, they can cry communism and emigrate *en masse* to Miami. Alternatively, of course, I could throw them out—save everybody the trouble of bargaining, since the net result would be the same, don't you agree? What's your opinion of that policy, gentlemen? Nationalization—it's simple, it saves time—and in the short run, at least, it's always enormously popular."

"But—" Dr. Imeldo de Rogua had gone the color of a duck's egg, and looked as if he were about to end his life right there at the conference table. "But that's unconscionable—the very people who supported the Lorcanistas, brought them to power—"

"Would undoubtedly applaud the carnival of the landowners, unseated by *my* revolutionary government . . . no, gentlemen, I'm no Castro, and I don't think even our friend Fidel would follow the same course of action today as he once embraced. My idea was to offer the *hacendados* large sums of money—as well as tax exemptions, favorable interest rates, et cetera—if they would take us, the government, into business as a kind of a silent partner. No coercion would be used: the landowners would be free to refuse, but their profit margins would be cut and their edge in the free market lessened by their unwillingness to go along with an incentive offered to their competitors. We, for our part, would apportion tracts of land to the *campesinos*, as well as development grants, long-term loans at low interest rates merely to keep the system solvent . . . I have some figures here which I think should clarify the general lines of my idea . . ."

And he handed around copies of a twelve-page document, neatly bound in clear plastic courtesy of Linz Industries, and pushed his chair back from the table and stood up.

"Gentlemen, I think that'll be all for this morning. I want some lunch, and you look as if you could all use some aspirin: there's some in a bottle on the sideboard, please help yourselves on your way out. Oh—" He turned at the door. "I'll be meeting with the American O.A.S. ambassador all afternoon, but please feel free to submit your responses to this plan to my offices to-night, I'll look them over tomorrow morning. If I don't hear from you, I'll assume you approve of the general direction of my thinking. Gentlemen, I'll see you all at nine o'clock next Mon-day."

That was how Ferdinando began his administration, with hospitality and aspirin for the oligarchs whose inherited power he intended to smash; and he kept it up, and kept his promises—to himself as well as to others—and didn't allow himself to fall into the twin traps of ruthlessness and melodrama, even while he was pruning the bureaucracy and granting the peasants the first dignity and freedom they'd had in their lives. With Camila and Battiste at his side, his unofficial vice-president and secretary of state, he began to make first tentative, then more rapid progress in alleviating the country's suffering—supplying housing for the victims of the earthquake, and nationalizing Buiztas Enterprises; instituting his program of land reform, and offering health and hope and the charisma of his own persona—something to believe in, a little joy in everyone's life. In those days he and Camila were always available, to the humblest *peón* and the most exalted *ha-cendado*, with a refreshing zest that came of their doing a job they really liked: it came to be said with admiration that the Lorcas worked for the people the way the *campesinos* worked in the fields, but that wasn't strictly true—the Lorcas were having a great deal more fun. Whether they were promoting tourism in Mayapán ("Isn't it time you came to worship our sun?") or set-ting up the Mayapanian Health Organization, the first charitable organization in Mayapán not conceived as a monument to ineptitude and graft, they communicated their enthusiasm to their subordinates with a directness of affection so appealing that the lowest government functionary was imbued with a sense of patriotic purpose—and indeed, patriotism itself began to stir in the arid hearts of the poor and the rich alike, for the first time in Mayapanian memory; and cynical radicals and major thugs like Lejo Costamendez wept like schoolchildren whenever they heard the national anthem, and during the first term of Ferdinando Lorca's Presidency the membership of the Mayapanian Communist Party and the Movimiento Nacional Socialista de Mayapán dropped by nearly one third.

Tentative, and then more rapid progress: free clinics in the provinces, the legal guarantee of rights for the peasants and the Indians, votes for women, the opening up of the National University (closed for a decade), and the establishment of scholarships for gifted students were all achieved during the first year of Ferdinando Lorca's government. The country, which had slumbered banana-joked through the news media in the thirties and forties, and which had then gouted, bloodstained, on the back pages of *The New York Times,* slipped back into a deliberate obscurity until the Lorcas had finished putting their house in order. Thus Mayapán was heard from sporadically and, for the most part, dully: land redistribution had brought the ratio of land ownership to population up 26 percent, and the G.N.P. up 38 percent; Amnesty International reported a significant drop in human rights violations (despite the residual carping of committed leftists like the communist student Martín Acchuirez, who ran a radical newspaper), and the Vatican scheduled a bishops' conference in Campeche as a significant sign of goodwill.

This was Battiste's doing, and what was not revealed at that time was that he himself had declined an appointment as Archbishop of Campeche, in favor of a candidate of his choosing. Tall and rawboned, his earlier fat pared to an ascetic leanness that gave his stark, pockmarked face a haunted, ugly grandeur, he had become a major figure in Mayapanian politics as El Lorca's second-in-command, as well as the preeminent power in the Mayapanian Church. El Lorca's instrument: but a man of scrupulous honesty, brilliant, learned, adept at conversational diplomacy.

The Vatican looked, and noted, and the aging Superior General of the Jesuits—a man whose thoughts were revealed to no one—offered him the archbishopric knowing he would turn it down to become instead, in the fall of that year, the Mayapanian ambassador to Washington: because the Church could take its time wooing such a gifted son away from his secular attachments.

And throughout the first two years of the Lorcanista Presidency, there were occasional hints of the glamour that was to come: mentions of La Señora Lorca in the fashion magazines, in November a four-page article in *People* (Camila, radiant in a Givenchy cloud of black satin, at a performance at the Montejo Opera House, and Camila in a man's tuxedo, with two-carat diamonds in her ears, entertaining the Saudi Arabian ambassador . . . Camila at her desk, with her hair brushed back, smiling . . . Camila in a bathing suit). In February Ferdinando granted an exclusive interview to *Playboy,* in which he discussed his theories of government (capitalist *laissez-faire* joined with calculated praise for U.S.-style democracy) and his favorite sports (swimming and polo, he and Camila had decided, dying with laughter, the night before. Fortunately, *Playboy* didn't ask for pictures of him at practice). His slender, aquiline features serious behind half-frame glasses, he presented an aspect of sober dedication, seated behind his desk . . . Camila and Battiste, Pisote and Jorge-Julio all knew with what suddenness that serious and somewhat grave demeanor could be transformed by his delighted smile when any of them came into the room. He was elegantly handsome, tuxedoed and smiling, in photographs with Camila; he was occasionally caught in candid poses, as once, laughing at dinner in a Campeche restaurant with Camila and Pisote; and he was never seen in either combat fatigues or a military uniform (unlike Colonel Enrique Zacapa and Generalísimo Ottavio Moroque) but always in a dark suit, hand-tailored by Dimitri of Italy, of which he owned ten, all in modulated shades of gray and blue.

But in those early years, Mayapán went relatively unnoticed, a mud-jungled tropical exile for dipsomaniacal foreign correspondents, who could write about the new El Señor Presidente without having to stop writing about the old (because Quintero de Buiztas remained alive and well, as a semipermanent resident of

La Miramar Prison). The Lorcas entered into a secret agreement with UNOCO Oil, whereby certain sums would be loaned to the country, under condition of certain rights being held in perpetuity by the aforesaid company whose representative, senior vice-president in charge of Latin America, Charlie Cox, flew down to Campeche in Alfred Linz's private jet to clinch the deal. They negotiated a loose, unpublicized tax shelter for MPE Communications, and shortly thereafter the entertainment conglomerate moved its prestigious Ocho Ríos recording studios from Kingston to Campeche, forming an umbrella company which came to be known as MixTech Studios. They wooed new talent—artists and architects, playwrights and poets—ferried into the jungle by the twin inducements of public funds and the massive canvas of an emerging nation on which to create their art. Among them was a young Japanese video artist named Isadore Ikemoda, who arrived from a position as resident consultant to the Misaki Corporation, and became the driving force behind MixTech Studios.

Because of his vision, and the vision of the Lorcas in putting their government and their private resources behind him, Mayapán in the span of a few years became a modest competitor in the explosive field of micro-electronics, while the majority of its people were still unable to read. He became as well the driving force behind the creation of the pop-iconographic myth of the Lorcas themselves as superstars: creating the dizzying barrage of video and film images, posters, graphics on every street corner showing the serene, smiling face of La Señora and the handsome, thoughtful visage—fingers propping a lean cheek, eyes mid-distance—of El Señor Presidente, which culminated in the vast, sixty-foot portrait of Ferdinando and Camila Lorca which came to dominate the Plaza Columbia in the fourth year of their first administration.

Oil made the Lorcas, as it made Mayapán, in its own image: dirty and fluid, drawing on an immemorial past to power a world still afraid of the future, fission and fusion, sunlight and nuclear holocaust. Ferdinando and Camila were part of its power, and so Mayapán flourished, as a small but vital link in the unpublicized profit-sharing that was sealing the fate of the superpowers. They succeeded in all things, save for a slight and disconcerting failure in the area of their cultural renaissance: because despite all their coolly voiced blandishments and their half-hearted requests that he return to Campeche, the world-famous poet Porfirio Cheruña refused to return to his native land and lend his public support to the new Mayapanian democracy: refused in fact to have anything to do with them, despite the fact that this hurt his sales (slightly) in Campeche, and disappointed the new Mayapanian public that was even then rediscovering his work.

In November of the Lorcas' second year in power, the Americans elected a President who shared their vision: an alumnus of the N.F.L., where he had been the highest-paid quarterback in the history of the Los Angeles Rams. In his post-football years, Duncan Farrell had gone into business, studied law, and become part owner of a fast-food chain called Krispy's, which had featured in its day a racist chicken with the slogan voice-bubbled, "Sho nuff good!" The chicken was gone, and Farrell in his midsixties was close-cropped and blond, a born-again capitalist and a muscular Christian with a Chamber of Commerce mentality and all the charm of ten years' experience doing shaving ads. His main principle of foreign and domestic policy was to give free enterprise free rein: in the first years of his administration, production of cars, rockets, satellites, and nuclear weapons was up 100 percent, and he looked on the pro-business attitude of Mayapán with approval. Indeed, as Alfred Linz remarked drily regarding the charming American President: "If Duncan Farrell hadn't been created by God, it would have been necessary for Linz Industries to invent him"—but he was a surprisingly canny and subtle politician, and Ferdinando treated him with respect: negotiating small treaties; signaling his willingness to compromise; resisting the twin lures of offensiveness and toadying; and waiting until Mayapán was strong enough to make use of his one-track enthusiasm for the profit motive to put him on their side.

Which happened—amazingly, it happened. Mayapán *did* become a modern state, one of the major oil-producing nations in the world, striving for the so-called goods of the modern age in a land which had once belonged to the gods and the chac mools and the timeless and secretive jungle. That was Ferdinando Lorca's gift to Mayapán: along with shouts of Here's to El Señor Presidente! Here's to the one who's done it all! The savior of his country, and one of the policy makers of the world, like Kennedy or

Castro. Ferdinando and Camila. The father and mother of their country, under the protection of the biggest military-industrial complex in history. The media stars of their generation, in one of the rare instances of two people being as good as their myths. Ferdinando and Camila. El Presidente and his wife, who comported themselves like lovers. Creating utopia in the mess of Central America, and a modern world in a place where, according to every rule in history, it should never have existed in a million years.

two

CAMILA DOS SANTOS LORCA (1957–1991) was First Lady of Mayapán for thirteen years, years of serenity and turmoil and the rapid lunacy of the world at the end of time, and throughout she conducted herself with the exemplary dignity and fleeting loveliness that characterized every moment of her life. She was never more radiant than at that time, never more adored by her husband and by her country than for the thirteen years when she was their spiritual figurehead and their major representative throughout the world, and after her death there was no single, clear memory of her—everyone possessed fragments, bits and pieces of a legend which was always contradicted by the presence of the beautiful, elusive woman who inspired it.

Battiste had been right in anticipating in her a born politician. She was charming, endlessly patient with the tedium of diplomacy, and adept at hiding her feelings with the skill of an accomplished actress and the candor of an ingenuous child. Adept too at the management of her time, for she kept as grueling a schedule as Ferdinando, with three offices in the city as director of the Mayapanian Health Organization, director of tourism, and executive director of MixTech Studios.

She and Ferdinando rose at 5 A.M., when the sun was just

fading the waves gilding beyond the seawall, filling the crevices of their enormous room in the Presidential Palace with its ridiculous bed of a viceregal governor with light, painting the watercolor strangeness of their beautiful life together in the pastel colors of another day. By six o'clock, when the sun was already warming the rosebushes outside the side door of the Presidential Palace, the trim, slender figure who stepped into the Presidential limousine was La Señora Lorca, immaculate, and authority incarnate.

Yet she was always playing off of her authority, incapable of sustaining any pose for long. It was her major fault as a political leader in her own right, a position she always shied from, skittishly uncomfortable with power. Sometimes she drove her own car, or one of Ferdinando's: he had six Mercedes, of varying vintages; she teased him about collecting automobiles like a little boy. She wired each of her offices, and played tapes of loud music for the annoyance and/or delectation of her staff; she surprised them with birthday presents, flowers, baskets of fruit when they were in the hospital, but she could just as easily forget that they were human, that they needed sleep, lunch hours, they needed to go home . . . and working for her they forgot these things as well, their tasks were great honors, and even many years later they spoke with awe of their daily contact with La Senōra Lorca, her wit, her sparkle, her carelessness with her own mystique, the abstraction which would suddenly fill her enormous blue eyes, as she stared at them blankly, in wonder, as if they were no longer there.

She still had accesses of her bizarre visions (nightmares in broad daylight, heady beauty mingled with the pain) but she had learned without consciously thinking about it to forget these brief interruptions . . . to think of them *as* interruptions, in fact; momentary headaches or cloudings of her vision (and she had them too). Pressed about it (and sometimes the devoted members of her staff *did* press her, Senōra, what is it, are you ill, are you just daydreaming?), she would laugh her marvelous laugh and shake her head, No, it's nothing, La Senōra is just crazy, that's all, didn't you know that? And she believed it herself . . . perhaps she was a little crazy, a slight chemical imbalance or the pressures which had been put on her in her youth (she smiled wryly when she considered them). I suppose I really should have gone mad, the percentages were certainly in that direction. She rarely spent more than a few moments on such morbid thoughts: her parents, her cloistered youth, and the horrors with Porfirio ... there were too many things to consider, too much to be done.

At 7 A.M. in the M.H.O. offices on the Avenida Cortés (bright-colored posters on the walls explaining hygiene and the practice of birth control, over Battiste's objections), Camila dealt with organizational minutiae so that by nine o'clock they could throw open the doors of the old mansion, which still smelled of bougainvillea and printer's ink, to petitioners and patients, many of whom saw the twelve resident doctors there as the first medical practitioners in their lives. Afternoons were split between the offices of MixTech Studios and the Mayapanian Tourist Board: learning media skills at the one, and applying them at the other. She had fun with the travel copy, which was submitted to her for approval: "Come visit Mayapán ... where can you find so much for so little?" which made her pencil her query across the top of the page: "Where else can you make fun of so many people who *have* so little? Let's not rub it in!" "Mayapán, the lure of the old, the magic of the new," which elicited her suggestion "Until we've actually built some new hotels, let's keep this magic of the new stuff to a minimum." And her favorite one, "Four hundred years ago, Cortés fell in love with our country! You will too!" which made her scrawl across the top of the typewritten page, "Four hundred years ago Cortés was nearly *shot* in our country, and went on to Mexico. Are you trying to give the *turistas* any ideas?"

Always her mind leapfrogged to the information that was the most vital, synthesizing and coordinating among her many responsibilities, and drawing the best minds in the nation to her side. She had the genius of a businesswoman, or a soldier, in keeping her eye on the final objective ... and all this so lightly, with such seeming ease, that it was inconceivable that she had not been doing this all her life, managing millions of pesos and hundreds of people marshaled to the higher authority of her husband and her country, which to her mind were patently the same thing. Battiste, who ought to have known her strengths better than anybody, was amazed at her skill and her grace: and working so closely with her, he felt all his old love and resentment and protective, hopeless jealousy coming to the fore. So he ran away from her—from both of them—in accepting the appointment as the Mayapanian ambassador to the new "football" president in Washington.

Ferdinando may have had that thought in mind, when he offered him the chance to escape, and at the same time to advance his natural ambitions. Caught up in the social rivalries and gossip of a city to which he was certainly no stranger, he came to know Washington now as a fascinated (and fascinating) insider: Father Battiste Tommassi ... who was an ordained Jesuit priest, and who wasn't above wearing his dog collar when it could win him points in a Capitol Hill argument, or a table at the Lion d'Or ... who was an expert on French wines, stocking the embassy with a mythic collection (two hundred? two thousand bottles?) and sharing it with his guests at lavish embassy receptions ... Father Battiste, who generally dressed in the impeccable style of El Presidente, but who could be seen occasionally on the towpath in Rock Creek Park, in shorts and jogging shoes (Q: What color sneakers does the ambassador from Mayapán wear? A: White. He's in training to be Pope). Father Battiste ... who had refused to hear the confession of an undisclosed Kennedy, claiming it would be a conflict of interest. An artist at the difficult game of gaining and supplying access (Q: Who doesn't want to go to one of Father Battiste's "little" dinner parties? A: The President. He's the only *other* man in Washington who has access to everyone). He played tennis as a guest at the Chevy Chase Club, and hosted a glittering dinner party before the Meridian House Ball, which was memorable for fourteen guests having such a good time that they stayed on at the embassy, and sent their aides to the ball in their stead. And he was beloved by Washington hostesses, as much for his tact as for his wit, and though he couldn't believe it, for his looks as well: for he had a touch-me-not reserve and a pale asceticism which went well with his sophistication and his poise, a painful shyness coupled with his education and a brilliant mind, all of which did nothing to alleviate the core of misery in his heart, which looked out with anguished sadness from his dark-brown eyes, and pulled tight lines around the corners of his lips.

So he ran away from her for three years: and she followed him, but in an official capacity, on a visit as a head of state to the White House. It was an invitation which was long overdue, and when it was finally extended, the Lorcas waited another six months before making the arrangements. Regrettably, El Presidente Lorca himself could not attend, being involved just then in the wage disputes of the chicle workers ... but La Presidenta Lorca would be delighted to accept the kind invitation of El Presidente Farrell, as part of an anticipated U.S. tour ... Father Battiste Tommassi would coordinate the arrangements through their embassy, for La Presidenta to remain at Blair House ... secret service personnel ... a visit to New York first (Camila wanted to buy some new clothes) ... and a state dinner on October 27 at the White House. Camila flew to New York for a week and took Battiste with her, a forced vacation for the ambassador in which he rediscovered the beautiful daughter he thought he had lost: chaperoning her through Bloomingdale's and Fiorucci's, having lunch with her at Le Cygne and Le Cirque (mobbed with reporters), and feeling his head spin with unreality as she asked him to hold, and later give his opinion on, emerald and diamond necklaces at Tiffany's. (Holding upward of one million dollars' worth of jewels in his hands, he alone caught her whisper in Mayapanian, "We can't afford any of these, but it doesn't do any harm to scare the American First Lady into wearing all *her* jewels! I shall shine in my simplicity by comparison, and save our treasury a small fortune!")

Her shining simplicity was an off-the-shoulder Halston gown of shimmering cream silk, worn with a single strand of pearls to accent her white skin, and an enormous, square-cut diamond ring on her left hand (the President asked her over dinner whether it was an engagement ring, and she smiled at him while she explained that for the six hours of her formal engagement she had been wanted by the police). She dressed in Blair House, standing at the window for a moment in the falling twilight to look at the *norteamericanos'* Presidential Palace across the street (floodlit and postcard effective) and turned at the knock on the door to say "Come in" without any thought of who it might be, secret service platoons to the contrary, because she was calmly unafraid, poised and pleasantly excited about the evening, and Battiste came into the room and kissed her hands.

"You look marvelous." He smiled. "The Presidente is going to make a pass at you."

"Do you think so?"

"I can't imagine any man under ninety who wouldn't." He prevaricated. "Besides, they say he has little in common with his wife. She's very plain—and doesn't like football."

"Well, I don't know anything about football." Camila smiled. "Do you suppose he'll mind? He was a very big star."

"He was also a Rhodes Scholar with a degree from Cornell. He's not a fool."

"Oh, no Presidente is a fool." Camila laughed. "It's like business, it merely makes some men look foolish."

She bent to the bed to pick up a long wrap of white mink, absolutely stunning, she wrapped herself in it with a laugh, twirling around like an ad for something, Battiste didn't know what, something outrageously expensive and elegantly sinful and he stepped up to her laughing and put his arm around her waist, and was transfixed by his feelings—delirium and shame, which of course she read like a book because she had always understood his emotions, better than he himself did. So she stood absolutely still, while his fingers for a moment felt the soft warm curve of her waist, and the blood suffused his face and left it as pale as a ghost's, and she felt the pain in him as he fought not to draw her to him, and he, the watchful care with which she did *not* move to withdraw from him, although her body had become taut and defensive with his first light touch. So they stood there for a moment, both scarcely breathing, until Battiste shut his eyes and murmured, "It's too much, it's got to be too much, I can't bear it," and she said with almost inaudible precision, "You've got to bear it, now take your hand off me, please," and he did take his hand off her and turned and walked to the window, a lonely man in a black suit and a white collar, pressing the back of his hand against his lips to keep them from trembling.

After a moment he reached in his pocket and said, "I've got a letter for you, it came to the embassy yesterday while we were in New York," and he took it out of his pocket and handed it to her, still not turning around to look at her.

214

She knew immediately who it was from, even as she looked at the spidery-thin handwriting that she should have remembered, even without knowing the hands that had written it. She found herself turning away toward the peach-shaded lamp like a sleepwalker, smoothly and gracefully, tearing open the seal as if she were reading any letter without giving away by the slightest word or tremor the consternation that was knocking like a sledgehammer at her heart. The letter was a single sheet, of light-blue, parchment-textured paper. *"Querida.* The moment when you and I could have been strangers was passed by years ago, and the persistence of your avoidance of me is something I find both incomprehensible and intolerable. Come to me at once. You know that there is that between us which can never be shared, and you know, if you have not lost all your honesty, that you will always want to be with me. Porfirio." She shut her eyes, feeling sick waves of warm moist air playing over her body. She shook her head. Battiste's voice cut through the periphery of her nightmare without dispelling it completely, quiet and striving for a conversational tone.

"Who's it from?"

"Nobody." She said it quickly, crumpling the letter up and dropping it in the trash. She was very white, and Battiste, turning finally away from his anguished contemplation of the White House to look at her, thought that his behavior of a few moments previously was to blame for it.

"Come," he whispered. "The Americans are always impatient. They hate to be kept waiting."

As they walked downstairs to the limousine he murmured, "The most important thing is the Taft-Grijalva Treaty," the trade agreement which they hoped to renegotiate with the United States government, and Camila smiled, nodding, as they got into the limousine, although she was already preparing her face for the coming meeting, smooth, serene, and unapproachable.

"Don't you think I've been well schooled in all that we want to accomplish tonight by Ferdinando?"

"I think Ferdinando doesn't realize what an asset you are. I think he takes you for granted."

"Oh, surely not." She was looking out the window, deliberately not looking at him. Her beautiful face taking the pale glow of a streetlight, the light of two small reading lamps within the limousine itself, she was unutterably lovely and all the darkness in him ached for her, empty and locked in his solitude as Ferdinando was—for they were both lonely men, and incomplete. We're incapable of loving anyone *but* her, Battiste realized with a start, and without her the ice would paralyze our hearts and turn us into monsters—but does she know that? Is she capable of understanding how a man could desire her, purely, selflessly, in a manner that goes beyond the body—although the body was certainly part of it?

"I love you," he whispered, almost inaudibly, through stiffened lips.

"Shh. Don't say any more. Don't you realize I could never choose between the two of you, and it would kill me to have to try? Besides—" Her voice took on an uncharacteristic, faraway tone as they drove up the street to the White House, up the curving driveway, and she stepped out of the limousine and up the steps to the side portico without looking at him, dreamy and unconcerned. "Of course you love me. All of my people love me."

Into an epicenter of power of a sort, however deliberately unpretentious, the residence of the first citizen of the land. The White House had undergone a discreet shift to luxury in the last three years and the awkward homespun niceties of the previous administration were gone: there were new deep-red and cream carpets and a lot more gold than had been allowed in the past; gold leaf decorating the cornices of the ceiling, deep gold draperies, floor to ceiling, in the East Room, a new portrait of the President and First Lady (posed before a fireplace with their several children and a dog), cream wallpaper warmed by a crystal chandelier, and candles and Baccarat crystal, gleaming white linen and a string quartet visible behind a screen. Camila entered on Battiste's arm in a corona of TV lights and thrust microphones, smiling and slipping her white mink back from her shoulders like a diminutive porcelain figure in that deceptively restrained, jewel-box setting—which no more than did her justice, President Duncan Farrell thought, as he stepped forward with a practiced smile to shake her hand. His own wife was absent with one of her inevitable headaches, so he took Señora Lorca gracefully from the arm of the distressed, unhappy priest, thinking, What's the matter with this asshole, doesn't he *like* getting invitations to the White House? while his smile won votes for his second term from the banked photographers, and her smile won renegotiation of the Taft-Grijalva Treaty from the same flash-popping voters. He turned to escort her into dinner, with a twinkle in his eye and an off-the-record quip for the press: "That's why I applied for this job, I get to have dinner with all the world's most beautiful women," and she murmured, slightly less audibly, for his private amusement, "I was about to say the same thing about my job, but unfortunately I seldom get to have dinner with such an attractive man. I'm lucky to be here tonight."

They hit it off immediately: two complete professionals, delighted by each other's company. They talked constantly throughout dinner, and Battiste, seated three tables away (Farrell knew enough not to clutter up his dinner with an ambassadorial chaperone), alternately pined with loneliness and applauded her successful negotiating technique. In fact, the President of the United States and the First Lady of Mayapán avoided any discussion of diplomacy for the entire course of the meal, in favor of a discussion of everything else. Duncan Farrell *was* no fool, as Battiste had said, and moreover he shared (although he didn't know it) a trait with Quintero de Buiztas, in that he was a voluminous and discerning reader. Throughout the coquilles St. Jacques (served with a Château Montelena Chardonnay 1977) they discussed the French structuralist critics, and the boom in Central American literature. Over the tournedos Rossini (served with artichokes St. Germain and a Château Margaux '66) they considered Heisenberg's uncertainty principle and the variables pro and con in conversion to solar energy. With the appearance of the Sacher torte (served with a Scramsberg Cremant Demi-Sec 1979, and accompanied by the U.S. Air Force Strolling Strings) they debated the merits of the classic "I Can't Get No Satisfaction," as performed by DEVO or originally recorded by the Stones. The President expressed his opinion that the Washington Bullets, although looking good this early in the season, would not be able to go the distance to the play-offs, and Camila murmured that perhaps they might, and as the Strolling Strings were strolling off and the orchestra was swinging into "One O'Clock Jump," he stood up and asked her to dance, claiming she was the damnedest First Lady he'd ever met and anything she wanted from him just name it, and it was hers.

Naturally, he didn't mean it, and naturally she didn't assume he had. He'd savored the excellent wines they'd had with dinner, and afterward switched to bourbon, but he was scarcely drunk— nor, of course, was she; although she'd matched him glass for glass, and now matched him shot for shot without succumbing either to sleep or obvious tipsiness. He was a good dancer, and they talked while they danced; and now they did talk politics, but generally, and theoretically. Camila said, "We've been trying to arrange evenings like this in Mayapán, but we could certainly use a little more money to bring them off," and Duncan laughed, saying, "What, with your oil resources?" and she said, Yes, but that wasn't liquid capital, no pun intended, but they needed investment dollars if they were going to survive. Duncan said he thought he'd heard they had plenty of investment dollars, he didn't want to say from where, and Camila said judiciously that they *had* made some deals with private individuals, but nothing detrimental to the interests of the United States; as a matter of fact she had an idea that a lot of the money for *both* countries came out of the same individual investors' pockets. They understood each other so well that finally they could laugh at the evasions and strange circumlocutions of politics—and finally, when even the band had grown tired, and the last guests were weaving out into the driveway, President Farrell suggested, more in the manner of a friend than as a head of state, that she join him in the Oval Office for a nightcap.

"I'd be delighted." Camila smiled. "I was just going to suggest that myself."

He put his arm around her shoulders as they headed down the plush, silently carpeted hallway. "It's very rare that one finds a kindred spirit to talk to. I hope you don't mind my saying that, Madame La Presidenta?"

"I don't mind at all, Mr. President. I was just about to remark on the same thing myself."

He fixed them both Jack Daniel's on the rocks, and sank into the big armchair behind his desk, sighing with a rueful laugh. "Good Lord, what a party! I don't think I've felt so pleasantly exhausted since the days of my misspent youth, getting sacked by the Dallas Cowboys."

Camila curled her feet up under her in one of the large leather chairs which provided a restrained, collegiate atmosphere to the room, and sipped her drink. President Farrell propped his chin on his hand with a tired smile and looked at her. "So, what do you want, Madame President? Everybody wants something out of my country. What are you in line for?"

She hesitated, timing it to a nicety, and then shook her head. "You're wrong. I don't want anything from you."

"You're got to be kidding."

"No, really, I mean it." She glanced down at her drink for a moment and smiled. "Mr. President—Duncan—let's be realistic. You're the President of the most powerful country in the world, and of course you have things to offer us, just as we have things—or anyway, one thing—to offer you. You could wipe us off the map. You also know what it would mean if we opposed you in this hemisphere—it would be suicide, but we could embarrass the hell out of you in the world press, and what for? We're not trying to prove anything, like Nicaragua or Cuba. Your country's the top capitalist country in the world, and we want to join! We're capitalists too! We want profits, and free exchange between our two spheres of influence—yours great, and ours small. Naturally, our desires and your own government's intentions are one and the same."

"You just want a free exchange—like an abrogation of the Taft-Grijalva agreement, for instance?"

"That would be very nice," Camila said smoothly. "I imagine you must have been considering just such a move, to be so familiar with the name of the treaty and its relevance to our present conversation."

"Just like that . . . I don't know why I don't have a dozen minds like yours in my cabinet, that's the loveliest double bind I've ever seen. I'm half tempted to give you what you want."

"You should always give in to temptation." Camila smiled at him. "I always do."

They continued to talk and continued to drink, as the night waned and finally birdsong began to be audible from the yellowing branches of the Rose Garden, and at 5 A.M. they finished the bottle of Jack Daniel's in a spirit of abiding friendship and great goodwill, and President Farrell sighed and got up from his chair and went into the bathroom to throw up. Camila got unsteadily to her feet. She was still sober, but light-headed with weariness, aching in every joint, and numb with verbal gymnastics. She borrowed a seat in the President's armchair and dialed a number on his outside line.

"Overseas operator."

"Campeche 6-1000."

The phone rang, and she heard Ferdinando's voice on the other end of the phone.

"Presidente."

She smiled to herself. From one El Señor Presidente to another. "*Mi amiguito,* I'm calling you from the White House. I just wanted to tell you it's all right, everything's fine."

She heard his intake of breath, but he kept his voice light. "Ah, then he hasn't declared war on us yet, I take it?"

"No." She laughed, although she was bone tired in every joint. "He's all right. In his own words, he's a kindred spirit. In a way, I liked him."

"That's good." She heard his answering laugh, and leaned her cheek against the phone receiver, her elbow propped on the desk.

"God, how I miss you."

"I miss you too." His beloved voice, musical as always, still with a hint of amusement. "I can see I was right in sending you in my stead. I can't imagine I would have charmed a connoisseur of Sho Nuff Good chicken in quite the same way as you quite obviously have."

"What—!"

"Just keep up the good work." His voice matter-of-fact as always, no indication that he'd truly missed her, or, for his part, how *much* he had truly missed her. "There's a man in D.C., his name is William Mynott, would you please contact him for me while you're there? He's already got clearance with UNOCO and he may be useful in effecting a deal with our far-off friends."

These were the Russians, she knew; he was right, of course, the phone probably was tapped. "All right," she said, rubbing her eyes, which felt like they were full of ground glass. "Anything else?"

"Nothing except take care of yourself." She could hear him chuckling, and she yawned again helplessly.

"God, I'm falling asleep on my feet! I'd better get some rest, I'll track down Mynott tomorrow . . . I wish you could be here with me."

"I'm with you in spirit," he murmured. "And in my dreams, *and* in the flesh, if you could be here to judge the truth of that statement in our bed at four o'clock in the morning. In the meantime, get some rest, you sound exhausted." His voice changed, almost imperceptibly. "How's Battiste?"

"Battiste's fine." It crossed her mind to tell him about the letter, but she didn't, putting it out of her mind. "Battiste's Battiste . . . you know how he is . . . I'll tell you all about it when I see you . . . God, I hate bourbon. I'd better get out of here before they want to use this office for something important."

"From what you tell me, the American President will probably want to sleep all day. And so should you. Get some rest, *amiguita*. You're my best diplomat. I don't know what I'd do without you." He paused and then added, "I love you. There isn't any point to my life if I don't have you beside me to share it."

He paused, and when she didn't answer, he said, "You sure you don't want to catch the next plane down here and have breakfast with me?"

"What?" Camila laughed, standing up and cradling the phone on her shoulder, while she stretched her hands up over her head. "God, no! I'm going to bed!"

three

FOR THE NEXT NINETY DAYS, Camila became a media star. She appeared on most of the major talk shows in the country, and was interviewed by every major and a number of minor journalists. She spent two hours telling jokes on "The Larry King Show," and two minutes talking politics on the "Tonight" show with Johnny Carson. She appeared on the covers of *Time* and *Newsweek*; she told her life history to Harry Reasoner and Barbara Walters; she smiled sweetly for Merv Griffin and Jane Pauley, and talked seriously with David Susskind and Phil Donahue. The wonderful *gringo* publicity machine adapted itself as easily to statesmenship as star-making, and she enjoyed herself in both respects: enjoyed herself yes and no, because the trip was scarcely casual, and very deliberately conceived; because the trip was probably the most exhausting three months in her young life, and accomplished the twin miracles of making her a celebrity in a foreign country, and a valuable political icon in her own. She streaked like a comet across the television screens and magazine covers of America, and after that she was famous: she didn't have to do it again, and looking back on the experience later she doubted whether she had either the sense of humor to repeat her itinerary or the strength to live through it more than once.

She smiled through her days and whooshed (pressurized, in first class) through her nights, and everywhere she went the lambs of publicist and press corps followed, because as the days went on it became apparent that the First Lady of Mayapán was an interviewer's dream, and wonderfully patient (waiting with a cup of instant Maxim and Cremora, for tape machines to function or a reporter to make it through crosstown traffic), forebearing (with questions of whether she spoke Indian or Spanish, and what did she call her husband, Ferdinando or El Presidente?), and tactful (as when she suggested to the host of "People Are Asking" that he wipe the cocaine off his nose before he went on the air). Her tactics were a mixture of calculation and incredulity; practicality and the purest caprice made her make the most of this unbelievable opportunity, and once she started the offers kept pouring in. The morning after her dinner at the White House she was interviewed by Libby Lanier for *Dossier* magazine, and by lunch the word had spread around Germaine's that La Presidenta Lorca was *the* hot interview to get (possibly through an erroneous impression, since Camila, light-headed on six cups of coffee and no sleep, punctuated her responses with pungent aphorisms and wicked asides too libelous to print, but wonderfully repeatable at subsequent Capitol Hill dinner parties. She toned down her *bons mots* thereafter, but by then her good/bad reputation had been irrevocably established).

Battiste coached her briefly on the vagaries of American taste in the last five years, and sent her off into the wilderness. She tippled *kir* and kiwi fruit with the reporter from the *Times* at the Four Seasons; sushi and rice wine with the Third World leftist from *The Village Voice* at La Divine Japonaise; hot dogs and cokes at Orange Julius with the representative of *The New York Post*. She spoke in ivied campus halls and white-glazed lofts, avoiding Columbia ostensibly because Porfirio still criticized their administration, and hitting her stride as she headed out, south from Chicago, down the mighty Mississippi from St. Louis to Memphis, Little Rock and Baton Rouge; looping north and west across the Pecos River to Roswell and Albuquerque, north to Boulder, Cheyenne, Great Falls, Montana (rerouted on account of snow); south to Salt Lake City (for an appearance on the Ohboy Family's Christmas special) and west to Las Vegas and

Reno and San Francisco, south past Point Conception into the spread labia of Los Angeles. Zigzagging across the United States, from plush television studios to plastic, kid-strewn terminals, zip locked between secret service men, hairdressers and makeup artists while she studied fact sheets at fifty thousand feet, nibbling Cheez-Ohs and sipping martinis and manhattans and eau naturel with a twist (whatever the airlines supplied), setting her watch by the clocks in rest rooms and feeling more and more, as the tour went on, that they were navigating by the stars. At a layover in St. Louis, she hired a car to take her south (disdaining airline repairs, quite correctly as it turned out, since she reached Memphis four hours before the plane did): past ticky-tack suburbs and rolling hills with the tape deck blaring salsa and her cabbie (Zito Ardilla, father of five, reluctantly self-exiled from San Juan and delighted to speak Spanish to this mink-coated señora), detouring past Cairo to see the confluence of the Mississippi and the Ohio rivers: brown boiling mud which gave her a slight sense of the country's power, but more, when they passed through Cairo, and saw the shells of the factories and rusted machinery silted up on the levees, the stale pallor of an overstretched industry which had forgotten its promises to the country and to itself. Poverty and waste, the increasing chaos at the end of a natural cycle. Secret service men having strokes when they caught up with her in Memphis, but when she left she took Zito Ardilla with her: hired him as her personal bodyguard, took him with her into Arkansas.

Where she picked up Norman Eyesler, teaching at the graduate center of the University at Little Rock: a four-eyed math whiz just out from a six-month stay at the state mental hospital, where he'd gone after trying to open his wrists. She stirred his Faubus-scarred heart, so that he recognzied he wasn't crazy to believe in his ideals, but just operating within the wrong system: and he punched his departmental head in the mouth and showed up at the airport with his *curriculum vitae* and flew with her to Dallas (to the secret service men's despair), prepping her on Farrellomics and the down-turn of the stock market. In Reno, Nevada, she struck up a conversation with Bob Bellson (ace camerman and film editor, until his station switched to videotape and relegated him to running boom mikes and carrying cable):

she paid his air fare to Campeche, and sent him to work for Izzy Ikemoda. And in Los Angeles (where she was joined by Pisote, who had a new album out of her singing and playing guitar, punk-scrawled across the cover in red and black, her favorite colors), she crashed the New Year's Eve special hosted by octogenarian Bob Faith, and boosted his ratings to a 40-share.

Carelessly generous: she seldom repeated herself from one interview to the next, and poured forth quotable quotes. Charmingly candid: although she curbed her descriptions toward euphemisms on the air, once off camera, host and crew (or reporter, once his Sony was unplugged) would be regaled with salty stories and frank expletives, graced with the local dialect of the region (which she cribbed from videotapes of newscasts while en route). Occasionally, luminously lunatic: as when she visited The Tight Squeeze in San Francisco and sang "La Golondrina" with the reigning diva, Long Dong Jones. But just as whimsically and thoughtlessly kind: as when she comforted the dipsomaniacal reporter for the *Chronicle* the next morning (he himself had been a patron at the same bar) and sat down with him at his Wang 9000, and helped him write his article about her.

She never quite believed in America for the course of those three hallucinatory months: and so America treated her gently, playfully. They were like two unacquainted lovers, who embark on a liaison deliberately short and quirky, which neither of them believes (or hopes) will last. Returning to Washington, at a gala at the Kennedy Center, she met Vice President Wilson Allen, the quiet former director of military intelligence who was the only member of her audience thus far to find fault with her performance.

They met in the long gallery fronted with glass doors, which looked out on the Potomac, ice-clogged and darkened under a clear black winter sky. The gathering inside was equally sparkling: with diplomats' wives vying with the crystal chandeliers for elegant fragility, and slim, sharp, tuxedoed men guarding the slender woman in white satin who laughed and sipped champagne, nibbled crab meat, and graced the conversation with wit and infectious good spirits. She was honestly having fun, and when she turned and recognized the reserved, attractive man in his middle forties who was waiting to be presented to her, she smiled at him with honest friendliness, and stretched out her hand for him to love her along with everyone else.

But it didn't work, and she was aware of it within two minutes: not with pique, but with a certain heightened curiosity, because this was the first time her charm had failed to ignite even the slightest breath of warmth in a companion. Not that he was in any way impolite: there was a poised, genuine smile on his lips, and even a certain sense of humor in his remarks. But she knew he didn't like her, and she set about wryly and thoughtfully finding out why.

"You must enjoy your life in Washington, Mr. Allen, getting to go to all these beautiful parties."

"I've never been one to waste my time on parties, Madame Lorca. Doesn't that strike you as puritanical? I can't help thinking there's a certain amount of frivolity in all of this."

"Of course," she said, smiling mildly, "but it gives people such pleasure, and there's no harm in creating beautiful images for people to dream about."

"Do you really believe that?" he asked her, slightly altering the emphasis in his smoothly cultivated voice. "That seems like a handy excuse for selfishness, if you don't mind my saying so."

"Oh, of course"—Camila smiled—"I'm only in this game for the money. My aunt and uncle owned half of Switzerland, but that never struck me as quite enough, I wanted to own a whole country . . . but seriously, Mr. Allen, if I had said, No, don't give me a party, I want you to send all that money to the Mayapanian Health Organization, do you think I'd have seen a penny of it? People do pretty much what they want to do most of the time."

"I presume that includes Mayapán's charming First Lady," he said, making it sound like a graceful compliment.

"Of course," she answered, equally gracefully. "Don't you like doing whatever it is that *you* do in the American government?"

If she had scratched needle-lightly on his surface, he gave no indication. He grimaced frankly. "Madame Lorca, as the Vice President I have no reason to be doing much of anything in the American government, and rarely any mandate to be enjoying myself at all!"

She laughed with him at that. He was a smart man, she thought, and so was Farrell: was that it, the impatience of his nominal successor twenty years the old man's junior, that had set a permanent stiffness on his sharp-hewn, superficially handsome features? She twirled her champagne glass around between her fingers.

"Mr. Allen, am I stepping across the bounds of every form of etiquette in suggesting you may not trust me?"

He raised his eyebrows and his thin lips pulled themselves in a half-smile. "No, Madame Lorca, you're not stepping across the bounds at all. You're quite right, I don't trust you."

"Would it be presumptuous of me to ask why?"

He inclined his head toward her with a charming expression of attention, keeping his voice low so that, from a distance, he appeared to be conversing or perhaps flirting with her. "Would you really like me to tell you?"

"Yes, I really would."

"Because you're far too beautiful."

She raised her eyebrows in clear surprise, because his answer was completely unexpected. He continued to hold her gaze with the same cool, thoughtful expression which gave nothing back, and she knew perfectly well he didn't find her remotely attractive.

"If you were a plain woman I could understand your desire for public display, or if you were a stupid woman, I could explain your publicity seeking as mere vanity, but I don't think you're either of those things. So I can see other options: your desire for public influence, or your attempts to wield power behind your husband's back, which is a laudable motive in some instances, but which puts a host government at a distinct disadvantage in getting your husband to live up to your promises. Conversely, you could be working as a team, his smoke screen, his good cop/bad cop. So you see I don't know. You could be doing any number of things, and when I don't have enough data for a theory I get suspicious."

"You don't think I could possibly be just what I am?" she asked him, looking up at him with her intensely blue eyes from which any coquetry had fled, but also any anger—she almost seemed to be asking him the question seriously. "You don't think this could be accidental, this fame, this adulation, this—what? Hyperbole?"

He shook his head. "Madame Lorca," he said, sipping his drink, "no fame is accidental, and if you don't think you're lying to your people just like the rest of us, then you're lying to yourself, which makes me revise my initial assessment of your quite obvious intelligence."

For some reason his words lingered with her for some time afterward, making her uncomfortable with the last whirl of parties of her visit: it was almost with relief that she quit the country and took a flight to Rome with Battiste. There they managed to avoid the ubiquitous *paparazzi* and have dinner by themselves at a trattoria out in the suburbs, several glasses of wine and a drive around the illuminated sights in his rented Spider, before ending up at her suite at the Grand Hotel at two o'clock in the morning for a nightcap.

Pouring them each a Sambuca, Battiste found that his hands were trembling. Weariness? He was forty-three, but lately he'd been assailed with bouts of exhaustion more typical of a man of sixty. He found himself less and less able to sleep, but the weariness was always with him, wearing down his strength.

"It's getting late, one drink and that's it," Camila chided him as she touched her glass to his, sitting relaxed in the puffy white leather sofa, the consistency of meringue. She had her shoes off and he was suddenly struck by her maturity, her worldliness. It was a little sad. She still looked like an adolescent angel, but she had become sophisticated: then he revised his opinion, she had always been sophisticated, it was he who had been naïve. He came and sat beside her and, almost without thinking, swallowed his Sambuca in a single gulp: warming and sickly sweet.

"I'm trying to get you an interview with the Pope," he told her. "It looks like it's going to go through in the next few days. I'll let you know in a day or so."

"Oh, God," she said, half in amusement and half protesting. "Do I have to? Isn't that a little excessive?"

He looked hurt: she guessed he'd been to a lot of trouble to arrange it for her. She changed her mind. "That's all right, I'll do it—I've got that Dior, that long black number with the tight sleeves, it's perfect, it makes me look like a Mafia widow. Will you promise to come with me?"

He nodded. She looked at him. He continued to look at his empty glass and she leaned forward a little on the sofa to read his expression, and then leaned back, giving it up. Whatever was bothering Battiste, he would get over it, or not, with the stubbornness of his self-inflicted martyrdom. She shut her eyes, feeling her weariness and the warmth of the Sambuca blur her mind with a tiredness which was not exactly pleasant. She'd been unable to sleep well for the past four or five days, and now her thoughts ran in circles of dizzy pointlessness: nightmares and visions which were indistinguishable to her from her memories, all equally repugnant, making her want to put up her hands in weak protest to fight them back. She heard Battiste saying something about the fame and adulation she'd gained from this trip, the love she and Ferdinando already possessed in such abundance from all their people, and it struck her as redundant: of course everybody loved them. Languidly she opened her eyes.

"What were you saying?"

"Just that you—you give them so much of yourselves, both of you. I was wondering why you had never thought of giving that love to any children of your own?"

"What?" She couldn't believe for a moment Battiste was saying this. And it struck her even as she stared at him that he was saying it almost at random, to cover for some other train of thought (perhaps his love? his unhappy, unconfessed love for her?) and that perhaps the best safety lay in cutting right to the heart of this other thought, and leaving the terrible question of children safely unanswered and buried in the back of her mind. She hesitated, and uncharacteristically lost command of the conversation.

"After all," Battiste was saying with strained, thin frivolity, "as a priest I should advise you against the practice of contraception! Surely the rhythm method should have failed for you and Ferdinando by now! When are you going to give me a little Lillita or Nando to baptize into the Catholic Church?"

And appallingly he meant it, or at least meant it as a pleasantry, to tease her. Behind his sad eyes and his ravaged, pockmarked face, there lay a hangdog decency, that made him want to spare her his suffering on her behalf, even as he felt compelled to remind her about it. Suffering, *his* suffering! When what he recalled for her was suffering past anything that he could imagine, or anything that she wanted to remember. She felt herself breathing very fast.

"Well, after all, we've been pretty busy with other things these last few years," she said, trying to keep her voice light, smiling at him with what she felt was a travesty of her usual ease. "When I get back to Campeche we'll see what we can do. Although I can't make any promises! I don't really picture Ferdinando in the role of proud *papá*, now that you mention it, do you? Kissing little *mamás* and dandling babies? That's never been exactly his style."

She wanted to get out of that room, the air grown moist and thick with remembered evil, scent of patchouli cologne and sex and blood: she must not, *would* not remember, although she had never forgotten. She looked around the room, trying to make herself believe that she was here in Rome, on the other side of the world and six years distant from that pervasive horror, but it didn't work. She felt as if she couldn't breathe.

"So you see—" What was she saying, she couldn't remember starting this sentence. "So you see I don't want to cast Ferdinando in a role for which he would not be ideally suited."

"You've got an available stand-in, you know." He said it so wistfully that for a moment she didn't know what he was talking about, and then she thought he meant an obscenity. It was only when she saw him continuing to look at his empty glass instead of her, and turn it around and around between his fingers, that she realized his heart longed not for her as an adult, but as a child: the safety of loving which he could recapture by loving her child, ideally her daughter, without the dangerous ambiguities of loving a mutilated, barren, deflowered, and complicated woman of twenty-six. He said softly, "Ferdinando will eat you alive if you let him. *He* doesn't care about children, I'm sure. Besides, he's so much older than you are. I know, I'm older than you too, so perhaps I shouldn't call him names, but I think I can remember something of the . . . oh, why not say it, the innocence of childhood, that you need for that wonderful insanity of trying to raise a child. I'd love to see you have a child, my darling. I think it would make you complete. You and Ferdinando both, but I'm thinking primarily of you. I think I would be the happiest man in the world to hold the child of my two greatest friends in my arms."

"I'm sure you would," Camila said drily. "I'm afraid I can't necessarily vouch for my own moral competence in raising an innocent child. Shall I tell you a little about childhood innocence, my dear friend, or would you like to maintain your illusions?"

Very simply then, brutally and with an absolute, unadorned lack of euphemism, she told him about the cruelties to which she had been subjected. She told him about the beatings and acts of humiliation, the endless, exhaustive explorations of her sex with fingers, objects, that could turn on a dangerous instant from pleasure to ruthless agony—with a change of her expression, or a change of his cold-blooded mind—or from agony to pleasure that was as piercing and as devastating as pain. She told him about the improvised but systematic damage that was done to her, such that the idea of her having a child was a medical impossibility; and she told him all this in such a way that he wouldn't know whether the events she described took place over a matter of days, or months, or years; and she found herself incapable of telling him her tormentor's name. She wept without realizing she was weeping, because unlike Battiste she didn't shed tears for effect: and her heart was a white-hot coal of unquenchable anger in her breast as she said to him with merciless clarity, "That happened to me when I knew you, and I wanted to tell you, but you wouldn't let me. You wouldn't listen. You turned me away with your demands that I be your *angelita*, your angel of purity, so I went elsewhere, and you know the results. They aren't necessarily results I regret, but I'll regret the events that preceded them for the rest of my life. You forbade me to come to you for help, and you made me what I am. Let me know when you want me to meet your Pope, now that I've told you that."

She continued to hold his eyes for a moment with her incandescent blue gaze, that struck him inconsequentially as very much like Ferdinando's, he wanted to reach out to her but he didn't dare, he didn't dare do anything but stare at her in absolute horror and after a moment she looked down and an expression of impatient contempt crossed her face, and she stood up and left

231

him. He saw her briefly and publicly in the next few days, leading up to her audience with the Holy Father (for which she did look beautiful, but oddly pale and fragile in the black dress, like a sacrifice); her reception of a papal marquisate and the Order of Pope Pius IX for Ferdinando, her smiling conversation with his Holiness and his gift of a silver rosary upon parting. Battiste was polite, practical, ashen, and businesslike on the way to the airport: limousined, with a representative of Linz Industries to accompany her to a meeting in Switzerland, for whom he was perversely grateful, since his presence precluded anything but general conversation. He saw her to the door of her plane (Zürich, Bonn, Helsinki—why?—then back to Campeche, and Ferdinando) and stood and watched as it took off into the bleeding sunset sky, and only after it was gone did he absent himself from felicity in the airport men's room and smash his hand with deliberate ferocity against the mirror, not once but many times, until he succeeded not in cracking the mirror but in bursting his knuckles and his hand was a mass of blood.

four

CAMPECHE WAS FEATHERING itself for Carnaval when she returned, its spring finery not merely man-made, but natural as well: explosions of flowers in the gardens along the Avenida Montejo and in the traffic circle of the Plaza Columbia, riots of bougainvillea and orchids surrounding the ministry of the Mayapanian Health Organization (soon to be renamed the Sociedad Camila Lorca) and the shining white palace—which she glimpsed from the windows of her limousine as they approached, driving beside the seawall past the National Museum, past the crowds of cheering Lorcanistas waving flags (some of them already costumed as skeletons and *brujos*, why did they give her a momentary chill? when all of their faces were smiling), flowers dizzing the air with the scent of a million blossoms, roses and passionflowers and lilies as she stepped out of the car, and up the wide white steps to the portico and into Ferdinando's arms. She had come home. Her visits to the United States and Europe had been an unqualified success, and that night the ball given in her honor was televised not only by MAYA-TV but by Cable News Network and the BBC as well. Such was the charisma she had at that time. In the months to come, the Lorcas continued their private drive to shake up the oligarchs and free their country from

233

its restraint as the world's chattel, while they soothed the opposition with their personal charm and the magnificent dovetailing of their talents: Ferdinando's will and Camila's innocence, Ferdinando's urbanity and the other-worldly intelligence of his wife.

It was an effective combination. Observers were moved by the degree to which El Presidente and La Señora relied on each other; their love was touchingly obvious, while never indiscreet or embarrassing. In private, Ferdinando would still awaken Camila with the light-drifting hands of a lover, and she would open her eyes to find him smiling down at her, his hands barely touching her shoulders, as if he were afraid she would disappear from him. Sometimes there was a frown, almost of pain, between the lightly drawn brows which arched half-questioningly against his smooth olive skin; sometimes his brilliant blue eyes would stare at her intently, as he murmured over and over again, "Who are you? Who are you?" smoothing her shoulders with his gentle hands, and burying his face against the satin softness of her breasts. She could not know how she hurt him, simply by existing: so fragile, so young—evanescent as the flame which she sometimes resembled, so that there was no way he could hold her tightly enough to satisfy his solitude, make her completely and irrevocably his. He found himself needing her more and more, not merely in his bed or in his work, but in the deepest recesses of his heart where he had no sense of himself any longer, no sense of reality without her as its centerpiece. He would take whole mornings off from work just to stay with her, finding in her both his reason to live, and the strength to move heaven and earth on her behalf. And she knew of this need of his, and answered it with everything she had—although they both knew that a part of her was fleeting and absent, even when she lay shining with love in his arms.

A part of her was reserved for anyone who laid claim to her, whose pain she felt with her instinctive wince and smile whether it was in her clinic or her bedroom, and felt compelled to assuage it. She didn't care about their troubles in the abstract; she didn't think about "the people" or dream of alleviating their unhappiness; she didn't see herself as a savior—but human misery triggered a reflex action in her which was too unconscious to be called compassion, although it accomplished the same effect. Baffled, irritated, or bemused: how many magi have understood the

234

power working through them, or have gone along with it blindly, without fear but without undue enthusiasm? A ragged piece of human offal would come up to her, worn with disease, and she would feel the shrieking complaints of its physical body, and soothe it, teach it to relax and love itself without restraint. A miserable psyche would reveal itself, sometimes masked between the taut facial planes and strung sinews of a smiling face, and she would weep the tears which allowed its tears to flow, allowing some interior dam to burst and leaving it clean and free and whole. Momentary—the touch of a cool hand on a cheek or a sudden embrace, a flippant word or a glance—and the chosen one was honored and filled with light, oddly joyous and at the same time completely at peace. And because they were human, they revered that peace in the person of the being who conveyed it: worshiping the doctor as though the morphia of easement were pumped from her own veins. That was the love that the people gave to Camila, clustering to be close to her because to be close to La Señora was to be close to joy—whether it was her picture in the newspaper (which in a confused way made them feel good) or her presence at the Sociedad Building (which was always jammed now with the sick and the indigent).

She didn't understand it; she was without need, but trip-wired into empathy she gave unstintingly of herself in individual fixes of love. There was a rumor of scattered cures, and it didn't take more than a few mentions of healings in the newspapers for her Ministry of Public Health to resemble Lourdes during tourist season: lepers packed three deep on the staircases, dysenterics out in the garden, heart patients white-faced in wheelchairs, and terminal cancer victims preferring her cures to Laetrile's. She was appalled . . . but some instinct told her to be gentle, when she stepped out of her office into that palpable atmosphere of human misery; and she sent away the truly ill to hospitals at her own expense, and laid her hands upon the less somatic symptoms, and gave the bum's rush to the malingerers, all with such an unerring accuracy that it *was* a kind of a miracle—as Pisote said as she came up the stairs, gasping at the unhealthy air to ask her, "How can you stand it?" and then hesitated, and looked closely at Camila. "You don't look so hot yourself, when's the last time you went to a doctor?"

235

Camila laughed. "I'm fine! I'm sick and tired ... of dealing with the sick and tired! It takes it out of you. Come inside my office and have a drink, and then we'll go back to the palace, there's a state dinner tonight, do you want to come? I'm done here for the day. I think the day has done for me!" she added, slipping into a chair behind her desk, curling her feet up and pouring them each a shot of tequila, in matching Baccarat tumblers. She pushed her hair back from her forehead with the back of her hand—she was wearing it short as always, like a *campesina*, artlessly and perfectly cut—and the gesture was that of a tired child, although there were little lines now around her weary sky-blue eyes. Pisote tried to think, How old was she now? Twenty-six or twenty-seven? Her eyes looked ancient, although they were beautifully tender, sparkling with their usual light.

"Have you heard the news from Managua? Seven hundred dead. It's a massacre. What does Ferdinando know? Here, here's the paper." Pisote passed along the late edition of *La Voz*, sipping her tequila and then draining it, pouring herself another. Camila's forehead creased as she read, and Pisote watched her eyes squint as though she disliked having to read the words, although she could scarcely have been surprised.

"Well, the consoling truth is that the Hondurans are themselves on the brink of a revolution—but how much American involvement was there in the Nicaraguan invasion, do you know? It doesn't say."

"Oh ..." Camila sighed and pushed the newspaper away, and looked at Pisote with a little smile. "How much do you think? Battiste told us about the plans for this operation a year ago."

"And you did nothing?"

"What could we do? Register a protest in advance? United Oil has subsidiaries in Honduras, mining interests in Nicaragua. The Sandinistas were fools, and the Hondurans, for allowing their country to become a base camp. Although the Hondurans have always done that, against Arbenz and against Buiztas," she added thoughtfully. "They must like getting in on the periphery of a fight with other people."

Pisote crossed her legs in their three-inch spike heels, her thin calves ballooned in a neon-orange flak suit, and lit a cigarette.

She had her own crew-cut hair dyed fire-engine red—an unbelievably fake, Play-Doh red—which didn't really go with the stark uncompromising planes of her face, a face too simple for beauty, although on a stage or on videotape it could look strikingly attractive. She looked at Camila sharply, with an irritating mixture of jealousy and fondness, insecure desire and less secure concern, and shook her head.

"What's the matter? You don't sound like yourself. Cynicism doesn't suit you, and I don't believe you couldn't do anything to stop the attack on Managua, if you had wanted to. Well, if not, then Ferdinando must have had a damn good reason for his actions! He's the most brilliant son of a bitch in this hemisphere—so? Then it becomes a question of statecraft. I can accept that. I'm not quite the refried hippie you seem to think I am!"

"I don't think you're a refried hippie," Camila said, smiling. "I told you, I'm tired. That's all. The view from the top of the pyramid is desolation, and it merely gives you a better seat. I'm going back to Switzerland next week. A tour of the country. Then Germany. Japan. If I'm not too damned exhausted."

"Why don't you take a break?"

"I should. I will. Do you want to be in the next batch of Mayapanian tourist ads? Carlos sent over some sketches, do you want to see them? And Izzy should do us a new image campaign, the big hotel is opening up at La Punta Nicchehabín next week and I want to have some spots running in the States about it. Do you suppose you could talk to him? I'm sorry to put all of this crap on you—" she added suddenly, reaching across the desk to clasp Pisote's hand with an abrupt, unstudied warmth that made the singer's heart contract, almost painfully, with love—although she couldn't help but notice that the hand that held hers was cold as ice, and really dangerously thin.

Camila stood up, a movement immensely light and graceful, weightless and seemingly renewed, not by the drink and the rest, but by Pisote's concern for her. She smiled, and it was a smile so gentle and so serene, so tender toward the world and its inhabitants, that Pisote caught her breath.

"Besides, I'm fine! When will you realize I'm doing exactly what I want to be doing? Come on," she added, linking her arm with Pisote's and leaning her head against her shoulder, "let's get you some new clothes for dinner tonight. I know you love to dress up. We'll go to one of the shops on Calle Guadana and get you something in dark green, and I'll lend you my emeralds, they look better on you than on me anyway. . . ."

Which was how it was: no one came away from her empty-handed (although some of her gifts were barbed, as when she asked the Argentine ambassador for his assurance his country wasn't really torturing Jews; knowing he couldn't give it, but that he wanted to; knowing he needed that excuse to sever his ties with Buenos Aires and apply for Mayapanian citizenship). Mayapán became a haven for political dissidents of all nationalities after the Honduran attack on Nicaragua: communists from El Salvador and lapsed Sandinistas, Miskito Indians and deserting Cuban soldiers. They were granted no largess, but a place in the Mayapanian work force at competitive (i.e., small) wages, so that everybody benefited—the Lorcanistas in particular, for they were hailed as liberators of the oppressed people, and enlightened capitalists at the same time. The United States government found itself blessed with a stable regime in an unstable region, and, moreover, one which was run by neither a sadist, nor a puppet, nor a madman; they kept silent about a few asylumed Marxists and poured aid into Campeche. Wall Street reported a twenty-point gain in UNOCO stock the first day drilling was announced in Piedras Negras. The Mayapanian standard of living skyrocketed, and Campeche outspent all other Central American cities in consumption of American hamburgers, Japanese whisky, German automobiles, and Bolivian cocaine.

Even Quintero de Buiztas benefited from the generalized euphoria—for it was impossible to cancel out thirty years of experience or, for that matter, thirty years of nostalgia for the bloodthirsty despot who had fouled their country like a pig in rut, but whose pictures had been on the currency and the postage stamps for as long as anyone could remember. A heart fibrillation released him from La Miramar: Ferdinando was generous, allowing him to retire under guard to his house on La Mancha Beach, but demanding the pleasure of telling Buiztas about it himself. He interviewed the former dictator-for-life in his own office, dark-suited urbane charmer meeting a restrained (but marvelously cheerful) generalísimo, in his same old combat fatigues and steel-rimmed spectacles, his Brilloed hair and beard now liberally streaked with gray. He accepted the chair that El Presidente offered; he declined one of El Presidente's Camels in favor of his own hand-rolled brand; he lit up, and flicked his eyes over the beautiful man in front of him in instinctive reassessment, much as El Lorca was doing with him (only more covertly, his graceful hands intent on sorting papers, a pair of half-frame glasses prop-balanced on his aquiline nose). Quintero coughed and smiled with an avuncular fondness which was very close to being genuine.

"So, how do you find it? The hot seat? The top of the greasy pole?"

"Disraeli was speaking of attaining power. One can't sit on a pole for six years."

"No and not be impaled, eh? Ha ha ha! You know, I have to thank you. Since you threw me out of office, I have had time to read, time to reflect—it's not at all terrible, this being a retired executive—isn't that appropriate? I was asked that question the other day, by a *gringa* reporter, I thought you might be interested in my answer, in case you have to try it yourself sometime."

Stained teeth gold-flecked a smile through his beard; the sun through the french windows warmed his khaki to a benign olive (he was thinner than before) and showed the dry lines of strain around his eyes, residual pig wrinkles, where the bloat beneath his spectacles had drained away, leaving them almost thoughtful. He folded his hands politely on one knee, seemingly prepared to spend the rest of the day talking to the President of the Republic if that was what the President wanted; but Ferdinando sensed his unease, and enjoyed the momentary pleasure of letting him wonder if he'd been summoned to that office to be sent back to prison, or tardily (but as he had expected, eventually) to be shot.

"I have here a Presidential petition to the Chamber, for your official pardon." Ferdinando smiled, beaming fondness not at Buiztas but at the piece of paper in front of him (which was actually a draft of his television speech that night, but a useful prop). "I thought you might be interested in *my* answer to your guards' use of torture on me, nearly twenty years ago. I *do* forgive, you see, although I don't necessarily forget."

Quintero was, for once, speechless. Ferdinando went calmly on.

"This pardon is contingent on two conditions: one, that you make no attempt to gain or hold elected office for the duration of my Presidency; two, that you make no attempt to leave Mayapán for any other country, without obtaining express permission from me first. Well? Do you agree to my terms?"

Buiztas was still having trouble breathing, but by now he had started laughing. "*Hijo de puta*, you *are* without a doubt the craziest son of a bitch I've ever met! What do you want to pardon *me* for? I can see you pardoning someone who's going to do you any good, but I'm just an old eunuch, what the hell good am *I* going to do you?"

"I don't know, I thought it was a humanitarian gesture," Ferdinando said mildly. "Partly I'm just being practical. You're a limited danger to me now, but the time could come when you'd be used by others as a titular leader. Partly I just want to stop this pathetic stream of whining about your health to the foreign press. And then again, partly, my motives are personal." He got up from behind his desk and came around it to stand beside the aging ex-President, forcing Buiztas to look up to him, calmly smoking and considering. "Why do you think I treated you so fairly, given the fact that you treated me like shit, and in fact, at our last meeting, tried to murder me? Do you know? I really have no idea," he mused, drawing in the smoke from his cigarette thoughtfully, and then slowly letting it out. "Perhaps it's that I'm curious about your mistakes. I want to avoid some of your pitfalls. Perhaps it's just my vanity. Thinking I can survive with you alive, and right beside me—visible for all the world—while you were forced to order my arrest, and my imprisonment, and even my extradition from the States, all to soothe your fear, all to keep me from opposing you."

He moistened his finger, and lightly drew a small circle with his fingertip in the center of Buiztas' forehead, almost like a caress, almost like a target. "I want to keep you well and truly alive, and perfectly safe—I don't know why. Perhaps just to please my own curiosity. Perhaps so you can taste my food. I'll see what I decide to do with you."

Buiztas involuntarily twitched like a dog from his gesture,

for which he felt little embarrassment, plainly reacting as he had been meant to. He didn't say anything, continuing dutifully to cast his eyes Ferdinando-ward, while inwardly smiling. So he was curious, was he, about a man who had been mainlining power for thirty years, speedballing "your excellencies" and *"mi generals"* while he was still teaching in his faggot-safe university? Ferdinando's own addiction was the size of Lake Superior, yet he wouldn't admit it; and so he was fascinating, like all blind parricides and mother-fuckers.

"Why are you telling me all of this now?" he inquired gently, his tone mildly solicitous. "Could it be because your term as Presidente is running out, and you're thinking about reelection? Could it be you're thinking that all the votes in the world can't be counted by you personally, and I might encourage my erstwhile supporters to cheat? Could it be you're worried I might oppose you, an old man like myself, in the pitiable state to which you have reduced me?"

"What!" Ferdinando laughed. "You must be joking. What on *earth* makes you think you could deny me a second term?"

"It was a silly idea, I suppose."

Buiztas heaved himself up from his chair, smiling at El Lorca with his tired eyes and resisting the temptation to salute. "Señor Presidente, I have the honor of accepting your offer of an official pardon." He had trouble keeping a straight face, but he managed. "It is indeed a generous gesture, and you may count on my unequivocal support, if you should ever be crazy enough to ask for it."

Which was true, he *did* support the Lorcanistas—at least to the extent of voting in the subsequent election, which was a Lorcanista landslide. Otherwise he kept to himself, out at his house on La Mancha Beach: engineering the perception of himself as a public joke—the former dictator, with his weak heart and his teen-aged whores—so they felt they could leave him alone, as he sat in the somnolent hours of early morning drinking his coffee and reading the world's newspapers with the same amazed attention as before; reading without rancor but without undue belief about the miraculous achievements of a beautiful woman with a face like an *angelita*, an adept political opportunist but whose entrancing blue eyes and fine-boned idealist's face stirred a memory in him too deep-seated and elusive for him to recapture. He read the accounts of her presumptive "miracles" with unconcealed delight, but something in her abstracted, pitying face touched something in him: here was someone who saw through the charade as he did, who realized that all charity was bullshit, yet who continued to play her part in the day-to-day charade of public life. He began to remember where he'd seen that face before. He was just starting to remember Juan dos Santos when he received his (grudging, extorted) invitation to attend El Presidente Lorca's second inaugural gala as El Presidente Lorca's special guest.

The palace was ablaze with lights, and packed with the world's dignitaries (including President and Mrs. Farrell, Vice President and Mrs. Allen), as Camila slipped her square-cut diamond ring on her finger, and opened a flat box to reveal an expected (but still breathtaking) collar of diamonds and sapphires, resting on a cushion of turquoise Tiffany velvet. She picked up the note that had fluttered out of the box: his familiar strong signature, just his initial *F* on a sheet of Presidential stationery. She smiled. She carried the necklace to the door of the bathroom in a shimmer of silvery satin and Arpège perfume, to slip her arms around Ferdinando as he stood shaving, and ask him to put it on for her.

He kissed the back of her neck, and her bare shoulders, leaving a trail of shaving cream which he wiped off afterward with his fingers. Taking the necklace from her, he deftly fastened it around her throat, and drew her back against his body, wrapping his arms around her.

"I love you madly, *amiguita*, do you know that?"

"I had a little idea you might."

"You're going to outshine everybody. There won't be another woman in the room who can touch you."

Which made her repress in that moment a shudder of sheer weariness, leaning back against him, shutting her eyes to let the warmth of his body get through to her, the electric tenderness of his lips as he kissed her temple, little playful kisses which tickled as he whispered, "You're so beautiful, so beautiful . . . so beautiful . . ." until she laughed and turned to face him, her blue eyes shining brighter than the sapphires.

"Shave and get dressed, or we'll never get downstairs at this rate," she whispered up to him, and added, "I'll wait for you outside," and slipped from his arms and floated back through the bedroom, and out into the hallway, where she discovered the former dictator Quintero de Buiztas standing and lighting a cigarette.

They were both caught off balance, although Buiztas recovered more quickly, taking the unlit cigarette from his mouth and bending to kiss her hand with a moist gallantry which was nonetheless honestly friendly, his big hand enveloping hers with a surprising warmth, and his breath warmly redolent of tequila and marijuana and cigarette smoke surrounding her like a cloud. She forced herself to smile, against a pain like unshed tears or perhaps like simple fury in her throat, and was about to say something when he beat her to it.

"Ah, Señora Lorca! You look radiant as always tonight—and ah, that necklace!" Trust him to notice the jewels, she thought; he did a brief double take back from their brilliance. Smiled and thrust one pudgy finger under them—in a gesture which was amazingly familiar, lifting them away from the smooth skin of her throat. "These are truly magnificent. An anniversary present, so to speak? Ah, señora, there's the difference between me and your husband—I never had such a beautiful *señora* to give presents to! Perhaps you would have made all the difference."

She found herself smiling with a pained stiffness by which she held herself back from insulting him more overtly, simply saying, "I find it difficult to believe you ever lacked *señoras*—or *señoritas*—to give presents to, Señor Buiztas. You can't have been trying."

"Ah, but with a woman like you, a man would be a fool not to try everything as hard as possible."

"You're flattering me. Aren't you afraid of making my husband jealous?"

"Jealousy, my dear Señora Lorca, is the emotion of a man who has *lost*. A man who has won as much as your husband—and may I say, if you'll forgive me, without missing a trick—deserves merely to feel complimented when someone envies him—"

He was dressed well, or at least better than usual, in a dinner jacket and a starched white shirt, and she watched as his oily, lined face became brick red and then white, as the color rushed and then drained from his face, and he fell onto the carpet like a stone. Camila knelt beside him, opening his shirt and feeling instinctively for a pulse, but there was no pulse, and his lips were blue, his face surprisingly white for a man who was so dark-skinned. . . . He must have had some Negro blood in him. . . . She found herself simply looking at him, with distant sadness and a complete lack of surprise. There were the big pores in his nose, the streaky gray in his hair . . . he might have been handsome once, there were the remains of that in his face . . . she carefully took his steel-rimmed glasses off and laid them on the carpet next to him. This was the man who had told Juan dos Santos to go home, not to worry . . . had guaranteed him safe passage out of the country, along with his wife and child . . . she had a sudden clear vision of her father, his fragile, aristocratic face overlaid on top of the heavy, brutal face of the former *caudillo*, like an image superimposed on film. Her hands hovered over his chest. Then she lowered her hands and unbuttoned his shirt completely, laying her fingers lightly on his sternum, still with the same cold, distant sadness and tightness in her throat as though she wanted to weep . . . pity and anguish so instantaneous and so intense that she couldn't comprehend them, rage drenching her in blood, a terrible sucking of herself down *into* him, into his bleeding chest, while a part of her mind remained distant like a bobbing cork, aware and not aware of what she was doing. The energy was all that was needed, energy seeping out of her now, no doubt about it, in the calm repeat-pressure of her fingertips while she felt herself opening the skin and rib-frame of his chest, cleansed the blood clot from his heart and restored the dying cells and relaxed the terrified muscles so diaphragm could move and lungs could fill, heart pump and brain clear and blood flow with a deep body rhythm regulated and encouraged by the light pressing down of her fingertips as her body registered the gradual diminishment of his terror, her breathing stilled and she sat back, removing her fingertips from his chest. And for a while there was nothing. And then Buiztas gave a great gasp, like a sob, and coughed and began to breathe in choked panting breaths, and he opened his eyes and looked at her.

From a great distance, he tried to draw back his words to speak, but all that came out was a sigh and an unintentional dribble of saliva. She continued to look at him. And then she smiled. It was a smile that held very little in it of compassion. There was ironic bitterness, and a twist of real humor, and her face was bone white to the lips, and he could see that she was trembling. She stood up, and her despairing smile was still on her lips as she turned away and made her way down the stairs, to where the Count Basie Orchestra was playing "Superchief" and a thousand guests were waiting to meet Camila and Ferdinando Lorca.

five

BATTISTE MANAGED TO CONTINUE to survive (more or less) by doing what he had done all his life: sublimating himself in his work, deft, precise, Cardinal Tommassi in all but name in the labyrinthine corridors of Washington politics, where he served his apprenticeship for the Curia.

It didn't help much, for the aridity of his life and the shameful devastation in his heart—but not a word of his private doubts clouded the smooth, glittering mirror of his mind, or muted the occasionally frightening, sharp impatience with which he dealt with obstacles, to his diplomacy or to his personal ambitions. He was a fair employer, but he demanded the same unflagging energy and immediate acumen of his associates as he demanded of himself: and as they were not priests (indeed, for the most part, not Catholics) there was a certain amount of good-natured railing at the ambassador, and his concepts of time management and human perfectibility. Battiste retreated from the society of his subordinates, becoming ever more aloof and detached: both traits which he would have cultivated deliberately, had he been a more traditionally ambitious priest. But he was miserably unhappy.

He socialized with the exiles—wealthy by this time, and not so much idealistic as vindictive—who had decamped from

Mayapán despite Ferdinando's best assurances that he intended to co-opt the oligarchy, rather than destroy it. He listened to their hate and their resentment, offering a pastoral ear with the added fillip of their knowledge of his friendship with El Lorca; and as he mitigated the fury of their misery he fertilized his own, not believing their ridiculous assertions (that his friend was a communist; was a fascist; was a running dog of the capitalist state), but listening to a tiny voice in his ear, almost inaudible but persistent: that his friend was not beloved by *all* the people of Mayapán; that he was not giving *everyone* what they wanted. That he was planting the seeds of discord, or ignoring a political wisdom not his own? Battiste wasn't sure. But that there was a crack, in the shining image of the man at whose right hand Battiste stood, like the archangel Michael. That Ferdinando might not be worth the extraordinary sacrifices he had made and continued to make on his behalf.

He visited the exiles to learn the extent of their activities in subversion, and in his ambiguous, failed priest's way to minister to them, at their parties for C.I.A. spooks and Mafia lieutenants and all the dubious people who might one day help them to regain their fortunes (but probably wouldn't) in Washington and in Miami and in New York. It was while he was at one of these parties in a penthouse on New York's Upper West Side that he met Porfirio Cheruña, quite by accident, shortly after he had arrived—met him without embarrassment, because he still knew nothing about his intimate connection with Camila—but with a certain curiosity, because he knew of his continuing refusal to support the Lorcas.

It was an opulent setting for a party: plush Oriental carpets softening the parquet floors and a huge walk-in fireplace on one wall, crackling with manicured logs, heavy German tables and a magnificent stained-glass window on another wall, backlit to a spectacular muted beauty, showing the martyrdom of an unnamed saint. The press of revelers was muted as well, soft voices and gestures disguising with elegance the high-toned frustrations of failed counter-revolutionaries. Battiste felt his stomach turn at the mingled aroma of crab quiche and chicken mole from the buffet table; he moved away to the slightly cooler air by the open door to the terrace, and came face to face with a remembered figure: spare, as he was, but with the ease of one who had always been slender, tall and crowned with a halo of beautiful snow-white hair. His high-bridged nose supported his remembered pair of steel-rimmed glasses, behind which his ice-gray eyes were as coolly distant as Antarctica. He stared at Battiste as if he had never seen him before in his life, and something, a momentary spasm of pain which crossed that epicene, aloof face, caused Battiste to feel an instant's pity for the old man—who must be in his seventies now, he thought, although he looked fit in his fragile, neurasthenic way—chalk-stripe charcoal-gray suit tailored to conceal or perhaps exaggerate his thinness, bone-white hands gracefully emerging from precise French cuffs. He looked in supreme and absolute control of himself, and Battiste had a moment of extreme discomfort, as he felt the embarrassed color flood his face.

"Señor—Señor Cheruña—I had no idea that we would see each other here—"

His voice sounded strained and unnatural in his own ears, and he couldn't tell with what frigid, false politeness his smile stretched his face; because he didn't know *why* Porfirio's presence should make him feel so uncomfortable, beyond his persistent, mild refusal to accommodate the Lorcas by returning to Campeche. It was something else—and it hit him with an access of misery that like everything else in his life it had something to do with Camila, it was simply that she had known this man, had lived with him and had been his student, in her all-too-brief and, he realized now, desperately unhappy youth. Perhaps she had deceived him too, her guardian: or perhaps, worse thought, she had been able to confide in him, as she had never been able to confide in Battiste. He stared at Porfirio with an expression of shock and obscure shame, as he remembered the terrible things Camila had told him (tried not to remember, wincing from them in horror) and wondered if she had told this man (*could* she have told him?), narrowing his eyes against the pain of a shared connection he wanted to deny, and at the same time unhappily wanted to confirm. Porfirio for his part read Battiste's painfully intent expression as something much simpler, and he shut his eyes, as if having trouble catching his breath, and then immediately began speaking in his raised, "onstage," slightly self-conscious voice.

"I had no idea either, Father Tommassi, but surely we are both men of the world, and can weather a slightly gauche social situation, by the simple expedient of pretending it hasn't happened. I'm sure you will excuse me—"

And he would have drawn away, had not Battiste put out his hand and detained him, his face ashen and his lips forming a soundless apology, perhaps a plea, which trapped the old man in the slightly comical position of an animal held invisibly at bay by the same social conventions he'd hoped to use as his escape. They were both painfully visible to everyone in the room, and Porfirio stared at Battiste almost with hatred, one corner of his bloodless mouth stiff, leaning heavily on his cane with the residual unsteadiness that had remained with him since his stroke. After a moment he said lightly, "I'm feeling a little faint, shall we go out onto the terrace for a breath of fresh air? I don't think the temperature's so inclement as not to make it a good deal less unpleasant than it is in here—" And Battiste found himself incapable of doing more than following the old man outside. The terrace was wide brick with a high stone balustrade that looked down nineteen stories, and when they stood by the edge, Porfirio turned to him and said in a sharp, high voice, "Well? What was it you wanted to say to me?"

"Nothing—I—" He hesitated before the old man's thin, working face, feeling the scalding shame of his own failure and something else, some less tangible feeling of distaste and repugnance, which he put out of his mind as incongruous. Yet a part of him was still the detached observer: seeing that there was a fleck of white on Porfirio's lips, that he was very pale, and that he was badly frightened, but his own unhappiness made him blind to anything else. He said quietly, "I did want to talk, but not if it makes you uncomfortable—" and something in his very diffidence stung Porfirio into a response.

"Oh, not at all, not at all uncomfortable—to talk to a representative of the government that's been so flattering in its attention, so insistent in trying to get me to support its regime—oh, no! My dear sir, do you realize that in the last five years of your

249

friend's term in office, my sales in this country alone have gone up twenty-five percent—I hesitate to mention the figure of my Mayapanian sales, for fear your beloved leader will require me to pay an excessive income tax *in absentia*! Oh, no, it doesn't make me in the least uncomfortable to chat with you, but I assure you I shall not go back— Señor Lorca and I do not, after all, see eye to eye on all matters. But I'm genuinely moved that he should ask you to talk to me, and I'm perfectly willing to talk to you as long as you like."

"This has nothing to do with Ferdinando," Battiste said with a painful smile. "I can see why you'd think that—I don't do much that isn't on his behalf—but I do have my own motives, and I can assure you this has nothing to do with him."

"No?" Porfirio asked in a nearly inaudible voice, and then for a moment he licked his lips, incapable of saying anything else. Finally in a stripped, flat voice he said, "What does it have to do with?"

Battiste moved to the high stone balustrade and let his hands travel over its rough surface, feeling the rough stone bite into his hands and thinking that he would have liked to grip it, feel the sharpness cut his palms to stop the unshed tears in his eyes, and give him back the clean, hard clarity of unthinking action. He said quietly, "You must miss her as much as I do. Forgive me for talking to you so frankly. I know you don't really know me at all, but do you ever have any contact with her? Of course not. Ferdinando wants you to come to *them* in Campeche, doesn't he? He's very inflexible about some things . . . and I know there's no friendliness between you, which must make it doubly incredible that I should be talking to you like this. I don't really know why, except . . . to remember her with someone else? You see, I suddenly don't know whether the memory I've had of her all these years is in any way the truth. How do *you* remember her? You knew her well, and—I knew that you cared for her deeply. But how do you remember her?"

Battiste's back was to Porfirio so he couldn't see the rictus of pain and rage that swept over his features so sharply that he put his twitching hands over his face, shrinking a little as if from a blow, and recovering himself almost immediately, in a state of deadly cold amusement. He said lightly, "My dear fellow, what do you mean? How do I remember her? I remember her as you do, as a beautiful child. Who was to know the heights to which she would climb? I give you my word she surprised me as much as she surprised you."

If there was a sharp twist to his last few words Battiste didn't notice it. He looked down at his hands on the stone and said with a certain amount of difficulty, "I may as well tell you she told me something that gave me a shock. It was something I knew nothing about, something that if I had known . . . my God, if I had known, but I didn't, and that's more or less exactly the point." His twisted smile was audible in his words, and Porfirio waited behind him, with his weak heart shuddering in his chest and his gray eyes fixed on him with an absolute stillness, because now was the time when you waited for the wheel to stop spinning, he was almost abstract in his curiosity as to what she had told him, and he almost confessed the truth himself for the sheer perverse fun of relieving both their anxieties, but he knew somehow with his predator's instincts alert that he was safe. Finally Battiste sighed and said quickly, as if to get it over with, "I was wondering if you knew anything at all about her health. About her being hurt—intimately—I mean, sexually, I mean—you see, I can't really believe—" And then he shut his lips sharply on a pain too large and jagged to have anything to do with questions of belief.

Porfirio relaxed and said calmly and perfectly reasonably, "I don't know what you're talking about."

I failed her, Battiste thought miserably, failed in the most elemental sense the beautiful grace that was given into my hands, but he couldn't tell him that, of course not, he stammered something, giving hints, vague circumlocutions, and after a while Porfirio pretended to get the general idea. He stepped to his side, to stare out over the lighted city through the double reserve of his steel-rimmed glasses, and his slightly averted face. He said very carefully, with slow, clear precision testing each syllable for its sound, "I thought I was the only one she'd shunned like that. By not telling me, and allowing me to help her. Pushing me aside, yes, denying me the opportunity to help her. I was devastated. And I forgave her, of course, as you'll forgive her. She is a bird of passage, an exquisite bird, not to be possessed by any man. I wonder if your friend knows that. It's dangerous to believe in people too much, they'll disappoint you, and ultimately the people we love most disappoint us most. I exempt Camila, of course . . . she is the *belle dame sans reproche* . . . and *sans merci* . . . but don't you find your friend exhibiting just the slightest trace of clay feet? I honestly wished to support him. You're mistaken that there was ever any enmity between us. But don't you find yourself disagreeing with some of his more radical propositions? I really cannot see that they will bring either his country or his people any good."

Battiste defended Ferdinando's government by reflex, without thinking about it, and gradually as they talked he began to feel true pity for the old man, as well as for himself: ashes of grief and loneliness in his heart, and a new stirring of bitterness, which hadn't been there before. Porfirio had a point, ultimately it was the people you loved most who disappointed you most. When Porfirio said that the oligarchs were maggots, and disappointed maggots at that, but that it was the socialists' argument he found most difficult either to refute or effectively ignore, Battiste found himself agreeing with him, and when he said with a convincing show of reluctance that there really was someone Battiste should meet, who would give him an alternate perspective and was in his own right a brave man and a brilliant political theorist, Battiste asked him with frank curiosity who he was. Porfirio laughed just a little lightly, and told him that he'd intended on meeting with him that night! He'd come there first, to see all his old friends and get up his courage, because at his age he was a little scared of becoming a true revolutionary! But if Battiste would care to accompany him, he would be happy to take him there now. And he looked at him, his thin, lined face stiff with his smile and a faint anxiety narrowing the corners of his eyes, and his hands twitched lightly as he laid them for a moment on Battiste's arm, and Battiste shivered he thought with the cold, and said certainly, why not, he'd be happy to accompany him.

Porfirio was silent as they rode the elevator to the lobby and found a cab on West Seventy-ninth Street, for which Battiste was fleetingly grateful. He was beginning to have the exhilarating/unreal feeling of making a trip spontaneously, which he hadn't experienced since his days as a revolutionary: he felt the same distanced unbelief in himself now, but also his age, and the numbing effects of his years as a successful bureaucrat. No delight, but rather a sharp nostalgia, as he looked around through the back of the cab at the retreating lights of Manhattan, toy miniature and benign, and they sped across the East River to Brooklyn. He would have liked to have made this journey by himself, in company with his former self: the naïve and hopeful and ridiculous young man he had been, five, ten, twenty years ago. He fought back the desire to stop, to ask the driver to turn the cab around, as they threaded their way through the darkened, still streets to an address on Lafayette Avenue which turned out to be an elementary school, paid the driver, and went up the old stone steps into the building. It was oppressively warm inside, with the dry smell of heated chalk and the buzz of overhead fluorescent lights jarring him with their modern glare (he had begun to develop a splitting headache) against the prevailing decor of green-painted walls, wide-planked wood floors, black chalkboards visible through the doors of classrooms, and faded crayon- and construction-paper cutouts. He felt that he had entered some time capsule of childhood, less his own than two or three generations of American children's, and he was reminded with uncomfortable poignancy of the Harley School, before he put that thought finally out of his mind.

They went into a classroom which was already full of perhaps two dozen men—Battiste noticed that there were no women present—most of them in their teens or early twenties: raw-nerved, ragged youths wearing the emblematic jackets and T-shirts of gangs, as well as some young executive trainees, in shirt sleeves and ties, and a few uniformed blue-collar workers, a gas-station attendant, a man in the baggy, sea-green fatigues of a hospital orderly. They were talking in animated Hispanic among themselves—Battiste took a moment to fully understand their elliptical, savage slang, mixing elements of English and Spanish and Mayapanian with the outdated rhetoric of sixties barricade *machismo*—and there was one among them who was speaking with more deliberation and also with more ease than any of the others. Battiste found himself studying him. He was perhaps twenty-six or twenty-seven, with the short, almost fat body of an Indian peasant, and a beautiful, smooth, classically Mayan face:

beak-nosed and wide-cheeked, his skin the color of burnished mahogany. His eyes were small and set close together, his lips sloping from a pronounced overbite to a receding but wide-jawed chin. His eyes were black and very thoughtful. He was dressed casually in an old guayabera shirt, the collar and cuffs stained with use and sweat, but he was unmistakably the leader of this free-for-all discussion—a discussion which seemed to be the denouement of some more formal business (if formal business there had been), with the men smoking cigarettes and drinking beer. They were arguing heatedly with the calm, soft young man who sat leaning back in his chair at a child's scarred wooden desk, listening to all their words, but also listening to the words behind their words, gauging their capabilities, his pudgy, work-worn fingers beating a rhythm on the ink-stained wood of the back of his chair, and accompanied ("guarded," Battiste thought with a flash of insight) by a dark, flat-faced young man with a thatch of black hair growing down almost over his eyebrows. This young man grasped his shoulder with a proprietary camaraderie, and their shared Indian blood was readily apparent (they might have been brothers or cousins), although this adjutant, or bodyguard, or lover (perhaps all three) was darker and much more closed in his expression, his eyes and lips narrowed, the latter over surprisingly long, almost wolfish teeth. He wore stained blue jeans and a paint-splashed shirt, open at the neck, and a plain wooden cross dangled on a silver chain around his neck. He was José Luaro.

When Battiste and Porfirio entered the room the quality of the gathering changed, both to include and to exclude them, and Battiste was struck by the immense, almost hypnotic power in the group leader's eyes, as he looked at him directly. He felt his headache and his weariness sap the strength from him, as if he were bleeding, and something else, the gelid misery which seemed frozen like an incurable and unnoticed tumor in his breast, stab him with physical anguish so that he winced noticeably, like a man with a bullet wound. All the while the calm, brown-faced man regarded him with simple curiosity, stroking his clammy brow with invisible fingers, palping his twisted abdomen with unseen pseudopods of impersonal energy until he relaxed, releasing his breath in a sigh of pain. He discovered, as he passed his hands over his face, that his cheeks were wet with tears.

The compact young man got up and approached him, looking from him to Porfirio with an inquiring and somewhat wary expression. Porfirio laughed nervously, settling his glasses on his nose (Battiste realized peripherally that he was somewhat ill at ease with the young man, a little embarrassed by him). He said, "Martín, let me present to you the Mayapanian ambassador, Father Battiste Tommassi. Yes, he's a priest, like your friend. Or rather *not* like your friend, I should say, in that he is, I believe, still a member of the Church. Isn't that true, Battiste? Battiste, let me present to you my good friend Martín Acchuirez. This is of course the gentleman I told you about."

This last could have been addressed to either of them, since Martín Acchuirez had plainly heard a lot about Battiste Tommassi as well. "So you're the Mayapanian ambassador, huh?" He came and stood very close to Battiste, looking at him with the same frank interest and impersonal attention as before, and Battiste felt a physical warmth emanating from his body, attractive and so comforting that despite the excessive heat in the room and his heavy overcoat, he found himself trembling, shaking like a man who comes out of a terrible, numbing cold to stand finally in front of a warm and all-consuming fire. He poked Battiste familiarly in the stomach. "You're getting an ulcer. You'd better drink milk. Lay off the hot food." His voice had the sprung punctuation of Indian cadences, overlaid with Americanisms. Later on, Battiste learned he was a doctor, doing his residency at Bellevue. But he was also an instinctive healer, and something within him sensed the priest's unhappiness, sensed it and touched it with impersonal curiosity, as something he might be able to use. He was exactly the same age as Camila Lorca.

Battiste smiled his bleak, distancing, and compassionate smile, murmuring, "Martín Acchuirez, of course. How pleasant, after receiving reports from our intelligence sources, to finally meet you face to face."

six

IT WAS CHARACTERISTIC OF the former dictator Quintero de Buiztas that he should, following his unpublicized and (possibly) unnatural resurrection from the dead, neither accept nor deny the possibility that he had been visited with a miracle. He neither reversed the whole course of his life, nor attempted to deny the fact that anything had happened. In the depths of his heart, he remained ambivalent about his "cure," but that such a cure had taken place was an undisputed fact (a team of heart specialists confirmed his having suffered a mild coronary occlusion) and the effect of that experience on his subsequent relations with the First Lady of Mayapán was embarrassingly immediate: from having been her caustic critic, he became her unabashed admirer. No task was too menial, no hours too long for the former dictator to seek in every way to assist her—with a self-deprecating humor which thrived on his knowledge of her continued dislike, indeed her continued exasperation with his presence, hanging around the Sociedad Building, until Ferdinando said with only scant sarcasm that she must have converted him, as the Spaniards had converted the Indians, and now why couldn't she use the same magic once and for all to get rid of him?

He said it lightly, because at that time he had scant attention to spare even for his wife's uncharacteristic silence, the deliberate vagueness in her eyes when he asked her what she'd done to win the loyalty of the old reprobate. He was too caught up at that time in the heady whirlwind of his second term as President, when so many things were happening at once that the people of Campeche had to subscribe to two newspapers to take it all in; when there was building and change and heavy industry going on in every inaccessible corner of the country; drilling in Cuchuma- tanes and Petén provinces and oil refineries pouring out thou- sands of barrels night and day; mining for minerals and steel plants and hydroelectric dams springing up in the untamed jun- gles where for previous centuries only quetzals had flown; and the biggest project of all, announced that fall and begun the fol- lowing spring: the construction of a new capital city to rise on the site of the ruins at Chichén Itzá.

It was a dream that had been evolving in Ferdinando's mind for a long time: a new capital, to signify the approach of a new century, and their freedom from the tyranny of the pirate-brothel capital of the past. He envisioned it rising on the site of the an- cient city, incorporating the ruins without defiling them, soaring skyward higher than the pyramids: a dream, but a pragmatist's dream as well, new construction further to stimulate an economy swelled to the bursting point with the influx of petrodollars, bloated with the profits of UNOCO and entirely dependent on foreign economic trends to control the roller-coaster sweeps of inflation and glut. It was an economy that couldn't last without the internal stability of private industry, so to stimulate the devel- opment of such industry, he mortgaged his country to the foreign banks: Linz's and UNOCO's banks in Germany, and Chase Manhattan and Morgan Guaranty Trust; the Bank of Tokyo and unnamed concerns in Switzerland; the Vatican Bank and anony- mous investors around the globe—to dredge this second Brasília out of the jungle. Madness? Or the daring and craft that still ran like quicksilver in his veins, as he spoke to the people of Mayapán in person, on television, over the radio, explaining his ambitious proposal in his rapid, melodious voice as if he were speaking to each and every one of them personally. "A city which will sym- bolize our new hopes for our country, as well as the technology

257

which enables us to make these hopes a reality. . . ." And of course they followed him, as they would have to the ends of the earth, into the jungle: while Battiste read about it in the newspapers in New York, read about it with an exclamation of admiring profanity because my God, there was no one but Ferdinando who would even have thought of such a thing! And Martín Acchuirez read about it in the emergency room at Bellevue, standing up stripping off latex blood-soaked gloves with his habitual, thoughtful smile; and Porfirio Cheruña read about it in the *Times* at breakfast in his apartment on Sutton Place, and nearly died laughing.

At that time Porfirio was becoming more openly critical of the Lorcas, and reestablishing his status as a protesting idealist by simple expedient of implying *his* ideals were more heartfelt and sterling than theirs. The effect was both annoying and negligible, and he may have been aware of it. No hint ever reached the press of his connections with Martín Acchuirez and the Frente Comunistas: his public persona was always discreet, and yet, in its own way, his continuing self-exile was an embarrassment to the Lorcas more effective than if he'd been publicly seen as a communist. Ferdinando even went so far as to offer him the Order of Santiago, their country's highest accolade, if he would return to Campeche to accept it. He hid his relief at his refusal from the beautiful woman who shared all his thoughts—and who didn't need to be told about his ambivalence. They never discussed the old man, and Camila never told him about the letters she received (occasional and peremptory, written in his thin handwriting on a single sheet of blue, parchment-textured paper) and which she always destroyed without reading. Save for one, which had shocked her by its sanity and the explicit instructions it gave for her to contact him, times and places which she ignored, but which remained in her mind as a horrible possibility, of armistice, of giving Ferdinando the alliance that he needed . . . and giving her something as well, the bittersweet No to the applause of the people who loved her. The private answer to the self that could heal her greatest enemy, and her personal response to the forces inside her that she could neither accept nor reject, nor accommodate nor begin to understand.

It was in connection with his new city that Ferdinando flew

to Washington, to meet with President Farrell and Vice President Wilson Allen. His meeting was heralded with considerably less fanfare than had greeted Camila's visit; but this was a private rather than a public summit. The President of Mayapán was flown by helicopter from Andrews Air Force Base to the White House, where he was ushered into the shining conference room, appointed with individual water carafes, pads of paper, and three packs of El Presidente Lorca's favorite brand of American cigarettes.

"All the comforts of home," Ferdinando remarked, as he unwrapped the cellophane from a pack. "However, if you expect me to smoke three packs in one hour, or stay much longer than that, I'll have a stroke." He smiled at the assistant secretary of state as he lit his cigarette, noticing how the young man (what was he, thirty-one, thirty-two?) was imbued with that terrible *norteamericano* assurance—square of jaw and clear of eye—masquerading as boyish charm. Why were they so implacably sure about everything? He was the President of an entire country, and he was rarely that sure about anything.

President Farrell, Vice President Allen, and Secretary of State Clarence Smyth came in in a group, and there was a moment of formal handshaking, with President Farrell commenting on the unseasonable chilliness of the weather, before the five men sat down. Ferdinando quietly drew on his cigarette and looked at them all. President Farrell aging, still fit, still attractive, and professionally charming; Vice President Allen politely impenetrable; Clarence Smyth self-effacing and affable. He had a moment of unreal amusement that he should be sitting there talking to them—a political artist, in a room full of nondescript businessmen—and he smiled and waited to hear what in the world they were going to say to him.

"Well, gentlemen," he encouraged them, "you have my complete and undivided attention."

"President Lorca," Duncan Farrell began without preamble, "You must be aware that we think you're doing one hell of a job with your country." Ferdinando mildly nodded, in acknowledgment that he thought so too. "But the rest of your neighbors are in a terrible mess, and I'm going to be frank with you, as far as our American interests are concerned, we're just stumped." He leaned forward, smiling, and Ferdinando thought, I could do without the man-to-man *bonhomie*, but what the hell. "We've been supplying money and arms to the factions we support—and I'm not going to deny it—but it's all going to waste because we don't have a stable enough ally in the region. Nicaragua's got one—Cuba. So where does that leave us? President Lorca, I'd like to know, just for my own curiosity and because I've never actually heard you voice an opinion on the subject, what exactly are your thoughts about Nicaragua?"

Ferdinando knew better than to hesitate, but he spoke lightly, seemingly spontaneously, with his usual, casual fluency. "Nicaragua's a country in which the rights of freedom and human decency were ignored for years, by a corrupt but . . . politically expedient? . . . dictatorship. Naturally, as an advocate of democracy, I applauded the downfall of Somoza. But since that time—" he paused to draw on his cigarette, "—I deplore the absence of any freedom and decency whatsoever in the country. Its people have been betrayed, and its leadership have been misled. It has become a casualty of what the Soviets refer to as 'liberating marxism,' and what you gentlemen, quite rightly, I'm sure, refer to as 'mindless communist expansionism.' "

"Right," Secretary of State Smyth agreed under his breath. Ferdinando practically expected him to add, "Hear, hear."

The President of Mayapán folded his long fingers together and continued mildly. "The Soviets have seen an area of potential influence in this hemisphere ever since 1959, and it's little wonder that they should be exploiting an instability in the region which predates their own existence, but which—roughly, but strikingly—imitates the peonage and oppression out of which their own Revolution was born." He felt like he was back at Columbia, teaching a class. "Your government, with its Big Stick policies, may have contributed a little to the image of the United States as a predatory colonial power? But in any event, the Soviets have a foothold in the region: they're perceived as being for the underdogs, and that's a potent position to take as regards a revolution, even if it *is* a lie."

Vice President Allen cleared his throat. "*Do* you think it's a lie?" he asked in his light, colorless voice.

Ferdinando leaned his chin on his hand, regarding him affably. "Of course I do. I never trust anybody who claims to have the best interests of Latin America at heart."

President Farrell shifted in his chair, and changed the subject. "The previous administration authorized limited aid to moderate regimes in the region—and to the moderate opposition in Nicaragua—but we've gotten beyond that now. The situation's too polarized, and since we are adamantly opposed to direct intervention on our part, we're left with a limited number of options."

"What a pity the Bay of Pigs invasion didn't work," Ferdinando said as if idly. "Havana is so much more convenient for laundering money than the Bahamas."

"Ahem—may I ask—" Secretary of State Smyth glanced around as if asking permission, and then said, almost apologetically to Ferdinando, "what are *your* objectives for your country, Señor Lorca? I mean, you've never made it difficult for communists or former communists to enter your country—"

"I don't prosecute those who are or ever have been members of the Communist Party," Ferdinando said, smiling. "Why should I? Our economy is stable, our people have peace, free elections, and a say in the direction of their lives for the first time since the conquistadores. It's a happy marriage."

"You have a talent for those," President Farrell said smoothly, with his best professional twinkle. "We all know your charming wife. That's what we want, another happy marriage, between your country and the United States."

"I thought we already were married," Ferdinando said with mild surprise. "Surely the history of our relations suggests something between a forcible rape and a prolonged, unsatisfying engagement."

"President Lorca—" Vice President Wilson Allen took off his tortoiseshell glasses with a somewhat more precipitous gesture than usual, near exasperation. "You yourself were a guest in this country for a number of years. You taught at one of our major universities: we are all well aware of your brilliant record as a scholar, as well as your incredible successes as a soldier and, if I may add, as someone who systematically violated the U.S. Neutrality Act for a number of years!"

"Thank you," Ferdinando said graciously. "But if you assume therefore that I must always be polite in my dealings with you, you are sadly unaware of the short memory that comes with the responsibilities of public office."

"Your military position is everything you want it to be, I take it?" the young assistant secretary of state drawled, adroitly respectful, not making it seem like a question.

"It's as strong as need be," Ferdinando replied a little sharply. "We have built up our armed forces by over two hundred percent in the last six years. That's not bad, considering we started out with a shambles!"

"Still, you could do more."

"We *will* do more. Seriously, gentlemen, you must give us time. After all—" he laughed, falling back on the obvious cliché, "Rome was neither built nor armed in a day!"

"Would you like your army to be?"

"What do you mean?" he asked, pausing with his cigarette held a scant millimeter from his lips.

"Built in a day—or rather, built up, which is really what we're talking about." Duncan Farrell gave him another one of his million-dollar smiles. "Pay your average *campesino* a better wage than he can make working on his little dirt farm, and you've got yourself a standing army. Get yourself American trainers to teach your boys how to parachute and handle modern explosives, M-sixteens and napalm, and you can whip anybody's ass up and down the Pacific and Atlantic coasts. You could become our most important ally in the region—better than Mexico. Mexico can't do shit for us, but you could become the key to our whole United States policy in Central America."

Ferdinando leaned his chin thoughtfully on his hand, unable to believe he was hearing any of this. "Better than Mexico, hmm?"

"I shouldn't say this, but the Mexicans don't know anything. Look at the mess their peso is in—they've even bungled their oil reserves, and you certainly haven't followed their lead in *that* respect."

"I have better business advisers," Ferdinando said quietly. "You really are serious about this. I'm sorry, I'm having trouble taking it all in . . . you want us to fight your battles for you in Central America. You are willing to train our army, with what—

however many millions of dollars it may take—to do what? Fight a war for you? Invade Nicaragua? I'm sorry, gentlemen, but what you're suggesting is so unlikely, it's really quite fascinating. What on earth makes you think we can do more for you than your Bowery Boys in Honduras and your Keystone Kops in El Salvador?"

President Farrell smiled. "Neither of those countries is headed by you, Señor President."

"Thank God! If I had to contend with the mess you've made of those two countries, I'd cut my losses and catch the next plane for Switzerland! Gentlemen," he said, leaning forward a little, still with his light smile, the intensity of his blue eyes catching them all by surprise. "Let's understand one another. Aside from the moral considerations, you're offering to give my country an army which can make mincemeat out of every other force in the region, and on top of that, enough matériel and training and—one presumes, although you haven't mentioned it—cold, hard cash, to keep this paradigm of military efficiency humming along till the millennium. In return, I presume, my men, rather than yours, will liberate those nations that labor under the communist yoke and protect those nations that labor under the capitalist yoke, pretty much on demand. Forgive me for saying so, but it seems rather unnecessary—why not do it youself? However, if you're determined to throw your money away on Mayapán, I don't see how I can reasonably attempt to talk you out of it!"

Apparently that was enough of a guarantee of national security to satisfy the American interests, and the deal was struck on those terms. Ferdinando was back on a plane for Campeche that night. His banker (factotum, ambassador-at-large) Felix Innocencio Agudo happened to be in Washington at that time (there were an increasing number of times when Felix Agudo happened to be where Ferdinando wanted him to be), and he arranged, quietly and efficiently, to superintend the bills through Congress authorizing an unprecedented figure in aid to be siphoned into Mayapán beginning by the end of that year. That money mixed with the rich red flow of life's blood from United Oil and Linz Industries, to fund the building that seemed more and more to be occurring as an act of God: an extraordinary interruption of the usual course of events, which experience, prescience, or care could not prevent. There was a similar-seeming permanence to the people's love for the Lorcas, but that survived a shock: there was an attempt on their lives on May 1, although the beloved Presidente and Presidenta of Mayapán fortunately survived the attack.

It happened in the early evening, as they were stepping out of the Presidential limousine to enter the Montejo Opera House for a gala in honor of the Argentine ambassador. It may have been the timing—May Day—or the well-publicized atrocities of the anticommunist Argentine government that contributed to the theory that the attack was Russian-based; but in fact the assassin was a lone man, and, it was proven later, mentally deranged. He was a truck driver, one of Lejo Costamendez's workers who had been laid off for drunkenness six months before, a slender, trembling man in his early twenties, as the Lorcas saw him when they descended from their car: pointing a gun at La Señora's head and babbling something incomprehensible about more wages and a bigger share of the profits, when Ferdinando grabbed his arm and pushed his hand up, forcing him to fire harmlessly into the air and incidentally breaking two of his fingers before the gunman was unarmed, and rendered summarily unconscious by the Presidential guards who surrounded him. He was quickly hustled away, and the Lorcas continued into the Opera House as though nothing had happened, but the incident had a strong effect on the domestic and foreign press: cries of "Assassin!" were screamed from headlines of *La Prensa* and *La Voz* the next morning, along with editorials demanding an investigation into this "foreign-based atrocity," while the opposition papers saw this attack as proof of Ferdinando Lorca's waning charisma, the first act of terrorism in what would, they claimed, soon escalate into a full-scale war against the government. Much was made of the gunman's having pointed his gun at Camila, as though he intended to kill her first; or perhaps to hold her as a hostage—there were conflicting opinions, but the *frisson* caused by a quick-witted photographer's image of the fragile, beautiful young woman with one hand outstretched toward the man who was pointing the gun at her, made sure the story got a wide and avid readership. The Lorcas decided to treat the attack as an unfortunate incident, and, characteristically, to discuss it with a certain amount of humor. Ferdinando asked Camila if she was going to make it a practice to be shot at, so he would know when to duck, and Camila replied that it was all the fault of *Time* magazine, since everyone knew that the best way to get in *Time* was to have your picture taken with Camila Lorca. They stayed close to each other that evening, but then they were always close: sipping champagne in the *entr'acte* with the Argentine ambassador, but excusing themselves soon after the opera was over and driving back to the palace with a military escort, keeping a low profile for the next few days. And they increased the guards at the palace and outside the Sociedad Building on the Avenida Cortés from the few unobtrusive, smiling policemen who had been there previously to a visible military presence, in sharp white uniforms, with bandoliers and rifles carried at port arms.

So it was at the time when Ferdinando was building the most modern city in Central America that he also contacted William Mynott with a view toward establishing a covert intelligence system in Mayapán. They met in the old Miramar barracks, which had formerly housed the military prison and which was now largely deserted, an unexceptional museum and sight-seeing stop for schoolchildren; and as they walked through the empty rooms and the high, echoing hallways of the fortress that had been built to expel the pirates, which had been reinforced with six-inch guns in the time of the building of the Panama Canal, and which had once served as the place of imprisonment for the country's current President, Ferdinando outlined to the ex-C.I.A. agent the parameters of what he wanted. Mynott was certain they would have no trouble implementing an internal security program which would interface easily with the intelligence-gathering capabilities of Linz Telecommunications, UNOCO, *et al.;* they could just patch right into the existing system, with a few minor changes (additional personnel to handle investigative minutiae, interrogations, and counterinsurgency; covers within the extant military and security forces, and a system of plausible deniability which would enable El Presidente to keep an exclusive eye on the proceedings). Ferdinando drew thoughtfully on his twentieth cigarette of the day, and tried not to laugh at the poor man, who was tragic and lonely in his way: what *did* you do when you were washed up in the intelligence community, but go pimp for a two-bit banana dictator, deal drugs, or retire to McLean, Virginia? Mynott took off his aviator sunglasses and Ferdinando saw the circles and pinpoint pupils of his eyes, and took *that* into consideration as a calculated risk (was it true, his being castrated by the Khmer Rouge? Jorge-Julio de Rodríguez swore it was, but in his melancholy way, Jorge-Julio wasn't the world's most reliable informant). He stopped at the door to the parade ground/exercise yard outside, backlit by the sun, his blue eyes in shadow, and laid his long tanned fingers on the American's arm.

"You understand, this is a precautionary measure. The people still love me." He smiled his light, charming smile. "I want you to avoid trouble, not to start it."

William Mynott stirred uncomfortably, transfixed by those extraordinary eyes. "Par for the course, Mr. President, I don't shit where I eat. No sweat, we'll do this one completely on the up-and-up. Oh, by the way, who do you want to head your side of the operation, Colonel Zacapa? He knows Fidel's style, so long as he doesn't wear a dress."

He stepped outside after Ferdinando, still looking like a non-descript businessman in his polyester suit, thinning kinky brown hair, and sweat-streaked, snub-nosed face. He had put his sunglasses back on again. Ferdinando smiled, but shook his head. "General Rodríguez is my closest military adviser, and the man I would trust most implicitly to carry a gun at my back. You'll work with him."

"Rodríguez . . .?" Mynott seemed to be having trouble remembering him. "I'm afraid I don't—oh, thanks, Mr. President—" as he accepted a cigarette and a light. "I'm afraid I don't remember him."

"You remember General Rodríguez," Ferdinando murmured quietly as he blew out the match. "You used to call him Julio, and an asshole. You see"—he smiled, bathing the *gringo* in the benediction of his chilly friendship—"I also have my sources of information. I am beginning to enjoy the prerogatives of not having to take any shit." His lips twitched. "So be careful. I want you to be *my* guard dog. Please don't let it escape your attention for a minute that *now* you are working for me."

seven

FERDINANDO BROUGHT BATTISTE HOME shortly after that; brought him home with what misgivings and divided loyalties Battiste alone knew, because Ferdinando knew nothing about them; brought him home to clap him on the back the minute the priest walked into the cool tiled foyer of the Presidential Palace, with its wine-red carpet and its white salute of the Presidential guard, because, as he said, he had a much more important job for him—even more important than being the Mayapanian ambassador to Washington.

"I've been wasting your talents, I decided—Camila can keep them happy with one visit every six months!—and I need you for something else." His blue eyes danced. "Besides, isn't it about time you started thinking about your own career, instead of wasting your time helping me?"

"I've got no career of my own," Battiste murmured with a painful smile. "I'm a jack of all trades, you know that."

"I know you're a liar, but it doesn't matter. There, what do you think of that?" He stopped before a display of pre-Columbian artifacts, new to the main hallway of the Presidential Palace, and stepped back to allow Battiste to come forward and examine them.

They were very beautifully arranged, with indirect lighting, and as a central figure a reclining chac mool, which Battiste noticed with surprise and a certain amount of amusement, because it was so massive, so starkly beautiful in its way (or was it ugly?)—bunched raised knees and a head turned at right angles to the body, wide-cheeked and clench-teethed and with its hands clasped under a flat surface over its abdomen used (so the tourist pamphlets theorized) as a stone of sacrifice, for cutting out the heart of a back-bent victim—it was a cliché of Mayapanian culture, and Battiste turned to Ferdinando with a laugh, saying, "Now you really *can* threaten your enemies with putting them to the sword, if they don't go along with your building proposals!"

Ferdinando smiled. "Do you like it? I can't decide whether I like it, or whether it terrifies me! At any rate it was a gift, so government auditors need question neither my taste nor my profligacy...." His light hands hovered over it, momentarily bemused, and then he turned with his dancer's grace, laughing, to embrace him. "Come on outside, I've got one of your fellow heresiarchs here. I've been entertaining him all morning with vague promises of your eventual arrival, and I'm sure he's beginning to think I'm one of those Central American tyrants who promises everything, and delivers nothing. *Amiguita*, what was his name?"

This to Camila, who had just then joined them, hugging Battiste with a little more lightness than usual, casually kissing his cheek. He stared at her in pain, remembering their terrible interview in Rome, replaying their last parting, and managed a sick smile.

"Camila remembers everyone's name better than I do," Ferdinando joked. "Who is this priest again? Cardinal Verrocchio? No, he was a Renaissance painter. What *is* his name?"

"Cardinal Vinolo"—Camila smiled—"who of course makes jokes about his being a teetotaler, and then drinks sherry like a bibulous nun ... okay, better put on a straight face, this is for real...."

And she stepped out gracefully onto the raised stone patio of tamarind trees which they had built on the site of the former stables of the Presidential Palace, with her face arranged in its perfect smile, slim in her sleeveless turquoise dress beside her handsome guayabera-shirted husband, and Battiste stepped between them, knelt, and kissed the ring of the tall, well-fleshed man who had been sitting awaiting his arrival, who was one of the most powerful men in the Vatican, an intimate of his Holiness and his Grace the Superior General of the Jesuits, and who said in Italian-inflected Spanish, "Ah, Señor Ambassador Tommassi, I have been hearing wonderful things about you!"

Battiste blushed like a brick. "These people are my friends. I wouldn't believe more than a third of what they tell you."

"Ah, in truth? Surely so little would in itself be flattering . . . but I have other sources who corroborate their testimony. Please, we will sit down and all be informal?" He gestured beautifully—he had very long hands, paler and softer than Ferdinando's, but similarly graceful—and the beatific hazel eyes of a born actor, one who dissembles without malice. Behind his eyes lay the shrewd mind of a Tuscan peasant who knows good value when he sees it, and who had traveled halfway around the globe for this meeting. "Felix Innocencio Agudo told me that you had been of great help to him in various spiritual matters, Father Tommassi . . . for which he was grateful, very grateful. His wife as well. . . ." Cardinal Vinolo added idly, referring (as Battiste was irritably aware) to a conversation of a scant two minutes' duration more than a year ago, wherein Battiste had advised the banker flippantly not to meet his wife's lover with a pistol unless he had enough ammunition to assassinate the *guardía*, and not to expect last rites from him if he persisted, since he wouldn't bury someone who was so foolishly bent on killing himself. The conversational gambit was a not-very-subtle way of saying that the Vatican had been in recent contact with the head of the Mayapanian Federal Bank, and Battiste raised his eyebrows toward Ferdinando, even while he wondered why the cardinal should wish him, as well as the Lorcas, to have this particular piece of information.

Ferdinando smiled and lit a cigarette, sunlight dusting the fine hairs on his arms, and the darker hair, visible through the open neck of his shirt, with gold; there on the terrace it was very warm, and Camila had a delicate touch of moisture in the hollow of her throat, and his Eminence sweated discreetly in his black soutane and red sash. They could look out over the ceiba trees and the lush green lawn of the palace (watered by sprinklers and tended by two short-clad Maya Indians) to the unreal clouds and hallucinatory blue waters of the Gulf, pelicans diving and long-tails soaring out beyond the seawall, sun sparkling on the rainbows in the sprinklers' arcs, warming a scent of ripe mangoes and papayas from the hidden fruit trees. It was very quiet, peaceful, with the distant sound of a radio playing the latest hit single by Pisote and the sound of the servants laying a cold lunch for El Presidente and his visitors, clink of china and soft Mayan whispers from the lower terrace. Ferdinando shut his eyes and chuckled quietly. "I'm glad Felix Agudo's visit pleased you, your Eminence. I'm sure he had no idea he was going to meet the Pope when I sent him to Italy!"

"No indeed, he was very surprised. But I think the visit with the Holy Father went very well. His Holiness is a keen judge of character, and not patient with the ill-prepared, but Señor Agudo is very cool—eh? A 'cool customer'?"

"Sophisticated," Camila murmured. "You make him sound like a criminal."

"Oh, scarcely. He made a three-day retreat with us, at the monastery of Monte Cassino, and later visited the Holy Father at Castel Gandolfo. Apparently, the climate in Bonn didn't agree with him, for he had a cold, but that may have been the abrupt change in latitude. They say last week in San'ā the temperature was one hundred and six."

Battiste tardily came awake to the import of what they were saying, although he kept his eyes attentively questioning, his features carefully circumspect. The connection between West Germany and the capital of South Yemen was oil and Linz Industries, which was also the connection between Felix Agudo's globe-trotting and the wells of Mayapán, and, apparently, the wealth of investment capital controlled by the Vatican. So the Church wanted to invest in Mayapán—but how much, and why? And why had he been brought here? He kept his hands folded loosely in his lap, and found himself staring at Camila, who was taking no part in the conversation, but leaning her folded arms on the table and watching them all with a queer, half-pained smile. Ferdinando shook his head.

"You know, I can't believe how much Felix enjoys complaining about his situation! You'd think he didn't *like* making fifty percent interest on his investments with the I.O.R!"

Battiste's skin bristled; the I.O.R. was the Vatican Bank, and in normal business had no reason to deal with a second-rate provincial financier like Agudo. He decided to risk a question.

"Your Eminence, excuse me, but wouldn't your Roman bankers be able to direct such investments on their own, without involving the Federal Bank of Mayapán? I mean—isn't that fairly unusual?"

The cardinal was so adept at statecraft, Battiste barely caught his hesitation. "Normally, of course, that would be the case." He smiled, tilting his head a little to one side. "You betray a great knowledge of our affairs, my son. Your friend was no less than just in his praise. However . . ." Studiously regarding his thumbs. "In such an instance as this, when the source of our funds would suggest an unfortunate tendency to take sides on our part, we prefer—"

"You prefer to launder the *norteamericanos'* money through Felix's little bank, and split the difference?" Battiste inquired sharply, surprising himself with his own anger. He was shaking, partly because he wasn't more surprised, because he blamed Ferdinando and Camila for his lack of surprise and the terrible, empty amusement he felt where his shock should have been.

"That is where you come in, my son," Cardinal Vinolo said without the slightest discomfort. "As you know, the Superior General of your Order is my friend, and my colleague. His health is precarious. The Holy Father in his wisdom has seen fit to appoint a papal legate, with full powers to direct the Society of Jesus in the interim. A man who has managed the foreign affairs of his country, and who could see his way clear to acting as liaison between the Vatican Bank and one of the larger oil-producing nations in the world, could pretty much consider his appointment guaranteed, pending the approval of the Holy Father."

Battiste looked around the table with a sick smile. "I have the feeling I'm being bribed."

Cardinal Vinolo was bland. "My son, sadly, we are all bribed by life. But I assure you this is merely business."

Was it? Camila still refused to look at him, studying her lacquered fingernails spread out before her on the tabletop, with her strange half-smile . . . surely she couldn't approve of this agreement to sell the country wholesale, when they had sworn to maintain their autonomy? But it was as if she had removed herself, as if . . . he thought with anguish . . . as if she were in another world, equally removed from pain and grief and pleasure. And because he rashly assumed that he had known her once, he assumed now that her change was due to Ferdinando.

"Why?" He discovered to his profound discomfort that he had asked the question aloud, but only Camila knew that he'd been speaking to her, and she turned to Ferdinando to allow him to answer it.

"Because I'm asking you to, that's why!" Ferdinando said, laughing. "The same reason I sent you to Washington! The same reason I'm sending you to the Vatican—if you'll go. My God, who do I have that I can trust besides you? Felix? He'll mess things up so badly that even the holy fathers wouldn't be able to put things right. Besides, he's not a priest." Ferdinando looked down and shook his head. "I know the Church has gotten more flexible in the last few years, but I don't think even *they* are quite up to considering Felito Agudo as a papal legate!" He laughed and put his hand over Battiste's, smiling at him with his extraordinary bright-blue eyes. "I need you enough to offer you the truth—which is that I need this investment, and I need you to handle the details. There, now if that isn't enough honesty for you, I don't know what is!"

Which left Battiste caught as he had always been on the horns of his devotion, unable to say no. Certainly, with a part of his mind, he recognized the possibilities: the scope for his talents, which had to come, if he didn't leave the Church. If he betrayed his people—but it wasn't of them that he was thinking, but selfishly of himself, his lost faith in the beautiful man in front of him, who had changed so little in the last seven years (still graceful and sinewy strong, shining with ambition and tanned and relaxed and holding his heart in thrall, in the questioning lines on his high forehead, the shadowed, deeper orbits of his eyes) while he had changed so much, and lost the last vestiges of his pride and his idealism. He found himself thinking about it quite calmly: I could do a lot for my country, in the Vatican. I could advance my own position. And if necessary, if the time came, I could oppose him.

"I don't know if I'm quite ready for all this holiness, Ferdinando." He said it lightly, so that Cardinal Vinolo might think he was joking or displaying false modesty, and deliberately refused to look at Camila, so that only Ferdinando knew that he was asking him to relieve him of this choice.

Ferdinando leaned toward him intimately and said, "Well, you know, I *could* hold off on this decision for a few weeks, while you go skin diving off Isla del Viento, but they really *do* need you now."

"Then I suppose I'd better say yes," Battiste said quite matter-of-factly, unfolding his clasped hands and shrugging as if it made very little difference. "If you're sure you want me to do this, I don't see how I can reasonably refuse."

Within a month Battiste was on a plane to Rome, as special envoy to the Vatican Bank in charge of the papacy's investment in Mayapán. He knew with a bitter certainty exactly how great an opportunity Ferdinando had given him, how exalted his position would be among the Jesuits; as indeed it was. The frail, aging priest, who had led the Society of Jesus for so many years, took his hand and asked that he be given an office next door to his rooms in the Borgo Santo Spirito. There were those, even in the Curia itself, who hushed their conversation as he walked past. He had arrived; and he began to build about himself the armor of indifference whose first, pitiful links he'd had to forge, instinctively, looking across the terrace at Camila and meeting her eyes, grown bittersweet and weary, pitying him (and what right had she to pity him?) and herself in the lovely golden prison of her fame and the exigencies of politics. She was never heard to breathe a word of complaint: indeed, even those whose veneration most nearly approached idolatry had to admit her unthinking devotion to her husband—if there were private contradictions, she kept them to herself. She was so completely indentified as his wife that she was never more valuable as an asset, more thoughtful and innovative, than while she was scripting her persona as *la llorona* who weeps for the whole world—though as to why La Señora Lorca should have to weep, with her country's love and her own private 727 jet and her army of assistants, no one could say.

She flew to New York in mid-September, unannounced and unaccompanied by anyone other than her private staff, makeup artist and hairdresser, private bodyguard and maid. She was there for a double purpose: to expedite the flow of currency from the U.S. Treasury to the Vatican Bank, and to present Porfirio Cheruña with the Order of Santiago on his own terms, in his adoptive city, and in a public ceremony. This last was at Ferdinando's request, since he refused to allow her to meet with the old man privately; and her presence there had been Porfirio's condition—and so she had gone, smiling and controlled as always, but it didn't work out, the ceremony had to be canceled because of La Señora's sudden and unexpected illness, and only the tactful bankers at Shearson Lehman/American Express knew that she had never shown up for any of her meetings, and only her staff knew that for a span of three days she had been absent from her hotel.

She took a cab by herself, to the Metropolitan Museum of Art, where the leaves were just starting to yellow and blow against the wrought-iron benches and cobblestones of the wide plaza, in front of its marble steps . . . a slight, elegant figure in a Russian sable cape, meeting a spare old man in a light-gray pinstripe suit, with a silver cane, steel-rimmed glasses, and an impeccable head of snow-white hair. They stood about twenty feet from each other, while the wind blew gusts of leaves and debris (candy and cigarette wrappers, bits of paper) around their feet and the impersonal fall sky arched cloudless and cobalt overhead; she couldn't look away from him, she was forced to stand rooted to the spot, while he approached her, walking with only a slight limp which strangely didn't offset but rather intensified his archaic and courtly grace; he stood only a few steps away from her, and stretched out his hand to touch a tendril of bright gold hair against her bone-white cheek and she shuddered, but didn't withdraw from him, staring at him with eyes that were wide and terrified, but for all that compulsively locked in his ice-gray, distant gaze. A sick span of endless time elapsed, which Porfirio ended with a slight gesture as much of command as entreaty, and turned away as if he were bored by her, although everything

274

about his tall, thin frame shivered with repressed expectancy. He started to walk away from her, slowly, as if he didn't care whether she followed him, and she found herself drawn forward like a sleepwalker, or like someone who follows after a figure in a dream: calling out, trying in vain to see that person's face, although the dreamer's object is always taciturn and evasive. That was the way she followed him, and he stopped and turned to face her, with a stern, cruel, mocking stare, saying, "You're coming because you want to, not because I'm forcing you," and she lowered her eyes and nodded, exposing her white, fragile neck deliberately, like a victim, and feeling the feathery touch of his fingers there, the light scratch of his fingernails against her skin. She shivered. She heard his voice change, becoming thicker and more intimate, "*Querida*, you have if anything gotten lovelier since the last time I saw you," and she wanted to scream as his hand encircled her neck completely. She thought, This is what I deserve, and then, This is what I've always deserved, as he helped her into a cab, and rode with her down Fifth Avenue in the bright flame and blue of the autumn afternoon, from which they formed something apart, a universe that was both secret and self-ashamed. She stayed with him for three days. She shut her eyes, trembling convulsively, the first time he touched her, and seemed both to want and to be revolted by a resumption of the intimacy which was inescapable between them . . . as Porfirio himself realized, at one point in the delirium of the next three days, staring at her with something like fear as he murmured, "Perhaps we ought to stop," and she shook her head almost violently, No, as she knelt before him, shivering, with tears running down her face. He was an instrument for her, he realized even as her tiny shoulders and buttocks reddened beneath the blows of his cane and her lips brushed the crepitating flesh of his abdomen, and he lost his mind. She slept curled away from him in his unmade bed, on the sheets scented with lavender, like a little child, and one morning less in lucidity than a strangely voluptuous innocence he found himself stroking her hair, and she turned to look at him with eyes blank with pain, and his heart stirred with an almost fatherly pity not unmixed with lust. I'm sorry, he murmured, and she shook her head again violently, No, and turned to touch him. He lay in an ecstacy of delight, gelid with guilt, but with the terrifying vertigo of a man who has lost all his bearings, and been raped by his own creation, and seduced in his fading twilight into the cruel illusions of love.

She left him after three days, as he had known she would, almost without a word, dressing with scrupulous care and slipping on the soft sable cape like a shroud without answering his pathetic questions of Will I see you again? except to whisper almost inaudibly, I don't know. She walked out the door, and instead of waiting for the elevator, walked down several flights of stairs like a somnambulist, with her eyes almost shut and a splitting headache knifing into her temples. For two weeks afterward she remained shut up inside a suite at the St. Regis, taking baths and sleeping for long hours of every day, remote, silent, letting her bruised mind and her body heal until she could go back to Mayapán with her generous spirit and her beautiful smile intact—or nearly so. She shut her mind to the memory and when she turned her head, smiling, to hear on the six o'clock news that OPEC had announced a 6 percent hike in the price of crude oil, she knew she was herself again. She appeared at Kennedy Airport two hours early and spent the time signing autographs, smiling for *Time* and the *New York Post*, before stepping aboard her private plane, and when she had settled into her seat with her shadowed eyes shut, Zito Ardilla asked quietly if La Señora was all right, and she whispered without opening her eyes, Yes, I'm all right, I'm perfect.

276

eight

SHE BECAME AN expensive friend for friendly governments after that, always traveling and expecting the best accommodations, state balls, a little quiet chat with this or that official figure which would, more often than not, result in a trade agreement or commitment of aid favorable to her country's balance of payments. No longer the passive pawn of airline schedules and other countries' media, she created her own media events, with her own cameramen, her own directors; and perhaps it was only natural, given her status in the world, and the inconceivable pressures impinging on any of the world's great public figures, that she should want to control what she could: no longer trusting to improvisation, scripting her triumphs and demanding her perquisites in advance.

She was still a frequent guest at the White House, where President Farrell remained her staunchest and, in many ways, her most important conquest. Likewise, Vice President Wilson Allen was also thawing toward her, to the extent of trading compliments and sly witticisms; he once asked her what perfume she was wearing, and when she replied Shalimar, he inquired if her husband intended to build a Taj for her, as Shah Jahan had done for his legendary wife Mumtaz Mahal. More cynical observers would have guessed that she was cultivating the straitlaced Allen as Duncan Farrell's heir apparent, after the aging football star's unchallenged eight-year term—and that may have been true; she was scarcely casual in her friendships then, and every smile was made to serve a purpose. But she was if anything even more tireless in her work for the poor of her country, and even her cruelest antagonists could not cite incidents of foreign monies and supplies going anywhere but into the hospitals and homes of her *porteños*, her *indios:* the mute throngs who had suddenly become vocal, with La Señora Lorca as their spokeswoman, shouting hysterically outside her Sociedad Building the moment she arrived, slender and beautiful (beautifully dressed and jeweled, but why not, she was rich), wan and tired from her constant traveling but with a handful of dollars, deutsche marks, or lire in her hand, waving to the crowd, smiling for the cameras of MAYA-TV before disappearing into the building.

She redecorated her offices with flowers, candles, big whitewashed walls, and holy pictures—so that it indeed resembled a church (comforting for the little *mamacitas* who came to her for birth control pills and clap medicines, but oddly disconcerting for her staff), including a big carved crucifix of the dying Cristo in her office, a wonderful, eerily lifelike statue, with ivory eyeballs turned up in death, and detailed, piercing thorns, each with its vibrant drop of blood. She attended more and more of the sick and the destitute personally, laying her hands on them: not with the brusque impatience of doctors, or the cloying tenderness of a childless woman (both of which might have been more easily understood by her associates), but with a deep, wordless wonder— reaching out to them as though to assure herself of their reality, or sometimes (Buiztas observed this, sitting at a desk in the corner, filling in invoices for medicines while his mud-brown eyes occasionally glanced in her direction, over the top of his steel-rimmed spectacles) as if to remember where they were, as if she were going blind or could no longer trust her own perceptions of distances. She hugged even the filthiest and most scabrous children to her breast (she began to keep three or four changes of clothes in her offices, so she could spruce up for photographs) and displayed real anger, rare to any of her adoring employees, who would have died for her, if anyone who wanted to was kept from

touching her. She worked longer hours, as did Ferdinando, sometimes neither of them returning to the palace before nine or ten
o'clock at night; usually to share a private supper in their rooms,
and stay up half the night working on plans for their city, a wage
dispute by the Truckers Union, or a new ad campaign to bring in
los turistas . . . sitting up in bed drowning in piles of papers, sipping brandy, smoking a joint, deciding the fate of their country
on pads of legal paper placed between their knees, *el padre* and *la
madre* of their country in silk pajamas, and getting up at 5:30 A.M.
to do it all over again.

Their status as a military power was growing even faster
than their phenomenal economy, and in Mayapán all the armed
forces were now under the command of General Jorge-Julio de
Rodríguez. It was his responsibility to coordinate not merely his
American-trained troops but the newly reorganized Guardía
Civil and the national police and the customs and treasury police
as well, along with the shadowy "intelligence police" controlled
by his nominal counterpart and former nemesis, William Mynott.
Late evenings, at nine or ten or eleven o'clock at night, General
Rodríguez would press the heels of his hands against his eyes and
drive his personal Mercedes to the two-bedroom bachelor's
apartment he'd bought in the *gringo*-style condominium El
Paraíso, a concrete high-rise facing the seawall, where he could
fall asleep with the sound of the ocean in his ears. He still had the
tall saddened look of an unhappy *campesino* in his uniform of an
army private, with the small gold star which Ferdinando had
given him, making him wear it, with a laugh, Yes, I know it
doesn't mean anything, but you have to wear something, otherwise how will they know to take their orders from you? his long
sad moustaches and his dark, sad Indian's face, the whitened scars
all over his body from his fighting for El Lorca and La Señora
during the civil war, and his rough hands—which he always kept
scrupulously clean, and the nails trimmed short, from the days
when he remembered them blackened with motor oil. He was in
many ways one of the most powerful men in Mayapán, certainly
influential, with the eternally inexplicable threat associated in
that latitude with the military, those in control of the Army, *el
generalísimo*. He walked apart, half government employee and
half government administrator, and no one knew whether he en-

joyed being a public figure, or whether he wanted the responsibility for the country's burgeoning military which had been thrust upon him, or even whether he believed in that burgeoning military at all.

The country's beliefs had an opportunity to be tested in May, when a national referendum overwhelmingly ratified the *gringo* intrusion (after all, the American advisers and their families, who were encouraged to join them, brought in a vacationing largess that made them big spenders, and outside Campeche no one could tell the difference between these *norteamericanos* and the businessmen who were there already anyway). For General Rodríguez and William Mynott and the two American G.I.'s and thirty-eight Mayapanian recruits who went on a training mission across the Lempa River a month and a half later, the situation was more complicated. For one thing, no one was absolutely certain afterward whether it had been a training mission: they had carried live ammunition, primarily M-16s and G-3 assault rifles, with a few private shotguns and pistols; they had gone into "active" territory, territory in which leftist guerrillas were known to be patrolling; but they brought the *norteamericanos* with them, a circumstance which suggested—at least officially—that they hadn't anticipated any real fighting. Then again, what happened? Could that bloody, and tragic, and finally inconclusive day be called an attack, or an ambush, or was it simply an accident blown up out of all proportion, not by the newspapers (who never got wind of it) but by the participants themselves?

They were airlifted in that morning by two American helicopters, which were scheduled to pick them up again at six o'clock that evening. They marched in a column down a sharp slope, into an area bordering a stream where it was minimally cooler under the trees (General Rodríguez estimated afterwards that it hit over 100 degrees) but swarming with mosquitoes. There was a good deal of offhand joking about the mosquitoes. The men were up, wired; they saw this patrol as a safe way to prove their *machismo*, even if they didn't meet up with anything more dangerous than the bugs and the wet heat and the haze which had hung over that whole part of the country since the rains started in May. They trained their guns on startled birds, and joked about getting a deer. The two Americans (who were a few years older than their trainees, perhaps in their early twenties instead of their late teens) walked at the front and midpoint of the group, holding their weapons a little self-consciously as if they were aware they were being copied, despite a deliberate informality of dress, a Phillies baseball cap and a two-day growth of beard on one of them, while the other carried a pack of cigarettes in his breast pocket which he politely handed around to anyone else who wanted them. One of the young recruits ahead of Jorge-Julio de Rodríguez turned to his companion and joked that the *gringo* had better have brought a whole carton: he didn't know how Mayapanians loved to smoke, look at El Presidente, you never saw him without a butt in his mouth. Jorge-Julio smiled, and although he would have liked a cigarette himself he refrained from taking one, partly out of a desire not to seem to ape Ferdinando too closely, partly to keep a semblance of discipline among this collection of children.

The man walking next to him was not a child, and Jorge-Julio had to admit that he knew how to behave himself on patrol. Well, why not, he'd trained in deeper jungles than this, walking lightly, keeping a careful eye out while keeping his body loose, relaxed, he might be a paranoid schizophrenic now but he was probably a good soldier once, well, what the hell, you could say the same thing about Adolf Hitler and I still wouldn't want him out on a patrol with me. He studied the *gringo*'s face, which was so unremarkable you couldn't even tell how crazy he was, sweat dampening his curly, receding hair and beading on his bulbous forehead, making his sunglasses slide down his snub nose, so that he had to keep pushing them up with his thumb, collecting on the short shelf of his upper lip, for he was unconsciously smiling. Why the hell had he come out with them? Jorge-Julio wondered, as he refused a proffered offer of Juicy Fruit (What were they going to do next, he wondered, cook hot dogs?) and watched as Mynott folded up two sticks and stuck them in his mouth.

"Sugar high," he explained. "Gets you into overdrive. It's better than caffeine, for somebody with my metabolism."

Jorge-Julio decided that the best thing for a guy with his metabolism was a nickel bag of heroin, but he didn't mention it. They were walking down by the stream itself, crossing over the shallows where the water was perhaps a foot to a foot and a half deep, green-brown and warm as a bath with parasites and mud, and the mosquitoes were as thick as a fog; he gave up trying to swat them on his face and grimly hurried his men across, up the farther bank of the river and onto a dirt road, which showed signs of recent travel, ruts and churned-up mud, but there was no sound, except the chirping of the birds and the omnipresent hum of the cicadas, and then they saw the body.

Or what was left of a body, presumably but not necessarily male, most of the face and genitals pecked away by birds and the body cavity swelling and bursting, disemboweled, they saw as they moved closer in horrified fascination, in the sign of a cross, and the absent intestines replaced with a living colony of maggots and something that looked like garbage, a paper bag, and a bottle of beer. One of the recruits turned away and vomited, and another one said, "We'd better bury him, *mi general.* We can do it quickly, it won't take very much time."

Jorge-Julio nodded, almost absently, chewing on his moustache as he glanced up and down the road in either direction, at the ordinary, dusty trees showing the hazy blue of the sky through their leaves, the banal, humid air stained with the smell of putrefaction, as it had been during the war. A memory he didn't want, either for himself or for these young kids. "Sure, bury the poor son of a bitch and let's get out of here." The words were barely out of his mouth before some sixth sense told him to hit the dirt, and the rifle shot that should have killed him smacked instead into the chest of one of the two Americans standing behind him, spinning him around and down in a spatter of blood like a fountain. Pure panic flattened them and started a disorganized counterattack; Jorge-Julio rolled over into the scrub on the side of the road and yelled, "Take cover, you dumb bastards, before you get your balls blown off!" and this exhortation apparently worked, because they all managed one way or another to scramble into the bushes to safety, leaving the dead *gringo* leaking blood into the dirt five feet away from the corpse they had intended burying. Jorge-Julio pulled himself up a few inches and surveyed the road, again silent, all trace of cicadas and bird noise gone in the after-echo of the burst of gunfire and in the flat stillness he could hear someone, probably one of his own men, praying to the Virgen to protect him and he whispered irritably,

"Jesus Christ, be quiet, *estúpido*," while he tried to see where the men were hiding who had shot at them. A sluggish breeze ruffled the leaves of the trees. He heard a rifle click, and he waited, very still, with his mind as blank as the mind of a dog while the soft wind died down and the buzz of a fly was stilled as it settled onto the gringo's wound. His own breath and heartbeat were suspended while he waited to see what the men were going to do next, down there about a hundred feet off in a stand of ceiba trees, a blue baseball cap visible for a moment, and the glitter of the sun, mirror-bright, on the barrel of a gun. There was a collective tightening of fingers on triggers (and of course the crucial question was, How many fingers on their side? how many guns?) and he felt a trickle of sweat running down his face as he lay flattened in the dust and a sudden viscous clot of rage in his throat because goddamn it what the hell was he doing here? He'd fought for his country years ago, and this was a repression without honor, with no beautiful señora to inspire them, and he felt the shame of fighting for the wrong side more keenly than a wound. But there was nothing they could do about that now.

A rat-scrabble in the dust of the road was his only alert, and he glanced up as Mynott scrambled forward and pitched a grenade into the stand of trees, tucked and rolled over to the other side of the road, and came up firing his Uzi machine pistol into the cover of the long grass with such violence that for a moment they all thought he'd gone crazy, and then the rest of the recruits started firing after him, and in a few moments the guerrillas came straggling out of the trees with their hands up over their heads. They were very young. Cheap crosses made of twisted wire around their necks, or American-style dog tags, ragged denim shirts and blue jeans or grimy combat fatigues, one of the young men badly wounded, blood running out of his eye and his head and the skin ripped off all along his arm, another young man staggering from a head wound and leaning on his comrades, two young women, both with their hair cut very short, one of them short and strong with a bandolier across her chest and the other slenderer, wearing a black beret with a red star on it, six children in all, and Jorge-Julio's heart sank as he wondered what in the world to do with them.

It wasn't as easy as it seemed. They had no provisions for

taking prisoners; moreover, the presence of the American advisers made everything more complicated. He got up and walked forward, looking at them with his sorrowful, hangdog eyes, and asked them who they were, thinking Dios, just say you're civilians and I'll pretend to believe you and tell you to beat it and we'll all save ourselves a lot of trouble. The young man with the flayed arm, who still seemed to be the leader, and who had a proud, snide expression on his bleeding, grimacing face, said in Spanish, "Revolutionary Brigade 251," and then noticed the Phillies cap and the M-16 of the remaining American and drawled, "*Buenos días*, Meester Asshole!" and gave him the finger.

"You little son of a bitch—" the American exploded, raising his rifle, and one of the Mayapanians said, "Lieutenant—" and even reached out as if to touch him on the arm. Jorge-Julio saw the recognition in the young man's one good eye, and felt a twist of nostalgia and misery in his guts because of course he knew the value of what they'd just said, he was a smart kid, and Jorge-Julio saw in him one of the rebels he himself had commanded just a few years before, although now, because they knew about the *norteamericanos*, there was no way he and Bill Mynott could possibly let them go.

"Come on," he said, jerking his head in the direction of the road.

"What are you going to do with them?" asked the American adviser.

"I'm going to get them the hell out of here, in case they've got friends in the hills. Jesus Christ, Señor, who are you to question my orders one way or another?" He looked at the fresh-faced American, who had a face like an uncooked pie, smooth as pastry and just beginning to be outraged by the notion that they were going to leave his countryman there lying in the dirt because it was too dangerous to bury him, as if it mattered to *him* one way or another where he was buried, if at all, and he felt vaguely sorry for the naïve son of a bitch from Des Moines or Philadelphia or wherever the hell it was but he felt sorrier for the young *campesino* with blood running down his face. Shit, what a mess.

"Come on," he said again, hopelessly. "Life is a kick in the ass, for all of us. Let's get the finger out."

They walked cautiously down the road, for perhaps another half a mile, and then cut across country, down into another gully of what might have been a former river, but this river must have dried up because all there was was a silt of mud and small stones. They walked more courageously along that, still with their ears alert for any sound and their rifles held at the ready, but they met no one. The captured guerrillas kept up as well as they could, and were fairly quiet, although after about an hour the man with the head wound started to get delirious, and gave loud groans, and finally sank down onto his knees puking blood and died. The miasmic heat and the thick stench of the mud of the riverbed and the presence of even more mosquitoes than before gave them all the feeling that they were walking in a dream, through thick overhanging plants and overarching trees which hid a sky now flat white, and on Jorge-Julio's orders his men helped the guerrillas who were wounded and even carried the young man who was their leader, when he could no longer walk, and the afternoon dragged on with the feeling that they weren't going anywhere, and the men started to get angry and disgusted and bored. Language itself became thick and heavy, and even after they had decided, for no real reason, that there was no more danger (because there hadn't been any danger for a while), the men didn't speak at all, and no one smoked any more cigarettes, although that might have helped to keep the mosquitoes away. Mynott and Jorge-Julio now walked at the head of the small column, Mynott consulting his map although it appeared to Jorge-Julio as if he had memorized the directions they were supposed to take, or then again as if he were making them up. They finally left the riverbed and climbed up to another road (apparently this was a "less-traveled" road, according to what Mynott said) leading to a small town, of corrugated iron shacks, a sad grocery with almost nothing to sell but a well-stocked Coca-Cola machine, which they gratefully patronized. The proprietor of the grocery watched them as they put dimes into the machine, and he didn't seem to register any surprise when he saw the wounded guerrillas or the lone American or the Mayapanian uniforms on the rest of them, but they couldn't be sure, and Jorge-Julio was pleased that everybody kept his mouth shut although he couldn't tell if it mattered, the town seemed to be deserted and perhaps it was except for this lone intrepid storekeeper, everyone else having been refugeed out, or "disappeared," or simply given up on a hopeless country and an even more hopeless situation.

They left the town and followed the road for another few miles, and as the afternoon got later and later there still seemed to be no *solución* to the *problema* of what to do with the guerrillas, who couldn't be taken back aboard the American helicopters, and there was no sign of what Jorge-Julio had been hoping for, which was a national guard *cuartel* or even a local police station, and finally it was coming to seem more and more meaningless *what* they did with them—the young leader was silent and nearly moribund and the sun was going down as they stopped beside a field of burned-out manioc and cassava and decided they were going to kill them. It was a decision that happened by itself, and Jorge-Julio couldn't say that Mynott was behind it, or the American adviser, or himself either, because it just seemed to happen. They lined the guerrillas up kneeling down and shot each of them in the back of the head, the women too, and Jorge-Julio was pleased that given the various options at hand (raping the women, mutilating the men) their deaths were neat and almost immediate: they might have hoped for worse from their enemies within their own country, who hated them. When they were finished, they marched the last four or five miles to the pickup point where they were supposed to meet their American air transport and met them right on schedule, piling into the cold metal but wonderfully secure interiors of the helicopters, and that seemed to release their tongues for they started talking animatedly about the day's adventures and their words were brave and young, and they talked easily about everything that had happened and Jorge-Julio started to bang his head against the hard metal side of the helicopter with his eyes shut, tears running down his face which in that culture didn't make him seem any less *macho*, but which oddly enough made him seem more serious and more respected, their commander in chief—because they were used to having someone else to weep for them, someone to take their sins upon himself, somebody else they could blame.

He left the airport, driving himself in his Mercedes, and after he had dropped Bill Mynott off at his office, (with the bright sunset fading over the seawall, so the *americano* had put his sunglasses on again, making him look more *gringo* and more matter-of-fact than ever, in a plain guayabera shirt like a businessman); after he had driven back to his own offices in the Ministry of Defense, and in his careful handwriting written up his report of the day's activities and his resignation; after he had said good night to his secretary and asked after her little boy and told her not to work late; he drove over to the Presidential Palace and parked his car, and asked to see El Señor Presidente on a matter of some urgency. He was shown at once into the President's office, where Ferdinando sat reading a long report, with his glasses giving his face a thoughtful, scholarly air, and he looked up with a delighted smile and put the papers down as soon as Jorge-Julio came into the room, gesturing to a chair in the circle of light from his reading lamp, which made the rest of the office seem very large, dark, and full of shadows. He looked tired, the beautiful thin face drawn and gentle, and he took the papers which General Rodríguez held out to him stiffly with a quizzical expression, and read them all through very politely before he put them down on his desk, and glanced up at his friend with a little smile.

"You want to quit?"

"Yes, *mi presidente.*"

"No kidding?"

Jorge-Julio withstood the bright blue gaze of his friend for as long as he could, and then sat down, clasping his freshly scrubbed hands between his knees and smiling a little in spite of himself. "I don't know. I want a drink, that's what I want. You know me, I don't drink a lot, but I'd really like to get shit-faced tonight, and pass out like a pig. I'd like to drink like a real *gorrón*, if you don't mind my saying so."

"So—" Ferdinando raised his eyebrows. "You have my presidential permission, if that's what you want."

"That's not what I want."

"*Amigo,*" Ferdinando said, reaching across the desk as if he wished to take his friend's hand. "Don't quit on me. I need everybody around me who isn't a fool, and I need you more than anybody."

Jorge-Julio shook his head. "Why did you do this, why did you send us out today? Or get us involved in this whole mess? We don't need to do this. Our country doesn't need to get involved in the messes that are tearing everybody else apart, why did you do it? Tell me, I'm just a simple *campesino*. If you explain it to me I'll understand."

"You really don't have to do that," Ferdinando said, looking at him with pain and seeming uncharacteristically at a loss.

"Do what?"

"Act the noble Mayan with me. I know you're worth ten of Mynott and every other *gringo* I ever met."

"Thank you." General Rodríguez looked down at his hands, swallowing, a shy man in everything, even accepting a compliment. "Then explain, please."

"I wish we *didn't* have to get involved in this whole mess," Ferdinando said ruefully. "Do you know what this is, that I've just been reading? It's the latest financial report from United Oil. They have twelve subsidiary companies in El Salvador. They had eighteen in Nicaragua. Six in Honduras. I could go on and on, but you get my point, if we want to go on pleasing them we have to support the United States' imperialism, if you want to call it that, because the United States is the country that supports *United Oil's* imperialism, and we're bought and paid for by United Oil!" He leaned his forehead on his hand for a moment in sheer exasperation. "Oh, I suppose we could just stop, cry poverty, but the Americans would probably just send us more aid! I wish I could make this country into a modern, American-style democracy without making American-style compromises, but I can't. I wish I could do it but I can't!"

Jorge-Julio had never seen Ferdinando defensive before, even with a thread of irritation in his voice (and it was probably just weariness and the myriad pressures of his office, Jorge-Julio decided at once with the immediate remorse of a good soldier for disturbing his commander). And what was he being after all but a sentimental fool, a womanish coward when, as he was to say occasionally afterward (and more and more with his sad fatalist's whisper), What does it matter if they hate me, so long as they don't hate him? You can't have one beloved leader and not have one who cuts the throats of some people, and he realized then what he had always known, that that someone was him, *madre de Dios*, what a shitty piece of news. He looked at Ferdinando with new eyes, and saw a man who didn't have all the answers, and that vision made him so depressed he gritted his teeth with a stoical sadness, as if he'd been told he had cancer, and felt the prick of a different kind of tears in his eyes.

"That's all right," he said with a certain amount of difficulty. "We're going forward, that's the most important thing." Ferdinando looked at him for a long, searching moment, and his eyes seemed to see into his very soul, as they always had, but Jorge-Julio realized with a shock that what they saw was the mirror that he wanted to see.

"Yes," he said finally. "We're going forward." He gestured at the papers that still covered his desk with the pleasurable smile of exhaustion of someone doing a job he loved. "Where we're *going* is anybody's guess, but we're going forward, that *is* the most important thing. Please leave me now. And keep up the good work. My wife and I are both very fond of you."

And General Rodríguez left him, without either of them doubting for a minute that he would go on doing El Presidente's wishes, that he would serve him as his faithful comrade—and as a matter of fact, he did, even after the people had started to call him Rodríguez the Butcher, and his name had become a symbol of terror and cold-blooded cruelty throughout the country.

nine

So MAYAPÁN SPUN OUT, spun out in ever-widing circles of influence like the ripples of the sea, sapphire bright and sparkling in the sun of a Caribbean vacation paradise on the eastern side, dark wine-colored as blood on the Pacific side, where the refineries operated day and night producing gasoline for the *gringos*. There was an interesting series of articles in *The New York Times* on April 28 through May 4 in which the writer described Campeche as both "evidence of the lapidary possibilities of grafting a stark modernism onto the complex rhythms and architectures of the past," and "a swollen metropolis of upward of three million inhabitants, a number which increases every day, as *campesinos* pour in from all over the country in search of the gold Rolexes and Sony Trinitrons which are seen as the new totems of Western industrialization."

He had a number of other apt observations as well: "Campeche is a microcosm for the problems and possibilities of Mayapán. It's the very antiquity of the city—outmoded sewage systems and cramped housing and inadequate utilities—which symbolizes the country's perverse potential: as an untouched resource, a dream as much as a reality, where anyone from the President and his cabinet to private industrialists, con artists, and *brujos* can wave his magic wand and transform the country into whatever he likes...." And further on, "Campeche's emblem should be the phoenix, for it has shown a stubborn resistance to being annihilated, despite the occasional best efforts of hurricanes and earthquakes, rioting and now the doom-saying of Western economists, who see the city, with all its vibrancy and its rapid, inconceivable growth, as reaching critical mass.... The biggest dream, and possibly the biggest problem, is the country's planned new capital at Chichén Itzá: rising out of the scrub jungle a hundred miles west of Campeche, virgin and inspired, quixotic and (possibly) a mistake."

It was a mistake which was never admitted in the continued euphoria of the country's burgeoning pride: pride in its wealth and its growing position, and pride in its leaders: above all, pride in Ferdinando and Camila Lorca. It was a pride which reached hysterical proportions when it was rumored from Stockholm that Camila was a candidate for the Nobel Peace Prize (she didn't get it, and it was suggested, probably after the fact, that she herself had arranged to be passed over for the honor, out of modesty or tactfulness or sheer perversity, no one could tell). It was around that time that she became more and more elusive, her disappearing acts staged sometimes for the press, sometimes for colleagues, sometimes for the nation as a whole, as when it was remarked by a half-million people that she was absent from the balcony of the Presidential Palace during her husband's speech on the anniversary of the Mayapanian revolution (as a matter of fact, she was in the hospital then, undergoing tests for an undisclosed ailment; some said it was an inflammation of the inner ear, some said a uterine infection; predictably, much later, her enemies claimed it was for an abortion).

Her willfulness or gaiety or simply her boredom with playing the role of La Madonna made her slip more and more through people's fingers; hagiographers and critics alike found her harder and harder to categorize, pin down, describe. Here was La Señora Lorca: ambitious, politically shrewd, making deals with the oil companies and Linz Industries and reputedly siphoning off millions into a private Swiss bank account; engineering her husband's election to an unprecedented third term (for which they rewrote the Mayapanian constitution, which had been out of effect for so long that hardly anyone remembered what it said anyway). Here was La Señora Lorca, jetting off to New York for unexplained weekends from which she returned pale and shaken, bruised with stigmata for which she never gave a single word of explanation. She was the symbol of her country, gossip item and newsmaker, her picture plastered on T-shirts, coffee mugs, ashtrays, and souvenir postcards; taped up in stores and in a special alcove in the National Cathedral; seen (along with Ferdinando and President Farrell and Battiste and President de la Madrid and a dozen other world leaders) cameoed in a videotape produced by MixTech Studios, with Pisote and Stevie Wonder, of a song called "One World": holding candles on the steps of El Castillo, the great pyramid at Chichén Itzá, in an exercise of commercial universality so simply moving it could break your heart.

She was above all and forever, with extensive press coverage, La Señora Llorosa, the señora who weeps: generous and compassionate to *los pobres* (which was axiomatic by that point), moved and devastated by their suffering. She would look at the people who came to her clinic with great sadness, and say, Well, now you know more about life than you did before, or God makes you carry a heavy load, doesn't He? and some people were disconcerted by her simplicity and some people thought she was becoming hardened and some people thought she was losing her mind.

She became a prey to all sorts of eccentricities and superstitions at that time: she would look at her hand after she had touched a man who was bleeding to death from an internal hemorrhage, and go to wash off the blood; she would rock a little girl to sleep in her arms, whose body was covered with terrible lesions and sores, and carry her around with her for an hour or more, pressing her cheek against her forehead and kissing her. She began to doubt the efficacy of any drugs, or any therapy at all save pity. Only Buiztas realized that she was getting lost in the labyrinth of illnesses which had no end because they were being created by her own government, and as fast as they wiped out malnutrition and gastroenteritis they were being replaced by automobile accidents and cancer and sooner or later they would all be replaced by napalm wounds, because that was the way life worked, people dropped dead whether it was from one damned thing or another and the "progress" of the Lorcanistas was leaving the people more unhealthy and dissatisfied than when they'd started. Because he remembered her fondly, he tried to distract her from the modern encroachments and advances of death, in the provinces and in the capital: bringing in gaily painted paper skeletons and carved wooden skulls on the Day of the Dead, and singing loud songs about the *difuntitos,* the poor little dead children, which had her convulsed with laughter; giving death all sorts of ridiculous names—"El Burro" and "El Blanquillo," the whitish one but also the egg, or the white peach—and telling stories about ridiculous or improbable deaths, like that of Lupe Valez, who had died with her head in the toilet. He had known death for so long that it held absolutely no interest for him: death was everyone's companion, and if it had been up to him, he would have put a bullet through the heads of the most terminally hopeless, and given rum to the ones who were dying by inches and told the families to bear up under their tragedy, God will reward you, while passing out little tinfoil stars and colored lights and sugar water and all kinds of worthless shit, because What was the matter? so they were dying, well, everyone was dying, only the ones who were walking around had to suffer for it.

La Señora moved him with her naïveté. He would tease her, as when he asked her, What about the festival her *chulo* husband was planning to celebrate his election to a third term as el presidente, even if he was just celebrating six more years of his reign as an elected despot rather than an honest dictator but what the hell, a week-long rock concert was a new way for a man to celebrate six more years in purgatory, and he wished him *cumpleaños feliz.* This was while they were standing out in the garden of the Sociedad Building, and what he said was quite true, the construction was already under way on a multimillion-dollar facility on the Isla del Carmen, with bands to be flown in from L.A. and Australia for a week-long event, in the warm waters of the Gulf of Mexico. She turned and looked at him with her eyes wide and smiling, under the bougainvillea, the overhanging vines, the tumult of flowers which threatened to engulf the Sociedad Camila Lorca Building because she would never have the flowers cut back, and her eyes saw right through him the way they always did.

"You know the island's owned by private investors, and they hope to turn a profit, and they probably will. *We* haven't had a hand in any of it—except to okay their building permits, which my husband has to do as President, and yes, *as* private investors and to give them an event with which to celebrate, and yes, we hope to turn a profit from it as well. So what's the harm?"

"No harm, I just wish I'd thought of a scheme like that while I was President!"

"You think we're crooks."

"I think you're pushing your luck."

"We're not crooks, you know."

He shook his head. "Little *mamá*, if you were crooks you wouldn't be pushing your luck. Crooks would be doing exactly what you're doing, but they'd be able to get away with it."

In the weeks preceding the uncontested election, there was an element of fiesta throughout the country, and abroad the anticipatory congratulations kept pouring in. From Washington, where ex-President Farrell cabled to guarantee his attendance, along with his successor, President Wilson Allen; from Moscow and Havana (whose cables of *felicidad* were a little more restrained, but nonetheless synchronized to Washington's within the half-hour); from Bonn and Helsinki and Riyadh and New York, the worldwide offices of Linz Industries and United Oil and Linz International and UNOCO Subsidiaries; from Isla del Viento; and from the Vatican, where Battiste sent his acceptance of their invitation through the diplomatic pouch, unable to risk a phone call, unable to trust either his voice or his emotions to the close scrutiny of the two people he loved most in the world.

Unwilling (no, *unable*, he admitted wtih brutal self-honesty) to let them hear his doubts: knowing he would lie again, be carried away by their enthusiasm, seduced into hiding the bottomless disgust he felt for himself and the sordid, unethical work he was doing. All of it was perfectly legal, in the convoluted legality of international finance: the loopholes that allowed him to launder money for Linz Industries, and transfer funds to support the rightest groups in El Salvador and Honduras that UNOCO and the United States favored to win; to siphon off funds for the *contras* in Nicaragua and trade information dollars for the data Mynott needed to establish his own death squads, with the dates the Sandinistas needed to avoid the next intercept raid for Soviet arms. All of which brought the Vatican a subtle profit, in fees, and investments through the UNOCO and I.O.R./Chase Manhattan pipeline, and brought the Jesuits once more into the absolute trust and preeminent inner circle of his Holiness's personal confidence, and brought Battiste Tommassi into a position of personal power second only to that of the dying old man who was his superior. He walked in the black isolation and severity of his unadorned cassock and strong-boned, pockmarked face through the opulent corridors and tranquil gardens of the new master whom he served: the shrewd, charming, and charismatic Pope, who saw his need to worship and wisely gave him an opportunity to change his allegiances. He loaned Vatican money to Alfred Linz's Panamanian bank, where it could be transferred to West Germany and invested in a UNOCO subsidiary that manufactured nuclear warheads, and he heard the claims for peace through nuclear deterrence, and he wondered if only he could see the cold hypocrisy of this rationale for endless arms buildup: which benefited nobody, but Alfred Linz, and UNOCO, and Mayapán and the Vatican and incidentally himself. He flew to Paris to watch thousands of young people—blond Nordic warriors and dark-skinned Italians and Galway cream-skinned Celts, all no more than twenty years of age—protesting the emplacement of Pershings and MX missiles; and he read with sickening dread the news that Cuba had been allowed to do what they'd been prevented from doing in 1962: create missile bases on their soil with targets in the United States, because the United States was building bases in Mayapán, with long-range warheads targeted for the Soviet Union.

He returned to Mayapán with this knowledge, to a country become sleek and elegant and polished as the new Campeche International Airport, with its plush red carpeting, piped-in Brandenburg, coolly silent air conditioning, and gleaming glass and chrome: from which connecting flights were available via Aero-Mayapán to Isla del Carmen in specially appointed 727's, painted with the colors of the national flag. He smiled to himself as he walked with his hard-learned, angular grace through the airport and saw how modern everything had become—no longer would you recognize the tropical, thirties-style terminal of the past, with its lazy flies, dusty linoleum, lounging *guardías*, and bilingual signs advising passengers not to spit. Now, hermetically sealed from the outside world, he might as easily have been debarking at Istanbul, or Orly, or O'Hare. He walked through the tinted-glass doors outside and felt the heat hit him like a blanket: that was something they couldn't change, and he felt a welcoming pain so deep he couldn't differentiate it from nostalgia as his eyes ached with the heat, the blinding light, and sweet-soft breezes mixed with the smell of increased pollution and exhaust fumes from the taxicabs. He found an older cab still with its hanging rosary and rates painted in garish yellow on the door and settled back into the interior before he remembered that of course they must have sent him a limousine, it was probably waiting for him now somewhere outside the terminal, but he felt so exhausted by the heat and the humidity he couldn't bring himself to look for it, he shut his eyes instead and thought with misery, I'm terrified of seeing them, I'm honestly scared to death to look at them now, start all that again ... the two people for whom he had compromised every principle and shred of integrity in his nature, but be honest, he had always been an empty man and dying for someone or something to fill him up with meaning. He had had the ill luck to meet the most beautiful woman in the world, and the greatest leader, and they had raped him without any compunction and without the slightest idea that they were doing him any harm, and filled his swollen heart to bursting.

"Where are you going, your Excellency?" the cabdriver asked, throwing the cab into first and cannoning out onto the highway, avoiding cars with the ease of a matador avoiding gasoline-powered bulls.

"Hmm?"

The question sounded so apt it seemed rhetorical. "I'm not an archbishop," Battiste murmured, and realized he wasn't even wearing clerical dress, and came awake belatedly. "How did you know who I was?"

"I saw you on television, your Excellency! On the videotape with El Presidente!"

"Ha! God, you can't escape it. No, never mind, I didn't say anything. Do you and your family have a television?"

296

"Ah, *sí*, your Excellency, everybody in Campeche's got a TV! We're a modern democracy!"

"How wonderfully progressive ... no, never mind, it's all right. Please take me to the National Cathedral. My God, it's hot ... wonderfully hot. Rome is nothing like this. Are they getting set for a big celebration?"

"Like nothing you could believe, your Excellency. Free food, free liquor ... parties in the streets and they're going to televise the concert! The *gringos* have to pay for it, but we get it free!"

"Sounds nice." Battiste gratefully let his mind go blank, watching the city crowd in more rapidly along the airport highway than it had before, taller buildings and, in their interstices, more and more shanties, bare sheds made by leaning a piece of corrugated iron against a wall, hundreds of grimy children but all of them carrying flags or toys or water pistols, pushing up to the car and banging on the hood in the excitement of the approaching fiesta and there were older boys wearing T-shirts with El Presidente's picture on them crowding up to the open taxi window with good-natured insolence to sell him condoms and Coca-Cola and postcards of Camila Lorca's crudely hand-tinted photograph. By the time he got to the Cathedral he was trembling. He got out of the cab, and thrust a handful of money and coins into the midst of the grabbing hands stretched out to him, and fled into the Cathedral, actively terrified of these sweat-stained, sugar-bloated kids, who were the children of the Lorcanistas: brought up on credit and empty promises; Ferdinando and MixTech Studios were all they knew. He shut his eyes, and breathed in the cool, closed air of the church where twenty-three years ago (my God! was he really fifty years old?) he had assisted at the mass with Cardinal Fuertes. Strange to think of all the time between, and all of it seemed a moment, picked out with the lustrous gold of a few bright memories and otherwise shadowed, dark as the interior of the Cathedral, which had neither the opulent insanity of the National Cathedral in Mexico City, nor the radical ugliness of the Metropolitan Cathedral in San Salvador. Picked out with gold light-flickering candles, on railings below the paintings of the Queen of Heaven with her crown of stars and the blue robe of a *Carnaval* beauty queen, were *retablos* of stark, simple awfulness, drawings and collages made of cutout cartoons, advertisements from newspapers, pencil sketches and painted scenes on pieces of tin and aluminum, thanking the Virgin for relief from illness, safety from disasters, the explicitly recorded pain which was so much a part of their enacted expiation that it dwarfed the kindliness of divine intercession with an overwhelmingly morbid, unintentional black humor. These were the kinds of drawings and prayers for intercession that he had seen all his life, primitive magic, tied with the sadness of love notes—but what horrified him was the softly lighted painting to one side of the altar, discreetly semireligious, without a halo but with a rosy cloud behind her, the kind of open-necked shirt that she often wore and her hair just so, short like a *campesina*'s, and her blue eyes gentle and remote as our Saviour's, surrounded by jars and cans full of flowers and candles, the woman he would have given his life for, Ferdinando's wife, the daughter of a Nazi heiress and a murdered journalist, Camila Lorca.

He stopped and stared, tears welling in his eyes and without his knowledge, running down his cheeks while he resisted an impulse to sink to his knees not in prayer but to fold his head in his arms and howl, as much with pain as with hysterical laughter. The sheer perfection of it, his little saint! And there was an old woman lighting a candle and placing a stiff decorated card in front of it, before crossing herself and walking briskly away. After she had left he came up slowly to the portrait and studied the cards and drawings asking for help, decorated with pieces of ribbon and carefully preserved flowers, all the hoarded minutiae of poor people's lives, stamps, and even money, photographs of deceased loved ones and numbers to be played in the Lottery. He wanted to give her something too, and he shut his eyes on the tightness in his throat before he realized that what he was thinking was an abomination, to elevate a mortal human being to the level of a saint was ridiculous, Camila wasn't a saint, and he turned on his heel and left the nave of the Cathedral as if he were being pursued by demons. The same tightened, anguished expression was on his face that it had worn all his life, but which he suddenly didn't recognize, as he passed a long, smoked-glass mirror set into the wall of the church like a *memento mori*—because he was middle-aged, and tired, and haunted-looking, and the brown hair that had always covered his head thickly had thinned and lightened to an ashen, silvery gray.

He didn't show up at the Presidential Palace until the inaugural gala two nights later—when he had to be there, dressed with severe elegance in an old-fashioned soutane and sash of black satin, with black silk-covered buttons imprisoning him from floor to throat. Ferdinando crossed half the polished reception room to meet him, with his hand outstretched and his blue eyes questioning him, discreetly, wordlessly—Was he all right, what was the matter?—but nothing so obvious was allowed to intrude on his conversation, which was light and charming as usual: "I was beginning to think I would have the evening all to myself, and gorge myself on praise, without having to share it with anybody! But now I see I'm going to have to be generous, and share my happiness with the one man without whom I'd still be back teaching history at Columbia University!"

"You taught me everything I know!" Battiste smiled, trying desperately for a light touch, and feeling that he failed utterly. Camila was sweeping up to them in a perfectly incredible dress, bare satin straps holding up a swooningly tight bodice and yards and yards of skirt, a filmy explosion of chiffon billowing out into ruffles and light scallops of lace around her tiny, delicately shod feet, and he took her hand and brought it to his lips, thinking with a shock how thin she was, fragile bones like a bird's at her throat and her beautiful, bare shoulders, her white face turned up to him in more naked concern than Ferdinando's, and as he looked down at her he fought the most devastating impulse in his life: to say to her, "You're young, you're beautiful, come away with me and leave all of these worshiping lunatics who are trying to kill you." But Ferdinando stood on the other side of her, and slipped his arm around her waist with the ease of long familiarity, saying, "Come on, we're going to have to talk to some of our other guests, otherwise all the people we've asked here for selfish reasons are going to get suspicious!"

So they talked to all their guests, among their number princes and presidents, heads of state and stars of every description—and even when compared to the elegance of all their parties, this one was described as being the most lavish, and the most beautifully orchestrated (swing music provided as usual by the

Count Basie Orchestra). Of course there was dancing, and as the evening progressed, even those whose natural dignity or shyness or age normally precluded their indulgence in such athletics were seen out on the floor doing the lindy, the stroll, the pogo, or the Jersey bounce . . . because the songs were eclectic, held together by an infectious beat and fueled by the best ganja money could buy. Ex-President Farrell danced so much that his wife complained she was fainting, and left him to be partnered by Camila Lorca; his now-visibly dyed blond hair grew dark with sweat, and his tanned, lined face became flushed and red, but there was no doubting that he would end his life as healthy and successful as he'd been for his eight-year term as President. The *norte-americanos'* new leader, President Wilson Allen, had been in office for too short a time to do more than ape the aspect of his more photogenic predecessor: and that night he did so as well, even going so far as to take his coat off, and dance with his wife in his shirt sleeves. The vice-president of United Oil, Charlie Cox, got expansive on margaritas and revealed to Colonel Enrique Zacapa that he'd always thought he looked "fantastic" in a dress. But the high point of the evening came when Ferdinando and Camila danced, all by themselves, in a fluid, flawless counterpoint to the music of "Night and Day." It struck Battiste with surprise to recognize that as the inspiration for her dress, Fred Astaire and Ginger Rogers in something, *The Gay Divorcee* or *Top Hat*? Dancing step for step to the tricky, intoxicating rhythms and was the comparison really that inapt? Ferdinando moved with a similarly expert grace, his head and body inclined toward his wife with the same serious attention, partnering her with the same effortless precision—and it had to be admitted, no man could have had a more lissome, delicately responsive partner. A shared intimacy more complex than lovemaking, for as long as the song lasted. No wonder I've ruined my whole life for them, Battiste thought with bittersweet clarity. They'd planted the same wild seeds of loneliness and longing, for a fleeting second, in the hearts of every other man and woman in the room.

In the next few days he began to have the feeling he was part of a lavish display for *Time* and *Newsweek*, so often was he photographed as part of the overall tableaux of Mayapanian unity, prosperity, and whatever else it was they were celebrating . . .

happiness, Battiste thought, having forgotten in himself what happiness felt like. He moved like a somnambulist through the bright days of dry heat and blue, vivid nights against which the carefully staged effects took place: Ferdinando and Camila, standing before a crowd of upward of a quarter of a million people, on the balcony of the Presidential Palace; Ferdinando standing before a crowd of scarcely smaller dimensions, at night in the Plaza Columbia, dressed in the plain white shirt he'd worn as a rebel leader; Camila, dressed as a *campesina* distributing gifts to the poor, spinning around on her toes to smile delightedly at the camera in the clothes she perversely made fashionable; Ferdinando and Camila taking communion from his own hands, in a gesture he felt was so confusedly ambiguous it was nearly blasphemous, in the National Cathedral while an entire country of the faithful watched them on television and cheered. They were presented with a stunning portrait by the government of Venezuela, which was also something of a joke. It showed the legendary Liberator of South America, Simon Bolívar, and his mistress and the great passion of his life, the beautiful Manuela Sáenz—but presented in such a way that their resemblance to the current President of Mayapán and his First Lady (or perhaps it was the other way around, Ferdinando and Camila Lorca in historical dress) was immediately apparent. Ferdinando took one look at it and burst out laughing.

"It's priceless. I want to hang it in the Salón Montejo, where everyone can see it!"

"You can't, you know," Battiste murmured. "The Chamber of Deputies would have a stroke!"

"Let them. It makes my wife look beautiful."

"I'm glad they presented me as your mistress," Camila said with her private smile. "I'm tired of everyone adoring me as your sainted wife."

She was too, in a way Battiste saw: a partial way—and partially she was just plain tired. He saw her exhaustion at the end of an endless day far more clearly than Ferdinando could, caught up in his own exhaustion but also in his own euphoria: thinking, electric with energy even when everyone around him was ready to drop. He had taken upon himself the organization of his new capital and his expanding government as a herculean, private

301

labor which challenged the very best in him, and he had little thought to spare for the weaknesses of anyone less brilliantly driven than himself, even Camila. Battiste watched and judged him and began to be filled with an overwhelming, unbridled anger. Damn him for being so blind, so unreasonable in his demands, although he could always see the other side, Battiste thought grudgingly, if you grabbed him by the shoulders and reminded him of it . . . reminded him you were tired, or sick, or fainting with the sheer impossibility of living up to the dreams and visions of a madman—because Ferdinando could easily convince you that he was mad, the priest thought with the newfound clarity of his distance: this beautiful, unyielding man who would never relinquish his grasp on the power of Mayapán, Battiste was beginning to realize that. (And did he censure him for it? He told himself he did.) He lived his life, whether he was in his office, or the Chamber of Deputies, or on the balcony of the Presidential Palace, or speaking to a crowd of *campesinos* in the middle of Plaza Columbia, in the clear white light of absolute certainty, turning his incredible intelligence to the image of worldly perfectibility which he had seen at thirty (or had he been even younger? Battiste wondered) and which he would never stop trying to give his countrymen, whether or not they wanted it. Camila had given him that, Battiste thought: her light, her warmth and certainty, but at what cost to herself? She was burning away like a vivid blue flame before their eyes and only Battiste felt that he was able to see it.

It was her distraction that frightened him the most, he thought as he dressed for the evening, for the final night of the concert on the Isla del Carmen to which they were going to be flown from Campeche by helicopter, because the island was too crowded, too wired for sound and light and direct satellite broadcast to allow for any earlier arrival, by any less spectacular means. "I wish we didn't have to make such an eleventh-hour entrance," Ferdinando said, seeming not to mind it at all, "but I suppose it can't be helped." He was dressed, as was his habit for state occasions, in black tie and an impeccably tailored tuxedo, his only ornament the narrow Presidential sash across his breast, and he was deeply tanned, his blue eyes sparkling as he spooned caviar onto a square of toast, sitting at his desk in his study. "Here, Eminence,

why don't you eat some of this? I'm a pig, but I can't eat it all."
Battiste didn't say anything. He was thinking how Camila's distraction reminded him of something else, something painfully,
sharply nostalgic he couldn't quite remember, as if she were always listening to another voice, seeing things he couldn't see. He
shut his eyes as the memory flooded back to him, not imprecise
but real and warm as blood flowing from a never-stanched
wound, his child, virginal and perfect at twelve years old, glancing up at him with clear blue eyes as lambent as the light of a
candle from a face already too wise and too politically subtle for
her years. How could he have forgotten her for a second?—overlaid with however many lapidary transformations, into an adult,
and a wife, and a political symbol, and God knew what else, an
astute labor leader and a skilled diplomat, and a whore and a
cold-blooded, cynical opportunist? But she had always been
there, drawn by a private, sad, self-contained knowledge . . .
like a saint, like a martyr, like a terminal patient in a hospital.
He shook his head. He didn't want to think of her like that,
certainly not sick, but not drawn either, to the ghostly faith he
didn't believe in anymore, fading away like a sweet, pale hys-
teric in the service of an Opiate who bled His victims like leuke-
mia. She had too much strength for that. He couldn't conceive
of any distraction from the world now save delusions: in the last
few years, he had gone lifetimes. Now he saw the world as the
text where God wrote His cryptic messages: the scribblings of a
lunatic, which man could alter, if he worked at it with all his
will.

He came out of his reverie to see Camila herself enter the
room, smiling and thirty-three and dressed in a straight white
gown like a Grecian statue off one shoulder and sewn with a profusion of winking, barely visible seed pearls, so expertly made-up
that only her shadowed eyes revealed anything less than perfection, and they were abysses, dark and tired, her age showing in
tiny lines at the corners and her eyes open a little wider than
usual, a little blind and blank. He was immediately frightened by
her eyes, although he didn't know why. She looked in all other
respects like someone to whom the world owed nothing but triumphs, and she realized it, crossing the thick white carpet to kiss
Ferdinando on the lips in the last perfectly graceful movement

the priest was ever to see her make, reaching up a hand as white as alabaster, to smooth the dark hair back from his forehead.

"Hello, handsome," she murmured. "It never ceases to amaze me, how beautiful you are."

Ferdinando laughed, and appealed to Battiste. "You see? What's a man to do with a wife like that? She spoils me! I could get the adulation of a million people, and it wouldn't matter to me half as much as one of Camila's compliments." Which was a lie, because it was the adulation of everyone that had him poised and shining like an eagle on the crest of a current of air only he could feel (no, of course, Battiste thought—Camila felt it), smiling and oddly enough more human than Battiste ever remembered having seen him—as if he had decided to let his intelligence relax for once and simply enjoy himself. He poured himself a glass of champagne, in the comfortable, high-ceilinged room which had once been Quintero de Buiztas' study, and leaned against the edge of his desk.

"Here's to conspicuous consumption!" He laughed. "My God, what a triumph! Charlie Cox said the Isla del Carmen makes Madison Square Garden look like a bowling alley ... do you know that we're sponsoring the biggest single concert event in history? Not bad for a little banana republic, eh, your Eminence?" He laughed at them with such unconcealed delight, such radiant happiness, that Battiste for one caught his breath: My God, he thinks they're doing this all for *him*. "We've put our country on the map in the most conclusive way possible—we've outspent the *gringos*!" He got up from his seat to offer Battiste a glass of champagne, not noticing that the priest hadn't asked for it. "In ten years' time we'll be able to offer quality education to everyone in the country, subsidized university training in information-processing and advanced technology, to outstrip the world's industrial giants—why should we pander to a nine-teenth-century revolution when we can be part of the twentieth century? The possibilities are *there*," he murmured almost with wonder, "and yet how many people are able to see it? *I* can see it. Is that vision so unique? Surely, you've always been able to see what I see, figure out what I'm talking about—but sometimes I have the feeling I'm leading a nation of children!"

"Those children elected you to a third term," Battiste said

drily. "What are you going to do if they don't want you to be President ten years from now?"

Ferdinando stopped short and looked at him with honest surprise. "Don't be an idiot, they're always going to want me as President."

"Sounds comforting."

"Just what are you driving at?" His blue eyes, alert, regarded him with a little smile. "You're trying to make me angry, aren't you?"

"Me? No, I wouldn't dream of it." He found himself trembling with a quiet, heartfelt rage which had come on him so suddenly he didn't understand it, so he sat down in one of the plush gray chairs and drank off the class of champagne that had been offered to him in a gulp. It wasn't a question of the Presidency, it wasn't a question of any of it, but because he could never say the things that were tearing him to shreds inside, he felt forced to go on parroting words he wasn't sure he meant.

"Is the twentieth century supposed to be the last one you're offering them?" he inquired sharply. "You're doing a pretty good job of involving them in a war that could wipe them out!"

Ferdinando shook his head, as if bemused and at a loss as to where all of this anger was coming from, and bent his mind and his oratorical skill patiently to debate the point. "Nuclear arms and nuclear deterrence are a fact of life—surely even the Vatican has been willing to concede that fact, despite the American bishops' schism, and you're an intelligent man, my friend, you don't have your head in the clouds of wishful thinking! What would you have had me do? Refuse the Americans permission to cement our alliance? When we are, part and parcel, owned and operated by an American-based conglomerate?"

"That's what your conception of freedom comes down to, isn't it?" Battiste snapped. "Service to one of a dozen masters, all of them *gringos* under the skin. You can phrase it any way you want, but you've always been a disciple of capitalist self-interests and you know it!"

"You're quoting somebody else," Camila said suddenly. "You never referred to capitalist self-interests in your life."

"Ex-excuse me," he faltered, losing the thread of his sarcasm in the face of her astute perception, and then regaining it. "I

305

didn't realize you knew my opinions so well, since you've always been so conveniently flexible in your own expedient philosophy!"

The moment he said it he regretted it, not because of her anger, which wasn't there in her face, but because of the corrosive recognition in her eyes. "I know that voice," she said, almost inaudibly. "I lived with it for four years, in New York," and turned away from them both, wincing, and putting her hand to her head, murmuring "Shit" under her breath.

He was immediately concerned. "What is it?"

"Can I give you a hint?" Ferdinando asked furiously. "Your dislike of myself or my policies is *fine*, we're men, we can have as many arguments as you like, but when you insult Camila you will find me a very implacable enemy, and not a terribly forgiving one."

"Stop it," Camila said, regaining her breath, and trying to regain the light tone of the evening, although her eyes glanced from Ferdinando to Battiste pleadingly. "I told you I can't choose between you, and I can't," she added, leaning her hand on Battiste's arm in an appearance of teasing which wasn't light and teasing at all, and he was surprised to see the look of entreaty in her eyes, as though she were asking for his help. "These are questions, and if the answers were easy, we'd all be saviors, and there's no need for you to agree with us on everything, you wouldn't be our dear friend if we couldn't trust your honesty." She was breathing rapidly, and there was a film of sweat on her forehead which had nothing to do with anybody's anger. "Darling, would you get me my silk shawl from my closet—I'm afraid I'm going to be cold tonight with all your expensive air conditioning—" she smiled, appealing to Ferdinando, raising her eyebrows to suggest she would pacify Battiste in his absence, and the moment he'd left the room she leaned her head against Battiste's shoulder and whispered, "Help me."

"Sweet, sweet, of course, what is it?"

"I'm sick—I've got such a terrible headache—"

He felt her teeth grinding together, as she pressed her forehead against him and hissed profanities under her breath. "I thought I could make it, but I don't think I can. Help me. Go with him. I know you're mad but forget about it, he doesn't care about any of those things, the only thing that matters is that the people love him and tonight is so important—everything's more fragile than anybody believes, treaties and presidencies, it's all a question of belief—the people's belief in him, his belief in himself—his belief in me—" She caught her breath and pressed her lips against his shoulder, in unconscious parody of the intimacy he'd always longed for. "Dear God I think I'm going to be sick . . ."

He managed to get her to be sick mostly on the white carpeting, not on that dazzling white dress, although his shoulder was not entirely unscathed. He gave her his handkerchief, and went to get them both some paper towels from the lavatory that was adjacent to the study—so when Ferdinando reentered the room he saw Camila crouched in a chair next to her own vomit, and Battiste emerging from the bathroom, drying his hands.

"What the hell have you done to her?" he asked, his voice sharp and deadly as a rifle shot.

"She's sick," Battiste snapped. "You self-centered bastard, she's sick and she didn't even have the courage to tell you!"

"My God, is that true?" he asked, sinking to his knees beside her chair to take her shoulders between his hands, so concerned and shaken in that instant that Battiste began to see what Camila meant: how high a wire he had been walking, for quite some time, and how easy it would be for anything to destroy him. She glanced from his face to Battiste's, and the priest saw her decide immediately.

"No, I'm fine!" she said in her clear voice. "I'm excited, and the two of you fighting—it was such a novel experience that it overwhelmed me. You can't fight anymore," she added, testing her voice for brittleness and finding it adequate, "or I'll throw up all over the helicopter, and the pilot will refuse to fly us anywhere! Come on, let's get going or we'll miss the whole concert— Pisote for one will never forgive us if we miss her number!" She laughed, getting to her feet with a swift movement which avoided both of them, and added, "See? I'm fine—" wiping Battiste's handkerchief across her bloodless lips. She smiled her million-dollar smile and shook her head. "You're both such wonderful fools, did you think I'd miss tonight for anything in the world?"

She was so good at it, she almost convinced Battiste, although she wasn't acting for him. Light as a feather, but strangely

307

awkward, almost giddily drunk, she bent to retrieve the long silvery shawl Ferdinando had brought for her, wrapping it around her body in a shimmer of iridescent light. "Come on—" she repeated to the two of them, so they went outside, to the helicopter's waiting whir, in the wet black night of the tropics in the palace grounds which seemed strangely silent, because everyone not at the concert was home watching it on television. They made the forty-five-minute flight in silence, Camila sitting up front in the seat next to the pilot so as not to crush her dress, while Ferdinando and Battiste sat behind her: so all they both could see was her perfect profile, greenly lit by the dials of the controls against the starry black sky, and Ferdinando quietly smoked one cigarette after another and Battiste felt as if he were swimming underwater, separated from Ferdinando by a transparent mass which weighed on his chest. "You're trying to kill her."

Ferdinando took a deep drag of his cigarette, and held the smoke in for a long time, his fine, drawn, sensitive face as still as a statue, poised on what interior forces of aloof pride and discipline Battiste couldn't begin to imagine.

"No."

Battiste felt tears start in his eyes, and thought they might be tears of rage. "She's sick. If you can't see that, you can't see anything."

"I can see that Camila is still my wife," Ferdinando said quietly. "Perhaps you don't remember that."

"Meaning?" Although Battiste knew very well what he meant.

"Meaning your touching concern for her implies I don't feel an equivalent concern." He didn't say anything more, turning instead to look out the window, the tip of his cigarette a glowing red light in the dark. Later he said, "If you want to cuckold me, you shouldn't make it so obvious."

They came in sight of the Isla del Carmen a few minutes later, flying in low over the refinery fields and the strip of unused jungle off Sabancuy and across Laguna de Términos to the flat tongue of land lying in the water, lit up to the sky with an arc of laser beams and packed like a foundering ship with over two million people—and because the pilot had turned on the broadcast of the concert on the radio, they came in with music, the amplified sound so loud they could hear it over the beat of the rotor blades as they set down on the roof of the facility, they could feel the beat through their shoes as they stepped out of the helicopter in a glare of lights and secret service personnel, they could feel the moist humid air throbbing with the beat of a million fans, swaying and stamping to Barbados funk. Battiste saw the light play over Ferdinando's handsome face and his proud, involuntary smile, and he turned quickly to look at Camila and saw the wrinkles of pain disappear from her face along with every trace of expression save one of distant serenity—he watched, fascinated, as she became someone he scarcely recognized, like the painting of her in the Cathedral, contemplative and unassailable as she and Ferdinando stepped down from the helicopter in the blaze of the security lights and crossed the flat roof of the building toward a service entrance with cargo doors and a concrete ramp, which would take them directly to their seats. He was escorted along with them, helplessly—step for step because he was as tall as Ferdinando—down a concrete tunnel backstage with bare light bulbs and the blare of sound and discreet murmurs of This way, your Excellency, this way, Señor Presidente, toward the enormous, open-air facility scooped like a crater into the island and ringed with bright green palms and bamboo trees and Battiste kept swallowing and swallowing to relieve the pain in his throat which wouldn't be relieved, he dug his nails into his palms to keep his hands at his sides and finally when they were approaching a carpeted, more public area, near the boxes which faced the stage he reached out his hands and grabbed Ferdinando by the shoulders.

"No, wait a minute, I'm not going with you . . . "

Ferdinando stopped and looked at him, the same searching look as when they had first met again, this last time, after the last few years had finally put a wedge between them. His blue eyes were as cold and as vivid as ice. "Why not?"

"Because this isn't what we wanted, this is a travesty, bought with blood, this whole place is bought with blood and you've been bought too—"

"So is your Vatican," Ferdinando said stilly. "So are you, as a matter of fact."

"I know." Battiste swallowed. "But you're killing the person I love. The people I love, because you're also killing yourself."

"You're a sentimental cretin." It was said without any teasing or any warmth at all. Battiste had never realized how terrible Ferdinando's anger could be, and he found himself getting angry in response.

"So that's it. You go out there and drink up the cheers of the multitude and fuck however many people you have to slaughter, fuck everybody so long as you hang onto your fucking base of power!"

Ferdinando's immediate response was a vicious slap across his face, which was somehow completely in character, as were the emotions that followed it: anger, remorse, and the denial of that remorse which closed in upon itself in an instant, leaving the reserve and distance of a stranger. "Get the hell out of here," he said quietly, as he might have said to a dog. He turned aside, composed and elegant, to where Camila stood with her back to them both throughout the whole altercation . . . a little at a distance, as if she hadn't heard, or as if she had decided to absent herself from both of them . . . and the color drained from his face, as he glanced back once toward his friend. But too late. Battiste had already left, walking back down the concrete tunnel with his hands behind his back because otherwise he would have touched his bruised face, perhaps wept, and he found he had no desire to weep, it was as if the tears had dried into a permanent wound in his throat and left him quite calm, thinking about the Vatican, his flight back, business he would have in the coming weeks with Linz Industries representatives and those of UNOCO. Also the Frente Comunistas de Mayapán, which was Martín Acchuirez's newly formed organization, with which he'd kept in contact through Porfirio Cheruña and José Luaro. The flat-faced, hard-spirited, idealistic priest, whose devotion to Martín Acchuirez amazed, inspired, frightened him. And whom he'd recently had transferred, from a parish in New York, to a position in Rome as his personal secretary and liaison in his contacts with the communist-inspired group. . . .

So Battiste wasn't there to see Camila and Ferdinando take their seats and receive the standing ovation of the crowd, and be picked up by television cameras and framed by lights as they sat there for the next four and a half hours, through nonstop acts, imprisoned in the glare of the public's love while Camila kept her head held high as the crucifying pain in her head blinded her to everything and made her want to scream out loud. She was vaguely aware of her husband sitting next to her, whom she loved more than her life itself; she was vaguely aware that she had let Battiste down, but it couldn't be helped, and she wasn't quite aware what it was all about because there were too many things in her mind, ever since getting off the helicopter when something had snapped in her head, and suddenly the pain had become unbearable. She kept her face still, floating on the pain, not free of it but gradually drowning in it, and gradually became aware of the soft sound of cries coming to her from the invisible people around her . . . audible through the cacophonous music. She strained to hear them, so sweet and sad like the singing of angels, We love you, we love you . . . what fools to love me, she thought, I can barely manage to *be* here . . . I didn't want to be here but now I'm glad . . . She came to herself standing next to Pisote onstage, and she whispered very quietly, "What am I doing here?"

Pisote looked at her for a long moment in silence. Her eyes were made up kohl black, and her hair was scorched red, and her cheeks were painted with blue hollows, and when she spoke her voice was very, very still. "I frankly don't know. There are two million people sitting there looking at us. I was about to sing the encore to 'One World.' What do *you* think you're doing here?"

Camila smiled at her suddenly, and her smile was very gentle, very loving and forgiving. "Let me sing it with you," she said. Which wasn't as strange as it sounded, considering her performance on the videotape. The conference between the slender, athletic singer and the slender, white and silver-gowned First Lady was strangely appropriate, like a conference between two professionals. "I'm not going to get another chance to do this," Camila added, and Pisote felt a shiver and acquiesced without knowing why she acquiesced, and cued her band, and the two women sang the song in harmony, Pisote's trained voice supporting Camila's untrained but sweet and clear one, which held until the song ended. And only Ferdinando and Pisote realized how truly sick she was: Ferdinando standing and watching her, realizing with tortured immobility the enormity of his mistake; and Pisote, who supported her, more and more, with her arm around her, keeping her standing up until the lights went down on the two of them, and she was able to get her to the side of the stage before Camila collapsed.

IV.
The Lady of the Turquoise Skirt

one

CAMILA WAS FLOWN TO Cornell Medical Center in New York the next day, and operated on for a brain tumor at four o'clock the following afternoon.

She had suffered another massive stroke in the helicopter on the flight back to Campeche, which left her in a coma; doctors at the brand-new hospital on the corner of Avenida Montejo could do no more than perform emergency surgery to relieve the immediate pressure before they made the necessary arrangements and sent her to the United States. For six hours a team of eight surgeons worked to remove a tumor the size of a baseball from her temporal lobe, pointing out the degree to which the tumor had invaded the cortex of the occipital lobe as well (which made it impossible to remove it completely); so great was the damage, both of the malignancy and the aneurism, that they were amazed she was still alive. Nor did the paralyzed, white figure that lay in a brightly lighted room after it was all over, her perfect, shaved skull wrapped in bandages and her face as still as a plaster mask, display any more signs of life than a corpse: flickering green screens displayed her thready pulse and the secret dreaming activity of her brain, but not for anyone to see, for the hundreds of newspaper reporters and television cameramen and well-wishers had been denied access to her room. That prohibition extended to the President of Mayapán, who had remained by her side during the operation in Campeche, and now stood in the hospital director's office, staring sightlessly out of the window into the darkness, smoking cigarette after cigarette. There were hourly reports issuing from the hospital to all the major news services, and everyone who could get to a phone had called someone at least a dozen times, in shock, in curiosity, in a stunned outpouring of sympathy, which turned into hope when she did not die during the operation; and morbid fascination, when the details of her illness began to filter out. She was the perfect symbol of the times, as always: vessel of cancer, holding the nightmare disease of everyone in her mind. So that the surprise as the hours trickled by was that she *didn't* die, as the perfect coda to their fear: cruel joke of a materialist world, where all beauty could be reduced to a malignant biopsy. She hung on, nourished by a thread of faith or a sediment of earth inconceivable to the Yanqui doctors who operated on her. In Mayapán, the people's faith was simpler: they came out into the streets *en masse*, to stand for hours, praying to the Virgin for a miracle.

Ferdinando hadn't said a word since he had relinquished Camila's hand, with such reluctance that they had had to pull his fingers away. He was standing quite still as he looked out of the window now, appearing to be his usual poised self without the terrible grief he had displayed in Campeche: when he had pressed his face against his wife's golden hair and let out a muffled cry, like that of a soul in torment; had heard the Mayapanian doctor's unthinking exclamation, "So long? What took you so long to get her in here?" and had had to whisper, with his eyes trapped like a man's at bay, "I don't know." He was standing looking with wide blue eyes down into the abyss of twinkling lights with no more than a line of strain between his eyebrows now, and a tightness in his lips which made him look, to the chief surgeon who came in to tell him about his wife's condition—to urge him to go to a hotel, there was nothing more they could do that night—like a man trying to remember a phone number, some precise but trivial detail that caused him a certain amount of insignificant irritation. He scarcely shook his head, not turning away from the window where he stood with a barely shaking hand bringing the cigarette to his lips, his eyes so narrowed and intent on the moving lights of the traffic far below him that a careless observer would not have noticed the tears that were coursing down his cheeks. The doctor was surprised, being unused to a culture that allowed a man to weep. He reluctantly cleared his throat.

"Mr. President, your wife's condition is stable, she's—quite frankly she's as well as she can be, which isn't bad. She's very young, and although she's run-down, severe anemia and a dangerously low leukocyte count, youth's the biggest factor in her favor. Always is, along with the will to live, you know about all of that. In terms of her age and general health the timing of this couldn't be better—"

"Ha!" Ferdinando said sharply, and then lapsed again into his high-strung silence, and this time the doctor saw his cigarette shake so badly he had to turn and put it out. "I killed her, Doctor, so please don't play diplomatic games with me. A pearl, richer than all my tribe, which I threw away because of my own blind ambition and idiocy. I worked her to death, and now I have no one to blame for this but myself."

"Oh, come on."

"If you don't like melodrama, you shouldn't have a Latin American *presidente* here." He tried to say it lightly, and his voice couldn't quite bring it off. He bent his head to light another cigarette and looked at the doctor over the blue of the match flame, and the doctor had never seen eyes so dark and miserable before.

"You shouldn't smoke so much."

"Why? Because I'll get *cancer*?" He laughed again, a little out of control. "What's the prognosis, Doctor? Does she have six months, a year? I've seen more people die than you have, so please don't worry, I can certainly believe you. I won't call in a second opinion, or sue you for malpractice. You can tell me your diagnosis in English. I am perfectly fluent in your language."

Although the chief surgeon recognized such pride as a self-inflicted punishment by this tortured man, he was still irritated by it. "Your wife has severe lesions of the temporal and occipital lobes of the right side of her brain, and a tumor which we removed in part; as an invasive tumor it has knit with the cells of the occipital lobe and it was impossible for us to remove more

317

than a portion of it without inflicting severe damage to the healthy portions of her brain. It will therefore probably spread to other areas. We don't know. Radiation treatments will help, chemotherapy will help, and we will probably have to go in a second and perhaps even a third time, if she lives that long. In the long run, your wife's condition is fatal, but I've been proven wrong enough times that I pray I am. I'm not about to give you a timetable. Those things are a lot of baloney anyway. Deterioration may be gradual, or it may be abrupt, or it may not be at all. You are *not* responsible for giving your wife a brain tumor, Mr. President. *God* is. I wish I could say He wasn't, because I'd rather blame you, and I can't punch God in the nose, but that's just the way it is."

"Walter Cronkite." Ferdinando turned abruptly away from him. "You fill me with admiration. Please leave me alone for a moment."

"No." Something in El Presidente's voice had disturbed the doctor more than anything he had said so far. "Come on, let's go get a cup of coffee, we've got some great people you can talk to, they're much more trained in counseling than I am—"

"For God's sake leave me alone!" His explosion of rage so intimidated the poor surgeon that he actually stepped back a few paces, before a voice that had shouted victory to a crowd in Plaza Columbia. "You tear my heart out and you want to give me *counseling*? What on earth do you think I am, an *idiot*? Bind my wrists with tape, to keep me from slaughtering myself or you or the whole world, but while Camila lives how can I tear myself away from her? Every second with her is precious, every instant! What can you know about that?" His smile curled again in that terrible pride which Battiste had recognized as being very close to madness, and his eyes were so wide and blank that the doctor was very much afraid of him, afraid that he was going to kill him. He stared for a long moment, searchingly, into the doctor's face, this man who had had his hands on his wife's brain, her mind, and yet hadn't been able to save her! and he saw that he was an ordinary man, who didn't much want to be there, and he came to himself a little, shutting his eyes and putting his long hands over his face. "I just need a moment to myself, Doctor, to learn how to stand this. I won't jump out of the window. Oh, dear God—" The hissing intake of his breath was the most terrible sound the surgeon had ever heard in the world, and he didn't know how to comfort this beautiful, dangerous, possibly crazy man who stood pressing his tanned, thin fingers against his face as if he would destroy his eyes, as arrogant as Lucifer in his grief, and as isolated.

For two weeks Camila floated in a state that wasn't death, but wasn't life either: serene as an effigy and drawn as a skeleton, her cheeks hollow and her lips drawing away from her teeth in an unconscious grimace, hollow eyes shaded so deeply they looked bruised, and her thin hands motionless on the blankets covering her body. Only the feathery-light rise and fall of her breast, and the noncommittal monitoring of the electronic machinery displayed any signs of life, and they were plant signs, signs of the body merely: there was no way of knowing whether she had any mind left at all behind the smooth white forehead the nurses wiped with alcohol, the attenuated limbs they moved, and spine they turned, to keep her supple as she lay on the bed curling into herself like a fetus, dreaming on a salt sea of oblivion which none of them knew about, because none of them had known her with Porfirio. She was hiding in a timeless time of blank waiting less painful than enforced, occasional ripples of impatience crossing the still, milk-white ocean of her mind, but there was nothing, no energy to enact them and they passed like winds over the unbroken surface of silence which covered her mind like a skin. She didn't know how long she lay there. Vague memories, uncategorizable as either pleasant or unpleasant, told her she had been there before, not once but many times: and she would be there again, but the whole concept of time was fluid in her mind like love or hate, connections that mattered merely for nostalgia, while she had a sense of waiting for something she couldn't even imagine, an imminent golden light, which pressed against her eyelids like fire and warmed her as she turned toward it as steadily as the sun. She waited and was still. Time flowed around her, but it didn't touch her, and she had no connection with any of the people who waited daily for her stirring with torment and whose lives were dripping away like blood through the wounds of her

319

stillness, her unconsciousness: otherwise she would have been concerned, and tried to communicate with them. She had forgotten all about them. And finally one day the world stirred, and came close to her eyes, and the fire that pressed against them was living and vivid with a very clear image of moist leaves and red plants and the steaming mist of a jungle which she nearly recognized—and she felt loss and time return to her in that instant, and she awakened to memory, and the consciousness that she was a particular human being, in a particular, finite body, and that she was going to die.

She knew it before they told her, when she first opened her eyes and saw the familiar objects of her hospital room—window, chair, and wall—all the commonplace things which were so shortly going to be taken away from her: she knew it, saw it, looking at it with the same stoicism with which she had faced her parents' death, life's glories and all its other uncertainties . . . it all came down to this, a single life in a hospital room, too commonplace for tears, too absolute and personal to admit of either the comfort or the intrusion of strangers. She looked at her death with clear eyes, a little sadly, and she was still looking at it when they came in with surprise and pleasure to discover she had regained consciousness, the nurses first, and then the doctors, and she came out of her reverie to tell them merely, "I don't want to see anyone . . . please don't let anyone in to see me . . ." because she didn't feel that she could bear it, the glass shell of her death was too fragile yet to bear the sledgehammer blows of love which would so inevitably and wantonly be dealt to it.

They respected her wishes, and kept everyone out, including Ferdinando, who had to suffer the terrible knowledge that she wouldn't see him, while she lay still and thought, watching the sunshine from her window make its way along the wall, a big bunch of blue irises in a vase on the bureau, the walls painted not white, but a soft blue-green . . . a beautiful, aqueous light filling the room, and the murmur of birdsong and traffic and the wind through the trees, invisible through her window, but audible nonetheless. Her perceptions, which were possibly distorted, but very beautiful, to be said good-bye to first; and then her memories; and only after that the thought of the people to whom she was bound, by cords as painful as veins: Battiste, Porfirio (yes), and Ferdinando . . . only approaching the thought of her husband as the sun was going down, because only then could she face the thought of leaving him forever without screaming, pressing her lips closed in the suddenness of her pain as tears finally forced themselves between her lids as she whispered, Ferdinando, Ferdinando, if only I could take you with me I wouldn't be afraid of death, but how can I go away from you and never see you again? Her heart longed for his touch then and his physical presence so much that she felt she couldn't bear it, she wanted to shout, I'm not a mystic, I'm not extraordinary, I'm a human being and I'm terrified . . . but death came for human beings, not saints, and the terrible fact was that death was ordinary. She had a bad moment of the body's anger then, rage beating like the fists which could do no more than clench on the blankets, the terrible unfairness of it all, she was young, she was *young* . . . but the habit of tenderness was strong in her, and saved her from self-pity. Breaths could still be drawn, released . . . it wasn't so bad, she was still alive . . . the beloved man for whom she had spent herself so wantonly and lavishly was still alive as well, somewhere in the hospital, and she could see him now if she wished. She thought of Ferdinando then, his pain, how could she have forgotten that? How much he must be suffering, his heart breaking at even this temporary separation . . . death taught her quickly, as she began to think normally again: each instant was a challenge to be conquered, an opportunity. She was alive at this moment, and everything she loved most in the world was within reach of her slender hands. She reached for the buzzer next to the bed, called the night nurse, and when she arrived asked her to bring her things, makeup, a mirror, the beautiful white silk negligée which had been brought for her from Campeche . . . and she dressed very carefully, expunging as far as possible the marks of illness and dying from her face. Only then did she glance up at the nurse with something like her old coquetry, Well, how do I look? and ask her if she knew where her husband was, could she see him, that is if he wasn't too busy, if he hadn't gotten bored with her already and left the country? And when Ferdinando was called, and came into the room, he found her two weeks after undergoing surgery looking incredibly beautiful, desperately sick, wounded but gallant and unfrightened and staggeringly alive, lying propped up on pillows doused with Shalimar.

"Well, so you decided to wake up?" His voice was no more than a thready whisper.

"Yes."

"They told me you had regained consciousness this morning. I've been here all day."

"You look tired."

"Do I?" He looked at her with faint surprise, and seemed incapable of pursuing that, or any other point. Unspoken, the question lay between them, Why didn't you want to see me? But Ferdinando felt he already knew the answer. He stood looking at her from the doorway, how beautiful she was, as if he could never stop looking at her, and for the first time she noticed his drawn face and the hollows and lines around his eyes, the thinning of his hair at his temples, the refining of his face and the weariness which had aged him. He was a man in his fifties, and the thought flashed across her mind, Thank God I don't have to see him die before me. Neither of us is going to live forever.

"Come here." She smiled. "What I have isn't contagious."

"I wish it were," he murmured, coming to her bedside and taking hold of her hand. She felt his warmth, all the love and tenderness which had nourished and sustained her every day of her life, shining in the inviolable reality of his concern for her; it was all there in the blue eyes that looked down at her with the same gentleness and care as they had always held—but there was a terrible tautness and reserve in his thin, smiling face.

"What is it?"

He shook his head. "It's nothing. I can't tell you."

"You can tell me anything."

"I want to quit." He spoke very quietly, as if idly, in a barely audible whisper. "I want to take you away, spend what time we have left together. I've given enough of my life to strangers, and enough of yours. I don't want to waste any more time."

She was silent, still looking at him. She knew better than to argue him out of it, and besides, who knew what they should do now? It didn't matter, nothing mattered, only that his terrible self-isolation should be broken.

"Please, tell me what's the matter. We've never had any secrets between us."

There was a struggle going on in his lined, anguished face, which was the more deeply felt for being nearly invisible. Only she, who knew him so well, knew what it cost him to maintain even the vestiges of his composure. "I did this to you," he murmured very quietly, as he turned away from her and drew a deep, shuddering breath, swallowing so hard she saw the muscle spasm in this throat. "I was afraid—I was afraid you never wanted to see me again—"

She was amazingly strong for a fragile woman and when she pulled on his hand she drew him down to her, snaking her fingers around his neck in an embrace no less convulsive than that with which he gathered her in his arms, pressing his face against her neck, her shoulders as he kissed her again and again with a terrible outpouring of passion for once so completely overwhelming as to make him oblivious to everyone else in the world. His strong, sinewy arms imprisoned her, his mouth claimed hers, hungrily, over and over, he wanted to hold her so deeply he possessed her, inside his body, in the enclosure of his rib cage, where he could keep her safe. He couldn't face losing her, wouldn't face it, and as he tried with ever increasing urgency to bind her to him, she felt the piercing sweetness of his desire for her, the floodgates of his discipline and duty overthrown for once in an excess of longing which was almost frightening: his mouth bruised her, his fingers clasped her shoulders, and he pressed her so tightly against him as if to shut out time and parting, everything else in the world but that moment. Because she was everything in the world to him, he couldn't avoid hurting her, and she, knowing this, gave him her ravaged body willingly, with all the loving courage of a warrior. He was her fate, this bony slender man who was not a conquistador but desperate as a youth in her arms, and she had always known he would be her epiphany, the beginning and end of the world for her, as she was for him, the destination and refuge of his life.

They went away to Isla del Viento as soon as Camila could travel, ostensibly for a vacation, to get her strength back and, as she joked to reporters, to let her hair grow back in. No one knew

323

the extent of her illness beyond the doctors who had operated on her; no one knew that Ferdinando intended to resign the Presidency of Mayapán and spend the rest of his life with his wife as a private citizen. Alfred Linz wasn't there, so they had the pink villa to themselves. They swam, and lay in the sun for hours, with their hands lightly touching, or made love on the beach or in their cool, mosquito-netted bed, lingering in their caresses like lovers newly acquainted with each other, memorizing the extraordinary moments that they shared with smiles, with gentle laughter, but never with tears: trying to do the impossible, pretend they were not who they were.

The weather was as golden bright and cloudless as it had been on their honeymoon: for a while, the illusion held. They played like dolphins in the blue water warmed by a sun so hot it played heat tricks on the eyes, and luxuriated in the coolness of the velvet-black evenings, as they sat on the terrace at the top of the world, Camila in one of Ferdinando's shirts and Ferdinando in a pair of swimming trunks (because they couldn't be bothered with what they looked like for nonexistent photographers), waited on by the invisible servants, watching the stars come out and Venus glowing in the sky like a liquid jewel, Quetzalcoatl or the Plumed Serpent to the Indians who had worshiped its cold, distant beauty before Columbus . . . as they both knew, and both refrained from saying to each other.

Time and the world were as near as the coast of Mayapán, toward which they never looked, except at sunset, when the sea was burning with red and gold and Ferdinando's eyes would turn toward it as helplessly as an addict's; and he would turn back to find Camila's eyes on him, not judging or condemning, but wide and blank, as the evening breeze blew the soft wisping hair which was growing back as light and blond as a child's against her skull, her wide, smooth forehead—the drowning light illuminating the lambent loveliness of her translucent skin, the pale immediacy of her smile. So radiantly, so quickly did Camila regain at least her superficial strength that he found himself staring at her with unbelief, a twisting filament of hope cutting at his heart because how *could* anyone so full of life be quenched, snuffed out, despite all the efforts of modern science and the flickering, indomitable energy of her will? He found himself wanting to be with her every moment, to kiss her warm, sweet mouth, the perfection of her breasts, her belly, her slender thighs; to take her in his arms in the shallow surf or the warm moist sand and feel the beating of her heart birdlike against his bare chest; to feel himself drowning as he always had in the exquisite mystery that was Camila, his beloved, his wife. He stared down at her beautiful face while she reached up, wondering, to touch his lean, tanned cheeks—his eyes in their laugh-lined orbits, the strong, indrawn brows—his hair falling loose and a little long over his faintly lined forehead as he looked at her, wanting to remember her by heart, every fleeting expression of her eyes and lips. He smiled at her, feeling her body's instinctual response, its slender arch to his, like dancers in a dance so perfectly joined they scarcely needed to move in the warm sun's rays and the sand's yielding pillow, ebbtide's lap and the rustle of the wind in the palms. And she twined her fingers in his black hair and brought his mouth down to hers with such urgency, such unconquerable happiness, that he lost all sense of time and grief and change and any thought at all save bliss, and lived for a moment in the paradise reserved for the gods.

The world was well lost for her—so he told himself, even when he sat reading the newspapers in the morning: all the major newspapers of the world were delivered daily to the island by private plane (Linz had a private news service to relay him information before it was published, but he liked the nostalgia of newsprint). He sat reading about the mess the world was in and the escalating warfare in Honduras, Costa Rica; he didn't need to receive messages from Campeche, to know of the spate of disorders in Mayapán, the ineptitude of Felix Innocencio Agudo, who had been elected Vice President for this his latest term and was serving as Presidente in his absence: he could read about it on the front page of *The New York Times*. Lejo Costamendez had called a truckers' strike and the major contracting teams at work in Chichén Itzá had gone out in sympathy; there were reports of violence in the interior, at Piedras Negras and Altar de Sacrificios; officials at the Chase Manhattan Bank and Citicorp had released a statement expressing their reluctance to continue underwriting loans to newly developing countries, in view of the current economic crunch. The statement was cosigned by half a dozen smaller banks, including, he read with furious amazement, the Istituto per le Opere di Religione—the Vatican Bank. He threw the newspaper across the villa's high-ceilinged dining room, where they were having breakfast, with a string of curses such as he hadn't uttered since he himself had been a revolutionary soldier in Honduras, and met Camila's gaze and, incredibly, her rueful smile, with the closest he'd ever come to irritation with her; he got up and left the table. For two days he tried not to read the newspapers at all, but Telexes and satellites kept murmuring in the far corners of the villa and humming in his head like the static of an untuned radio, and he had no peace. He sought relief in swimming far out into the sparkling water with its strong current, farther than Camila could follow him, fighting the ocean like a living presence and returning trembling with weariness, gasping for breath, and looking back at the invisible strip of land that haunted him like a nightmare, the cruel ambitious dream which he had loved before he loved Camila, the country he had tried to serve. The sacrifices of his youth and his sanity had seemed a small price to pay once (what ambitious man did not sacrifice at least a part of his sanity, his detachment, in pursuit of his life's goal?), and Buiztas had read him well in knowing how deeply he was hooked on the insidious highs of power. He had never had practice in denying himself any addiction, either to his pride or his genius at politics, or his wife. He truly didn't know what to do, and the experience was so novel that it terrified him, as he put a smile to his lips for Camila's sake, pretending that his thoughts weren't a million miles away; sitting with his chin leaning on his hand as he stared at the ocean, its restless ebb and flow echoing the confluence of his thoughts; refusing to see the obvious conclusion of all his twistings against fate until he stood with Camila on the high white-washed terrace and read the answer, bittersweet, in her shining eyes.

"You know, don't you?"

"Of course. I'm not blind."

"It's not what I want, it's just—"

She put her fingers to his lips. "It just is. This thing with me isn't what I want, but it just is too."

He cupped her face in his palms, blinking tears from his eyes and ignoring them on his cheeks. "I shall love you every instant of my life, until the day I die, and nothing can ever change that."

"Oh, I know that," she said softly. "I'm not stupid either."

His lips twitched. "You always have a gift for understatement."

She couldn't tell him how terribly sick she felt at that moment, pain lashing her head and visions surrounding her with flames, with blood-red gelatinous leaves and a hideous smell of burning flesh. She shut her eyes in what he thought was passion, to shut out the terrifying sights which had assaulted her, with ever increasing frequency, ever since she had left the hospital: visions of death, annihilation, the end of the world in a convulsion of blood, and a jungle so primitive she walked through it with only an uncomprehending sense of wonder ... climbing steps to an enclosed stone chamber of densely painted walls, in a world newborn where she was the only sentient being left alive.

two

WHEN FERDINANDO RETURNED to Campeche he dealt with the truckers' strike by putting Lejo Costamendez in jail, threatening the union leaders with fines and tariffs so merciless they would have bankrupted any less powerful and well-protected labor organizations than those in Mayapán, and contracting with cheap Mexican firms to supply the workers necessary to continue the construction in Chichén Itzá, and in forty-eight hours the strike was over—the first instance of union-busting tactics in the history of Mayapán, and the first occasion when Ferdinando Lorca was seen (and criticized) as having betrayed the very common people who had first put him into power.

That was what Ferdinando was like in those days, steely precise and driven with more than his usual tenacity to get things done, less and less patient with delay, haunted by the passage of time. His aides noticed the change in him right away, soon after his return from Nuevo York with La Señora Lorca: who was ill, but it was nothing serious; yes, it was something serious; perhaps; no one knew for sure, the full resources of the Lorcanista security and informational services were employed to cordon off the question of her health from the general public and even from the press. But word got out, it leaked through the cracks, and added to her mythology, and his: the First Lady who was wearing her-

self out for her people, and El Jefe, who was leaving his wife behind for his ambition. Subtly, as if a cloud had passed over the
city, and an unseasonable *norte* begun to blow, the unanimous
good favor that the Lorcas had always enjoyed began to disappear, and people began to remember disappointments and lies
that they'd never thought of before: Why was the national debt
higher than ever, if the oil profits were continuing to roll in? Why
were key positions in the refineries, the entertainment and tourist
industries held by *gringos*, Japs, Cubans: all sorts of foreigners?
Why was the Fundación Camila Lorca a privately incorporated
financial entity, if their madonna truly had no economic secrets to
hide? Why were they involved in a foreign war in Honduras and
El Salvador? Why were they harboring American military advisers, and leasing their soil for American army bases, and helping the Americans train foreign, counter-revolutionary troops?

With sweeping suddenness the people began to question the
government they'd previously worshiped, and since it happened
at the same time as the changes began to be observable in El
Lorca himself, it took even the most astute observers a long time
to realize the damage was coming from outside: the breeze of
doubt was blowing in off the foreign presses, books and pamphlets of the Frente Comunistas, which were suddenly visible
and readily accessible, well written and plainly, clearly phrased,
with the subtle look of cheaply printed broadsides, although they
were printed in the millions and shipped into the country (as
Jorge-Julio de Rodríguez discovered) from Miami. He went to El
Lorca with the news, Ferdinando, these bastards are organized
and they've got money behind them and more than that, they've
got a purpose that has nothing to do with revolution or any other
kind of change, they don't want to make anything better, they
just want life to conform to their political theories, and Ferdinando looked at him with his clear blue eyes, in which the liquor
of bitterness and cynicism was starting to collect like rainwater, and
said, What do you think, that we did things any differently? Wait
till they get their hands on what they want, then they'll see what
reality is like. He turned back to the papers on his desk, Arrest
the ones who are accepting shipment of the pamphlets, and find
out who's working for them inside the country, you can do that,
get Mynott to help you, and Jorge-Julio de Rodríguez protested,

But, Ferdinando, it doesn't matter who's accepting delivery for this propaganda, what matters is that we refute it, open every corner of this government to the ordinary light of day and show the people that we're on their side, and Ferdinando took off his glasses with a sigh, You naïve son of a bitch, we're not on the people's side, we're not on anybody's side, no government in the world can stand the light of public scrutiny and certainly not mine—so use your agents to control this infestation of fleas as best you can, because these things always happen, it's a summer problem and what's wanted is a good strong pesticide, get rid of it for me, what the hell do you think I made you Minister of Defense for anyway?

That was what Ferdinando was like at that time: cutting through knots he would in other days have carefully untied, solving with a glancing blow problems that in former times he would have solved by thought, diplomacy, and guile; and for all that, pensive, careless, disillusioned—sitting for long moments with his chin on his hand, listening to the sound of the rain falling on the terrace of the Presidential Palace outside his office. He and Camila were still in complete agreement on all things: they were the team who ran the country, and no decision was taken by El Señor Presidente without his conferring with La Señora, and no decision was taken by La Señora without the full knowledge and support of El Presidente. She had to rest more, so he brought her reports, detailed analyses of current governmental business which they read together, or which he read to her, when her eyesight began to fail, touching her hand lightly with the tips of his fingers, or brushing her forehead with his lips, when she fell asleep, and stealing away to work in the next room with the door open, to hear her if she awoke and needed anything. He was the one who administered opiates to her when she was in the worst pain, cradling her head in his lap and rubbing her temples until he felt the tension in her relax; the terrible fight to keep from crying out which made her grasp his hand so tightly that his fingers became numb.

With everyone else he became so forbidding in his severity, and the imperious snap of his commands, that his aides began to take small liberties in the anticipation of his wishes, never going against the grain of his intentions, but circumventing the necessity of disturbing him whenever possible. The first time he realized they were doing things without telling him about it, he was relieved; it saved time for them to show some initiative, and it was about time they learned how to get along without him in any case. But later on he began to be convinced that they were distorting his desires and compromising the integrity of the revolution which was his life's work, and that was when he decided to take all effective authority in the country into his own hands, extending the duration of his Presidency for an unspecified, indefinite period: a period of national development, which his advisers, and the Chamber of Deputies, and even the majority of the people hailed as a victory, because his was the spirit and the inspiration of the government. That decision reinforced in him the dangerous illusion that he could do anything in Mayapán, and cut him off even more from the ordinary human lives of his associates, so that when Generalísimo Ottavio Moroque asked for permission to be excused from a diplomatic function so he could attend a dance with Colonel Enrique Zacapa, he looked at him as if he couldn't understand what he was talking about: Of course not, what do you think we're doing, running a whorehouse for transvestites or a modern democracy? he snapped, Permission denied, and I don't want to see the two of you in each other's company anymore either, I'm transferring Colonel Zacapa to Punta Herrero before the world thinks we're nothing but a bunch of fairies.

That was what his decisions were like at that time, immediate and irrevocable but giving the impression they were arrived at spontaneously, while he was letting himself be seduced by the bleak loneliness of glory, the terrible isolation of power into which he was sinking. He observed but made no particular move to influence the changes in policy of Duncan Farrell's successor, Wilson Allen, as President of the United States: sitting looking into the mirror of his own thoughts even when Felix Agudo commented that President Allen seemed to be thinking along different lines from President Farrell and he didn't mean just because he didn't play football. Agudo cleared his throat, sipping a martini in the Presidential study, and ventured the analysis that Allen had been waiting a long time to be taken seriously, surely it was just a matter of his unique perspective but he could well imagine a Vice President getting impatient with the ludicrous restraints of his secondary office, and Ferdinando merely lit another cigarette as he sat reading the newspaper at his desk and said, If you hate it so much, why not quit, I'll appoint Camila as my Vice President like Perón, why not, what difference does it make? and Felix Agudo was so upset by the idea that he might actually do it that he was never heard again with anything but praises for his job.

Wilson Allen *was* a different President from his charming, photogenic predecessor, but initially the differences were cosmetic: he looked like a bank accountant at news conferences, and he dealt with Congress like an investigator for the I.R.S. Someone else compared him to a chameleon who knew all the colors of the rainbow from brown to beige, and he was so completely accessible as a target of journalistic boredom that it took them a long time to realize how intelligent he was. Subtle and absolutely unconcerned with seeming to be a strong leader, he had been organizing and overseeing the policy of the Oval Office for years, but he'd been compelled to abide by some of Duncan Farrell's foibles: for instance, his affinity for big business, his love for Third World fawning, and his fondness for the Lorcas. None of these were tastes that Wilson Allen shared: and it may have been that Ferdinando recognized this from the beginning, and saw him as a challenge or a foil (for he was never prouder of his political skills than at that point); he may have seen him as his adversary, because he began more and more to think of his life in symbolic terms, with enemies and allies, staunch friends and duplicitous rivals. Or he may have seen him as his nemesis, for he began occasionally to put his head in his hands and press his fingers against the sides of his head like a man who wishes to wake himself out of a dream—although he still hadn't fallen prey to the insidious impulse to think about his imaginary successor, as Buiztas had. He kept up with his incredible, exhausting schedule, regulating every aspect of his government from the most minute to the largest, with his careful precision and his sleepless leadership giving himself the illusion that because he couldn't live without his country, his country couldn't live without him, while he sank deeper and deeper into the warm mud bath of unacknowledged despotism which scalded him with shame and trapped him like cement.

When General Jorge-Julio de Rodríguez came to him with the report that they knew at last where the pamphlets of the Frente Comunistas were coming from, he listened impassively, not just the pamphlets but guns and ammunition and *contras* borrowed from Nicaragua and located in the highlands and It's that foreign journalist, Ferdinando, the one we all talked to, but he's gone back home and his liaison's still in the country, I'm sorry, Ferdinando, but it's Carlos Molina, he said it without inflection, standing immobile without coming to attention because he didn't want it to be a military matter.

For a long time Ferdinando didn't even look up from the papers he was reading, and when he finally did he took off his glasses and steepled his fingers and said quite calmly, "Arrest him, but tell Bill Mynott to take it easy on him, he's got a lot of information we could use and it would be a pity to short-change ourselves too quickly."

Jorge-Julio had the sensation that he was talking to a total stranger. "But, Ferdinando," he said quietly, "it's against nature not to feel something," and when his commanding officer reached for a cigarette and lit it with an unsteady hand he took this as a sign of compassion and added, "We could let him go, deport him to Miami and that would probably keep him out of trouble."

Ferdinando blew out his match and said sharply. "Don't be ridiculous, I was held in La Miramar for six months and they didn't have half the evidence on me that you say you've got on Carlos."

Only then did General Rodríguez realize how far away Ferdinando had grown, and he shook his head and said softly, "No, I guess we've got enough on the poor bastard, if you think so," and he ran his tongue ruminatively over his teeth as if he wanted to say something else but didn't have the nerve, and he saluted instead and walked out of El Lorca's office.

Carlos Molina resisted the idea of his own capture by pretending that nothing had happened, arriving at MixTech Studios at seven-thirty the following morning, where he had coffee with extra sugar and milk as he always did, two sweet rolls, looked over the layouts for several ads and storyboards for a new video for Pisote, and escaped down the service staircase five minutes before the officers sent to arrest him burst through the front doors with unslung rifles and an order signed by the Minister of Defense. It was impossible to believe that General Rodríguez had relented to the extent of warning him in advance, since in fact he was the person who captured him two days later, hiding out in the guesthouse on Luis García Mores' estate—filthy, his hands bloody from having broken a window and sick from having eaten some meat that had been left in an unplugged refrigerator. General Rodríguez had his men give him a chance to wash, comb his hair, and pull himself together before he was driven in an unmarked van to La Miramar Prison under the mistaken impression that delaying his arrival would be an act of charity, and by the time William Mynott and his men had stripped him and drenched him with water in the basement of the old barracks, whose whitewashed walls had been covered with zinc and extensively rewired, he had had time to lose all the deliberate bravado he'd maintained for the past forty-eight hours and become badly frightened. Still, he was strong, and intelligent, and aware, even in his terror, that his only remote chance of reprieve lay in keeping his valuable thoughts inside his mind, so it took them a long time to extract the information they wanted from him: a process of teaching by demonstration for the trainees, whose knowledge of interrogation procedures stopped with beatings; and a chance for Mynott to explore the tangled synapses of his own memory, and see what techniques of the Khmer Rouge and the KGB he remembered in his own flesh. It was a lengthy, brutal, well-orchestrated, and deliberate escalation of nightmares and in a preliminary sense at least it was hideously effective: although Carlos continued through pride or *machismo* or idealism (or, impossibly, innocence) to refuse to give them any concrete facts, his screams and inhuman, blood-choked pleading for mercy echoed throughout his whole quarter of the prison, especially when they pulled his fingernails out, one fingernail at a time, and then broke his hands, when that didn't work, smashing his talent to jelly with a hammer; poked an electrical prod up his ass and applied shocks directly to his prostate, and hung him upside down from a crossbeam, swinging him back and forth until he became terrified with the idea of drowning in his own vomit.

What was happening to Carlos at that time was that two things were intruding on his mind with strange insistency: blinding laughter at life's absurdity and rage at the people who had put him there. This rage included both the Comunistas and the Lorcas: he was ecumenical in his disillusionment with politicians and political philosophies, but as his flesh descended to a level of animated agony the inconceivable pain which he was suffering struck him as so excessive that his actions against the Lorcas began to seem more and more reasonable. He was really quite surprised at himself. He had never considered himself a hero, and didn't consider himself one now, but he felt no threat in losing every last vestige of himself in the flashing black darkness of his physical terror because goddamn it he was *right!* and he felt privileged to have stumbled on a circumstance of absolute morality in a relative world. In that instant his gadfly's radicalism became a moral certainty, and it was that certainty which kept him mute, along with the fatal punch line that he could have stayed at home in Cuba if he'd wanted *this*, and resulted in his sense of humor remaining intact while his body began to fall apart. He had long since passed the landmarks of pain known to the haunted man who had ordered his arrest . . . and who sat watching the proceedings on video surveillance from another room, smoking one cigarette after another and not saying a word. Finally, he divined his unseen observer, and began passing on remarks to him.

"Is this what you wanted us to learn at Columbia, Ferdinando? You must have thought we were blind!

"You'll have to have your dogs kill me now, I'm too dangerous a victim for you to leave me wandering around unattended!

"I could do holocaust drawings after this—are you trying to give me some new material?

"You've become just as bad as Buiztas—worse, because you told us you were going to be something different! You built up our hopes!"

When it was a little after nine o'clock Ferdinando ordered Mynott to stop torturing the prisoner and said that he would interview Molina alone. When he came into the room, the cartoonist was breathing through his mouth in moist snores, because the guards had broken his nose, and he turned his eyes without moving his head to look at his former leader with the dreamy stare of a man who had given up hoping for anything.

"You can't leave me alone for a minute, can you?"

335

When he articulated these words, with the difficulty of a man who's been beaten especially hard around the face and mouth (and it occurred to Ferdinando to think that he'd never told Mynott not to mark him; when the Buiztanistas had tortured *him*, they'd been told not to leave any marks), the Presidente felt his heart assailed with an impersonal pity which had nothing to do with his having ordered the interrogation in the first place. He remembered Carlos Molina in blue jeans and a ponytail at his seminars, he remembered him casual and joking, saying, You wouldn't have caught me out in the hills with Fidel and Raúl, even if my parents hadn't dragged me out of Havana in the first place, and because he remembered all of that, his voice had the coldness of absolute certainty as he said, "I would never have betrayed you, but it's you who have betrayed me."

"Go fuck yourself."

Ferdinando was still immobilized by the dispassionate sympathy he felt, which was for neither a friend nor an enemy but rather what he would have felt for a stranger, a visceral wincing from the pain of those purpling swollen bruises that made Carlos Molina's face almost unrecognizable. So he gently said, "It doesn't matter what you think, old friend, this had to happen so that the stability of the whole country wasn't lost. It's better to hurt one man than to jeopardize a whole country's peace just when it's starting to believe in itself."

Carlos Molina continued to look at him with his swollen artist's eyes, registering the intact sense of humor behind them, although they were swimming with the glazed weariness of absolute contempt. "You've made your point. So what are you going to do with me now?"

"Do? What do you mean?"

Mindless exhaustion had taken the place of every other physical sensation, and Carlos forced himself to look at the graceful man whose athlete's body had been tortured within these very walls (a long time ago, Carlos Molina knew; how long must it have taken him to recover from, if not forget, such pain? Perhaps you never could) and whose handsome, patrician face was looking at him with such sorrowful compassion that it would have moved anyone less brimming with hysterical laughter than Carlos Molina, or anyone less filled with the certainty of rage. "I mean you've tasted blood. You know what it's like now. On the other side of the whip. I can understand that. I want to know too. What it's like. To do this to someone else. You can do this now. Whenever you want. Whenever you need a fix of making someone else feel exactly what you felt. I'll bet you got a hard-on just watching me shit myself."

There was the smell of blood in the room and it overpowered the other smells, of excrement and sweat and vomit, the nauseous smell of fear . . . and Ferdinando shut his eyes. He said quietly, "If you give us some names, I can let you go. Right now I have no purpose to show for having arrested you, so I'm going to have to keep you here, and eventually I'm going to have to kill you."

The cartoonist continued to look at him, blinking the blood from his eyes and feeling the rush of absolute morality searing his lungs like a breath of pure oxygen. "Then go ahead and do that. I'm sick of painting lies. You go ahead and paint this shitty arrest any color you fucking well want."

The next morning Carlos Molina was reported as having flown to Los Angeles to undergo minor surgery, and his friends in the Frente Comunistas learned that he'd been transferred from La Miramar to an unnamed prison in the interior, after which everyone lost all trace of him. Investigators of the special security forces turned up a quantity of illicit drugs and obscene videotapes in his apartment, but aside from some copies of the offending pamphlets which had already been discovered, there was nothing to connect him more seriously with traitorous or criminal activities within the country. There were several dozen portraits of world leaders and celebrities, done in his usual quick, pen-and-ink style, and some more elaborate and delicately tinted watercolors, including a beautiful portrait of Ferdinando. There were also some paste-ups for the latest campaign to promote tourism in the country . . . including one which had been designed as a joke and which was responsible for the one time when anyone could remember hearing Bill Mynott laugh. It showed the artist snorting mounds of cocaine and surrounded by a pharmacopoeia of drugs, and the caption read, "Come to Mayapán, where you can get away with anything."

three

IT WAS AROUND THAT TIME that a meeting took place between Battiste Tommassi and Martín Acchuirez in the Vatican.

It wasn't the first meeting between them, but it was the first time they had met in the opulent, gilded rooms put aside for Battiste's use, down the corridor from the bare cubicle where the Superior General of the Jesuits was dying. Battiste was his *de facto* successor, and had even begun to be referred to as "The Black Pope": a case in which the legendary colloquialism for his office was particularly apt, for the tall, gaunt, gray-haired priest, dressed in the severest black, seemed to give off a visible aura of darkness and intransigence. In reality, his mind was still a maelstrom of conflicting emotions, of terrifying ideas. He felt the thick taste of his discomfort, like a physical nausea in his mouth, as he received his guest in the cool, high-ceilinged room which seemed both to welcome and to trivialize this matter-of-fact and unimpressed young man, who looked at the priest directly, with the same mixture of arrogance and candor which he always exhibited, and said, "You look good. You've got better color in your face, for one thing. Are you sleeping better than you were in New York?"

Battiste winced. "Yes, much better," he murmured, indicating a chair. "Would you like some tea?"

He sat down as well, arranging the folds of his soutane in careful pleats over his knees. Martín continued to look at him thoughtfully. He was a gifted diagnostician, and he knew much more than even his followers gave him credit for; he read Battiste like a book. Nothing mattered, or rather everything mattered and each fact played its part, in the eventual Marxist liberation of Mayapán to which he had dedicated his life, but he saw the priest's pain and some spark of contempt pulled up the corners of his lips—although he felt toward Battiste and everyone in general but his *compadre* and fellow Mayan, José Luaro, nothing but the merest indifference.

"I can give you some drugs," he said familiarly to the older man. "But it's not good for a man like you to take too many pills, you're too prone to the side effects."

"Yes, that's always been my trouble," Battiste said, smiling thinly. He could still be betrayed by the physical revulsion of his body—although he was getting better at controlling such things, he thought as he rang the bell for Sister Angelina to bring them tea. He was eating again, as Martín had noticed, and he didn't look so wretched, although his ulcer had perforated shortly after he'd gotten back to Rome and he'd needed a series of operations. He was finally adult, and thought in compromises: half-loaves of tangible good for the country he still loved with every waking breath. It could not come from the Lorcas: even to himself, he never thought of them anymore as Ferdinando and Camila. But he felt a sharp emptiness in his heart that nothing could fill—not service to his Holiness, or collaboration with this undemonstrative and impersonal young man whose physical presence was uninspiring, and who yet radiated a warmth and magnetism that drew him like a fire behind a glass: but he had learned not to reach out his frozen fingers anymore to touch another human being.

"You've come at a good time, another week and I wouldn't have been able to spare five minutes without causing ripples of gossip to spread through what is, contrary to popular opinion, a very small and insulated pond." He smiled, pouring tea, handing a plate of amaretto biscotti to Martín, and added, scarcely casually, "The Holy Father is due back from Castel Gandolfo next Monday. I intend to tell him to sell all of his shares of Linz Industries and UNOCO stock."

"Oh, really? I thought you weren't so sure."

"I'm so sure."

"He's not going to like that, without any explanation."

"Oh, I'll give him an explanation—close to the truth, as a matter of fact. Mayapán's instability . . . Exxon's refusal to sell oil to Nicaragua . . . he'll agree to diversifying the Vatican's assets. Our Panamanian banks will transfer a lot of the money into U.S. Treasury bonds, in anticipation of the American's 'windfall' in foreign oil, and a certain amount can be laundered through Buenos Aires and go to you. Not, I regret to say, a princely sum, but you can take a cut from the C.I.A.'s nest egg, I should imagine."

"It occasionally strikes me as funny," Martín said candidly, "that the Americans are so pliable. El Lorca must have experienced the same feeling when Linz agreed to foot *his* bill."

"It *is* the same feeling, because it's the same thing," Battiste murmured, his hand hovering over the plate of biscuits and his eyes shutting in a wave of nausea. He withdrew his hand. "The Americans would rather deal with an illusionary enemy than a real one. President Allen is tired of saying Marxism is the ultimate enemy in the region, and propping up United Fruit—read United Oil, but you know what I mean. That lie's gotten too thin. They've committed their military help to the Lorcanistas, but they'd prefer for your side to win." Battiste narrowed his eyes, and sighed almost inaudibly, a curious, whistling sound as if his throat closed around his pain in the moment of its trying to escape from him. "Ferdinando always said we could never oppose the Americans—meaning the capitalists, thinking they were the same thing. It's the only serious mistake I ever remember him making."

"The Americans can't make up their minds whether they want to be millionaires or saviors," Martín said, munching on a cookie and drinking his tea, glancing at Battiste's ravaged face and settling his compact, warrior's body more comfortably in his chair. "Your friend had the same problem."

"Shut up," Battiste snapped, turning aside quickly. "What do you know about it?"

"I know he got rich."

"Ferdinando never wanted money in his life. Who do you think he was—Trujillo? Somoza? Camila was rich. Her uncle was as rich as Croesus, she came to school in a lamb's-wool coat and Alfred Linz himself was her . . . I don't know, some sort of relative . . . oh, my God!" He turned away from Martín, biting his knuckle, whispering to himself, "My God, my God, how I miss them!"

"You've never gotten over either of them, have you?" Martín said, eating another cookie. "No wonder you're such a mess." He smiled his ambiguous smile, looking at the priest with what might have been contempt or distant compassion or sarcastic concern.

"Of course I never got over them—they never gave me a chance," Battiste murmured. "They still don't, living in my heart like a cancer that throbs and aches with everything they do, every breath they draw—every word I have of them. Oh, what can you know about it? It's my business who I love and what I do about it . . ." Battiste got up quickly from his chair and walked, with the grace that he had learned so imperfectly to master, over to the window, looking down at the Via della Conciliazione while his ungainly shoulders shook. Martín was thoughtfully silent. Gradually, taking a deep silent breath, Battiste managed to control his emotions and his voice.

"I think the United States is frankly frightened of the power of some of these multinationals, like UNOCO, and Linz Industries, and Linz International." He pressed his fingers over his eyes once, sharply, and swallowed, returning and sitting in his chair. "And so long as United Oil has a private oil field in Mayapán, for their unlimited use, Washington's analysts have a right to be frightened." He refused to think of how brilliant Ferdinando had been, in giving himself such a weapon. He refused to remember his own amazement, listening to his friend tell him the intricacies of his plans in the pink villa on the Isla del Viento, Ferdinando standing up to his waist in the warm blue water, smiling at him, putting his arm around his shoulders and telling him, "Who do I have, but the two of you? Who can I trust completely, besides you and Camila?"

"That's why Washington is willing to accept a Marxist government in Campeche, is even willing to accept an open alliance with Havana, if you want one—if you're willing to nationalize the oil fields and strike a private deal with the United States. Are you willing to do that? I have to have your answer now, in which case not only will the Vatican pull out its money, but the major American investors will pull out as well, and Allen will go to bat for you with covert aid and Israeli arms for your people when the time comes. But they've got to know they're getting their money's worth, and if you double-cross them later, I promise they'll destroy you."

"Why should I double-cross them?" Martín shrugged. "I'd rather make a deal with Wilson Allen than the Soviets, they're too far away. And let's face it, the United States is a far less powerful master than United Oil."

"Exactly." Battiste dipped a biscuit in his tea and ate it without a qualm. "Your propaganda efforts are going strong, I see—you're not going to win over a large number of the *campesinos*, but some of the middle class will join you, and the dispossessed oligarchs will join anything that moves. It's mainly useful as a cover for the United States' involvement, it gives the appearance of inevitability. How's the old man?"

Martín made a face.

"I know," Battiste said with a bitter smile. "I don't trust him and I never have, but after Ferdinando and Camila he's the most famous Mayapanian in the world, and people read his stories who've never heard of the place, or of either of them. I think he's thinking of backing out, he wrote to me, Should he or shouldn't he send you some material? Did you get him involved in that other thing by the way?"

Martín nodded. "He'll go along. He's too far in it to back out now, and he knows it. I've got enough on the old man to land him in jail."

"So it's settled?" Battiste suddenly felt the stillness in the room, less echoing than oppressive, lined with draperies and rugs, thick glass and the gentle, golden, polluted Roman sunset, and he felt as if he couldn't breathe. "You won't—you won't take any ..." His voice closed up and he couldn't say it. "You won't take any action against her—or have you decided?"

Martín rubbed his nose thoughtfully, and looked at the priest. "No, I haven't decided, as a matter of fact." He hesitated, and then added, relenting, "I can't be accountable to you for what I will or I won't do. But she probably won't live that long, so it doesn't matter. As for the other one—"

"It doesn't matter."

"It better not. I can't afford to leave Ferdinando Lorca alive for five minutes after we get into power."

"No, you can't," Battiste said quietly. "It makes sense. I'd thought of that. Don't worry, you haven't said anything that surprises me. Only—"

"Yes?"

"Give him a quick death. Don't let him suffer unnecessarily. After all, he was once my friend," the priest said with a twisted smile. "And I would willingly and happily have given my life for him in his place."

four

So THEY DECIDED on their course of actions, and the campaign of financial and political isolation of Mayapán began. Camila found out about part of it, in the offices of their private broker at Goldman Sachs in New York, and her reaction was as immediate and decisive as it had been in the days of her full strength.

Not that she had anything like her former health: she was there, in fact, against doctors' orders, having walked out on her latest round of chemotherapy with the snapped comment that I'm dying anyway, why do you have to make me glow in the dark while I'm at it? and gone to their offices to distract herself, with the meaningless concerns of their great wealth, and the unexpected company of the former dictator Quintero de Buiztas. She'd had no idea that the profits of his tyranny and their triumph were being managed by the same brokerage firm, and perhaps they weren't: he might have come there simply to annoy her, to spy on her, or perhaps to look out for her, so pale and thin was she that the bankers accepted him as her escort . . . and she didn't have enough strength to argue with them. She sat and heard about the vagaries of the stock market and began to be aware of the trend behind the trends they were following: the unspoken subtext of the shift in capital away from Mayapán, which the discreet men and women who managed the world's assets could hint at, but never admit. She heard them through in silence, and finally when the message was as clear to her as a billboard, she simply said, "The United States doesn't trust Mayapán anymore, and the banks don't trust UNOCO, so they're pulling out, right?" And the brokers hemmed and nodded, and she asked them quietly, "Who's behind this, can you tell me?" And they couldn't, but by then, she had already guessed.

She was very quiet, and only Buiztas, lounging in another chair, could see the old blue light like a match flame in her tired eyes, as she gave them a few small transactions to put through, concluded her business, and stood up with something like her old briskness. They ushered her out—and she stalked to a waiting elevator and streaked earthward, with Buiztas barely having time to get in beside her, because he knew economic trends as well as she did, and was dying to see how she answered this betrayal by her beloved priest.

"Señora—where are we—excuse me, but I'm getting a little old for this—" He laughed as she stepped into her limousine, and he just made it, to slip into the seat beside her.

She didn't say anything, staring out of the window with her slender legs crossed and her thin hands clasped over one knee, a muscle contracting in her fragile throat in time to a rapid, internal beat; Buiztas was fascinated, he'd never seen her so furious before. They got off at the Plaza, where she'd checked in (according to the newspapers) the week before in a lavish suite; and he rode up with her in the elevator, still without her saying a word and her black hat hiding or revealing her chiseled, lovely, immobile profile (he tried both sides to see which was the more interesting). The lips untouched by lipstick and the eyes very lightly made up; she was wearing less mascara and shadow as illness provided the shadows for her, and he was reminded by her beauty and her anger of both her parents, but especially that crazy *caballejo* her father: that old nag with his yellowing white hair, and his crazy morals, Don Quixote in a guayabera shirt, sacrificing himself and his wife and his child for a principle. Yes, this was his daughter, and the daughter of his young wife, the pure Aryan beauty who had escaped to peace or boredom or a second chance in Mayapán? Married to an idealist, which meant death in any case, but a legacy of ambiguity in this *angelita* First Lady with her Halston dress, her pearls and her black hat and her eyes shutting in a grimace of pain at the ascent of the elevator, blood draining from her face in a pallor which might also have been that of rage, forces beneath the surface of her fantastic calm which he couldn't begin to imagine, but which intrigued him, as he'd always been intrigued by her mystery, her delicacy, and that part of her that called out her kinship to some buried, ambiguous part of himself.

They got off the elevator and Camila again moved past him, not running but walking with incredible swiftness and precision down the hallway to her room, unlocking the door and leaving it open less in hospitality (he had the idea she was scarcely aware of his presence) as thoughtless haste: slamming through her sitting room to the bedroom and the telephone which she snatched up, dialing and securing an overseas line, Italy, the Vatican: Get me Agostino Brinisi on this line, hold on, please, I'd like to make this a conference call, give me Cardinal Vinolo at the offices of the Vatican Bank, yes, I'll hold, Signore Brinisi, I don't have time to mince words, as the lay leader of Opus Dei, how would you like to gain control of the Vatican Bank?

Buiztas lit up a cigarette and sat down quietly in a Louis XV chair to see if she could pull this off. For half an hour she spoke, first to one party and then to another, speaking in English, Spanish, Italian ... rapid-fire, pacing the room with the phone cradled against her shoulder and sometimes sitting cross-legged on the bed, running her hand unconsciously over the soft stubble of blond hair which covered her head like a crew cut. "*Digame!* Who do you think controls the price of crude oil in Mayapán and who do you think can change it? I told you what I want, I want the investments secured by Father Battiste Tommassi to be *worthless,* and I'm going to get that, it's just a question of whether you want me to bankrupt the Vatican while I'm at it! *Claro,* of course I want your Society of the Holy Cross to benefit ... we would not be talking like this if I did not think ... yes, of course ... his reorganization of your investments right now could be *excessively* dangerous, but a unique opportunity for *you* ... *verdad,* Cardinal? You do not want me to reveal certain things about the sources of those funds, certain things that the files of Linz Industries would make *uncomfortably* clear to the European press? Very well, then give me what I want . . . !"

It was a bold move, and in its own way a brilliant maneuver, striking right at Battiste's power without wasting time on inconsequentials, lashing out with all the impacted rage and steel-sharp fury of her illness and her pain at the man who had so inconceivably betrayed her. Buiztas reflected that he might have known she wasn't the kind to get angry uselessly: her fast, staccato voice on the phone was dealing telling blows against the opposition that was hounding her, and who cared if it was all bullshit? At least she was doing something. Why, nine *muchachitas* out of ten would have been weeping, and here she was, sitting on the edge of the bed with her legs crossed in their fine silk stockings, and her eyes fixed on a single, immobile point while her mind fished up facts which even *he* didn't remember, it was ridiculous and a waste of time and in its own way it was wonderful, who cared if it was all too late . . . and he was stirred by something that in another man would have been an atavistic tenderness, and reached out his hand tentatively to touch that shaved, white-golden head.

She barely noticed, and stood up a moment later to cross the room again, talking quickly, sharply, rapidly . . . hung up and hurled the phone across the room with all her strength (which was considerable) to smash against the peach-colored molding and fall apart on the floor. She was shaking with rage. "How dare they? How fucking dare they! Don't they know who I am, who Ferdinando is, what we can do to them!" She was trembling as if she were feverish, and speech gave way to movement: she grabbed any small objects within reach and began throwing them with deadly accuracy at all the breakable targets in the room. Buiztas shielded his head and exploded with laughter, cheering her on with cries of *"Olé! El toro!"* although he was a little daunted by her fury, her tantrum which must surely be bad for her, but what the hell, it was what those *pendejos* deserved and hadn't she suffered enough to have earned every right to be angry? It was a good question whether he could have stopped her in any case, and being Quintero de Buiztas, he had no intention of stopping her, although he finally rolled off the bed and reached to grab her shoulders just to steady her as she sank gasping with dry furious sobs of near-hysterical laughter onto the floor . . . slipping between his hands like a doll, and it was then that he noticed her clenched hands opening, furling back like petals and the wounds opening like tulips inside her hands, one on each palm, splitting open as he watched like the parts of a woman or a flower, pouring blood like the hands of a saint, like a *crucifijo*, he was very frightened, Shit what was going on here? He went to get a towel from the bathroom, huffing and puffing, no, that would take too long, and when he turned around she was sitting, very still, her face listening and intent, all anger gone, and a moment's flicker of recognition in those enormous blue eyes like the eyes of a serious child, wide open, as if she saw something he couldn't see, before her eyes rolled up into her skull and she became limp, and lost all consciousness, and lay for two days scarcely breathing as if she were dead.

After that they became more frequent, those instances of paralysis, trance, as if she were (depending on your perspective) being claimed by an insistent and devouring enemy, or battered, with a force scarcely less brutal, by a power she refused to admit. Each time she awakened, she laid claim more fiercely to the world that was slipping away from her: the power she had never sought, world acclaim and the love of her people; power to punish her enemies, and reward her friends. She worked as tenaciously as her strength would permit, touring the massive free medical clinic being built in her name in Chichén Itzá, all glass and chrome like the clean cold surfaces of a morgue; she jetted off to Washington and Bonn and Zürich as like as not to end up in some emergency ward, with a terrified internist jump-starting her heart; and her flutterings grew smaller and smaller, more and more restricted, as her body was broken, bent, and beaten down by the power that was trying to kill or make her new. Still she wouldn't admit it, still she pretended blindness although she was forced to see: that what was attacking her was the same world of hallucinations and visions that she had always known, stronger now and much more compelling, possessing her like a seizing hand and turning her face toward the light relentlessly, impatiently, till she got the message and stopped struggling against the transformation within her.

She saw it, and didn't want to see it. Saw it as the hallucination of peeling flesh on the corpse-face of Alfred Linz, standing with her in the gothic hall of his ancestral home in Mainz, and she pressed her brain shut on the concept of buying up Linz stock until her tumor exploded and sent her into seizures. She saw it in the deceptive twilight of a pastel Washington evening, riding in a limousine up Pennsylvania Avenue with soft lights pricking out of the blue-hazed, tender sky, but all she saw were time-zero flashes and mushroom clouds: arrived at the White House hallucinating and somehow managed to walk inside, talk and comport herself normally, until she was alone with President Allen, at which point she started to speak in a bell-clear voice in the words of the prophet Isaiah, "Thou has heard, see all this; and will ye not declare it? I have shewed thee new things, from this time, even hidden things, and thou didst not know them. They are created now, and not from the beginning; even before the day when thou heardest them not; lest thou shouldest say, Behold, I knew them." She saw it most of all on her return to Campeche, when she stepped out of her gleaming plane into Ferdinando's arms and saw his face split open, blasted apart like a bomb by rifle shots, and only then did she close her eyes and accept the power that was growing in her, accept it like a rapist and baptize it Death, because she had no other name by which to address it.

Ferdinando saw her eyes shut briefly, and the spasm of pain that followed, mistook it for the physical pain of illness and so kept his arm light and steady around her waist, his voice privately desperate, "For God's sake, don't faint until I get you in the car," and there was no way she could explain it to him . . . but there was no way she could ever explain it to him, she realized as she lay back against the cushions of the limousine and looked at his drawn, thin face, his sensitive lips . . . no way in the world she could explain something she didn't understand, but which was calling her away from him. She looked at his profile as he turned to face the driver and the white, chalky road ahead of them, the prominent nose and farsighted eyes which made him look like a bird of prey, the slender hands clenched in helpless rage against the impeccable blue pinstripe of his trousers, and knew him so well she felt that every breath they drew was shared between them. The world was the same again—perfectly ordinary—but now at last she couldn't doubt the truth of that other world which was equally real but indescribable.

She reached out her hand and took his tenderly, squeezing it. "I love you." He jumped as if she had stung him, and looked at her with fear, anxiety that she was all right, trepidation perhaps that she was losing her mind (her thoughts felt easier and strangely light, she could even consider the joke of the political liability of a mad wife), and she smiled and shook her head. "I'm all right," she whispered. "It comes and goes. Don't worry, there's life in the old girl yet."

Fading, diminishing. Relaxing the terrible battle she had fought. She appeared to be distracted but Buiztas (and sometimes Pisote, who stayed close to her, helping her dress and apply her makeup) realized she was paying very close attention to something they couldn't see. Listening, watching. Called back from a trance, like death, with difficulty, and a terrible expression of loss. Oddly enough, Ferdinando was the only person close to her who didn't recognize her absences: she was seldom absent with him, and he resolutely refused to see her symptoms, although he spent more time with her than anyone else. Slept with her in the same bed, but got up at four-thirty in the morning to read reports, sign decrees, and helicopter off to Chichén Itzá to oversee the building of his lakes and plazas, the blazing white steps and sheer facades of his city which was taking shape and making the pyramids look small and grubby by comparison. Striding through the halls of the Presidential Palace, snapping orders, or sitting at his desk with his fingers propping his forehead, with his half-moon glasses pushed up into his hair while he read the newspapers in several different languages, all of which told him the same thing, how he was losing the support of the people through outside agitators so he stepped up the duties of the internal security forces headed by William Mynott; he read how the *norteamericanos*' military insanity had clotted his armies in Honduras and El Salvador so he ordered General Jorge-Julio de Rodríguez to Get me some soldiers who can *fight*, goddamn it! If we lose ground now the Americans will abandon us altogether; and he read how he was being abandoned anyway by outside investors, so he put all his eggs and faith in the combined corporate baskets of Linz Industries and United Oil, and met with Charlie Cox once a week in the Presidential Palace to plan their strategy, their responses to the drying up of World Monetary funds and the increased difficulty of obtaining men and machinery for the hellish wells that operated day and night, seven days a week, in the jungle, in temperatures exceeding 120 degrees. Killing men on an average of ten a month, but there were always more to take their place, silent Indians with the high cheekbones and lithe bodies and jet-black hair of El Lorca himself, but bloated with drink, drugs, salt, the promise of french fries drawing them to the *gringos* but not so much, because they were disappearing, fading into the jungle, joining an Indian *brujo* with the face of a classic Mayan statue, who had recently landed in the region, and set up his headquarters along the Aguán River in Honduras. And when Ferdinando read that in a report he stopped and sat quite still, massaging the fold of skin between his eyebrows, savoring the near-perfect collusion of past and future which he could still appreciate with intellectual and bitter mirth ... and then refusing to believe in the repetition of history, he smoothed his hands over his thinning hair, pressed fingertips to his eyes to shut out demons, and continued to govern the country as only he could, brilliant politician and tactical genius but all the brilliance in the world couldn't save him from the storm clouds massing all over the hemisphere against him.

Camila saw those clouds, couldn't miss them. She was hallucinating and dying, but she wasn't blind. The protests in the capital, the desertion of all the other oil companies to OPEC, leaving Mayapán and UNOCO monogamously conjoined. The storm clouds in her husband's mind as well—thought-monsters and the enemies of memory, conspiracies so farfetched even Bill Mynott couldn't believe in them, although he continued to arrest and torture, send prisoners to Jorge-Julio in gasoline drums with unabated enthusiasm. She saw it all, and sometimes she saw more: walking down the stairs of her Fundación building, she saw the apocalyptic burning of flamed faces, napalm wounds in the upturned palms outstretched toward her, the vistas through the open doors of worried faces creased with smiles and hands crossing themselves which charred to blackened stumps as she watched, and the garden's green bursting into flames (she was

351

beginning to have a certain poise even in the midst of horrors), sending livid orange plumes to blossom with gasoline smoke, among the bougainvillea. She saw it all. Saw the burgeoning of faith in old religions, the *chacs* and the *tzitzimitl* as well as *candomblé* and *umbanda* imported from Brazil, Argentine *espíritisimo*, Haitian voodoo and the cult of the Virgen ... dime-store statues and blood-smeared feathers crowded next to the tinfoil fragility and paste-fake jewels of La Madonna and the Niño in country churches, white-clad children in hand-embroidered smocks singing to Santa Camila in the National Cathedral. She saw them all ... didn't need to hallucinate the last, because it was already happening; standing in the Cathedral incognito in a black silk scarf, she heard them sing and it filled her sick heart with outrage; she shut her eyes and saw a gargantuan picture of herself ten stories high, and didn't understand it until she went out into the street and saw the enormous blank wall of the old Grand Hotel and knew that's where it would be, a billboard-cum-memorial lit with floodlights, her portrait, after her death. She saw everything in the midst of massive doses of pills and pain-killers, which did nothing—didn't even affect the brilliance and tactile reality of her visions, much less lessen the pain—her always uncanny resistance to drugs and alcohol coming full circle to haunt her with unremitting agony. But she discovered a threshold beyond pain, she learned how to fall backward and upward through it to a level of distant clarity where she knew immediately which things were false and which were true: so she knew immediately, when there was a report of the death of hundreds of workers in the jungle, that they were Indians; that it wasn't an accident but a massacre; and that she had to go there.

five

S̲HE HAD BEEN WARNED against going: by her doctors, by Pisote and Jorge-Julio, and most of all by Ferdinando himself.

"You'll die, the jungle itself would kill you. It's at least two hundred miles to Piedras Negras and then farther upriver to Altar de Sacrificios—" Taking her face between his hands as he stood with her in his office, the air conditioning muting the scented darkness of a tropical night outside the windows. "What is it? What's up there?" Casting his eyes searchingly over her face, as if he would read her thoughts, but all he could read now was a reflection of his own. "Do you blame me? Is it for that that you want to leave me, because I caused it, because I should have done more for them?" He smoothed his fingers over the fragile skin of her forehead, trying to see what was in her mind with all the persistent love at his command. "Tell me, my darling. You know I'd do anything to make you happy, but you must see it's impossible, I can't let you go up there. I can't run that risk. Tell me, my love. Tell me what's up there, explain it to me—"

She couldn't explain it. She knew they were trying to "pacify" the region, but it wasn't that. Knew about Project Quetzal, aimed to annihilate the remaining Mayas because they were a threat to the government (or perhaps merely nightmares in the mind of the C.I.A. paranoid who ran the Mayapanian death squads), but somehow Bill Mynott seemed to retreat in importance too, a symptom, not a cause . . . and she felt instead the terrible beauty of the world that was calling her to it, the jungle to which she'd always known she would return.

Which was how she arrived, in the steaming jungle, on a train with burst plastic seats and women with baskets and chickens and undershirted *pachucos*, and sweat-soaked whores, and men selling ices and empenadas both lukewarm and speckled with dirt. The train seemed to stop and start continuously, and once it stood for six hours in the middle of the jungle for no apparent reason, even though it was impossible to see anything, not merely because it was night, but pitch dark with the thick black stench of night in the middle of nowhere. She bore it all not merely in silence, but with a freshening and lightening of her spirits, so that when they began moving again and the light revealed towering trees and lianas looped like cables through the verdant green, she started at the flash of a quetzal's feathers through the trees. She drank the same amoebic water and ate the same corn broth and tortillas as everyone else, and she continued to lose weight, but she didn't mind, because when they got to Piedras Negras and stood on the train platform the people who had traveled with her for a hundred miles finally recognized her, and the Indians standing by the trees in white shirts and the workers sweat-grimed in their undershirts knelt down in the oil-churned mud of the jungle, and the machinery came to a stop, and the drilling in the interior was suspended as of that instant, and the world grew still. They helped her down from the train, supporting her faltering steps, and an awed *mestizo* in a leather jacket tried to give her a cup of chocolate and broke three mugs before he could hand her one, stammering, "Señora, you have done us a great honor, you are our savior, please sit down, señora, save us all, we love you, please sit down—"

Oh, my God, she thought, with a mixture of sadness and poignant terror, they really believe I can help them.

They really did. Risen from the dead, although she was dying, on the route between the little villages of the interior,

Naha and Yaxchilán, down the Usumacinta River away from the derricks in a single-engine boat covered with a canopy of palm fronds, sunlight sparkling on the oil-smeared water. Listening to the throbbing of the engine and the crackling of the radio, barking coughs of howler monkeys and the receding boom of the refineries after they left behind the nightmare city of Altar de Sacrificios . . . with its oil tanks and its corrugated iron sheds built over the crumbling ruins of its truncated temple, its bridge which had been blown up by the Frente Comunistas, and its barracks of troops under the command of a Green Beret colonel who came down to the water's edge along with his soldiers and half-breed Indians snapping out questions of what was going on, and went white when he saw the fragile blond woman with her sculpted pale face and her beautiful eyes, sitting in a wicker chair under the canopy of palm fronds. He saluted and cleared his throat. "Madame Lorca, I don't know how you got here, but you're in a lot of danger. This is a disputed area, and we've been taking a lot of sniper fire—"

Camila smiled, barely moving her lips, but it was a smile of great tenderness. "I've always been in danger, ever since I was born. Under whose orders are you operating?"

"General Welsh, ma'am, Commander Special Forces."

"I see. So it really is a lie, isn't it?"

"I beg your pardon?"

"The story that the *norteamericanos* are here as our advisers."

"Your husband is fighting a war, ma'am."

"Yes, but against whom? Do you know? Altar de Sacrificios is no longer drilling, but the United Oil investments in our country already total millions. They can't afford to stop now." An understatement: the refineries were operating day and night, to fuel the pacification/resettlement of the Mayas. She looked into his eyes and saw the Indians he had killed, perhaps even his regret, the promotion he'd received after the evacuation of Saigon, the wife and kids he'd left back in the States. She shook her head. "Where is Martín Acchuirez?"

He licked his lips. "I can't tell you that, ma'am."

"Do you really think I'm his spy?" She searched his eyes,

355

and then inclined her head. "Go on," she murmured to the pilot of her boat, and he started up his engine and pulled away from the wharf.

A light rain was starting to fall, pattering on the palm-frond canopy and filling up the river and the encroaching jungle with mist—the surrounding jungle that massed even here, against this huge plant lettered with the big block letters "UNOCO." The jetty was crowded with grimy men, a few filthy women, and children in torn white smocks and matted hair who stood a little ways off, all of them silent as the Green Beret colonel saluted and disembarked, and who set up a low, whispering murmur as the boat cast off. Camila glanced back, and glimpsed the burning gas of the refinery like an insubstantial torch, garish against the drizzle. It surely couldn't be that lianas, creepers, and vines had already choked the abandoned rigs, and substantial trees had sprung up, quickly as weeds, to dwarf the crumbling, green, moss-spangled buildings? She shut her eyes. The boat churned slowly around a bend in the endless river, and when she turned to look again the ruins of Altar de Sacrificios had disappeared.

They continued up the river, in the hallucinatory heat and moisture and dripping greenery of the forest, and she felt her mind slipping away from her, sapped leechlike by the primordial lethargy of this timeless, motionless journey. She stared up at the leaves, a ghostly world of huge hanging fronds, ferns and branches that arched overhead to the dizzying height of the mahoganies, massive rubber trees oozing their gum along with the chechem, or weeping tree, whose sap could blind a man, a riot of flowers, scarlet, yellow, pink, and parrots taking flight while clouds of butterflies and gnats blew above the dark-green water and spider monkeys chattered like human children in the trees. A twilit, blood-warm world of gelatinous leaves and monstrous, elephantine, exotic plants, voluptuous orchids whose velvet tongues lolled from soft throats like the mouths of panthers, thick-petaled, livid, firm-fleshed lilies, with living veins engorged in their beating hearts, fragile, quivering passionflowers falling in clusters over the strangling embrace of vines, and figs and cassavas fallen to rot where they'd been half-feasted upon by monkeys, tapirs, and insects. Red ants devouring a dead paca that heaved like a mountain of iridescent satin beneath its mantle of pincers and filaments of death, shimmering pools of oil undiscovered by man, five-foot iguanas that threw themselves from the overhanging trees to crash like human divers into the secret river that bubbled with the sulfur of decay and flamed with the lush, slimy green of moss and shivered with the passage of snakes, black and yellow toucans who soared overhead into the rain-misted firmament of the cedars. For what might have been two days or two years, they went up the Pasión River, her reluctant guide steering for shoals and hidden rocks, salamanders skittering like dancers in front of their boat and the oily blood of the sliced water lilies leaving a trail of darkness in their wake. They remembered the sun in the haze that filtered down through the curtain of overhanging trees, and Camila slept and her profile became sharp, and her skin became the color of alabaster and she looked like a wax effigy of herself.

She had almost abandoned herself to the passivity of death when suddenly the river opened up, widening into a secret, glass-clear lake, and there was a wooden canoe poling toward them, and Camila opened her eyes and said with quite certainty, "I've been here before."

six

CAMILA'S GUIDE SHUT OFF the engine and let the boat drift on the surface of the lake, as the canoe poled gracefully toward them. There was a young man standing up in the bow, dressed in a plain white tunic that reached to his knees, with long black hair down to his waist and a thick oar with which he maneuvered his craft with remarkable dexterity: a small, childlike man, scarcely five feet tall, with bare feet and serious eyes and a beautiful, high-cheekboned face. He poled his canoe until it rocked lightly against the side of the boat, and looked at Camila for a long moment curiously, as if she were someone he had heard described, and was interested in finally meeting face to face.

"My father, Nuxi', was told that you were coming, but he wasn't sure. He sent me, because my father is an old man, and waits for you in the god house. My mother, Nuk, sends you this."

He held out a gourd full of a brown frothy liquid like dark beer. "My father says a woman may have balche if she is a *t'o'ohil* or a teacher, but I don't know how that can be, since all *t'o'ohils* must be men like my father. So I think maybe my mother sends you balche because she knows you are just a woman, and because it will make you strong and brave and you will walk across the

358

water like Our Lord Hachakyum!" He laughed, showing big white teeth, and Camila took the gourd between her hands and drank, like a communicant, with her eyes closed.

"Now." The young man laughed as she finished it. "Now Our Lord Hachakyum will see that you are one of the true people, and He will not kill you."

"No?" She opened her incredibly vivid blue eyes, and smiled a little. "That's a good trick. Forgive me if I don't believe you."

Across the lake there was a settlement of thatched huts, and behind them an immense, overgrown temple of lichened stone, which towered to dizzying heights above them, half hidden by vines and mantled with moss and trees. There were about twenty adults, and as many children living there, and they greeted Camila with pleasure but no undue surprise: it was as if she were arriving from the other side of the lake, rather than another world and time, and they directed her to climb to the top of the crumbling pyramid, which she did, rising above the trees (sometimes on her hands and knees), pulling herself up by vines and roots to the top of the jungle-clad ruin. There was a small temple at its summit, its roof struggling to shake off the embrace of the trees, its carved walls home to troops of spider monkeys: its labyrinthine rooms painted with murals in every color of the rainbow, she saw as she entered it, and in the dim light and the smoke of the incense burners, there was a tiny, filthy old man sitting, smoking a homegrown cigar, who looked up at her through a tangle of matted jet-black hair, and she knelt down in front of him and sat for a long time without saying a word.

"Tell me who I am," she said finally, and he held out another cup of balche, which she drank, desiring to be drunk or unconscious. "I'm not what they say," she added, to deny the myth, the spectral presence of La Madonna Lorca which she felt even there.

The old man looked at her for a moment more thoughtfully, and then didn't answer, instead looking down at the ground where a praying mantis had alighted close to Camila's knee. He laughed. "That must be your *onen*."

"The praying mantis?"

"Yes, or else he'd bite you. *Xaman*, are you going to bite her?" He bent toward the insect for a moment, as if he were truly

359

asking it a question, and then he glanced up. "The *xaman* says you aren't what *you* think you are either. You are one of the ones who remember when her eyes were clear."

"What do you mean?" She shivered, and clasped her hands around her knees like a child.

The old man's eyes were very dark, shining like polished onyx in the half-darkness of the god house.

"Long ago, Our Lord made men and women out of clay and sand, and Akinchob, who is the god of the corn and the *milpa*, gave them teeth out of corn and the first men smiled. These were the true men, the *hach winik*. They could see everything, even the gods coupling and going about their business, so Hachakyum took out their eyes and burned them in a pan until they were cloudy. Now, men cannot see the heavens and the gods making love, but they remember and sometimes they see things again, even when they are awake, as if they were dreaming."

"You think I can do that?"

"You are a *t'o'ohil*, K'in Ah. You are one of the *hach winik*. But you are also a woman and a foreigner, which is why your body fights with you and gives you no peace."

Camila shuddered, shutting her eyes on a giddy wave of sickness. "I don't believe you," she whispered.

The old man didn't press her, but told her other stories, about the jaguar and the sweet potato, and the woman who had cut off the jaguar's claws. He told her about Kisin, the god of death who was also called Tezcatlipoca, the god of the Smoking Mirror; Quetzalcoatl, who taught men time and writing; Chac, the rain god, who lived in a lake in the jungle (perhaps in all lakes); and the goddess Ixchel, the white goddess—jade or turquoise skirt, the goddess of the moon.

"She is our mother," he said seriously. "Under her protection Our Lord Hachakyum sleeps throughout the night, safe from Kisin. But when she ruled the world, the earth was covered with a great flood, and the sky fell down, and the waters of the earth were let loose. The place of the gods was destroyed, and all life was washed away, and that was the ending of the fourth sun."

As he spoke, several other men had come into the god house, lighting cigars while the night fell with tropical suddenness outside, filling up the god pots with smoldering incense so that the air became fragrant with the pine scent of copal. They sat on the ground and tore up bits of roots or vegetable stems, grinding them in small bowls into which they mixed small dried chilis, chocolate, and broth. The old man placed a gourdful of the bitter chocolate liquid on a leaf in front of Camila, and encouraged her to drink. She smiled, thinking that between illness and recreation, she had consumed most of the drugs known to the Western hemisphere, and all to no effect. She closed her eyes without hope or fear, and drank.

At first all she felt was a chocolate high, from the cocoa, and a trembling, vertiginous euphoria—she felt as if she were drowning in a river of tiny, elusive beings, laughter bubbling up inside her like carbonation in a shaken bottle. Her heart was racing a mile a minute, and she struggled to catch her breath, control the twitching that animated her fingers with a palpitant life of their own, and hold herself together as diaphragm, sphincters, and facial muscles all threatened to give way. Her body gave a deep, convulsive shudder, and she was drenched in sweat. As quickly as her euphoria began, it was replaced by alertness. She glanced around, becoming aware of the murmurous night and her intensely sharpened hearing: she heard the splash of tree frogs, the drip of moisture, the almost inaudible slither of a snake through the leaves. She shivered, feeling the not-unpleasant quickening of her heart. Sitting in the pyramid, she felt scarcely separated from the immensity of the forest all around them, which pressed in, alive, seemingly pouring with rivers of eyes. She shook her head, trying to maintain her perspective, but the eyes kept sliding away from her, and she caught her breath at the strangeness and beauty of that vision, multicolored and timeless, pouring like endless streams of globules incandescent and luminous, each with its own intelligence and soul. She looked at that vision for what seemed an eternity, until it faded into the ancient, smooth faces of the descendants of the Classic Mayas: who had built their temples in the jungle, and burned copal to their gods, not in huts, but on altars of jade and limestone, and mapped the stars in their courses, and never been conquered by Cortés. Their lined, ancient faces became lit with the flickering light of the god pots, and it made perfect sense, when the old man began to speak, that she was able to understand him.

He told them how, after the death of the last sun, Hachakyum gathered all the gods together in Teotihuacán, the ruined place of the gods, including Kisin and Quetzalcoatl and the white goddess and all the lesser gods. He made a great fire, and the gods debated who should cast himself into the flames to become the next sun. All the gods were afraid, because of the terrible heat of the fire, except for two of them: Teucciztecatl, the warrior, and Nanahuatl, the pimply one, whose body was covered with sores. Four times Teucciztecatl tried to cast himself into the flames, but each time he retreated at the final moment. Then Nanahuatl ran past him and threw himself into the heat of the fire, and his body was consumed with a great cry, and he became the fifth sun. His age will end with earthquakes and fire falling from the sky, and his will be the last age, after which all life on the earth will be gone.

"The sun will burn like a torch in the sky, and all men will see it for an instant, before their eyes are struck blind. There will be a great cloud, and the earth will be burned away, and Hachakyum will cut off the heads of men and use their blood to paint His house, if it is good. If their blood is bad, He will throw it on the ground, and jaguars and eagles will eat the bodies of all men. Their hearts will go up to the heaven of the lesser gods, where there is no sun or stars, and they will be given no pine torches to comfort them, but remain in darkness, the good and bad together. Blood will drip from the trees and stones, heaven and earth shall burn up, and all the cities shall be blown away like ash, any settlement of people whatever, the great towns, all over our land of Maya Cuzamil Mayapán. This will happen when the earth is tired and the cold becomes too powerful throughout the world, and men fail to be what the gods want them to be, and Akyantho destroys the world."

The old man was silent, filled with the thoughts of the people there assembled, and there was a sadness too deep and desolate for words, seeing the end of the world, the flaming sun and terrible wind which would end the last age of human existence. They all saw it, such was the *t'o'ohil's* power and the power of the drug, but they saw it with recognition, a timeless farewell to the calendar their own ancestors had developed. They knew it was going to happen. Complete in a world of earth and leaves, the yearly round had led them once to look up into the sky—compute the cycles of the planets and of time, foresee the end of time and glimpse Armageddon. Over the years this vision was refined: there would be men who worshiped oil and paved the forest floor with asphalt, but ten centuries before them the Mayan astronomers saw the pointlessness of lingering in the monuments they'd built; they left their palaces a prey to vines and monkeys, and went to live in the jungle and wait for the bombs to fall. Camila saw what they had seen: she was one of the *hach winik;* she was a praying mantis who forecast rain by turning instinctively north, and in seeing what they had seen, she realized that she had always known it. She opened her mouth but there were no words to speak, and she closed her eyes and saw. The silent arc of rockets, obliterating everything she knew. She felt as if she were walking alone in a place too new and primitive for speech, ascending stone steps to a ruined room, which she entered without fear, and saw the paintings on the walls. The pain of death, of the animal fear of the greatest and the least, in the face of this most terrible devastation. She felt an aching compassion for the people who would suffer far more than she, those who would be alive in that unimaginable instant; and knew, finally, pure love which was synonymous with pity: no evil was so absolute, no good so flawed, as to deserve so incomprehensible a punishment. She touched the faded paintings on the walls, and saw what they might have been: mirroring artists and pockmarked, flayed martyrs; warrior-kings and *t'o'ohils* who saw beyond the stars. It might one day come, that they became those things, but it couldn't be now: they were trapped, in a soulless, exhausted time, and time itself had to stop before they could begin to dream a higher, purer reality.

She felt as if she were standing on the steps of the pyramid, looking out at the endless green sea of the jungle, and she felt a presence beside her and turned to see the clear, farsighted eyes of the man she loved alone in all the world . . . his face serene and smiling, his forehead crowned with a circlet of small jade stones. Ruling a realm set free from war and fear, and beside him others: an old man, set free from cruelty and narcissism, and a young woman, set free from the limits of her sex; a sad-eyed, sad-moustached Indian, set free from the mechanics of torture, and a trim, bearded second lieutenant in army fatigues, set free from the constraints of cynicism and the bitterest, most active sense of humor in the country. She saw the richness of the earth and the primordial light mist of an endless morning rising high over the jungle, which might or might not have been at the beginning or the end of the world, and she couldn't know where *she* was except that she was there and not there all around them: in the proud eagle's gaze of a king robed in quetzal feathers, and a brown-skinned servant with motor oil dirtying his hands, and an arch symbolic poet and an ardent *querrillita* and a federalist with cartridges in his belt, but also in a naked man whose body was covered with sores . . . whose ulcerated flesh was obscenely visible like the suppurating flesh of a crucified man or a leper or a man who'd been buried in a ditch, or an imperfectly embalmed relic of a saint in a crystal coffin, as he crept toward them and held out his hands saying, Take, eat, this is my body which is given for you, and his miserable eyes said, Kill me, help me, make me stop, but there was no one to stop him, because this time he was the one who would kindle the fire, and stop the sun.

Camila gasped—she could *see* it so clearly—but in that instant her sight was dimmed, and she was lifted up on a cloud of painless unconsciousness into a realm of shining clear and invisible light. After the ceremony, the Indians carried her down to her boat. In two or three days up the Usumacinta River, they made it to Piedras Negras, where a military helicopter was waiting to take the still-living Presidenta to Campeche.

V.
The
Flayed
God

one

So PRESSING ARE THE NEEDS and rules by which a public myth sustains itself that a curious phenomenon began to be apparent around that time: although Camila Lorca was plainly incapable of making public appearances after her return from the jungle, the Lorcanistas had no trouble keeping up the fiction of her presence. She began to be clearly and unmistakably visible, not merely in one place, but all around the country at the same time: working in her office in the Fundación building and driving her car down the Avenida Montejo, handing out medicines and gifts of food to the hungry people of Cuchumatanes Province, and giving a six-minute interview on MAYA-TV (although following the broadcast, no one could remember exactly what she had said). She was always seen from the middle distance: radiantly pale, smiling with her usual expression of compassion, giving the people hope although she was seen at one and the same time on the balcony of the Presidential Palace and in a ward of the tubercular hospital in Santa Cruz; the dying black man who'd been stabbed in the Cantina del Flor saw her in the reflection of his own shimmering blood, and the hard-drinking journalists staying at the Sheraton saw her strolling by in a bath-

367

ing suit. She was everywhere and nowhere at the same time, and only the Presidente's closest advisers knew how much it cost to maintain that illusion: knew how much it cost El Presidente, who looked up at them with his terrible, parched smile, saying, "I don't know what good it does to delay the inevitable," at the same time as he was asking them to do just that. Sitting at his desk for long moments, he smiled to think that he'd thought of her once as a candle flame: She's not a candle, she's a blowtorch, she cuts through solid steel, pressing his long, thin fingers over his working face, thinking, My God, she's worth ten of me, what am I going to do without her? He worked late, concentrating on details to avoid seeking her in his memories: Camila in the surf, in the bath-warm water off the Isla del Viento; in his bed; standing at his side on the balcony of the Presidential Palace. He bought a reminder of her only once, in the person of one of the little whores to whom, as El Jefe and an attractive man besides, he had immediate access: satisfying his body with a military precision as perfunctory as his signature, while he paused to look down at the girl with a strange, fleeting tenderness, touching her pinched, child's face to murmur softly, "Aren't you afraid?" and when she answered No, señor, he smiled, and didn't pursue the reference.

He was never more beautiful than at that time, when he behaved with impeccable courtesy toward ambassadors and prostitutes alike, staring at them with the visionary brilliance of his eyes intact, while he tightened his stranglehold on personal freedom. He needed Camila to give him balance, and without her he lost his equilibrium, although he kept his instinctual grace. He took to reading the poetry of Porfirio Cheruña, getting a slight and pitiless glimpse into the harrowing loneliness of the old man; and he became bemused, somewhat self-consciously, with the life of the man whose career his exploits loosely paralleled—the Liberator who had freed his country and died in exile abandoned by his followers.

He was often heard, by General Moroque and others, to compare his exploits sarcastically to Bolívar's—but the most telling indication of his mood at that time was a quotation of the Liberator's, found copied out in his strong, precise hand on his blotter after his death:

You know that I have already been in power for twenty years, and I have drawn from it only a few sure conclusions: first, America is ungovernable by us; second, he who serves the revolution plows the sea; third, the only thing one can do in America is to emigrate; fourth, this country will inescapably fall into the hands of a mob of petty tyrants almost too small to be noticed, men of all colors, of all races; fifth, devoured by every kind of crime and beaten down by savagery, we will be disdained by the Europeans, who will, however, not disdain to conquer us; and sixth, if it were possible for a part of the world to return to primitive chaos, America would do it.

He copied that and other things, on the papers put forward for him to sign, and as the days went on he spent more and more of his time simply staring out of the window: at the pelicans diving in the ocean, at the brazen harshness of the water, and the white, hot blankness of the high, impenetrable sky.

Gradually, Camila recovered her last shred of strength, and with it a light stubbornness, gentle but absolute: the conviction that she had to make one last trip to the United States. Ferdinando didn't question her decision. The news caused a stir around the world. Camila Lorca was alive, and coming to Washington, not with discretion, but with the shameless publicity of the early days—no interviews, no talk shows, but a million press releases, columnists suborned to write about her from a dozen different angles, including medical (her heroic fight with cancer), personal (her appearance, clothes, and jewels), and political: the First Lady of Mayapán, coming to the White House to threaten/plead bankruptcy for her country.

She made no secret of the urgency of her mission: the United States, by increasing its yearly deficit an unprecedented 35 percent, had jerked global interest rates out of reach of the overextended Third World: this move was seen as a direct attempt to break the back of the Mayapanian economy, while other key borrowers (like Brazil and Argentina) would (theoretically) be slipped some World Monetary funds under the multinational table. Whether this scenario was feasible was moot: the assumption was that the fall of the Lorcanista government would change a great number of things. Reporters spoke of Mme. Nhu, Imelda Marcos, and Mme. Chiang Kai-shek, other lapsed *presidentas* come to intercede for their fading, dictatorial spouses, but Camila Lorca was different because the reporters liked her; they felt sorry for her, and their readers and viewers, in general, assumed that the United States *would* help her husband: it was still not widely perceived that the President of the United States could back a communist. Nor could the newspaper and magazine photographers have hidden (if they had wanted to!) the cost of the visit to her personally: emaciated as a skeleton, with her short hair combed back from her dry, white, pain-wrinkled skin, she looked twenty years older and fragile as a moth. But she was still the same star performer as she had been in her golden days, smiling for the cameras as she was escorted in a wheelchair through Dulles Airport, sagging back into the seat of a limousine to shut her eyes as she was sped through a crisp November turn around the beltway, accompanied only by a White House press secretary, who sat with his briefcase on his knees and looked at his hands for the entire course of the drive, too embarrassed to meet the eyes of the dying woman his boss was so thoroughly abandoning.

Camila looked out the window of the limousine at the wintry landscape as it flashed by. I could never have managed to live all my life in this country, she thought, it's too cold, too barren, no wonder these people are puritans, their land is too bleak. They passed smooth squares of concrete and glass, flatly situated, in this season, in dun-colored landscapes with leafless stands of trees, architecturally deliberate and lifeless as artists' renderings of proposed elementary schools or industrial parks, save for the occasional letters identifying an arms manufacturer, computer dish sweeping for secrets, or a low, windowless roof indicating that the bulk of a building lay underground. Turning into town they passed stark new rowhouses and elegant Georgian residences discreet in lawns and shrubbery, a school, several churches, a glimpse of the Washington Cathedral; passing the embassies in stately review: Brazil's glass box, and Churchill's striding statue in front of the British embassy, smallish India's bookish office and grandiose Iran's enormous faience tomb. They passed the beautiful marble building Battiste had bought for the Mayapanian embassy (moving them from an ignominious address in Maryland), which they couldn't pay for now (but they couldn't pay for anything) and which was circumspectly curtained in the Mayapanian colors, to disguise the fact that it was empty and up for sale. Camila felt a distant floating sadness as if she were traveling on air without direction, letting the car with its soft, silent ride carry her wherever it wanted to go, watching memories slip past without either ignoring or holding onto them, as detached an observer as if she were looking at the screen of a television set. She felt cushioned in mist, floating through a city she had never liked and which she could scarcely believe was still alive, intact and inhabited and bustling with its secrets, its lies. The limousine sliced like an efficient knife down Pennsylvania Avenue and turned with a whisper up the circular driveway to the White House, and Camila said, "No," to the press secretary's movement to offer her assistance, saying, with a smile, "It's not good to be helped into the office of a head of state. I won't be able to walk much after this. He must not see me be hesitant."

Wilson Allen was struck immediately by the devastating change in the beautiful, worldly woman whom he had first met eight years earlier—and found unfriendly, arch, and brittle, but scarcely so unpleasant that the wreck of her poise and grace could be viewed as anything but a tragedy: an impersonal, almost aesthetic one. He felt an instinctive desire to help her, even if such help was purely medicinal. Did she need a chair, a doctor, could he offer her the services of N.I.H. *et al.* (although they said she was terminal), or perhaps, quite impossibly, his sympathy? the one politeness irony precluded he extend. Shown in by an aide, she stood dressed in a plain dark suit with a gardenia in her buttonhole and flat dark shoes and she looked like a child, like a Katharine Gibbs applicant for a job at seventeen, but her shadowed blue eyes were ancient.

President Allen crossed his office with his hand extended, and said with more than his usual friendliness, "Señora Lorca, please sit down, can I get you anything to make you more comfortable?"

371

"Money," Camila whispered, as she sat in one of the brown leather chairs she remembered (was it in this office that she'd gotten drunk with President Farrell? But she'd never gotten drunk) and glanced up at Wilson Allen. "You could give me some money, but you're not going to do that, are you, Mr. President?"

"Señora Lorca?"

"It doesn't matter." She smiled, her voice barely audible; he had to lean forward a little to hear her, and she didn't help him, leaning her head back against the leather and looking at him thoughtfully, almost casually, like an old enemy or friend.

"It really *doesn't* matter, you know. They all think I'm here at the eleventh hour, but the eleventh hour has passed and it's midnight now, so what's done is done. Don't you think so?"

He didn't know what to think. It crossed his mind that she might be irrational (Alzheimer's disease, or something similar?). Could she simply have forgotten whatever it was she'd wanted to see him about? He couldn't risk insulting her (not yet) and he'd never underestimated her intelligence (like Duncan Farrell), but he was uncharacteristically at a loss. He moved a conversational pawn.

"Señora Lorca, I understand your husband's issued a challenge to the other major Third World debtors, to stand with him in boycotting the International Monetary Fund, until global interest rates can be significantly lowered—"

"He said in jest that if Mayapán and Mexico and Brazil all told the I.M.F. to go fuck itself, the I.M.F. would have to comply. He was speaking in *jest*."

"Yes." Wilson Allen smiled, crossing his legs. "Well, they're not going to do that, which puts your husband in kind of an awkward position, doesn't it?"

"Does it?" Camila looked at him, sitting perfectly still, discipline giving her rail-thin body a shadow of dignity and strength. "Sodomy rather depends on your perspective. You obviously like the male dominant role."

She abandoned fencing the moment she had stung him, and leaned forward, clasping hands together that really looked like bones, he thought, still sparkling with that enormous diamond ring. "Mr. Allen, I don't have much time. I didn't come here to ask you to stop what you're doing in terms of my country. My country's small, it doesn't count. But you're dancing on a knife blade and I don't think you know it, and there may be nothing to be done to stop it, but at least you should have a choice."

She stopped, ordering breath and thoughts and giving him the chance to murmur, "I'm afraid I really don't—"

"No, of course you don't. No one does. We're not monsters or madmen, but you know, I really suspect that it doesn't matter. I'm sorry I'm not being clear. But you know, we truly tried to do good, and I'm sure you did too, and look where we are today? There may just *be* too much death in the world, the slaughtered martyrs' ashes or just too much cold . . . but a crisis is coming very soon, the likes of which you can't possibly imagine, and I think you ought to be ready for it . . . although you're already far too efficiently armed."

The President of the United States debated a number of options, the mildest of which was to make no move, and simply ask coolly, "What sort of crisis?"

"I don't know." She smiled at that, shaking her head and rubbing the back of her hand across her forehead, with a paralytic stiffness she hadn't previously shown. "I know that sounds idiotic. There's a man, a priest in the Vatican, his name is Father Battiste Tommassi—yes, he used to be our ambassador—he's involved, and it involves our country in some way, I myself don't completely understand it. . . ." She paused, and glanced up at him with a sudden intimacy, leaning forward, intent on making herself clear. "I won't be alive much longer, you know. I'm not going to be around for any of this. I just . . ." She shook her head, annoyed at the difficulty of trying to say what she saw. "There's going to be a war. It will start small, and seem to be a limited conflict, but it's going to get out of hand, the missiles you've placed in my country and El Salvador and Honduras, the Soviets in Cuba and Nicaragua and later in Mayapán . . . it'll seem too easy, to steal the oil and the money, once you wipe out Linz and UNOCO, and us, there won't *be* any nice, clean figurehead for you to support and label a communist, but the remnant of his followers, and ours and yours . . . there won't be any borders anymore, but a bloodbath from Texas to Colombia, and after all the only answer will be more weapons, because you'll be more threatened and more in need of reassurance, a gun, a slogan, a phrase, a bomb. . . ." She paused, looking at him with her eyes very clear and luminous. "You're not going to be able to stop this one." She held his eyes for a long instant, glancing aside finally in a moment of abstraction to murmur, "It's already started. It's a waste of time talking about it. I can't heal wounds." She looked down at her hands, and made up her mind, looked up, although she couldn't rise, and said quietly, "I'm sorry, I've wasted both our time, and that's my shortage. I think I'd better say good-bye."

Much later, when an emissary of the papal commission approached President Allen and inquired if there was any evidence he could add to substantiate the claim of Camila Lorca's saintliness, the President of the United States replied that Camila Lorca showed no unearthly or mystical attributes whatsoever, and, further, categorically denied that she had displayed even the most modest of precognitive or clairvoyant powers. But at the time he held out his hand and said seriously, "Thank you, Mrs. Lorca, you've given me a lot to think about. I appreciate your candor. May I be candid in return? I think you might be more comfortable here in the States, Sloan-Kettering or the Naval Hospital might be able to do more for you than—"

Camila looked at him as if he had lost his mind. "You don't understand, do you? I don't *want* to live through that! Why would I? I don't know whether I believe in God, but God Himself would want to close His eyes at that final moment. You haven't heard a single word I've said, have you, Mr. President?"

That afternoon she flew to New York, where she disposed of the assets in her private accounts with the order of Sell everything, and transfer the money to the Mayapanian national treasury, including her jewelry (she stripped off her rings in the offices of Goldman Sachs, saying, Here, take these: a briefcase with her sapphires, pearls, and emeralds, the heavy gold cuffs off her wrists and her two-carat diamond earrings. You can get rid of these, can't you, I don't want them), all but her big diamond solitaire, which she took with her to the Harley School, and left on the altar of the little chapel with the note, Please pray for my soul, I can't think who else I would trust to intercede for me, Camila Lorca. When she came outside, the chilly day was becoming raw, early dusk was beginning to fall and the sky was black-gray, the color of stone. She shivered as she stood leaning against her bodyguard and driver, Zito Ardilla, as he helped her into the limousine which here too had been put at her disposal.

"You want to go home, señora?" he asked, meaning the airport, their flight back to Mayapán.

"In a minute. There's one place else I've got to go. Take me uptown to Columbia University."

A well-remembered drive. She shut her eyes, to stop the tears that she no longer had the strength to wipe from her cheeks, because she had exhausted herself at last, there was nothing left, she could feel the pressure building up behind her forehead as though her brain were being packed in layers of cotton, the prelude to pain which she couldn't fight, Please don't let me die here, she prayed, and it abated slightly, the limousine windows were tinted from the outside for privacy, giving her interior view a smoky haze, and she sat and looked at the numbered streets go by, Eighty-sixth, Ninety-second, Ninety-eighth and she whispered, Stop here, and the driver pulled over to double-park. There were students going about their business, tweedy professors and butch, masculine women, boys and girls in sweat shirts and down jackets and jeans and fur coats, My God, they're so young, she thought, transfixed, gazing out through the window with her bare, stiffened hand pressed unconsciously against the glass she could no longer feel. There were pimpled young men and unsophisticated young women with their hair pulled back with scarves, Hasidic Jews and prep-schooled Ivy Leaguers talking in close knots, their arms burdened down with books, and they were all so innocent, ardent and brilliant and in love with the future of the world, she felt not bitterness, but a faint forgiveness for her former self, and slight amazement: Jesus Christ, we actually went out and did the things you're talking about. She experienced a mild shock: there, advancing down the sidewalk, with his spry gait of a predatory old man while leaning briefly, unobtrusively on his cane, was the very man she'd come uptown to see, and she watched him stop and speak to a young girl, apparently a student, fluttering excitement of a pale hand readjusting his glasses, the flattering attention of his white-haired head bent in exaggerated interest and the bloodless, queasy insincerity of his smile, and she felt nothing: neither revulsion nor tenderness, but, unbelievably, a distant sense of humor. Come on, Porfirio, she thought, you can do better than that. She smiled, feeling her smile lift only half her face, and she didn't mind. I surprised you all, didn't I, she thought. I gave you a run for your money, and the best man I ever met will love me from now until the hour of his death.

She suffered another stroke on the flight back to Campeche, and by the time the plane arrived that night she was paralyzed. Zito Ardilla carried her off the plane to the waiting motorcade which had been planned for her arrival, and there was nothing for it but to thread their way through the packed streets because there was no other approach to the capital, no way they could call for an ambulance without provoking a panic among the massed throngs who had come from far and near to get a last glimpse of their beloved señora. Last if you believed the lies that she was ill, that God would not cure her who had cured so many others, the frail white *angelita* who sat with her eyes shut in the back of the car, praying, Get me out of here, Get me out of here, while the crowds rocked the car, pulled open the doors, and pulled her out because La Señora had come home, she was going to solve all their problems. She was like a *muñequita*, a doll in their hands, and they lifted her up and several people fainted and many more were trampled in their effort to get close to her, because she was *la reina*, the Queen of Heaven, who sat so still on her throne of a kitchen chair which someone had hoisted up, with her eyes open and her gentle smile of *la bendición* fixed forever on her face, and only her eyes moved, turning to the left and the right as they carried her down the Avenida Montejo toward the Presidential Palace. Ferdinando saw her coming, standing on the steps of the palace like a statue of *el dictador* himself in the glare of the spotlights, and when he saw what was happening he started forward and General Ottavio Moroque, who was with him and who was dressed not in any costume now, but the fatigues of the governmental militia, laid his hand on his arm and murmured, "Let them carry her. I don't have enough men here to protect you, if you try and stop them." Ferdinando bit his lips and stood still, while the crowd surged forward, reaching up to touch the tiny, suffering woman who swayed above their heads in a small chair with her head on one side and her hand stiffened over her breast, and when he saw her eyes begging him for help he calmly pulled away from General Moroque and walked down the steps, an un-armed, slender man in a dark business suit, his handsome face that of a stricken widower . . . and though there were many there who hated him (who had lost relatives to the death squads, lands or livelihoods to the rapacities of UNOCO, faith in *him*) no one stopped him, and they fell back as he reached the ones who were carrying her and told them to put her down, reached over their heads as they were lowering her and took Camila in his arms. They were afraid to interfere, for he was touched, still, with his lonely charisma, the aura of a man apart. He carried her back up the steps and then turned and said, "Thank you for bringing my wife home," and entered the building without another word. It was the last public appearance of either of the Lorcas before Camila's death, and the last time the people of Mayapán, who adored her as their savior, were to see Camila Lorca in her human form at all.

two

LIFE NARROWED DOWN to a hospital bed, and a monitor of her heart; Ferdinando watched the monitor and the world did too, but he had forgotten about the world and lived only within the circle of his wife's still living, beautiful eyes. He never left her room. She could blink to communicate with him, and they developed a sophisticated code, and held long conversations with his gentle, resonant voice punctuated by thoughtful silences, although sometimes her replies were incoherent—incommunicable not from drugs, but because of the immense, unfathomable distance she had gone. She lay still and looked at him, as if she could never tire of looking at his face. For his part, he slept in the same room with her, and forgot that he was president of anywhere at all, refusing to answer telephones or letters with his gentle smile of complete finality, saying, No, my friends, you can't possibly want anything from me that's remotely this important. Mayapán stopped still. In stores and restaurants, plazas and villages and the disordered chaos of the half-finished buildings that were crumbling into the ruins of Chichén Itzá, one question hovered over every activity: *¿Esta muerta todavía?* Is she dead yet? *Todavía no.* Not yet.

Porfirio Cheruña made an unprecedented attempt to get into

the country, only to have his visa denied by the government. He was a national monument, and he hadn't visited his country for fifty years, but when he was turned away from his flight at the Mexico City airport he got on the phone and called the man he hated with every trembling bone in his body, and got General Jorge-Julio de Rodríguez on the line. General Rodríguez was surprised to hear by his voice how old and exhausted he sounded. He said that he would do anything for a twenty-four-hour visa, that he promised not to disobey any of the statutes of the government and would put up with all sorts of humiliating strictures, but that he begged General Rodríguez as a compassionate man to let him see Camila one moment more before she died. General Rodríguez had to explain that Señor Lorca couldn't come to the phone, and moreover that he had left explicit instructions that Porfirio Cheruña was never to be allowed inside the borders of the country again, even to be buried. Porfirio then asked that he be allowed to visit the capital and stand outside the palace, among the crowds who were gathered there day and night and whose vigils with candles he had heard described, and General Rodríguez had to repeat his original message. He heard a long silence at the other end of the line, and didn't know whether Porfirio had hung up or was weeping or had walked away, when finally he heard the old man's thin, devastated whisper, "He doesn't forgive anyone anything, does he?" and Jorge-Julio had to shake his head and answer, No, he never does.

In the Vatican, sibilant whispers of silk on stone and murmured prayers surrounded the offices of the Superior General of the Jesuits, who went about his business with a tranced, cold efficiency which left no room for any intimacies at all, I'm sorry, but the difficulties of taking over this position at this key time have left me no leisure to follow the events in my own country, and spent long hours in prayer that God would spare him his reason, for he felt that he was truly in danger of losing his mind. Sometimes he shut his eyes, and saw her face so clearly he thought he would die with the accumulated pain of losing her in his life, and now in hers; but for the most part he saw Ferdinando, the devil who had taken her away from him. Father José Luaro was a distant comfort, supplying the warmth of his fanatic's loyalty as a fading echo of the counterpoint which had played so piercingly sweet between them: but the majority of the time, Father Battiste Tommassi sat working alone in his office, in his severe black cassock, chained to the telephone he knew would ring only with the news that his beloved Camila was dead.

The Archbishop of Campeche offered masses for her immediate recovery, and in Cuchumatanes Province an old man even went so far as to publicly offer his life for hers; since he was ninety-seven and nearly blind, apparently the offer was declined. Inside the Presidential Palace, time began flowing more slowly, in hours and minutes instead of days: there was time to share a remembered word, a joke in the privacy of the bedroom that, although of necessity filled with the paraphernalia of death, was still their bedroom with its damasked walls and gentle, iridescent light, filled with flowers which Ferdinando insisted be changed daily so she wouldn't grow tired of them—arranging them himself with his own deft hands so she could see them, taking a blossom and brushing it against her cheek. She was being fed intravenously, but he opened a bottle of champagne for her to sip through a straw. He played music for her, and once, late at night against doctors' orders, he held her in his arms and they danced, with her head pillowed securely against his shoulder, moving her in slow, sensuous circles around the room in the soft moonlight as he whispered, "You look very beautiful, I don't think I'm going to let the doctors look at you anymore, I'll get too jealous." He held her hands during the worst of the physical examinations, and laid his cheek on the pillow beside her to murmur, "Who are these people? What do they think they're doing? They can't touch us. We're as far away from them as the moon."

No amount of drugs had any effect on her: they pumped enough narcotics into her body to kill her, and it was as if they were injecting water into her veins; she lay, completely conscious and in agony, a victim of her freakish sobriety, but she was gradually fading ... the flickering light that had burned in her was dimming, and her eyes lost their translucent fire and became very wide and pale blue, turning in, lost in wonder before the visions that were now all she could see. Ferdinando saw it happening, and couldn't bear to lose her, even to the power he knew would win: she could still hear his voice, and he held her for three days with a constant flow of talk that reduced his fine baritone to a whisper, refusing to let her slip into unconsciousness, although she was in devastating pain; and she stayed with him, as stubborn as he was, silent and immobile and giving no other indication but her life that she was listening.

He told her everything he could think of, the history of the country and a list of its principal exports, military strategy and off-color stories, and he sang her songs: "La Golondrina" and "La Barca de Oro" with its murmured lines, "You'll never see me again, nor hear my songs, But the seas will overflow with my tears, Good-bye, my love, good-bye," and "Mairzy Doates" and "Ain't Nobody's Business If I Do." Finally, his voice was just a breath of pain that tore like a rasp against his throat, and he looked down into her face and thought she looked as if she were sleeping.

"I love you," he whispered, bending to kiss her pale, beautiful lips.

Camila blinked. "I. Love. You. Too." And then, "Sing. Something. Else."

So he pressed her face against his chest and put his arms around her, and sang very softly for only her to hear, "You are the promised kiss of springtime, and someday, I'll know that moment divine, when all the things you are are mine," and when he finished singing he continued to press her face against his chest and there was a terrible silence in the room, worse than the screaming of a soul in hell—and the doctors and nurses had the courage to enter the room only much later, when his shaking shoulders allowed them to realize he knew that she was dead.

three

THE MOURNING FOR Camila Lorca was excessive, baroque, a *velatorio* that had something of the hysterical energy of a fiesta. It was tragic, it was funny, and it was minus its central player, because Camila wasn't there, at least not her body—which gave rise to the terrible rumors that she was still alive, that she hadn't died but had simply gone on a trip, one of her elusive flights to somewhere, a fiction which Ferdinando didn't invent but which he didn't bother to deny either, because after Camila's death he seemed to have lost the ability to think at all.

The doctors wanted to examine her, and perform an autopsy (for their own protection, as well as for their memoirs; who knew what incompetence *el dictador* might accuse them of, when he'd gotten over his first shock?), but Ferdinando wouldn't let them touch her; in fact, when they murmured *Permítame, señor*, and tried to grasp his shoulders and encourage him to let go of her and stand aside, he simply looked up at them and said, "What else do you want from me?" and looking down at the lovely woman whose porcelain-clear features were smoothed with the serenity of death, he whispered, "She was the only one who could rescue me from this darkness, and now that she's gone I can never be free from it."

They thought he was exaggerating. He told them of her desire that her body be destroyed after her death, because she feared the people's reverence for her corpse, and, moreover, hated the idea of being examined when she was unconscious. "Or dead, obviously," he said with more than his usual courtesy, his timbreless voice enclosing a devastated smile. "She told me she had had enough of that, and not knowing how much is enough, I have no choice but to believe her. She told me what she wanted me to do, and I'm afraid, gentlemen, she wanted it to remain a private matter between us."

Pisote confirmed that he wasn't making it up. She had been hovering around the palace for days, unable either to intrude or go away, and in the terrible, unimaginably long hours of the endless night following Camila's death, she was one of the few people who could make rational decisions. Muffling her face in Kleenex, her white, hungry features bare of makeup but bruised around the eyes and with her eyelids and nose swollen with tears, she nonetheless was able to find the key to Camila's desk, which contained her will (leaving everything to Ferdinando), her approved obituary (drawn up after her first operation), and her favorite photograph: a gently smiling three-quarter-turn portrait in a white, open-necked shirt, with her hair pulled back from her face, a loving madonna dressed as a *campesina*. She got the doctors to leave Ferdinando alone with Camila, and substantiated his story that Camila had asked to be allowed to disappear after her death. "She was looking at her hands once, and she said, You know, Pisote, when I'm dead they'll want my fingernails for relics, isn't that ridiculous? And I said, Not so ridiculous, it gives them something to hold onto. And she shook her head. Not me. That won't be me anyway, I'll be gone with the wind. And then she laughed and said—" Pisote's eyes filled with tears again, and she bit her lips and murmured, "Shit. . . . She said, When I'm dead why don't you just throw me away? That won't be me anymore anyway."

Ferdinando told no one when he called the pilot and told him to get his private helicopter ready, and ran his fingers for the last time over the delicate lips and wide, smooth forehead of the woman who was entwined in his heart as intimately as his blood, and kissed her, feeling his tears scald his lips and tear at his throat with pain, whispering, "Sleep, *amiguita*, I'll be with you soon." He could feel her warm flesh cooling and becoming not so much stiff as simply less pliable to the touch, and he knew he had to do what she'd asked him to do now, before he could never bring himself to do it. Not allowing himself to think, not allowing himself to feel beyond one simple action and the next, he smoothed her hair and wrapped her in the sheets and blankets from the bed, and lifted her tenderly in his arms and carried her through his deserted office up in his private elevator to the helipad on the roof, where he held her close in the winds from the whiffling blades, as if she could feel their chill. He shouted, Open the door, and the pilot, terrified but unaware of what was happening, scrambled down to pull open the passenger door.

"Where to, *mi presidente?*"

Ferdinando barely answered him, and seemed to be lost in a dream. "Just take us up." The pilot, less disturbed by his inexplicable bundle than by the stark, ravaged misery which scarred El Señor Lorca's face, held back and started to protest, when Ferdinando snapped with his inimitable soldier's voice (hoarse though it was), "Just take me up, goddamn it!," changing his order with a stab of anguish as he realized he could never speak in anything but the singular form again.

The pilot took off without another word. He flew in silence, waiting for instructions, and after a while Ferdinando said in a scarcely audible whisper, "Just fly north, I'll tell you when we get close," and then sat staring out of the windshield without saying anything more. The pilot glanced from time to time at his haggard passenger, his face gaunt with suffering and his hands, so motionless but so tender with the burden he was carrying, that sometime after they'd left the coast behind he realized what he was doing, and then looked away because he couldn't bear to look at El Lorca's eyes anymore. The flew out over the clear waters of the Gulf of Mexico, lit to a phosphorescent brilliance by the moon, and Ferdinando said softly, "I think this is far enough, don't you?" and the pilot brought the helicopter down, until he was hovering fifty feet or so above the water, and he saw El Lorca reach blindly to open the door.

"Here, Señor Presidente, let me," he said, and reached across Ferdinando to open it.

"Thank you." For a long time Ferdinando didn't say anything else. The pilot looked away, out of respect for the man he'd served like a god and the Señora, who, he realized now, Ferdinando must have loved more than anybody, until his passenger gave a little laugh and said, "I don't think I can do it, isn't that ridiculous?" He took a deep breath, and the pilot felt his whole body shake with a convulsive shudder, and then he felt the change in the helicopter's weight, and a few moments later, he heard the splash. He waited, praying that El Lorca wouldn't take it into his mind to follow her, and finally, after what seemed like an eternity of silence, he heard a sigh and turned to see Ferdinando staring down at the illusory brightness of the waves in the darkness.

"It's very beautiful, isn't it?"

"Very beautiful, *mi presidente.*"

"Do you think . . . would it embarrass you to take my hand for a moment? You can fly with one hand for a little while, can't you? I just . . . I need somebody to hold onto for a minute."

The pilot willingly grasped one of El Lorca's hands, which was very thin and as cold as ice. Feeling his own sight dimmed, he flew back, not looking at the man who sat beside him, who held his hand like a man with a mortal wound but was otherwise silent, his face turned to look out the window. When they set down again on the roof of the Presidential Palace, Ferdinando took a deep breath and let it out soundlessly. "So," he said thoughtfully, as if to himself, "now it starts."

"Now what starts, Señor Presidente?"

He turned and looked at him with his luminous gaze, his light eyes shining like blue flames, and there was something so uncanny about his expression that the pilot was the first person to think (although certainly not the last, in the next few days) that perhaps El Presidente Lorca had lost his mind. "The madness," he whispered. "Did you think I wasn't going to do anything to honor her death?"

If he *did* go mad with grief in the days that followed, then the whole country joined him, and it was in many ways the last, greatest hour of national unity, as *campesinos* and capitalists alike stood long hours in the broiling sun to enter the National Cathedral and pray for the soul of their beloved Señora. He decreed a period of national mourning, during which time it was forbidden to drink liquor or wear any color of clothing but black, have sex, eat meat, or go out on anything but the most necessary of errands, and rather than chaff under these restrictions, the people imposed far more stringent mortifications on themselves, cutting their hair and smearing their foreheads with ashes, going without eating entirely and spontaneously naming every street, square, airport, and bus terminal they could find after Camila Lorca. They besieged the palace to kneel for hours in the street, beating their breasts and sobbing, and the sellers of sweet rolls and fruit drinks began to set up regular stands to feed the faithful who, in the interstices of their fasting, ate standing up with the ravenous hunger of wild animals, since what was empty was not their stomachs but their souls. In all this Ferdinando was, if not exactly demanding, in no way discouraging of their sorrow, and he led them by his own example, charismatic as always, even if he was leading them now into the pathways of his own lunacy. He decreed that there should be a special Camila Lorca Day, and a billboard ten stories high (he had no way of knowing her vision) on the side of the old Grand Hotel in downtown Campeche, which he unveiled himself, standing in the spotlight of a brilliant black night while the people cheered beneath him and he stood looking up at her, his face as drained and awed as all the rest of them, and General Moroque, who was standing on the platform next to him, thought, Shit, he's starting to believe she's a saint too, it's the only way he can deal with losing her.

And he gave her a bloodletting, because no amount of suffering was enough. I want you to imprison every last member of the Frente Comunistas you can find, every sympathizer and everyone who's given them aid, or money, even silence, do you understand me, I want you to do everything that's necessary to get confessions out of those people and I want you to execute all the ringleaders, do you follow me, everyone you suspect of being a force against my government. He looked at General Jorge-Julio de Rodríguez with such feverish intensity that there was nothing to be said, no recourse against a tyrant especially when that tyrant was bent on destroying himself, and Jorge-Julio went away and drove to the basement of the Miramar Prison and started interrogating prisoners, with his usual loyalty and habitual patience of an Indian working his *milpa*, using rubber hoses and cattle prods to obtain El Presidente's confessions. You're a rebel against the government, aren't you? No? Well, you are now— And he did all of this with such a sad, penitent thoroughness that Bill Mynott realized after a while, You're turning into a monster, and Jorge-Julio de Rodríguez looked down at his hands and said, No, I just know who is, that's all. And after he had executed thirty-two prisoners, including a young woman and a twelve-year-old boy and a pregnant girl (who had died unintentionally, while they were beating her with a tire iron), he said, Excuse me, and went upstairs to his office, and rolled a piece of paper in his old manual typewriter, and typed out a letter.

Dear Ferdinando,
You have been my friend ever since we were six years old, but I've got to tell you I think you aren't worth the courtesy of being saved from dying in your own vomit, and the people are going to slaughter you like a dog one day, which is what you deserve. I never believed in you for an instant, but I believed in your wife, and I pray she will forgive me for what I'm going to do. I would have died a million times for you, but now I think just once will be enough. Please forgive me for doing this, but somebody's got to show you what a complete and utter bastard you've become.

Then he got up, leaving the paper in the machine, and got his pistol out of the drawer in his file cabinet and shot himself in the mouth. Bill Mynott brought Ferdinando the typewritten note sometime later.
"He was a sentimentalist," he said, staring down at the piece of paper with surprise, as he unwrapped a stick of gum. "I never realized it until now."
"Yes," Ferdinando said. He ordered a full military funeral

for General Jorge-Julio de Rodríguez, a hero of his country, who had died in the defense of El Presidente in an ambush, and a medal of the Order of Santiago to be awarded posthumously, for services to the republic and because of the deep respect that El Señor Lorca felt for him personally. But he didn't weep for him. His face had become thin and hard, fine and drawn as a piece of tanned leather, and his remarkable energy, though undimmed, was now unimpeded by any pity whatsoever. General Moroque had a moment of painful surprise a few days later when he entered his office, because he could scarcely recognize him.

four

I N THE LAST DAYS of his Presidency, Ferdinando governed with more ruthlessness than before, but also, even his critics had to admit, with more efficiency than he had displayed at any other time in his political life.

He was aware how closely he was being chased, the hounds of international amnesty groups being loosed against him at the same time as his credit was drying up for good. Even Charlie Cox, when he met him for breakfast, told him, rather shamefacedly, about a recent meeting of the UNOCO board of directors, and admitted he'd been hard pressed to justify their continued involvement with a demagogue. Ferdinando merely leaned his chin on his hand and looked at him with his intensely blue eyes, which could still be very attractive.

"Do you think I'm a demagogue?"

Charlie Cox swallowed. "No. I don't."

"Good." Ferdinando lit a cigarette and thoughtfully inhaled. "We knew it was going to be difficult, we're fighting both Moscow and Washington now and your board of directors has got to understand that. But I've been thinking of a way to help things, distract a certain amount of attention, and perhaps, at least, gain us a little time."

In the devastation of his heart, he began to think again. Those who were loyal to him helped him: General Moroque, Nucho Ortega, Izzy Ikemoda, who still made sure El Señor Presidente could be seen at least once a week on every program broadcast by MAYA-TV. Pisote helped him most of all, throwing herself into this new role with her customary, chameleonlike haste, as a way of assuaging her own grief, but also as a way of staying close to him. She served unobtrusively as his secretary, amanuensis, confidante, and representative, in those circumstances where El Presidente Lorca either was unable or didn't want to attend to something personally, and she realized in her heart why she liked it (of course, she was no fool; she knew how dangerous it was), skirting the edge of a hopeless love for the only man in her life she'd ever really liked, while she played with the necrophilic, consoling idea of taking her beloved Camila's place.

If she had any illusions about Ferdinando's feelings, he cleared them up for her at once; he was polite with her and sometimes, in his old way, charming, but the only times she ever heard a note of tenderness enter his voice were when he said to her (as he did to almost no one else), Camila always thought this, or Camila would have done that ... warming himself before the cold, thin flame of his memories, like a man who presses his fingers to a stove in order to remember what it was like to feel anything at all. She didn't kid herself. Camila wasn't diminished by her death: she was inviolable. But he was a man who needed a wife, to give him support and also as an aid to his failing image: he needed Camila or somebody, and he seemed to intuit this himself when he looked at her once, as if he finally saw her for the first time in how long had it been? perhaps years? and said, I like your hair like that, soft against your face, but why don't you try lightening it a little?

She went to the best makeup artist at MixTech Studios, and had her hair lightened to Camila's color. She dyed her eyebrows blond, and although her eyes were the wrong color, greenish hazel, the effect wasn't too disconcerting; she bought a small fortune in cosmetics, and learned how to apply them at home, working to achieve not a copy of Camila's features, but a subtle echo in her own face: fragile mouth, hollowed cheeks, and delicate, bone-white forehead. She did it gradually, knowing as an actress that the trick was not in the mask but in the expression; working for a hint of Camila's gentle grin, her tender, lyric lunacy: she couldn't match her fire, or her wounded, shimmering vulnerability, but she gave herself a slight, disturbing similarity to his dead wife, and she left it at that. Ferdinando spent a lot of time with her, and she kept it light: giving him her own, tart comments on the actions of world events and political leaders, bending her head when she felt his gaze for a moment, thoughtful and quizzical, to let him look at the bony, translucent profile which was attaining an unintentional loveliness. She never asked him for anything, fearing his ridicule as much as anything else: she had known him since Columbia, and had always encouraged him to think of her as tougher than she was. But he had to have noticed, a stone would have guessed what she was doing, and so she wasn't surprised so much as cornered when he looked at her late one night, over a drink in his office, and said quietly, "It's very beautiful, Pisote, but I don't know how much I can respond."

She shook her head. "I'm not doing it for you, I'm doing it for me, fuck your feelings, I miss her."

Ferdinando smiled. "Not that it's a bad idea."

"What isn't?" She knew what he was talking about, but she didn't want to know. She didn't look at him.

"The people adored Camila. They wanted to believe in her: they still do. There's a rumor, you know, that she's still alive, that she'll come back one day.... It wouldn't be offensive to their sense of reverence, if you appeared in her place ... as my wife." He looked at her as if searching for something to believe in, some spark of love which would serve him in place of faith. "I can't ask you to do that, can I? It wouldn't be fair to you. I can't love you except for ... the part of you that loved her ... and I don't think I can ever be a husband to you, and you have every right to expect that, you're a beautiful woman. Well, so you are, Pisote, my God, any man would have noticed—oh, my dear, please don't cry ... come here, let me hold you. ..." He put his arms around her, and whispered against her hair, "It feels so good to hold onto someone. You have no idea how *empty* my arms have felt. Oh, Pisote ... I need someone to take her place, it's true, and I should prefer it to be a friend, although it's a terrible thing to do to a friend, don't you think? Shh, don't answer. I think this is the first moment I've felt at peace for weeks. It's dark all over the world, and the light's very far away. Do you think it's possible to wait for the light, like two soldiers in a foxhole, feeling no more than the distant companionship of your shared fear, your horror of the darkness, that's out there, waiting to claim you and devour you? Hmm? What do you think?" He kissed her hair lightly, companionably, and without the slightest trace of passion, and she shut her eyes to force the tears silently between her lids, telling herself It was enough, it had to be enough, he was here and he was alive and hers for a few minutes, even if his heart was in the ocean, or in the stars. "I always used to wonder what it was like to grow old, and I could never imagine it. My hair's getting thin, you know, but I still feel inside like a young man, so perhaps that's it, we never do grow old and we don't have that serenity to look at the darkness and not mind it, we're still terrified, we're still drawn to it, we still wonder what it's all about. I thought Camila could show me, I thought she'd show me a way out, but now that she's gone I find myself hiding in labyrinths of madness—meaninglessness! What earthly difference does it make who runs this country? Yet it does. I'm like a horse on a treadmill. So, what do you think? Would it be fair to ask you to help me? I don't know, little Weatherman, I don't seem to be able to judge those things anymore. You'll have to figure it out for me."

She told him it was a wonderful idea, of course she would help him, they both would honor Camila's memory and keep her alive while they were serving the dreams she'd helped to build, not knowing if any of it was more than a load of bullshit but feeling a desperate need to bind herself as close as possible to this beautiful man who'd first given her soul something to believe in. They were married three weeks later in a private ceremony, and she moved in with him at the palace, avoiding a public announcement and trusting to the winds of Campeche gossip to leak the fact that El Lorca had a woman with him, not some *puta*, no, *Pisote*, who was a pop star (and what better icon could he have married!), although the people saw very little of either of them, because they were both busy with the endless details of keeping the ship of state afloat when it was springing leaks and rebel garrisons all over the place. General Moroque said, We can't arrest everybody, sir, the prisons are already full to bursting, and he looked at him with his thoughtful gaze, murmuring, Surely you know how to relieve that, what do I have to do, tell you how to do everything, and the people read in the newspapers how although things were in a state of flux because of the great strides they had made, El Señor Presidente still had given a speech before the Chamber of Deputies, and his wife still made a special appearance before the Ladies of Charity, and so the people pretended to be deceived by the everyday evidence that despite all their fears things were going on in the usual way and the government was smoothly in control, when everyone knew that the country was falling apart and nobody knew it with a greater certainty than El Presidente Lorca himself. He met the rebel forces with his over-spent army to such good effect that although they made gains in the provinces, the northern cities were unscathed, and he could still place a division with such precision that it could outflank a regiment, even if he didn't have General Jorge-Julio de Rodríguez to help him. Perhaps the greatest testimony to his military skill was that he was able to outmaneuver an army funded by both the United States and the Soviet Union, but he knew it couldn't last. And so finally, when the rebels blew up a bridge twenty miles from the capital, even though it was an isolated incident and the men involved were caught and executed at once, he stood in his office, thoughtfully smoking a cigarette while General Moroque and Security Director William Mynott and former dictator Quintero de Buiztas all stood around waiting to see what he would do, and he said to them, Gentlemen, how would I send word to Commander Martín Acchuirez that my government was willing to negotiate?

General Moroque started to protest. "*Mi presidente*, it isn't necessary, we can turn them back or at least put ourselves in a far superior position—"

"Don't do it, Mr. President," Bill Mynott warned. "You can't trust them. They'll just nod their heads and blow you to kingdom come. Wipe 'em out or pack your suitcase, you'll never win by trying to believe in them."

"Besides, they don't need to negotiate, they're winning," Quintero de Buiztas said reasonably. "You can't have forgotten how much fun it was to kick someone out of your chair. Give somebody else a chance."

Pisote was with them, taking no part in their conversation; she was there as window dressing, she thought ruefully, not because she could add anything, but because Camila had always been present at such a vital discussion. She looked at Ferdinando's face, and thought, My God, he could do anything, he's got no human feelings left at all. He said quietly, "Don't contradict my orders, just do it, or join the rebels yourself if you disagree with me. Tell Commander Acchuirez I'll meet with him here in Campeche, to discuss terms for a negotiated settlement. Tell him I offer him safe-conduct and guarantee his freedom to come and go as he pleases, regardless of the outcome of his visit. Now leave me alone with Security Director Mynott."

It was the biggest gamble of his life, and even his detractors had to admit its audacity. Trapped in the jungle, mired with his forces in the desperate struggle just to stay alive from one minute to the next, the short Mayan doctor paused and tried to listen to the voice of his clairvoyance, but that voice was stilled, muffled with practicality and slaughter, and he could only send a telegram to José Luaro via Washington and the Vatican which consisted merely of the words, What should I do? José Luaro showed the telegram to Battiste, whose fingers shook while he read it and then he crumpled it up into a ball, snapping, Shit, I don't know, we're on the other side of the world, tell him to do whatever he feels like doing, and eventually he did, coming to the conclusion that he would meet with El Lorca but in his own way, flying out from the interior to New York and then disappearing, going underground, arranging through his followers and his contacts in Washington to fly first to Mexico City, and then to Campeche on an unknown flight. He would pick the time of his arrival, because he feared duplicity and even his arrest, despite the crowds that would be there to greet him, and on the night before he left Mexico City he wrote two letters, one to José Luaro and one to his followers at large, telling them to go on fighting even if *el dictador* imprisoned him, because they were fighting in a just cause and God would stand by them and see that the right prevailed. Then he drove to the airport the next day in an unmarked car, and walked to the plane unmolested, and found his seat in coach and drank a glass of orange juice, refusing the light lunch that was served on the short AeroMexico flight to Campeche, which touched down a little after two o'clock in the afternoon, but there was a slight trouble debarking from the plane, *por favor* all the passengers would have to wait and it was then that his clairvoyant voice came back to him, and he stood up and said to the attendant, Look, why don't I get out first, I'm the reason you're held up, tell them I'll get out here and they can take me wherever they want. He was allowed to do as he wished. A portable escalator was rolled up to the plane and he was escorted down to the runway by two *guardías* of the Lorcanista government, where he was shot with seventeen rounds of ammunition which pierced his body from several directions at once, so that he stood for a moment like a jerking puppet before the impact of the bullets which themselves kept him standing up, and then he fell down and the *guardías* took him away, and the airport crew had to wash the runway down with brushes to get bits of him out of the cement.

five

T HE SHOCK WAVES of that blast echoed
around the world, in Washington and in the Vatican. Horror and
revulsion were the principal reactions, and for President Allen, a
chill of ominous memory. "There won't be any nice, clean figurehead for you to support . . . but the remnant of his followers, and
ours and yours . . . there won't be any borders anymore, but a
bloodbath from Texas to Columbia." Well, even if she'd known,
this was the action of a madman and demanded a set response:
condemnation in the U.N. and the breaking off of diplomatic relations. Since Martín was a communist, there was a still, cautious
waiting for the Soviet Union to make their move, and when they
did (condemnation in the world press as well, but an elegant evasiveness of everything just short of direct intervention), a slight,
quiet emission of global breath . . . because the world wasn't
going to end yet, not for a little greaseball country that nobody'd
ever heard of, no matter what kind of a lunatic was running the
show or courting his own destruction. Let him remain in power
for just a little longer, because he was a danger to everyone living
but far more dangerous if he was dead. President Allen was heard
to remark publicly that he didn't support failing fascists but pri-

vately he withdrew a little of the *norteamericanos'* support for the Frente Comunistas, because without a leader they were useless to him, an unpredictable element, they might take the country anywhere and he didn't want that. The fading comet of El Lorca's power seemed to be diminishing of its own accord, degenerating into repression until it snuffed itself out in the 'airless vacuum of his own desperate measures, and the drowning torrents of his people's hate. Only those most directly involved knew that it would flame like a torch for as long as there was breath in Ferdinando's body, because it was fueled not by the simplicities of hatred, but by the contradictory complexities of love.

In Rome, Battiste heard the news in silence, feeling the thin, terrible wound of his certainty even before it was confirmed that an assassination *had* taken place: he knew what Ferdinando had done, because he had always known that his friend was capable of anything. He closed his eyes for a moment in thought, and then met the stunned gaze of José Luaro with a resolute bitterness which was his only substitute for compassion. "Be at peace, my son. I have faith that some brave man will avenge Martín Acchuirez's death."

He must have known what he was telling him to do. That afternoon, José Luaro dressed himself in civilian clothes and booked a flight to Mexico City, carrying enough plastic explosives to blow a hole in the Presidential Palace the size of a truck. He planned to follow his friend's example of caution, and take one of the many commercial flights from Mexico City to Campeche when he could be certain he wasn't being followed. In the meantime he knocked around the Zona Rosa, and walked all the way from Río Consulado to Chapultepec Park, and was on the point of going into the Anthropology Museum when he ran into Porfirio Cheruña.

The old man had lost the spryness of illusory youth, which had enabled him to fight off the depredations of stroke and arthritis and failing kidneys and a dying heart, and now he walked very carefully with the discreet steps of a man who doesn't know what will happen next, looking shabby in an ancient gray pinstripe suit and a white shirt which was far from clean. His hands trembled, and his eyes had lost the direct malice of former times and wandered now to anything, a bird flying by, a child running in the street, but he had arrived at the terrible finality of old age with all his marbles intact and he took one look at José Luaro's stolid, flat-planed face and could not repress a shudder. He greeted him with false cheerfulness.

"José, my dear friend, I thought you were in Rome! Are we two exiles, then, both forbidden from entering Campeche? I feel like an excommunicant, no, of course the Church doesn't do that anymore, I wouldn't know, but certainly it's strange to be in limbo here, don't you agree, stranded on the edge of the country we both love and waiting to see what will happen next? Although, of course, they say they're lifting the travel restrictions to encourage *los turistas*. My dear boy, humor an old man and come and have a cup of coffee with me, there's a little restaurant not far from here, we could sit and chat, I'm anxious to hear the news from our mutual friend in the Vatican, what does he say, does he think they'll go beyond the vote of censure in the United Nations to something concrete like a trade embargo? Although, of course, there really isn't any more Mayapanian trade at all, is there! They're starving in any case, perhaps it would be merely redundant to make it official by imposing a governmental sanction. My dear boy, I'm terribly sorry about Martín."

His anxious eyes flicked over the younger man as they sat down in a café, and he saw with increasing concern that there was no change in the priest's expression, not even a flicker of sadness, he was like an automaton and well, yes, you had to admit that it had needed something like that at one point, but not now, because they were all dead, the best and the brightest, and what was the point of plunging their country into chaos? He was surprised in himself to discover not patriotism, but grief. Mourning for the past, he found himself unwilling to relinquish any thought so long as it bound him to Camila: even thoughts of El Lorca, even thoughts of that man who was still in power, *el dictador*, El Jefe. As miserable as he was, certainly, yes, possibly more so! and he deserved it! and he would suffer, oh, yes, but why destroy him when there was no longer any need? He found himself thinking these things and wishing he could say them to the young man while his heart was beating with uncommon rapidity, really it was frightening and he had to shut his eyes because no, no, no, he

398

still didn't want to die, and he took a deep breath and sipped his coffee and murmured, "So? What are you doing in Mexico, my dear friend?"

José Luaro told him something imprecise about a vacation, which neither of them believed, and Porfirio watched him with the vertiginous feeling that he was hypnotized, while he searched for some key that would unlock his labyrinthine, unfathomable mind and enable him to say the right thing to call this whole thing off. He couldn't find it, or couldn't bring himself to say it. He thought, I'm not the worst, I'm not by any means the worst . . . but still he couldn't say to this hardened man, No, if you try to fly out of the country I'll stop you, I'll report you to the police. He found himself sitting there mute and listening as José Luaro said calmly, "I have some business to attend to in Campeche at the end of the month, is there anyone there you want me to call on, anything you'd like me to do?" and he stammered something inane like No, no, nothing at all, staring at José Luaro's wolfish, dangerous smile, as he got up and threw some money down on the table to pay for coffee. He was sitting there much later when the waiter approached him to ask, Señor, is there anything else you want? and the old man simply waved him away with his white, stiffened hand, staring into the abyss of memories that terrified him with their tenacious clarity.

Ferdinando was unaware at that time of the currents of uncertainty and passion that were swirling around him. He continued to fulfill the duties of his office with something of the calm, gentle thoroughness of other days, because after the death of Martín Acchuirez his heart seemed to be eased, and he spoke occasionally of events that were far in the future, the turn of the next century and his own retirement from office, as if those things were possible and he could make plans in which they figured. Pisote began for the first time to relax. He was lighter in his dealings with his subordinates and colleagues, even going so far as to invite Colonel Enrique Zacapa back from exile at the garrison of Punta Herrero, and when General Ottavio Moroque tried to thank him he smiled and said, Well, what do you think, everyone's got to have a friend in this life, if you don't have that you might as well go live in the trees with the monkeys. He was seen to smile more frequently and sometimes, occasionally, to laugh, and he appeared one day on the terrace outside his private apartments in a pair of swimming trunks and lay in the sun for an hour, with his eyes shut and a film of sweat soothing his temples and easing the little dry white lines around his eyes. He was playfully teasing with Pisote as when he asked her once, Don't you want me to give you any diamonds? Camila always appeared dressed up like a Christmas tree, and he said her name so easily that even Pisote might have been deceived into thinking he was starting to forget her, except that only she knew he sat up all night thinking about her, and could only bring himself to lie down as the dawn was brightening the sky to toss in light-sleeping, terrible dreams and torture the air with his cries, until one night she looked at him quietly and said, "I don't think I can stand it anymore," and he gazed at her with his tender, compassionate eyes and whispered, "You must, my darling. There's no way for either of us to be free without going through this ridiculous charade for a little while longer."

One night she was disturbed by the light from his study, and walked through from their bedroom in her robe. He was sitting at his desk, reading the newspaper, and he greeted her with something of his old, light banter, saying, "Mmm, I like that, are you trying to tempt your old celibate widower husband?" His eyes were very clear and blue. He offered her a drink, and immediately started to talk about the future.

"I think you ought to take a trip to the States, try and see President Allen and introduce yourself, you know, see what kind of an impression you make. . . . Camila always said he was an untrustworthy snake, but you've had enough experience dealing with snakes, and who knows, you may do better than she did. I don't need you here for any of the official functions coming up in the next few days, and we can certainly see that you're kept in the newspapers, perhaps an article in *People* magazine—"

He smiled, indicating the newspaper lying on his desk, and she said sharply, "What's wrong? You're trying to get rid of me!"

"Of course not!" He laughed, with very nearly the same honesty as in happier days, and standing by him in her light robe, she was aware of how warm and alive he was, not chilled with the coldness of death which had made him shudder and say, My

God, don't come near me, it's like spending time with a corpse. He was alight with his old, vital fire, and she knew he was lying to her.

"What's going on?" she snapped, suddenly losing patience. "You said you wanted me to be there tomorrow, full Señora drag for the press, and now you're telling me to forget it? I know I'm not Camila, and I know you never lied to *her*—" She swallowed and went on, regardless of how much she tore up her heart. "So don't lie to me. I know I'm not her, and you can't even bear to look at me, and tomorrow we're going to stand there on the steps and people are going to say, Ah, there is *la señora segunda*, his secondhand wife, but goddamn it it isn't just that, because I know you, and you're not so fucking sensitive with other people's feelings, so is it a death threat, or a warning of a *demostración*, or what?"

Unexpectedly, he laughed, this time completely honestly, hiding his face in his hands. "Oh, God, Pisote, you've caught me again. I can't get away with shit with you, can I?" He sobered up and looked at her seriously, the tousled hair and the white, sharp-boned face, the intent hazel eyes which could never have Camila's beauty, Camila's magic, or Camila's fire, but which were the intelligent eyes of a brave and uncompromising woman, a warrior in her own way all the same.

"All right, no more lies," he said, smiling. "I've received word that there might be a disturbance tomorrow. Nothing you can pin down, but who knows? But it wasn't just for that that I suggested you might want to get away from me. If you do want to stay, I assure you you're very welcome, and I'll ... I'll be very glad to have you by my side tomorrow, when we speak to the Chamber of Deputies and pat them on their backs for doing nothing. After that, if you want, we can both take a vacation from this shit-pile of a country, and go someplace where we can draw two breaths together like decent human beings."

When he said it, he really meant it. He felt freed from the past, and could see as if it were an accomplished fact the existence of a new life, there or elsewhere, for himself and Pisote. That night for the first time he slept without being tormented by atrocious dreams, and he was so far unaware of the nature of the omen that he awoke the next morning feeling completely refreshed. He shaved with special care and put on the plain, dark-blue business suit and white silk shirt that he always wore for state occasions, with the sash of the President of the Republic across his breast, and as he looked into the mirror he wasn't exactly displeased with his reflection: for all he looked like a man who'd come through a debilitating illness, and perhaps a spell in a madhouse, he was still tolerably handsome and the dark hair lying against his olive forehead didn't look too thin, his eyes didn't look too lined, their clear, blue light was dimmed without being entirely quenched, and his smile still had a light, thin filament of humor in it, something he'd salvaged in spite of the wreckage of his life. It might very well be possible to go on living, if not here, then perhaps someplace else; he looked around his private dressing room, and thought that it might not be difficult after all to give it all up, go back to teaching or obscurity on someone's pension (UNOCO, Linz, or the *gringos*, someone undoubtedly would pay). He wondered what the members of the Chamber of Deputies would do, if instead of congratulating them in person on the steps of Constitución Hall, he tendered his resignation, *Permitame, señores*, but I've decided to leave you all in the lurch, excuse me, but I've had enough of fucking myself up and whoever wants to come after me in this job is welcome to it? Of course it couldn't be done, like that, but it was a delicious idea. He would follow the formalities, and arrange for his exit from power to be accomplished decorously: packing a suitcase and fleeing like every other *presidente*, but only when he'd arranged for his succession, a constitutional assembly, leaving the groundwork of some kind of freedom for the people who had believed in him, and who would be disappointed enough to learn that El Presidente was a man just like everyone else, and was tired of his job, and wanted to quit.

He was so elated by his idea, and amused by the image of shock he'd conjured up on the faces of the imaginary deputies, that he was able to bear the unmitigated pain of seeing Pisote dressed up in a white linen suit with her hair pulled back, diamonds in her ears and a necklace of pearls at her slender throat, her face, lips, and fingernails hinting at the exact shades worn by Camila Lorca. He was able to conquer his sorrow and link his arm in hers, to whisper almost inaudibly as they walked down the stairs, "There, you see, nothing secondhand about you, you look tailor-made," and he smiled as they got into their limousine with the same gentle, tender smile of a loving leader as he had worn through the most glorious revolution and bloodiest dictatorship in his country's history. The streets were crowded, and the sky was the perfect blue of morning, clear of the brazen heat which would descend later in the day but warm enough that the people were wearing shirt sleeves and light summer dresses. He enjoyed the few minutes' drive to Constitución Hall with the private knowledge that it was the last time. Bill Mynott's security forces escorted them inside and through the warren of the old viceregal building that housed the Chamber of Deputies, to the entrance out onto the wide, white marble steps, for the ceremony of the Presidente's address was always performed outside, if the weather allowed, to give a better setting for the camera crews. Ferdinando stepped out into the blazing, Campeche sunlight, and walked the few steps down to the temporary platform with his customary grace and the knife-thin elegance which had characterized him at every moment of his public life, and met the massed, catastrophic cheers of "El Lor-ca! El Lor-ca!" with a gasp of the purest, unfeigned pleasure because Oh God he loved it, how could he have imagined for an instant that he'd ever give it up! He held out his hands to embrace them all, and Pisote looked up at him from her position standing directly at El Lorca's side and saw his worn, beautiful face shining in the light of the sun.

"My friends, I thank you from the bottom of my heart for coming here today."

He looked around, still having the instinctive knack of appearing to love them all, and thank them all, individually. There was something wrong. A man was trying to get through the security forces that ringed the bottom of the steps, and he braced himself not so much for death as for an attack, stepping between the assailant and Pisote when he saw with a combination of mirth and fury that the man was a revolting old sinner whom he knew, a filthy pervert who put his hands into little girls' pants and who had hurt his wife past imagining and denied him children, and because he was who he was, he didn't think for an instant of striking the old man or having him dragged away, but instead simply looked at him with his shining blue eyes, as he said with far more kindness than he actually felt, "What is it, Porfirio? What the hell do you want?"

From an open window in Constitución Hall José Luaro had a moment's fatal hesitation, as he had to choose whether to kill the old man or El Lorca. He froze, and something, certainly not Porfirio's babbling but the concentrated lodestone of his fate, drew Ferdinando's eyes up to the window, where he saw perfectly clearly the light of the sun shining on a rifle barrel. He stood completely still. He was a leader, and he wouldn't run. He narrowed his eyes a little, to see if he could see the face of the nameless assailant who was going to kill him (the window was almost close enough for that), and he saw instead the pure clear beauty of his wife Camila's face, and heard her sweet voice telling him not to fight the inevitable in a fluid, glottal language like birdsong that left a residue of peace and serenity in his heart. He was surprised in himself that he wasn't more frightened. He closed his eyes and whispered in place of a prayer, Camila, Camila, I miss you so, and then he turned to the assembled crowd with great love and started to say something absurd about the solemnity of the day.

He never finished his sentence, because the rifle shot that ended his life cracked across the plaza like the order of an implacable judge and shattered his skull and pitched him forward, spattering those standing nearest him with blood. In the moment's stunned silence that followed, two more shots were fired, as José Luaro, who had discovered with what deceptive ease you could kill someone, put a bullet into the head of the second Señora Lorca and the distinguished white head of Porfirio Cheruña, whose glasses caught the light for a deadly instant even as he was pushed aside by the crowd. Then he detonated the plastic explosives he was carrying and blew himself to God.

EPILOGUE

IN THE VATICAN, heavy velvet draperies muffled the cheering of the crowd, and Battiste's hand fell from the curtains in the action of drawing them, thinking how Camila would have loved it, the perfect irony, taking all those who loved her into death except for him, leaving him here to mourn her and canonize her, guard her memory as he had tried to guard her in life . . . but she had escaped him as she'd escaped everybody, and now she belonged to the world, and to no one. He heard a footfall and a respectful "Reverend Father," and he turned with his practiced, distant, serious gaze.

"Yes, my son, what is it?"

He was a very holy man, the young priest thought, newly arrived from San Salvador and looking for a Third World Jesuit to believe in: with his gray hair and his lined, pained, pockmarked face, he seemed to have suffered much, and he knew about the misery of the poor and sought to alleviate it with practical change; he was a dutiful religious but he was also a man of the world, for hadn't he been in politics once, a man of social realism, and for all that kind, understanding, and wonderfully patient, comprehending the faith of *los pobres* in miracles because, as he said, I too was the beneficiary of a miracle once, I knew a saint. He couldn't understand the reverend father's bitter, painful smile, but he respected it.

"Reverend Father, the Holy Father sends his best wishes on this most blessed and solemn occasion, and requests that you should join him and the holy fathers in prayer."

They were waiting for him. He didn't know whether Camila would do any good as a saint. The world seemed daily to be careening out of control toward chaos, and there were *gringo* troops in Campeche now, the military maintaining a fragile, puppet-mastered hold; the once-richest nation in Latin America was reduced to begging for aid from the International Red Cross, and all that remained besides the body-strewn roads and the burning buildings were the missile silos and the rhetoric: so many Marines dead, so many Cuban advisers. It seemed that when mankind's madness ever *did* cross the threshold of annihilation, it would be on his native soil that the final conflagration was launched. He had to smile. They had escaped that too, and left him alone to face a world he'd helped create. They had given the people hope, and its aftertaste was as bitter as gall. Their glamour alone was intact: you could still see it on every bullet-scarred billboard in Campeche.

He hadn't pushed for Camila's beatification in the anticipation of any personal gain, or to increase the status of his order, or even because he really believed she was a saint: he wasn't sure he knew what sainthood was, but he believed Camila had ended by going beyond any of his categories. It was simply a debt he felt he'd owed her, and the beautiful man he had helped destroy. A debt to his friends, and even more so to himself. For in exalting her, he had placed a crown of thorns on his own head which he knew would never be removed, never be diminished in the exquisite torture of his loneliness; and which would go on wounding him until death, which was exactly what he deserved.

"Tell the Holy Father I'm ready," he said with his bleak, pained, martyr's smile, and went out into the corridor in his black soutane, to join in the hymning of the heavenly choir.

ABOUT THE AUTHOR

Adrienne V. Parks is the daughter of a stockbroker and a swing musician, and the granddaughter of a Catholic priest. She is a graduate of Princeton University *summa cum laude*, and is the wife of William C. Bowman, an independent video producer. This is her first novel.